The Black Dragons' Chronicles III

M. R. Lucas

Copyright © 2023 M. R. Lucas

All rights reserved.

Contents

Legal Stuff i
Dedication i
Acknowledgement / Special Thanks iii
Glossary iv
Introduction v
Blessed, Precious Memories... 1
The First Elders' Will 11
Dragonosophy 24
An Honored Tradition 30
Fate's Favors.. 45
Scarred Memories 54
Luna Fendasse... 64
A Misunderstanding... 69
Secrets Unveiled 74
Hell Hath Much Fury 88
One Hundred Daughters and Sons 105
Tol'Tarei 125
Choices for Death 145
Meeting Death 161
Reunion in Death 194
Blessings and Forgiveness..202
The Eighth Hell 208
Reconciliation and Redemption.. 231
Homecoming 239
Inheritance 249
The Last Chapter 260
Still United and Strong...270

Epilogue.. 290

Legal Stuff

Copyright © M. R. Lucas, 2022

All Rights Reserved. This book is protected by the copyright laws of the United States of America. Any reproduction or unauthorized use of the written material or artwork contained herein is prohibited without the express written permission of M. R. Lucas.

This story is a work of fiction. Names, characters, places, and incidents are either the product of the author's imagination and/or are used fictitiously. Any resemblance to actual persons, living or dead, companies, events or locations is entirely coincidental.

Dedication

This book was also started after I transitioned into semi-retirement. After working full-time for over forty-two years as a business management consultant, data analyst and legal project manager, I still had extra, uncommitted time on my hands. I wanted to do something more "fun". I believe that everyone, regardless of age, has at least one story to tell. So, I decided to tell a story, one that I would enjoy reading had someone else written this book.

As I was finishing Book II which was actually the first book completed of the trilogy, I started this project. By pure chance, The Black Dragons' Chronicles II, when finished, profoundly resonated as the second part of a great story. Though Book II required several years to complete, Book III was mostly finished in just four months thereafter. Concurrent with the capturing of ideas for Book II's sequel, I also compiled a number of ideas that would eventually be incorporated in Book I.

This writing is dedicated first to my beloved family. I love you all and wish you much happiness.

Secondly, this book is also dedicated to those readers who enjoy finding themselves submerged in a good story, getting attached to interesting characters and anxiously waiting to discover intriguing subplots' twists and turns. I do hope this book meets that criteria and you find much enjoyment reading my tale.

Lastly, I wish to dedicate this book to all the aspiring, did-not-really-expect-to-become authors who have accumulated hundreds of note pages. Writing to tell a great story is a wonderful journey.

Enjoy!!

Acknowledgement / Special Thanks

Humble and grateful acknowledgement for this book's inspiration came from a variety of sources including some authors who tell great, transforming stories. These motivating authors include:

    Dan Brown

    Jim Butcher

    Frank Herbert

    Robert E. Howard

    Christopher Paolini

    R.A. Salvatore

Four very special friends also joined me on my incredible journey during the development of this writing project. Their editing, listening, encouragement and inspiration were very important and helpful. I appreciate and value our many years of close friendship. Special thanks to the following:

    Elaine R. Nawal

    Jeffrey R. Lucas-Nihei

    Jeremy J. Pettit

    Lewis C. Rhodes

Lastly, the fantastic cover art was developed by the amazing Denise M. Vlahos whose manifested creativity inspired portions of my writing. THANK YOU too!

Glossary

It became evident after a while that certain "words" or specialized "terms" were being "created" in order to adequately express certain thoughts. So, this glossary was needed to document those particular words or terms used in this book:

Belf	Young male elf; less than two hundred ten years old
Dragon Life Stages (Years)	Young (Birth -two hundred fifty), Adult (two hundred fifty-one – five hundred), Elder (five hundred one – seven hundred fifty) and Ancient (seven hundred fifty-one - Death)
Fah	Unit of measure; the "average" length of a forearm or about twelve inches
Felf	Adult female elf; two hundred ten years of age or older
Gelf	Young female elf; less than two hundred ten years old
Hand	Unit of measure; about eight inches
Melf	Adult male elf; two hundred ten years of age or older
Moon / Full Moon Cycle	Unit of measure; thirty days
Step	Unit of measure; three feet
Stone	Unit of measure; fourteen pounds

It may be important to also note that to simulate the realm's spoken Dwarfish language, the words' "th" sounds are spoken as "d" sounds. Further, words normally ending with "ing" are spoken without the "g" sound effect.

Introduction

This is a story of fantasy. More specifically, it is a sword and sorcery fantasy tale of great adventure.

This story takes place in the mythical and magical land of Canae, a world filled with many great wonders. In this world, many different creatures live. Both creatures of magic and those that are not inherently magical live, struggle and survive together. This world is also a world of magic where dragons reign supreme as the most powerful and magical across all the lands.

Canae is ruled by a queen and king. Canae's capital city is Rhodell, founded by the ancestors of House Rho. Canae also has many powerful families of nobility called great Houses. Although there is a queen and king who is royalty and wishes their bloodline to continue to rule the kingdom for centuries to come, the true power of the kingdom, as well as the noble great Houses, is often wielded by the leading or ruling matriarchs of the families. These House great mothers are formidable and focused upon enhancing their family's status, power, and wealth through a variety of means. Most methods used are overt, such as building strong relationships or alliances through marriage. Other, covert means can sometimes lead to violent acts.

House honor and reputation are cherished and fanatically protected. One who belongs to a great noble House has an inherent duty to protect, enhance and grow the House. The well-being of one's House is prioritized higher than the individual family member. Even love can be ill-fated should it conflict with the House great mothers' strategy and direction. On the other hand, love, shared or unrequited, can be used as a weapon to achieve House goals.

This story is the continuing, great adventure saga of Houses Je Luneefa, Nui Vent and Ona Feiir. Though they live in the Aboveworld land of Canae, an ancient and mythical land, they are challenged by a powerful unforeseen enemy of the dark, mysterious Underworld.

Blessed, Precious Memories

Looking out the window to witness what was to be a glorious late winter day, House Nui Vent great mother Nui Honei could still see the patches of scorched earth where her sons had been cremated by horrific, yet blessed dragon flames. The burned earth there reminded the felf that neither that earth nor her torn heart would ever fully recover soon.

Tears started forming again in her mournful eyes as she recalled that day of battle at the Borauec Mountain. The long-time feud with Houses Tou Ahn and Si Moina was finally over; the enemy Houses were completely destroyed. *"My sons, only in their third century of life, surely did not deserve to be taken so soon. They were not supposed to die, only me, if anyone... Did I give my consent to them to die? No! Did I, the matriarch of now, the noble House Nui Vent, give them my final blessings? No!"* her mind screamed again as she pounded her fists upon the windowsill. Fresh new tears of great sorrow started to flow. Today, like many others, her heart was in agony. Yes, Nui Honei realized reluctantly she would still hold onto her anguish for a long time.

She recalled, "In that very private ceremony conducted in the Nui Vent stronghold east courtyard, the bodies of her fallen sons, Nui Danka and Nui Rei, had been cremated by dragon flame. Her two once living, strong and healthy melfs had been reduced to less than a stone's weight of ashes in just a few moments. My sons' ashes were then reverently collected, placed in urns, and presented to me. I knew I did not love easily; but when I did, it was unconditional and powerful. Though I was not my sons' birth mother, Nui Danka and Nui Rei, like Nui Jooba, became my beloved sons through adoption. Through some wonderous miracle, the former thieves stole my heart from our first fortuitous encounter."

Nui Honei's time with her fallen sons had been relatively brief. That very short time of less than two decades though was enriched with many fond memories. She pondered again, *"Even when they were most annoying, trying to garner favor or attention, my love for them never waned. In fact, it grew deeper. Their childlike pranks they played on each other, or the sons and daughters of House Je Luneefa were humorous to observe. My adopted sons most greatly enjoyed annoying my beloved Ona Noirar by slightly moving his cherished weapons in his private study. My precious sons, especially Nui Rei, felt the pranks aimed at my beloved Ona Noirar were justified since Ona Noirar seemed to have displaced my sons as their mother's 'favorite!' Foolish, foolish males.*

"In truth, I also secretly enjoyed the special attention my sons bestowed upon me," Nui Honei admitted inwardly. "The former thieves had truly stolen her heart. Nui Danka, a woods elf, the former thief gang's unofficial leader and spokesperson, attempted to always set good examples by taking the lead. He was the oldest and usually first to greet his adopted mother with flowers or a lengthy, affectionate salutation. He was extraverted, handsome and so very charming. Nui Jooba, a mixed dark and rock elf, however, was introverted, a very quiet melf of great strength. He was a learner, seeking knowledge. Nui Rei, a woods elf, was the youngest and craved to be his mother's favorite and receive her attention often. His large, deep blue eyes and wide affectionate smile could warm my dark heart at any time despite my foulest mood.

"All my sons were tall, each reaching over six fahs in height. Nui Danka and Nui Rei both had long blond hair and blue eyes. Nui Jooba has short dark brown hair and brown eyes. This middle son, though slender in stature like his brothers, is very muscular. All were intelligent, brave, courageous and completely loyal to me and my House. All my sons have had a profound impact upon me that I recognize and acknowledge. I deeply loved and love you all."

After placing Nui Danka and Nui Rei's urns in the House Nui Vent crypt, Nui Honei was greatly saddened that the youngest of her family was the first to die and placed there in memorial. Again, her deceased sons continued to lovingly anger her by denying her that first honor.

Whenever the House Nui Vent great mother visited her special sitting room, after staring out of the window to see the scorched earth, Nui Honei would eventually look upon the portraits hanging on the walls. First was a portrait of her beloved grandparents, Nui Dreza and Nui Teru, who truly loved and raised her. Most importantly, they accepted her warrior's spirit when the young felf did not follow her parent's more "noble-like behavior" examples and directions. Her grandparents, unlike her parents, were warriors trained and experienced in many battles. Like her grandmother, Nui Honei trained to become an elite warrior and battlemage. Nui Dreza and Nui Teru's knowledge of weaponry, magic and ancient elven martial arts were passed on to their granddaughter and grandson.

Nui Honei smiled knowing that her grandmother, Nui Dreza, had also gifted her fiery spirit to her granddaughter. On the other hand, Nui Teru had more of a calming disposition like her older brother, Nui Samu. Though both melfs had quiet natures, they were very deadly and fierce warriors. Both elders were wise, brave and fearless in battle. Nui Honei was so very thankful she had grandparents like Nui Dreza and Nui Teru. Their honored teachings and memories would always remain with her.

Next to that portrait of her grandparents is a portrait of the House Je Luneefa first elders, Je Buel and Je Taeliel. Nui Honei acknowledged to the portrait's captured images, "Though long deceased, you Je Buel and Je Taeliel, my real beloved parents, still impose your love and excessively protective natures over your family. You accepted me and gave me the needed guidance and much needed unconditional love. You were strict, loving, extremely kind and loyal to family and dear friends. In contrast, you also inflicted, without remorse, complete deadly force upon enemies who threatened your family and friends." Nui Honei momentarily smiled evilly.

After a long sigh, she sadly continued her soliloquy to the portrait, saying proudly with lifted spirit, "Mother Je Buel and Father Je Taeliel encountered, persevered and overcame many life hardships to ensure that *all* in your family would flourish.

"Then living in the kingdom's capital, Rhodell, you first elders of House Je Luneefa were blessed with a daughter who further blessed House Je Luneefa with the births of five granddaughters and grandsons. Rhodell was generally peaceful and lawful; however, evil and injustice were still pervasive in the world. To help safeguard your young family, you did the unthinkable. Though you were high noble, woods elves of House Je

Luneefa, you courageously defied high noble, societal standards when you chose to adopt certain rock and sun elves, the daughter and sons of Houses Nui Vent and Ona Feiir and even Diazae Alleina, all outcasts, orphans of war and secret enemies of the Crown.

"Fate too greatly favored you when you became dear beloved friends and eventually extended family of the famed Clan Battle Hammer, the mightiest Dwarven clan of the Blood Tears Mountains realm in northeastern Canae. Further, Je Taeliel and son-in-law Je Maron established family ties and strong allies with the five great, united orc tribes of Canae's northern frontier.

"Hence, Houses Je Luneefa, Nui Vent and Ona Feiir stood and will still stand, strong, united and very well protected behind your formidable Toronwalein. Mother Je Buel and Father Je Taeliel, the first elders of House Je Luneefa were indeed wise, very wise. Thank you."

Nui Honei next recalled the chance first meeting with Je Buel. Smiling, she silently remembered, "After first arriving in Torondell, a much younger felf then, I stopped at an inn to eat before continuing my journey to find my brother. Torondell was still quite unorderly and lawless then. Many ruffians and rogues boldly roamed the streets of the city causing trouble.

"By chance, Je Buel had also stopped at the same inn earlier for a meal. She had already dismissed her escort, citing her lingering time at the inn would be brief. The elder felf, upon noticing a knife throwing contest in the tavern area, had been slowly drawn to the competition. So, Je Buel finished her meal and then decided to throw knives herself in the next contest. She smiled as she accepted the previous contest winner's challenge to all the tavern's patrons. Throwing knives at a ten-steps-away target of concentric circles had brought back several fond, old memories the elder felf conveyed later to me.

"Je Buel won the next contest and a small bag of coins as the prize. After leaving the inn, a gang of ruffians and rogues decided to attempt to rob the felf of her winnings. The eight rogues, armed with swords or axes, were fifteen steps away. The gang blocked her way in the street and claimed she needed to pay a 'street tax' first before leaving. The tax was to be her contest winning purse of coins plus any other valuables she might have.

"Like other patrons leaving the inn about the same time, I also stopped to watch the brave felf face the gang of would-be thieves. Je Buel was in the middle of the street across from the corral where her horse was stabled. Unafraid, Je Buel calmly and confidently remarked, 'I won these coins fairly. So, I will not give them to you. Try to take them if you must but that will be far more difficult than you imagined. Some of you, if not all, may very well die in your stupid attempt.' All the foolish rogues then laughed.

"'You do realize there are eight of us and only one of you. We like these odds. Besides, you look like you are not armed,' the gang leader loudly declared, continuing to laugh at his next, supposedly would-be victim.

"'Know too that Jura there is a mage; so, we have the numbers and other advantages. Avoid getting hurt or even worse, perhaps dying. Are those coins truly worth that much to you?' A second rogue boasted attempting to further intimidate the lone felf.

"Unimpressed and unafraid, Je Buel returned the menacing glare of the gang leader. 'Thank you for pointing out that mage; she then will be the first to die. Also, know that the females of my House are always armed,' calmly scoffed Je Buel. She then quickly pulled her long sword from the inside of her cape. She also had first immobilized the gang's weaker mage with a paralysis spell. The battle-experienced felf had already and easily recognized that mage and knew she had to be eliminated first. Fortunately, the gang's mage had not recognized Je Buel for being a more powerful battlemage. Unlike Je Buel, the gang's mage had not blocked her magical 'aura' which identified her as a practitioner of magic.

"The outcomes of battles are heavily weighted by skilled battlemages. The battlemage's magical aura was typically 'hidden' from enemies. Battlemages, the adept and wise ones, did not foretell their magical skills lest they would be initial primary targets in battle. Those battlemages who were not careful usually became the battle's first casualties. The gang's mage was at most a level eight, an advanced novice at best, in magical power and skills and most likely had not ever been in war. Her low skills and training were evident, a great disadvantage that can prove to be very fatal.

"On the other hand, Je Buel had been officially ranked as a level two battlemage in magical power, skills and experience from many battles. She also naturally masked her magical aura well.

"From the side street, two more rogues joined their gang. The gang leader smiled wider then at the felf with evil intent, pleased that his odds had now increased more to ten-to-one. 'You should now relinquish all your valuables. My odds have again improved. And I do not believe anyone else here would want to help you,' the gang leader arrogantly announced.

"At that moment, Nui Honei pushed her way through the crowd watching the attempted robbery and stood by the lone Je Buel. 'I am Nui Honei. I will improve your odds if you like,' I said and then drew my twin scimitars from my sides. 'I will kill those six in front of me and you can kill those three in front of you.'

"The gang leader angrily shouted, 'There are ten of us, not nine; you are meddling hag! You should choose your fights more carefully. You too will now suffer the same fate as your doomed friend there.'

"The gang leader then noticed too that their mage was not responsive to his calls nor commands. 'Boss why can't Jura move?' another rogue frantically inquired.

"'I paralyzed her first fools,' Je Buel said. 'Know that I am a skilled battlemage and fought in many battles where my odds were much worse. Cease with your worthless attempt to rob me and be gone. I will release her afterwards. Continue your foolish attack and she will be the first to die. Now, you should choose wisely.

"'May I join you for your evening meal? I am still famished from traveling,' I then requested.

"'What say you gang leader? Will we battle or not? I need to make haste; I will have guests for dinner and need to return home quickly,' an impatient Je Buel remarked.

"The gang leader continued glaring at the two felfs with his menacing stare for several more, long moments. He was again reevaluating, I imagined, his so-called favorable odds. Never had he encountered such difficult victims despite assumed overwhelming odds. Before the gang leader could utter another word, Je Buel threw another hidden long knife at the inattentive gang leader. Her knife was thrown with such speed that the gang leader did not see it until it was just a hair's breadth away from his exposed throat, suspended in the air.

"Several gasps then came from the surprised gang members and the crowd of spectators. 'If you move towards us now, you will surely die first,' Je Buel announced to the gang leader. The elder felf then quickly pulled another hidden short sword from her side. 'What say you?' After more careful thought, the gang's leader made a hand gesture, commanding his followers to back away slowly. Even one sly gang member, hiding amongst the spectators, joined his gang members in the street. Je Buel's knife slowly followed the gang leader as well, staying fearfully close to his exposed neck.

"Moments later, Je Buel recalled her long knife to her outstretched hand and placed it inside her cape. She also returned her swords to their sheaths.

"The gang, now about fifteen steps away, continued backing away slowly down the street. The gang leader pointed to their paralyzed gang member and Je Buel released her.

"'Argh!' Jura screamed loudly. 'I will repay you for this insult. In fact, I will start by first killing you and then your precious daughter and...'

"'Jura, hold your tongue!' screamed the gang leader.

"Too late. In less time to blink an eye, Je Buel instantly transformed from her once relaxed, calm demeanor after avoiding a senseless robbery to a blood-raged, hellish warrior. Je Buel immediately broke the gang mage's neck with a spell, killing her instantly. Je Buel then turned her attention to the remaining gang members, now crazed and angry, who screamed battle cries and charged at the two felfs. In response, Je Buel, engulfed in her own battle rage, charged. Upon witnessing this instant transformation, I joined Je Buel in attacking the gang.

"Je Buel quickly learned that I was indeed fearless and a skilled warrior. My battle rage was also intense and powerful. Though extremely outnumbered, Je Buel and I killed each gang member mercilessly. These warrior felfs' first "dance" in battle together left them alive with no serious injury and all the gang members very much dead.

"After the battle, I looked at the House Je Luneefa first great mother covered in blood and gore and quietly laughed. I surmised had that gang's mage not threatened Je Buel's family, the gang may have lived to steal another day. Unfortunately for them, this gang had threatened a very protective and very deadly mother.

"Nui Samu had said, in one of his letters, that this House first mother and grandmother resembled their own beloved Nui Dreza in many ways. This was a great honor her brother bestowed upon Je Buel, the first great mother of House Je Luneefa. As such, I would fight by her side anytime despite the foes and odds. I also realized then this mother would indeed kill without hesitation anyone who threatened her family, especially her daughter... I greatly admired the elder felf for that protective trait, a trait I had not ever known from her own mother. The daughter of Je Buel was indeed very fortunate to have such a strong mother's love, a love I had not ever known from my real birth mother.

"Looking at Je Buel, blood covered and panting, I said, 'You dance very well first great mother of House Je Luneefa.'

"'As do you too, great mother of House Nui Vent,' Je Buel replied smiling. 'Your brother has told me much about you.'

"Great mother of House Nui Vent – that had been the very first time the full weight of that title and responsibility struck me. I was now the ruling matriarch of my family. I, like other House ruling great mothers, must lead my House, be formidable and focused upon enhancing my family's status, power, wealth and prosperity. I am also now responsible for the well-being and growth of House Nui Vent!

"I was awestruck; for it was the first time anyone had acknowledged me with such great respect. I was young and moved to tears then realizing that I and my brother were the last of our House. The weight of those responsibilities would be difficult for me to bear. I humbly responded, 'Thank you. Your words mean much to me.'

"I was pleased too knowing that my brother had become friends with a noble House whose first great mother had a warrior's fiery spirit like hers. I then anxiously looked forward to becoming more acquainted with Je Buel, the first great mother of House Je Luneefa. This elder felf was the one my brother had fondly mentioned several times in his letters to me while I was away training in the Underworld.

"After joining my brother in the northern kingdom, the elders of House Je Luneefa sincerely welcomed both House Nui Vent daughter and son. After some time, the House Je Luneefa first great mother and father became Nui Samu and my true beloved 'real' parents. The love I had lost from my real parents was recovered in the House Je Luneefa first elders. That parental love, strict and caring, was unconditional and ever present, regardless of my lack of noble character at times. So, it was overwhelming when I learned Je Buel and Je Taeliel wanted to adopt me and my brother. It was a great honor."

Je Buel and Je Taeliel, the first elders of House Je Luneefa had adopted several felfs and melfs into their family long ago when their granddaughters and grandsons were young. Nui Honei, Nui Samu, Ona Noirar and Diazae Alleina became the House first elders' beloved daughters and sons of House Je Luneefa. Through life's ordeals, each had proven unconditional loyalty, love and devotion to House Je Luneefa. They all gained the love, wisdom, unwavering commitment and guidance of beloved elders in return.

"Je Buel and Je Taeliel gained three of the kingdom's deadliest blades, a mighty dragon and a gifted healer. Ha, ha, ha. Je Buel and Je Taeliel were truly very, very wise. The overly protective, Je Luneefa House first elders somehow knew their House – their granddaughters and sons – would be well protected and flourish after they were gone. Yes, these elders were very wise. Beloved mother Je Buel and beloved father Je Taeliel, you will always forever hold a very special place in my heart," Nui Honei whispered.

Nui Honei bowed again, paying silent homage to all her elders enshrined in the portraits. Returning to the present, Nui Honei would lastly gaze upon the third portrait. Shortly after her sons' adoptions, Ona Noirar had that particular portrait secretly painted of her, himself, Nui Samu, Ona Drachir and her sons. All were in their finest House red and black uniforms. Nui Honei wore her finest red and black robes to compliment the males, all formally dressed in their House uniforms. Nui Honei sat with Ona Noirar holding hands in front of the other melfs. Her face held a rare radiant smile, one that genuinely revealed her great joy then.

"My sons vied for my attention, each claiming at different times to be my favorite. Nui Danka, Nui Jooba and Nui Rei all quietly competed against each other in small ways. From escorting me to and from the market, giving me flowers for no special reason, preparing meals for me to just spending time with me asking me about my past, hopes and dreams. The young melfs constantly demonstrated their great appreciation and affection for their mother," Nui Honei confessed tearfully.

"That portrait was a surprise gift from her beloved Ona Noirar who had given her the portrait for no special reason other than just 'to see the joy of the House Nui Vent great mother's response,' Ona Noirar had claimed. However, I thought that he gifted me that portrait to permanently annoy the three troublesome melfs by reminding them that *he* was my true favorite!" scoffed Nui Honei. "*Foolish, foolish males.*"

Displaying a small smile, Nui Honei next recalled, "Ona Noirar's presentation of the portrait and declaration produced much laughter and fueled more friendly competition thereafter. In their own humorous way, my sons sought revenge by moving one or two displayed weapons Ona Noirar had on the walls of his private study. The great warrior was very orderly and each of his weapons had a very specific place on the walls. Any movement of his weapons, even over a small distance was a tremendous source of annoyance. Yet, my beloved did not ever complain but just accepted the mischief as signs of her sons' endearing affection."

How ironic she thought that her then future sons' first encounter with her future husband would be such that they would try to kill the then unknown Ona Noirar for being an assumed threat to her. Nui Honei quietly laughed as some new tears fell. "My sons were quite overly protective of me, as well as all the females of Houses Nui Vent and Je Luneefa. Whether noble or servant, strong or weak, her sons took great pride in protecting their Houses! It was a solemn duty and responsibility they all gladly embraced and upheld. All my sons brought much joy to me," the great mother of House Nui Vent quietly declared.

Weapons and martial arts training had been difficult for her sons if either of them had to face their adopted mother in a match. Nui Honei, being an elite warrior herself, was adept in several different martial arts, as well as many weapons. The House Nui Vent great mother had even secretly trained as an assassin. She would lead many training sessions. Her sons had difficulty competing against her in martial arts or weapons challenges for their "fear" of potentially losing their mother's favor. Still, her sons valiantly tried their best and still lost the contests every time.

All the melfs, except for Ona Noirar and Ona Drachir, were "lowly," being born of peasant or commoner blood. Ona Noirar and Ona Drachir of House Ona Feiir were of noble blood. *"Yet while gazing at the portrait on the far wall, the melfs of House Nui Vent all looked so regal,"* she thought. Nui Honei could only smile whenever she looked upon that portrait knowing that she had been blessed by Nui Danka and Nui Rei and would always cherish their memories.

Upon hearing a soft knock on the sitting room's open door, Nui Honei turned around to see her smiling nieces. "Good morning our beautiful Auntie," Je Danei first greeted.

"How do you feel today? Did you sleep well or were your little ones unsettled?" Je Leena inquired.

"Well met my dear beautiful nieces, daughters of House Je Luneefa. Good morning. I do feel well and very pregnant. The little ones were not too restless this past evening. I was able to sleep comfortably for most of the night. I do believe your uncle's singing to them may have helped," Nui Honei responded.

"Will he then be joining us for our meal also?" Je Danei asked.

Nui Honei replied, "Yes, he will. Both your uncles, in fact, should be there. They wanted to see all of you before you left on your sojourn into the mountain." Each niece walked over to their aunt, hugged her affectionately, and took an arm. They all then slowly walked to the main hall for their day's first meal.

Before leaving the room, the House Nui Vent great mother glanced back at the last portrait another time and smiled.

The First Elders' Will

The House Je Luneefa stronghold hides and protects many family secrets. The stronghold is a mighty fortress, purposely built into Mountain Toron not only for its protective properties, but also to provide well-guarded escape routes should the Je Luneefa family ever need to use such desperate alternatives. Besides the numerous, hidden passageways laden with deadly traps, powerful ancient magic is also constantly vigilant guarding the House Je Luneefa secrets throughout the great mountain.

One such secret of the House Je Luneefa are the family crypts. Deep within Mountain Toron, crypt Ardal Buel, holds family historical artifacts and is also one repository for the family's fortune.

Ardal Tae is another secret crypt; but it is used primarily as a secondary, family fortune storage repository. Not only are more gold reserves stashed there, but there are also relatively large quantities of extremely valuable diachrom hidden within this vault. Less important, but still valuable are some weapons used by other family ancestors. A few former enemy weapons there were either taken and/or won through honorable combat. Some weapons had even been gifted to the House Je Luneefa first elders from respected enemies and friends of esteemed honor. These various weapons adorned the crypt's walls. Beneath most of these weapons were scrolls describing the weapon's distinguished history.

House Je Luneefa great mother, Je Pagi, and her daughters, Je Danei and Je Leena, had made the day-long journey together to the secret crypt of her deceased father, Je Taeliel. After passing through several, magical protective walls, the House great mother and her daughters entered a large, well-appointed room. With the felfs' entrance, certain magic was then evoked illuminating the large interior by many fire globes placed across the room. Throughout the room on shelves and tables were many large and small bags. In addition, there were several large chests scattered around the room.

As Je Pagi looked around and collected certain items, she placed them into the large, old, plain looking, leather bag she carried. Her daughters walked around the crypt investigating its many wonders. For the daughters of House Je Luneefa, this was only their second journey to any family crypt. Their last visit was well over a hundred years ago.

Je Danei was drawn to inspect each of the different, exquisitely crafted blades she saw. Je Leena, on the other hand, just wandered aimlessly around her grandfather's secret cache and shrine. She eventually peeked into several of the many bags and discovered they were filled with unrefined gold. Je Leena also found other bags containing pure, unrefined diachrom ore.

After some time, both daughters noticed that their mother had stopped at a table on the far side of her father's crypt. Je Pagi was there quietly weeping.

"Mother, why do you weep?" Je Danei asked.

After a few more moments, the House Je Luneefa great mother turned to look at her daughters and replied, "Come here and see what my father truly treasured most of all." Je Danei and Je Leena both quietly walked across the room to stand by their mother in front of an opened chest. After peering inside the plain, ordinary-looking, wooden chest, both daughters' eyes started to fill with tears. Je Pagi started removing from the chest different gifts her daughters and sons had given their grandfather. Some of the gifts Je Pagi had given her father when she was a gelf were even there too. All these gifts were only simple drawings, paintings, structures and tokens she and the Je Luneefa granddaughters and grandsons had gifted "Papa" over the past several centuries. Each item was carefully taken from the chest, fondly recalled through tearful eyes, and placed onto the table. Many cherished memories of their beloved Papa returned and recaptured the three felfs with great sadness. All started weeping anew while hugging each other. After some time, comfort did come and rescued them from their latest grief. Je Pagi then meticulously returned her father's most valuable treasures to the chest.

"Let us prepare to leave soon; I have collected what is

needed for the meeting," Je Pagi announced. "Let me again remind you too that we do not discuss the treasure you saw here outside of this crypt. Here though you can speak freely." Both daughters nodded in acknowledgement.

Je Danei asked, "Will we also go to grandmother's crypt?"

"No. Your father and brothers have that honor. The pain of visiting my mother's crypt again would be too great. The sorrow I bear of losing her is still a constant reminder of someone who was so much more to me than just a mother," Je Pagi quietly responded. "Your father and brothers will retrieve the necessary items from that vault."

Now wanting to change subjects and hopefully lift her mother's spirits a bit, Je Leena inquired, "Mother, there are well over three hundred bags here. Are they all filled with gold?"

"Yes, most of the two hundred fifty-six brown bags are filled with gold. Thirty-two black bags contain raw diachrom," Je Pagi replied. "And those bottles on the far wall's shelves contain precious dragon's blood."

An astonished Je Leena gasped. Now, a shocked Je Danei looked up from the dagger she was examining with awestruck eyes after hearing her mother's last words. "Mother, how did our grandparents accumulate such wealth?"

Je Pagi replied, "Through your grandparents' perfidy with the Crown and with the aid of one then very mysterious Ona Noirar and his great dragon, Ona Kei Kuri Ryuu," Je Pagi nonchalantly replied. "Well over two centuries ago, Ona Noirar and Keiku lived in Taurus Mountain. They first discovered the rich veins of these precious metals. For many decades, they secretly mined and hid the treasure for their future use. After becoming very close friends with our House, they decided to secretly gift large amounts of the treasure to your grandparents who used that fortune to first build our stronghold and the Toronwalein. Ona Noirar and Keiku's gifts also funded the construction of the House Nui Vent stronghold too."

Both sisters then looked at each other somewhat amazed and puzzled after hearing such words, especially about their beloved grandparents.

Recognizing the puzzled looks on her daughters' faces, Je Pagi further explained, "As you know, the Crown has not been a *true* friend of Houses Je Luneefa, Nui Vent or Ona Feiir. They harbor great jealousy and distrust over your grandfather's miraculous accomplishments here in the North. Our support of Ona Noirar's relationship with the deceased princess angered them too. The king and queen were further enraged when our House adopted Nui

Honei, Nui Samu, Ona Noirar and Diazae Alleina.

"When Ona Noirar discovered the gold and diachrom in Mountain Taurus, 'technically' the Crown was due certain taxes on the find. Taurus Mountain was supposedly part of the Canae kingdom then. However, your grandparents chose not to disclose the discovery. Fortunately, the *official* northern border of the Canae realm was later declared to be leagues south of that mountain. Your grandparents were very wise to always hide the true facts of our family's wealth. You and your brothers also must always guard such family secrets."

Je Leena's attention now was quickly drawn to the dagger her sister held. Two small red points glowed brightly near the base of the blade. Je Danei handed the fine weapon to her sister after Je Danei noticed that her sister's piqued interest had been unusually aroused. After handing the dagger to Je Leena, the youngest Je Luneefa daughter closely examined the blade. As she suspected, this sinister looking weapon was imbued with magic. What exactly the magic is was unknown to the young battlemage. There at the base of the blade itself, a small spider had been placed. This spider had small red gemstones for its eyes. A spider's web was also etched on both sides of the double-curve blade. Upon receiving the dagger, Je Leena also noticed that the etched spider's eyes no longer glowed. The dagger's pommel also held the image of a small spider. After her examination, she returned the weapon to Je Danei. The spider's eyes immediately glowed again when the House Je Luneefa first daughter received the blade.

Je Leena asked, "Mother, do you know the blade that Danei holds? Papa left no scroll for this weapon."

Je Danei held up the blade for her mother to see. Je Pagi looked at the weapon but did not know the blade's true history. "I do not know that blade nor do I recall my father ever speaking about such a unique weapon," Je Pagi remarked. "Anyway, I have now finished collecting everything needed and packing my bag. So, let us now leave this place and return home."

"May I take this spider fang dagger with us and ask Auntie about it?" Je Leena inquired. Je Pagi nodded in response knowing that her sister, a renowned battlemage, could possibly answer any further questions Je Leena might have.

As the House Je Luneefa great mother and her daughters left the crypt, Je Pagi checked the magical seals of the hidden repository again with all its magical protective wards. She briefly thanked her mother too for also gifting her with a bag that can easily hold many items after greatly reducing their size and weight through magic. The bag could even conceal its precious contents as well within its hidden compartments. Under normal circumstances, Je Pagi removed from the crypt a wagon's load of weight and items. However, on this special occasion, the House Je Luneefa great mother was able to easily pack and carry all the necessary things within her large, plain looking, but very magical bag. As before, the felfs traversed back through the mountain's depths quickly returning home in less than one day. They still needed to prepare for an important event.

The House Je Luneefa elders invited the House Nui Vent elders to a late-night meeting in the House Je Luneefa stronghold two days later. Je Pagi and Je Maron had also invited Alleina, Ona Noirar, Ona Drachir, the Canae northern army commanders and the Houses armies' commanders along with all the daughters and sons of both Houses Je Luneefa and Nui Vent. All would assemble in the House Je Luneefa stronghold's great hall.

Even the great dragon, Ona Kei Kuri Ryuu, had been invited and would attend albeit she would watch and listen through a window overlooking an enclosed courtyard. Keiku's magic blocked the night's weather from entering the great hall. Even though the air was still cold, the weather presented a welcoming invitation to three young dragons playing cheerfully with each other in the courtyard around their mother. Keiku's offspring Nui Kei Dan-Rei Ryuu, Ona Tae Kuri Ryuu and Je Ri Kuri Ryuu just played like young elves without any cares.

The final days of winter were passing; yet soft, knee-deep snow still blanketed the land. The House Je Luneefa great hall has two great fireplaces at each end of the room and the roaring fires maintain a warm temperature within the large space. At the front of the room on a dais, Je Pagi and Je Maron sat with numerous scrolls and several chests laying on the main table. Four other large tables were in the hall too facing the front of the hall. Family members and honored guests were seated at these other tables.

Following the instructions of her deceased parents, House Je Luneefa great mother Je Pagi congregated together these select individuals for them to hear the House Je Luneefa first elders' last wishes. Since the first elders' deaths, six moons have passed. Given her deep sorrow, Je Pagi had postponed this sad duty a few times. But now she thought the time had finally come when she could fulfill her last responsibility to her parents without too many sorrowful tears being shed.

The reading of Je Buel and Je Taeliel's will was to be done that night. All those attending this meeting were still in some stage of mourning. House Je Luneefa great mother, Je Pagi, was still greatly affected by the passing of her dear parents and still cried each day. However, her tears became less with each new day. The grief she bears slowly fades away as the joys of Je Annaei and Je Kei's Dwarven wedding celebration approached. *"I still am so amazed that my youngest son, the one who would bury himself studying scrolls and tomes for days, somehow miraculously found his 'one' at the infamous Dwarven Heartstone Architectural and Engineering Academy. Born a woods elf and orphaned but raised by Clan Battle Hammer dwarves, this felf brings great joy to our House,"* Je Pagi pondered from time to time.

More joy entered her saddened heart too as her adopted sister, House great mother Nui Honei, approached the delivery time of her twin elf infants and her wedding celebration. The House Nui Vent great mother was a fearless warrior and battlemage; however, the unknowns of pregnancy and childbirth frightened Nui Honei. So, Je Pagi, a "veteran" of five pregnancies and childbirths herself, is of great comfort to her sister. Je Pagi's given support also lessened her grief's toll which decreased each day as her attention was required for the remaining family and dear friends. With each new day, Je Pagi healed a bit more, recovering from her great loss. Reading her parents' will was another barricade she needed to remove to continue her healing. *"This sorrowful duty had been postponed long enough,"* she thought.

House great mother Je Pagi rose and addressed the group "Thank you all for joining us for the reading of my parents' will. Also, thank you all again for your words of encouragement and on-going support as I continue to heal from this great pain of losing my beloved parents. I know we all share this pain of losing our House's beloved first elders, but I do hope your pain, like mine, decreases with each new day.

"This is my last responsibility to them... No, my true, our true last responsibilities to them are to continue to live well, protect the Je Luneefa, Nui Vent and Ona Feiir families and dear friends, and be happy. These sacred responsibilities are truly life-long." After pausing again a few moments seemingly reflecting upon some private thoughts, she continued, "Despite the great sorrow we share over losing the House Je Luneefa first elders, my burden of sorrow becomes less as I look upon my dear daughters, sons, nephews and friends who are still very much alive, safe and well. May we all mourn less with each passing day. Thank you all again." Je Pagi then raised her glass in a toast to her family and friends. In response, the group all raised their glasses in a silent, respectful response.

    Je Pagi continued, "Let us now begin. First, Je Maron and I will give you the personal letter my parents wrote to each of you. Each letter is addressed and sealed; so, we do not know the contents of your letters." Je Maron started passing the designated personal letter to each meeting attendee. After distributing the letters, Je Maron quietly took his place again at the room's center table, next to his wife.

    "Secondly, I will now read my parents' will," Je Pagi then said and selected a scroll in front of her, broke the seal and started reading aloud, "I, House Je Luneefa great mother, Je Buel, and I, House Je Luneefa great father, Je Taeliel, herby declare this to be our last, final will and testament…"

    The House Je Luneefa great mother stopped, now with eyes full of tears, and handed the scroll to her husband to continue with the reading. Je Pagi sat down again and softly cried overcome again with the weight of her great sorrow.

    Je Maron first consoled his wife for a few moments before continuing, "To Alleina, the finest healer in the kingdom, the House Je Luneefa first elders thank her again not only for having enough courage to leave Rhodell with House Je Luneefa so many years ago, but also for being a loyal and devoted daughter to their House. Having the healer join them on their journey to the northern desolate lands of Canae provided great comfort to the first elders, as well as to their young daughter then. Alleina, you became like a second daughter us, a dear sister to our lonely daughter, and eventually a beloved aunt to our granddaughters and grandsons."

    The House Je Luneefa first elders bequeathed to Alleina two large bags of gold. The elders noted that the gold was for compensation she did not receive from the many Torondell poor citizens who could not pay her for the medical services she provided over the many decades. Alleina was generous with her medical talents and cared for the rich, as well as the poor equally. Alleina had also sacrificed a wealthy and promising career in Rhodell to journey also to the dangerous northern frontier. Her loyalty to House Je Luneefa was exemplary.

    In addition, House great mother Je Buel left her a book containing secret family recipes for the preparation of many delicious foods. After Alleina graciously accepted her gifts, she started immersing herself in the precious recipe book once she noticed that Je Buel had personally magically sealed the book and penned each page. This book was most precious and greatly valued by the humble healer, for it personified many pleasant memories of her cooking with the House Je Luneefa first great mother and Je Pagi.

Similarly, the House Je Luneefa first elders next thanked House great mother Nui Honei for becoming another dear "daughter" to them, a loving "sister" to their Je Pagi, and a beloved "aunt" to their granddaughters and grandsons. The elders quipped that Ona Noirar is truly worthy enough to be her husband; so, she should consider marrying him now. Further, the first elders proclaimed, "And according to Canae law, his possessions would become your shared possessions. So, Keiku will formally and officially become your dragon – which we know she already really is."

"Even now, House great mother Je Buel still continues to derive humor at my expense," remarked a quietly laughing and tearful Ona Noirar, touched by the words of the House Je Luneefa first great mother who had become like a mother to him too. Keiku stretched her neck into the hall and quietly roared in acknowledgement. Ona Noirar stood and placed his arms around Keiku's neck and declared loudly, "Mine!" In response, Keiku snorted, and Nui Honei just scoffed shaking her head. All the others laughed.

The House Je Luneefa first elders bequeathed to Nui Honei a diachrom, gem-studded necklace and matching bracelets. The precious necklace contained two diamonds, seven emeralds and ten rubies. Upon receiving her gift, Nui Honei studied the necklace closely and realized that the gems were a representation of the first elders' "family," immediate and extended. She also immediately recognized that the necklace and gems all encapsulated different blood-magic properties.

Ona Noirar and Nui Samu too received similar jewel-studded chains and matching bracelets. Further, a small bag of gold was bequeathed to Nui Samu for the "specific use of buying new, custom-made attire made by Zhen Lae," Je Buel and Je Taeliel stated.

"So, they evidently knew about my closely guarded, secret feelings towards Zhen Lae," Nui Samu quietly remarked turning to look at his blood-brother, Ona Noirar.

"Brother, I would not ever willingly divulge any of your secrets; but House great mother Je Buel had her quiet, clandestine ways of gently wresting secrets from us without our knowledge. She was a master of bribery and using subtle arts of *encouragement* ranging from food to trading information. Surely, we all have been her target at some time. I honestly believe she used my beloved Nui

Honei as her accomplice to gather and analyze information with her," admitted Ona Noirar attempting to redirect Nui Samu's irritated attention to someone else.

"Dear Samu, Noirar may be completely innocent. My mother utilized all the females of our Houses to gather facts for her. No secrets you males had would ever remain secret from her for too long," Je Pagi remarked.

"Besides, I realized you liked Lady Zhen Lae when you went to her shop three times in the same seven-day time period to get the same vest coat 'adjusted' supposedly," Je Danei contributed.

"And you personally accompanied her home from her dress shop at least sixteen times over the last ten moons," added Je Leena.

"I have also noticed that you seem to get nervous when she stands close to you," Alleina said quietly chuckling.

"And you missed hitting a distant target that you had hit five times earlier this year after Zhen Lae joined us on the training field requesting personal self-defense instructions from you," added Sochae, First Commander of the Canae northern army forces.

"You also joined our House soldiers many times when we needed to escort her to and from the traders' market or Zhen Laehua's concert appearances," House army First Commander Somai also commented.

"So, dear brother, as you can see, House great mother Je Buel had many eyes watching and ears listening over her family," Nui Honei concluded.

"The females of our Houses are truly formidable. Je Annaei, will you too become cunning like the other females of our Houses?" Nui Samu asked.

"Yes. Me pledged to House great moder Je Buel to be a *dutiful daughter* of de House Je Luneefa. Me be and will continue to do so aldough me not be as skilled yet as de oder females of Houses Je Luneefa and Nui Vent; but, me learnin'," Je Annaei responded proudly and without hesitation.

"Ha! Father, uncles and brothers, our *war* against the females of our Houses continues," Je Jero declared.

"Oh Jero, please understand that you males can only win a few battles against us. The females of our Houses continue to win the *war*. You just need to realize and accept it," proclaimed Je Danei.

Together, all the females raised their glasses and shouted, "Aye!" Even Keiku stood on her hind legs, spread her wings, and then roared in agreement. Her daughter, Nui Kei Dan-Rei Ryuu, too imitated her mother, but could only emit an annoying, nonintimidating loud screech.

Continuing, Je Pagi read that each granddaughter and grandson, including Annaei, Ona Drachir, and Nui Jooba, was bequeathed a bag of gold.

To the great dragon, Ona Kei Kuri Ryuu, the House Je Luneefa first elders bequeathed full payment to commission the manufacturing of new, diachrom-enhanced armor. The armorers of Clan Battle Hammer had constructed her first armor and they already had started constructing the dragon's new armor. The early mining operations at Taurus Mountain had gone remarkably well. Much gold and diachrom had been mined, not only to replenish the Je Luneefa family crypts but also to provide the diachrom enriched gifts. When Keiku goes to attend Annaei and Je Kei's Dwarven wedding celebration at the Blood Tears Mountains in a few moons' time, the final fitting will take place then.

Each northern army and House army first commander received a small bag of gold which represented thirty years' worth of their salary. Je Pagi and Je Maron knew that the House Je Luneefa first elders greatly valued the loyalty, dedication, and unwavering commitment these commanders displayed to their duties and responsibilities over the centuries. Je Buel and Je Taeliel were greatly appreciative, and these gifts were another small token of the elders' deep gratitude. The commanders also promised that they would personally deliver the deceased Commander Baka's gift to his widow.

Further, each soldier of the northern army and House army were bequeathed four gold coins. These gifts were to be awarded in a ceremony over which House great mother and father, Je Pagi and Je Maron, along with the commanders, would preside. Again, the House Je Luneefa first elders wanted to reward all the soldiers for their unwavering loyalty, dedication to service and exemplary commitment. The stunned commanders repeatedly thanked Je Pagi and Je Maron again, praising Je Buel and Je Taeliel for their leadership, loyalty, and dedication to the Canae northern and House armies.

Each House servant was to receive three gold coins which was the equivalent of six years' salary.

Lastly, the large plot of rich farmland outside the Toronwalzwei by the Toron River southern tributaries was bequeathed to Je Pagi and Je Maron for the sole purpose of providing shelter and occupation to the homeless of Torondell. The House Je Luneefa first elders had bought this land long ago not knowing then how to use it. As time passed and the city's homeless population grew, Nui Danka gave the elders the idea of using that land as a farm and providing shelter for the homeless of Torondell. Large dormitory-like buildings had been constructed and most of the homeless left the city and found welcomed refuge at the Torondell's Estelridhaus, "Farm of Hope." Those living at the farm worked, learned a trade, and received fair wages for their efforts.

Je Pagi then dismissed the army commanders with more thanks and gratitude on behalf of the House Je Luneefa first elders. The remainder of the meeting would pertain to personal family matters only.

The House great mother Je Pagi resumed the meeting by next telling the daughters and sons of Houses Je Luneefa, Nui Vent and Ona Feiir that each one would receive a pair of blood-magic enhanced, diachrom enriched bracers. The steel bracers, infused with diachrom, would greatly protect their forearms. Unlike the elders' bracers, the daughters and sons of Houses Je Luneefa, Nui Vent and Ona Feiir received bracers containing only two bloodstones.

"So, grandmother's 'routine' extraction of our blood every ten years had serious purpose, so it seems," Je Danei pondered out loud.

"Most definitely. Our bracers have remarkable capabilities and yours will be bonded to you through blood-magic. The Houses Je Luneefa, Nui Vent and Ona Feiir families' wellbeing and protection were always the House first elders' first priority. Even now after they are deceased, they continue to perform that sacred duty. We are truly blessed to be part of their family," Nui Honei proclaimed.

Je Pagi resumed reading the House first elders will. Je Pagi and Je Maron received several manuscripts Je Kei had authored when he was younger. Of the four original manuscripts, only one resulted in a published book, *The Mathematics of Tunneling*. The original manuscript also had some unpublished map drawings of mountains that Duenor Heartstone had surveyed many years ago.

Je Buel bequeathed all her clothes to Je Pagi, Nui Honei and Alleina. The House Je Luneefa first great mother also specified which daughter and granddaughter would receive the pieces from her jewelry collection. This House elder also bequeathed all her books, journals and artifacts pertaining to magic to her granddaughter, Je Leena.

Je Taeliel's clothes and other personal belongings were bequeathed to Je Maron and his grandsons. Je Taeliel had collected and received different weapons over his lifetime. Some weapons were family heirlooms; some weapons were gifts received; and others were haunting reminders of his sometimes evil and dark past.

Je Jero received a pair of scorpion blades with matching long knives and daggers. Je Tero received Khopesh blades, falchions, and shields. Je Danei received several different naginata, butterfly swords, throwing knives and shuriken. Je Kei received several spears, shields, and knives along with books and scrolls pertaining to ancient elven construction principles. Je Leena received spears, knives, a long bow, and a quiver of arrows. Annaei too received knives, a long bow, and a quiver of arrows. Ona Drachir received battle maces, spears and a bladed Manriki-gusari. Lastly, Nui Jooba received spears and a bladed Manriki-gusari. With each weapon, the House Je Luneefa first father also penned a scroll detailing the weapon's history and any special inherent, magical capabilities.

House Je Luneefa first great mother Je Buel wrote:

Your aunt or mother, Nui Honei, will bond the designated weapons to you through blood-magic rituals. Also, magically welcome Annaei to our families and Houses. Please get this done very soon!

The last page of the House Je Luneefa first elders' will ended with a directive to their granddaughters and grandsons:

Though we are no longer there to watch over and guide you, fiercely love, protect our family and support each other. Know that we greatly loved you all and are immensely proud of each of you. Honor us by remembering and maintaining the valuable lessons we tried to teach you. Love fiercely, live honorably and be happy.

Lastly, your parents want to know and enjoy the great honor and privilege of being grandparents. So, make baby elves and grow our family too!

Lastly again, definitely the last this time, we will still be watching over you...

All the Houses Je Luneefa, Nui Vent and Ona Feiir family members started weeping quietly as the meeting concluded. After many hugs, each left the hall.

On their silent return to Je Kei's room, Je Annaei asked, "Kei, wat be dat part in de will about 'magically welcoming me to de families and Houses'? Me did not understand."

Je Kei quietly responded, still saddened with memories of his deceased grandparents, "Beloved, there are numerous magical wards protecting our Houses and the passageways of Toron Mountain. These wards also constantly guard our family crypts. Should anyone or any living thing attempt to pass through such guarded tunnels, they will be destroyed. Any living thing attempting to break into a family crypt would also meet its death. Only the living blood of a family member can safely pass through these guarded passageways. Through a blood-magic ritual, our aunt will share our family blood, taken from our grandparents, with you."

Je Kei started laughing to himself and continued, "Remember seeing those statues of my grandparents in our stronghold? Those statues and some others are imbued with magic and will defend this House when called upon. My grandparents truly are still watching over and protecting us."

Dragonosophy

Ona Kei Kuri Ryuu looked upon her three young offspring with great pride and admiration. Before her stood her daughter, Nui Kei Dan-Rei Ryuu, Keiku's first born. The great dragon's sons are Ona Tae Kuri Ryuu and Je Ri Kuri Ryuu. Daughter Dan-Rei, named after the House Nui Vent's fallen sons, Nui Danka and Nui Rei, is eight moons old. Dan-Rei is bonded to Nui Jooba. Taeku and Riku eggs both hatched about the same time but are not twins. These infant dragons are just four moons old. Taeku, named after Je Taeliel, is bonded to Ona Drachir, the last son of House Ona Feiir. Riku is bonded to Je Leena, the second daughter of House Je Luneefa. Riku also bears the second name of Je Buel, "Ri", the House Je Luneefa first great mother.

Through magic, all could communicate with each other mentally since they all shared Keiku's blood. High atop Mountain Toron, the great dragon continues instructing her young ones on what it means to be a dragon. Most importantly, Keiku is teaching them what it means to be *her* offspring. The elder dragon would often say, *"Young dragons, you are my offspring. I and the elders of our Houses hold you to the high standards I have set. My expectations are that each of you will be noble and aspire to greatness like me. And hopefully, you will even surpass my renowned accomplishments in the centuries to come."*

During these same training sessions, Keiku, with the aid of an attending felf or melf, would read from the *Chronicles* of Siida, her mother. Siida was another great dragon that had many adventures and acquired much knowledge, especially knowledge of magic. The great tomes looked like any other slab of unremarkable rock – when not touched by a dragon or elf carrying her blood. However, when touched by one sharing Keiku's living blood the "slab of unremarkable rock" transforms into the great tome. Siida and Jaale wrote and left two great tomes. The first was dedicated to capturing the dragon and dragon rider's histories and adventures. The second tome documented much of the wonders of magic, not only its principles but also many of its mysteries. In addition, much of the ancient Elvish language, the world's first language, was documented. This second tome also contained many incantations which can only be evoked with the first language.

The young dragons, as well as their riders, would all learn of Siida and her rider's, Jaale, feats and adventures. Siida and Jaale too had learned much ancient Elvish language, language that would be invaluable to know when casting certain spells.

Also present were the newly bonded dragons' riders, Nui Jooba, Ona Drachir and Je Leena. In Keiku's lair, there were few distractions; yet the young male dragons' attention seemed too easily drawn to playing with one another as opposed to listening to their mother's instructions. Fortunately, Keiku was patient, very patient. To no fault of their own, Taeku and Riku are still very young, and today's lesson focused upon more of the ancient Elvish language which none of the young male dragons really enjoyed.

"Why must we learn the ancient Elvish language?" Taeku questioned again.

"Magic, especially ancient magic, may only be evoked with incantations spoken in the ancient Elvish tongue. We dragons are the embodiment of magic, powerful magic. So, you will learn this, as well as several other useful languages. I am fluent in the twelve languages spoken across this kingdom. So, I will expect all of you to become fluent in at least the most popular four languages besides the ancient Elvish dialect," Keiku would respond.

Dan-Rei would add her support, "We are the offspring of the world's greatest dragon. Our mother too is the descendant of another great dragon. We will not be ignorant and shame our ancestors. I, Taeku and Riku will be immortalized not only for our noble, heroic deeds and fighting skills, but also for our vast, comprehensive knowledge. Mother, as your blessed offspring, we too will also acquire great knowledge."

Keiku continued instructing, "Energy to fuel magical incantations is drawn from the one casting such incantation or spell. Little spells require little energy; whereas more powerful, big spells require larger amounts of energy. When a spell is cast, the needed energy is taken from the spell's caster. That internal energy is primarily sourced from one's blood. And one's personal, internal power source or energy amount is limited and can greatly vary from individual to individual. Further, as one's energy is depleted, time is required to replenish one's internal power resources.

"Long ago, mages also discovered that nature's crystals could be used to capture and store primal energy needed to power magical spells. Whether from the wind, water, fire or even lightning, nature's primordial sources of power can be absorbed and stored in quartz rocks. Mages learned thereafter to utilize this stored energy for their magical purposes. Quartz rocks are like power cells and carried in a special belt that a spellcaster wears. Mages can draw upon the needed energy stored in the crystals to power their magical spells before utilizing one's internal energy.

"Different crystals, based upon size and color, store different amounts of energy. When depleted, these crystals' energy requires replenishment from primordial sources of energy like the sun, fire, water, and wind. Even energy generated from life and forces of nature could be captured to store in the crystals. As you might imagine, crystals have their advantages as well as disadvantages as energy sources needed for magical spells. Using one's blood as the energy source for magical incantations can have far greater advantages when the spellcaster's blood has been enhanced with the blood of dragons.

"Dragons though are blessed being great creatures of both nature and wonderous, mysterious magic. We have an extraordinary amount of magical energy and that wonderous energy also chiefly comes from our blood, our main life source. Further, know that dragon's blood, especially the blood of a black dragon that has been fully blessed and freely given is extremely powerful and is an unequaled source of magical energy. Even with no blessing, our blood is still powerful. However, the blood's power is greatly magnified by the Massicenae, one of the first dragon riders, blessing cited in the ancient dragon's language. Following the ancient tradition, a full blessing, or the truest blessing, requires the dragon to incant the Massicenae spell fully three times when its blood is freely given:"

> Blood of my ancestors, blood of mine.
> To these friends, I freely give.
> I beseech thee my ancestors; bless my gift.
> Let my dragon's blood be transformative.

Keiku also instructed the young ones that their blood will be requested from time to time by their riders, "Blessed dragon's blood holds a power unlike any other. Yet the blood's potency will slowly dissipate with time. So, know that freshly drawn and blessed dragon's blood will be needed by your riders or even our family members to bring their health, strength, stamina and dragon-enhanced senses to their full potential."

Then Ona Noirar added, after drawing his scimitar, "Your blood too, after taken by your rider or family member, can then utilize that power to greatly enhance certain capabilities of his or her blood-magic weapons. The joining of your dragon's blood with your family member restricts only her or him to call upon the magical capabilities of the weapon." The melf then quickly struck a boulder, cutting it into two pieces. Upon displaying his weapon to the young dragons and their riders, they all noticed that the blade displayed not the slightest damage. "As you can attest, my blade suffered no damage."

"Just as important, if not more, your blade made no sound when you struck that boulder," Dan-Rei recalled. "When stealth is of vital importance, killing an enemy silently could also be very critical." Dan-Rei's keen observation was awarded with small smiles by both Keiku and Ona Noirar.

"How long will it take before I master flying? When can I breathe fire? How do you make red flame-spears? When will I be able to make red flame-spears? When can we go hunting again?" Taeku and Riku would ask incessantly and almost daily to the point where it would sometimes become quite annoying. Other than flying, hunting, or play-fighting, the young male dragons cared for little else.

Taking a deep breath, either Ona Noirar or Keiku would respond, "Patience, little ones. The time for you to do those things will come. You first need to devote time and effort to learning many rudimentary things. In time, you will learn how to master those things you desire most and much more."

On the other hand, Dan-Rei, a young, smaller, mirror image of her mother, listened intently to her elders' instructions. Dan-Rei was obsessively committed to fulfilling, if not exceeding, her mother and Ona Noirar's expectations. Indeed, this young female dragon wanted to become a scholar as well as a great warrior, just like her renowned mother.

With spending additional time with Je Kei helping him translate some ancient Elvish language scrolls, the young female dragon started to excel in the language arts. Je Kei introduced Dan-Rei to his dwarf grandmother, Urtha Dal, who was not only a renowned battlemage, but also another great scholar. Urtha Dal was now the first great mother of Clan Battle Hammer and a highly valued resource of great knowledge. During scrying sessions with Urtha Dal, Je Kei and Dan-Rei learned much about the ancient Elvish language. Urtha Dal also informed the young ones that the portion of the great Dwarven library pertaining to the ancient Elvish language would be copied and sent to them later this year. Dan-Rei was most pleased with the news. She could thereafter study ancient Elvish more easily. Je Kei needed only to recompense his grandmother with a great granddaughter or grandson soon and four bottles of Napa brandy.

After today's morning lesson concluded, the young male dragons started romping around the lair. While the morning lesson took place, Ona Noirar instructed the bored Je Danei in the preparation of a dragon's meal consisting mainly of deer meat. The House Je Luneefa first daughter often accompanied Nui Jooba to Keiku's lair. Dragons still fascinated the House Je Luneefa first daughter. She too secretly wanted to become a famed dragon rider. Much to her disappointment, none of Keiku's eggs had hatched for Je Danei, but the warrior felf was still pleased to be welcomed at the dragon lair and dragon riders' lessons. Keiku still had one last unhatched egg, and Je Danei still had hopes that one day, she too would be bonded with a dragon. When the House Je Luneefa first daughter visited the great dragon's lair, Je Danei would periodically silently slip away from everyone to touch Keiku's last unhatched dragon's egg.

Not all were pleased when Je Danei visited the dragons' lair. Dan-Rei was not overjoyed with Je Danei's presence. Dan-Rei would insert herself between Nui Jooba and the felf whenever she could, nudging the felf away. Dan-Rei had become quite fond of Nui Jooba and was jealous of Je Danei's ability to redirect her rider's attention away from her. There were even times when the young dragon would bare her fangs at the felf, especially when Dan-Rei's menacing behavior would hopefully go unnoticed by Nui Jooba or her elders.

Nui Honei devoted time to educating the young dragons and dragon riders in the exploits of Keiku, herself and Ona Noirar. The elder felf would often read from Keiku's Chronicles. Their history conveyed many important lessons.

Each day Keiku would fly with her young dragons. Her sons would only be allowed to fly short distances with their mother.

However, Dan-Rei, being older and stronger, could fly longer distances and at greater heights and speeds. Keiku also started battle training with her daughter. She instructed her young ones in the dragon's version of martial arts. She reminded them often that there will be times when they must be able to fight not only in the air but also on the ground using just their claws, fangs, and tail. The young dragons greatly enjoyed these particular lessons.

With each passing moon, the young dragons and their riders became stronger together, more knowledgeable in the dragon arts and became more committed in accepting their great responsibilities.

An Honored Tradition

It was pre-dawn and a bit cold within the House Je Luneefa stronghold. All was quiet; no one, not even patrolling House soldiers nor servants, could be heard performing their early morning duties.

A lone, dark cloaked figure crept silently unnoticed through the hall from the first floor to the main stairway and moved quickly up the stairway to the second level of the stronghold. Stealthily, this hooded one, who also carried a covered tray, continued to move silently to the bedchamber of the House Je Luneefa youngest daughter. Je Leena's bedchamber door was partially opened, and the lone hooded figure entered the room silently, closing the door behind her.

"You are late," Je Leena said.

"Apologies, but me took longer dan expected to find everythin' needed from de kitchen," responded Je Annaei, the dwarf-raised, female woods elf, after removing her hood.

"Do you really think this tactic will work to uncover whatever secret they are hiding from us?" Je Danei questioned with certain doubt in her voice.

"The males of Houses Je Luneefa, Nui Vent and Ona Feiir are planning something for tonight and we need to know what it is. They must again learn they should not keep secrets from us," Je Leena declared. Turning to Je Annaei, she continued, "You volunteered to wrest whatever secrets Kei might harbor using your preferred tactic of 'feeding him his favorite foods in bed'. You are our last hope since Danei and I failed in our more straightforward attempts already. Mother cannot divulge any information either since she too is unaware of the intent behind tonight's meeting. Our aunties are unaware, and both prescribed we should rely upon and use our own *exclusive female talents* to get the information we want."

"Be de 'exclusive female talents' dey be talkin' about refer to sexual talents?" an exorbitantly smiling Je Annaei asked.

"Yes, of course," Je Leena answered nonchalantly. "Go now sister and report back here after you uncover their secret."

Je Annaei covered her head again and left Je Leena's room silently. After returning to Je Kei's bedchamber, Je Annaei silently entered the dark room and closed the door. After her eyes adjusted to the darkness, she immediately noticed that Je Kei was no longer sleeping in their bed. Upon hearing the door to his private water room open, she turned and stood motionless, just gazing at Je Kei. There stood her husband in the doorway, wet, completely naked and glistening from the candlelight behind him in the water room. The young felf smiled just gazing longingly at her husband. "Ye be hungry?" she then inquired, extending the tray she carried.

Je Kei returned her devilish smile and replied, "Oh me darlin' beautiful wife, me be ravenous now!"

A few hours later, Je Annaei returned to Je Leena's room to report to her sisters about her attempt to uncover the secret hidden from them. "Me failed," Je Annaei sadly immediately admitted after entering the room and seeing her new sisters waiting anxiously for information. "Kei be waitin' fer me, and he outmaneuvered me wid his own clever 'talents'... Me did try hard. He anticipated me would try to trick him into tellin' de secret, but he would not. Me tried real hard too, but he kept distractin' me wid more of his clever talents... Oh, how me love me husband! He did dough say dat all us females should meet at de door of de great hall at sundown tonight."

"Then stop grinning so much," Je Leena said disappointingly. "We should have targeted our other brothers or Jooba last. Their defenses would not be so formidable. Kei, it seems, is still unlikely to succumb to your charms Annaei. Drachir knows my tricks; so, he would not be easy prey either." Turning and looking at her older sister, Je Danei, Je Leena continued, "And you failed too with your initial meal attempts. Why do you still feel uncomfortable using sex to extract information? Sex is a powerful weapon of our female powers; we must wield all our formidable weapons to gain victory! Remember sisters, we are constantly at war with the males of our united Houses. We must show the males we are always in control and know everything. Our grandmother, the House Je Luneefa first great mother, Je Buel, would want it so. We must vigorously maintain the tradition she started. It is part of our sacred duty in protecting our Houses. Let us go now and meet Mother and our aunties for the day's first meal. Maybe they can then share what information someone else may have gathered."

Disappointed, the young felfs left Je Leena's bedchamber and went to the main dining hall. There inside were the House Je Luneefa great mother Je Pagi, Nui Honei and Alleina. House Nui Vent great father Nui Samu was there too. Now that Nui Honei was in her tenth moon of pregnancy, she is always accompanied by a family member whenever she left her stronghold. Given the extremely rare occurrence of elves having multiple births at one time, there was great concern for her health and the health of her unborn. So, Je Pagi, and Alleina gave strict orders that Nui Honei was not ever to be left alone during this late stage of her pregnancy when many complications could possibly occur.

"Greetings honored elders of Houses Je Luneefa and Nui Vent," Je Danei said after entering the hall.

Nui Samu briefly smiled and nodded to welcome the young felfs. "Well met my daughters, good morning," Je Pagi said warmly with a smile. "Any great news yet?"

Je Leena quickly responded, "The young melfs of our Houses are planning..."

"Daughter, no. The only *great* news I would wish to hear is that one of my daughters has conceived my glorious first granddaughter or grandson. Well?" Je Pagi inquired impatiently with eyes reflecting joyous anticipation.

The young felfs walked to elders and hugged each affectionately. They all reported too that no one was yet pregnant.

Nui Samu chuckled and added, "Daughters of House Je Luneefa and my beloved nieces, the advantages of pregnancy would be great. For example, as our Houses' weapons master, your training schedule would be significantly reduced, and..."

Je Pagi quickly asserted with a commanding voice, unconsciously using her mother's authoritative voice, "Ha! Dear brother Samu, as the ruling House great mother, any of my daughters bearing *my* granddaughter or grandson will have no training during her pregnancy!"

"I told you Samu. Now pay me since you lost the wager!" Alleina declared. All laughed.

"Why must you be so much like your mother?" Nui Samu

asked Je Pagi. "She did not want you to continue training either even when you were pregnant at the very early stages."

Smiling pleasantly at Nui Samu, Je Pagi concluded, "My mother was so very wise."

Je Leena added, "Dearest Uncle, should there have been any mishap possibly harming *her* granddaughter or grandson, whom do you think would bear the consequences of my grandmother's great anger which could last decades?" Je Pagi's cold stare certainly indeed reminded the House weapon's master Je Buel would have indeed punished him severely for any accident that may have occurred to her most precious, pregnant daughter.

"Nui Honei joined in and whispered, "Take the hint dear Brother. There will be *no* weapons or martial arts training at any time for any pregnant daughter of Houses Je Luneefa and Nui Vent." A bit surprised, Nui Samu looked around at the united females of Houses Je Luneefa and Nui Vent, succumbed to the immense weight of their collective stares, and nodded, acknowledging the House Je Luneefa great mother's directive.

"Where is Uncle Noirar?" inquired Je Danei.

"No doubt, he is still sleeping. I had several requests requiring his attention throughout my past night's unrest. He is still very attentive and fulfills my every wish. My beloved did not sleep well. Our unborn elves were quite unsettled during the night; so, we walked throughout the stronghold for hours to quiet these restless ones. My little ones also craved pie twice last night," Nui Honei reported. "When I look at you my nieces, my spirits are lifted knowing that my young ones will become great little ones despite my current discomfort."

Je Pagi exclaimed, "Hah! Mine were all restless too at my late stage of pregnancy. Danei was my most restless; she began fighting unknown battles even in my womb. My mother and father knew then she was destined to become a great warrior. Leena's restlessness was more at night and subtle. She fought quiet battles, it seemed against enemies. All daughters are truly remarkable and incredibly special. My mother was very much a part of raising Danei and Leena. I see much of Urtha Dal in you too Je Annaei. My daughters are extensions of my mother mostly in strange ways. Grandmothers meddle more perhaps. They want to ensure they leave their mark on this world, especially through their granddaughters, I believe. Honei, I do hope you have daughters; our families need more battlemages. And females make the best!"

Nui Honei chuckled quietly and said, "Pagi, be honest; you really want your chance to play *grandmother* with all the new infants born into our Houses! You too want immortality like great House mother Je Buel." With that proclamation, all the females joined in laughter now knowing that House Je Luneefa great mother Je Pagi anxiously awaited becoming a proud grandmother.

"Who are your attendants today, Sister?" Je Pagi inquired.

"I believe Jooba has the honor this day," Nui Honei responded. "According to my son, the great dragon Ona Kei Kuri Ryuu and her young ones should arrive here shortly after our meal. They too want to visit with me."

"By the way, where is Zhen Lae? Why is she not here yet?" Je Danei inquired. All eyes then turned toward the House Nui Vent great father who immediately felt some unwanted pressure of discussing his supposedly "secret" romantic relationship with Zhen Lae. Nui Samu stopped drinking his tea and before he could conjure some clever answer to hopefully distract his female relatives, the doors to the dining hall opened and the males of House Je Luneefa, Ona Drachir and Nui Jooba arrived. In their midst was Zhen Lae and her daughter, Zhen Laehua, too.

"Elders and sisters of Houses Je Luneefa and Nui Vent, greetings. May this good day's blessings be upon you all," Je Jero announced in ancient Elvish, the highest form of respect and honor.

"On our way here, we met Zhen Lae and Zhen Laehua and personally escorted them here to your meeting," Je Tero continued.

"Uncle Samu your wisdom and counsel are greatly needed now. So, would you please join us? In exchange honored females of Houses Je Luneefa and Nui Vent, we will give you another hostage of great value. Our House Je Luneefa great father, Je Maron, will gladly exchange places with our uncle whom you females were about to subject to uncomfortable questioning I strongly suspect," Je Kei announced. "House Je Luneefa great father, Je Maron, has been subjected to your type of scrutiny and interrogation many times in the past by Mother and will not likely succumb."

"Thank you, my dear nephews, your timing was impeccable," a relieved Nui Samu said as he stood and left the table smiling goodbye to the females. As he passed Zhen Lae, she grabbed the House Nui Vent great father and kissed him. Now completely embarrassed by the usually reserved Zhen Lae's surprising action, Nui Samu hastened his steps to join his nephews while the females quietly laughed at the ever-serious Warden of the North. "Thank you too Maron for the hostage exchange."

Je Pagi rose and declared, "Sisters and daughters, mark this day as another rare occurrence when we have again been outmaneuvered. Our new hostage, my husband, does not have any secret information to share. I already interrogated him thoroughly last night. We will not gain any new information. My sons have learned their tactics well from my father!"

"Dear elders and sisters, grandfather taught us many lessons. One of these lessons he imparted was to not divulge the entire secret to everyone. He had learned from his centuries-old relationship with Grandmother that she was very adept in compiling and analyzing facts and bits of information. To counter Grandmother's mastery of gathering secrets, Grandfather knew he had to develop new tactics. Whichever male masterminded a secret had to only share small pieces of the total secret with the other males to safeguard the entire secret's privacy," Je Kei triumphantly declared. "And Father does not even know the secret either; so, your attempts, as anticipated, Mother to wrest information from him would fail."

"Me told ye he be clever, very clever," Je Annaei said to her female companions at the table.

Now grinning, feeling like he and the other males of the united Houses Je Luneefa, Nui Vent and Ona Feiir had just won another battle against the House Je Luneefa females, Je Kei announced lastly, "Please all be here just outside the hall's doors at sundown. Wait for us there. Also, please dress very nicely. The attire befits our grand, secret surprise." Now that the unsuspecting captive had been successfully recovered, Je Kei closed the doors to the hall and left with his companions to finalize their plans for the evening's surprise.

Later, a short time before sundown, Je Leena went to Je Danei's bedchamber upon request to give counsel to her older sister. After entering her bedchamber, Je Leena first inquired, "What do you plan to wear tonight?"

"I am still undecided; maybe I could wear the red and black dress grandmother had made last year," she responded quietly with some nervous uncertainty.

"Or you could wear that new red dress. I believe that would better serve you to heighten Jooba's cravings for you," Je Leena interjected quickly.

"And why would I want to do that? I do not want to further stoke desires I cannot fulfill." Je Danei said seriously.

"Can or will not? Dear beloved sister, why will you not fully embrace your female powers? What may trouble you so? Please be honest with me," Je Leena asked quizzically.

The House Je Luneefa first daughter took a deep breath and

then quietly responded, "Although I do care for Jooba a great deal, I still am unsure if I can, hmmm, meet his expectations. I fear I might fail terribly in my attempt. Every day, I chance his patience will end."

Je Leena scrutinized her sister's dejected countenance, "Sister, why did you not spend more time with Grandmother having these discussions? She was a formidable warrior on and off the battlefield. She could have helped you overcome your fears. How do you think she managed to keep Grandfather's exclusive devotion for over four centuries? It was not by chance I assure you.

"Further, why do you think Jooba even has such high expectations that you cannot fulfill? Like most of the males of our united Houses, I believe Jooba is not greedy nor craves affection and attention from many females. He only wants you. Though he may yet be unfulfilled now, he will not leave your side. Rejoice sister; you are indeed fortunate. However, do not take his patience for granted; it is not limitless. Our most wise grandmother imparted males will lose interest or cheat primarily for one and/or two reasons: they are either greedy and/or unfulfilled. Closeness or a simple touch conveys much. If he is your *one*, I would suggest you try to learn and fulfill his desires. In so doing, you teach him how to fulfill you. You might just enjoy wielding your female powers..."

"How are you so wise when it comes to male-female relationships? Did Grandmother counsel you?" Je Danei asked.

"She and Papa were both paragons of wisdom. They both bestowed their wisdom upon me numerous times when I asked them questions or was troubled. I missed them both very much," Je Leena reflected with a sad voice.

In an equally sad voice, Je Danei said, "We all missed them. I now wish again I had spent more time with them."

"Well, there is no time for regrets now. We have our cherished memories, and we should continue to honor them by 'loving fiercely, living honorably and being happy'. Let us follow the examples they set for us so long ago. So, be of good cheer. Our mother, father, aunties, and uncles are still with us. They too would gladly share their knowledge and wisdom with you too. Rejoice also for we have surprises and maybe gifts too to receive this night," Je Leena remarked lastly now trying to uplift their spirits.

"Agreed, let us turn our attention to preparing ourselves for this evening's event," Je Danei responded with a small smile trying to be less anxious and dreary.

That evening at sundown, Alleina, Je Annaei, Zhen Lae,

Zhen Laehua, and the females of Houses Je Luneefa and Nui Vent congregated outside the House Je Luneefa stronghold great hall's locked doors. All the females were attired in fine formal dresses or gowns of mostly black and red, the heraldic colors of both Houses Je Luneefa and Nui Vent. Though not formal members of either House, Zhen Lae and her daughter Zhen Laehua, were invited to this evening's event since Zhen Lae and Zhen Laehua were now the hearts' joy of Nui Samu and Je Jero, respectively.

Moments later, Je Tero arrived with Pi Liu, the second daughter of noble House Pi Zhou. Pi Liu was beautifully attired also in her formal purple and gold gown. After meeting Je Tero at the Rhodell Military Academy, the young felf developed strong feelings for the quiet and reserved House Je Luneefa second son. Unbeknownst to him, she had declared to her family last year that Je Tero was her "one." Fortunately, Je Tero too had developed strong feelings for Pi Liu over their five-year relationship and considered her to be "a very important part of his future."

Commander Somai Adrien, formally attired in his House Je Luneefa army uniform, arrived shortly thereafter. He was also a dear, longtime friend of Houses Je Luneefa and Nui Vent, being the newly promoted first commander of the Houses Je Luneefa and Nui Vent army, as well as the long-time love of Alleina.

Looking about, seeing smiling faces around her, hearing cheerful conversations, and feeling quite pleasant with anticipation herself, House Je Luneefa great mother Je Pagi wondered again about the surprise the males had planned. "Leena?" Je Pagi asked.

After closing her eyes for a moment and reopening them, the youngest House Je Luneefa daughter, a noted battlemage, reported, "No one is currently inside the hall."

Low noises erupted down the hallway. Voices of the males of Houses Je Luneefa, Nui Vent and Ona Feiir could now be heard as these distinguished males began walking towards the great hall. Like Commander Somai, these males were also formally attired in their House army uniforms. House great fathers Je Maron and Nui Samu were in the forefront leading the all-male entourage.

When the males were close to the doors of the hallway, they were all greeted by warm, big smiles from the females.

"Mother and aunties, please correct me if I'm wrong; but Houses Je Luneefa, Nui Vent and Ona Feiir do seem to have some of the most, if not the most, handsome males in the kingdom," Je Leena proclaimed.

"They are indeed most striking and impressive in their House uniforms," concurred Je Pagi staring approvingly at her fine-looking husband, sons, and nephews.

"Agreed," Nui Honei concurred with a wide smile as she gazed upon Ona Noirar.

"Yes, I too must agree. These males tonight look incredible," Alleina declared.

Je Annaei, Zhen Laehua and Pi Liu contributed compliments too acknowledging the fine features and splendor of Je Kei, Je Jero and Je Tero, respectively. Je Danei offered no vocal complimentary comments, but just displayed a small smile at Nui Jooba.

Je Kei made his way through the group to the locked doors of the hall. Before opening the doors, he turned and addressed the group, "Thank you all for joining us this night in honor of an important tradition Grandfather, the House Je Luneefa first great father, started long ago. After sharing portions of this night's secrets with my father, uncles, and brothers, we all wanted to practice Grandfather's wisdom by again doing something he started centuries ago in courting Grandmother. Whether your relationship is relatively new or centuries old, know that you are all very much appreciated, highly valued, and loved. So, esteemed females of the great Houses Je Luneefa, Nui Vent, Pi Zhou and Zhen, we welcome you all to an evening of enchantment and wonder befitting you, our precious and dearly loved queens."

With that said, Je Kei turned, unlocked, and pushed open the hall's doors. Each of the nine felfs was then personally escorted into the hall which had been marvelously decorated in the colors of the early spring season. Shades of green, yellow, and blue could be seen throughout the hall. A fire roared at each room side fireplace making the hall comfortably warm. Three large candle chandeliers hung from the ceiling, and these provided soft accent lighting along with the tables' candles that enhanced the rich spring colors of the hall's decorations. Pleasant aromas from the flowers placed around the hall filled the air.

The felfs were seated at two long tables perpendicular to the front table resting on a dais. This center table was also richly adorned like the two main tables. After the felfs had all been seated and poured a glass of wine or water (in the case of the pregnant Nui Honei), Je Jero went to the front of the hall to address the group. There, he raised his glass and said, "Honored females of the noble Houses Je Luneefa, Nui Vent, Pi Zhou and Zhen, we, the males of Houses Je Luneefa, Nui Vent and Ona Feiir, salute you. We honor you not only for being our hearts' true loves, but also for being our esteemed and dear mothers, aunts, sisters, friends, and comrades in war. We are just lowly males and we wanted to make time to show all of you our sincere appreciation for what you do for us. Your dedication and commitment in the big and small things you do, are all noticed. We are humbled and most thankful. So, to you, our queens, we salute you." All the males then raised their glasses and joined the toast to the felfs.

Je Tero then rose and walked to the front of the room after his elder brother retook his seat. The second son of House Je Luneefa looked upon the group, smiled warmly, and raised his glass for another toast, "I too am very much honored to stand before all of my loved ones to raise my glass to toast such beautiful, intelligent, capable and strong females. As Grandmother often said, 'great females make great males even greater'. On behalf of my father, uncles, brothers and cousins, thank you all for helping to make us greater with all that you say and do. We again salute you."

Again, all the males then raised their glasses and joined the toast to the felfs. Ona Drachir, Nui Jooba, and Je Kei were then next to stand and go to the front of the hall. Ona Drachir slightly smiled at the seated group, reflected inwardly momentarily, and said, "Jooba and I are not as eloquent as our elder brothers; so, we will keep our toasts brief." The three young melfs then raised their glasses to the felfs and said in unison, "We love you all."

Nui Jooba continued, "Some of you may not know, but first House great father Je Taeliel was an exceptionally good singer and would sing to House great mother Je Buel on rare occasions. The three of us here, on behalf of all the males of Houses Je Luneefa, Nui Vent and Ona Feiir, would like to serenade all the Houses' females with a ballad House great father Je Taeliel would sometimes sing to his beloved Je Buel." After clearing their voices, Ona Drachir, Nui Jooba, and Je Kei sang an ancient Elvish love song. The small group of baritone and tenor voices first sang two verses of the love song, "Pinarsevi". As they started to sing the chorus, the other males there joined the three starting singers at the front of the hall. The entire group then sang a third verse together as a choir, blending harmonious, varied vocal ranges. At the conclusion of the song, the singers received a standing ovation, cheers, and big smiles from the felfs.

All the melfs, except for one, returned to their seats where they were each affectionately greeted. Je Kei had remained at the front of the hall and addressed the group, "Even more surprises await you felfs this night. Behold, a glorious feast, befitting royalty that you all are, will now be served." Je Kei then nodded to a servant standing by the door leading to the kitchen. This door was opened, and more servants entered carrying plates of a variety of well-prepared, beautifully presented food. "This meal was specially prepared by us too for all of you. We do hope you will enjoy."

Je Kei retook his seat next to his wife who greeted him saying with tearful eyes, "Me husband, ye never cease to amaze me. Dat song be beautiful. And ye cooked too. Me do love ye so very much."

For the next few hours, the group ate, drank, and engaged in numerous happy conversations. More toasts were dedicated to the felfs for less important reasons as the night went on. After the meal was finished and the tables cleared, exquisite Napa brandy was served with some rare berry desserts.

House great mother Je Pagi stood, raised her glass, and addressed the group, "On behalf of all the females gathered here, you males promised us *more surprises*. Well, where are they? We females impatiently wait." In solidarity, the other females released a loud "Aye" in unison.

Je Tero stood and asked the group, "Would my father, uncles, brothers and cousins please join me at the front of this hall." All the remaining males then rose from their chairs and joined the House Je Luneefa second son. After a few moments of quiet discussion, the males turned towards the females, and started singing again. This time, the song was a joyous Dwarven love ballad. It was a tale of a great dwarf warrior who fought and won many battles but was finally defeated by a dwarf maiden in a battle of the hearts. At the conclusion of the song, after the clapping and another standing ovation from the females, a cloth was removed from the front table. Concealed underneath were bouquets of rare flowers. Each male took a bouquet and presented it to his respective beloved.

Je Kei again went to the front of the hall to address the group. He said, "This evening began with the singing of an ancient Elvish love song, a meal prepared by our hands and another rendition of a Dwarfish love song. The flowers are just small gifts of our love for you. This is another tradition Grandfather started long ago and we wanted to honor him, Grandmother and you in this same manner."

"Wait! So, that you all know, some of you males had committed several small wrongdoings earlier this week. If you think you are forgiven, you are right! However, tomorrow is a new day!" Nui Honei proclaimed. Laughter erupted throughout the group.

"Please forgive and forget too?" Ona Drachir requested with

doleful eyes as he gazed at Je Leena.

"But me Kei did nothin' wrong dis week. He be perfectly wonderful!" Je Annaei proclaimed, frowning.

"Despite what you may think, he is far from being perfect. Surely, he committed some small transgression?" Je Danei inquired.

"Hmmm... He did everythin' right. Me meal was even prepared de way I especially like. It tasted just like me Grandmoders! Even if he did somedin' wrong, it be somedin' so small dat it be not important enough to squabble about," Je Annaei quickly countered while grinning at her Je Kei who nodded in appreciation.

Je Danei then looked indifferently at Nui Jooba who just smiled at her acknowledging that his transgression, he thought, had been too small for their mildly angry discourse. Yet, he still wanted the felf to forgive him and most importantly, forget his small slight. In his mind, his reasons were just!

Je Pagi stood and addressed the group, "My husband, my one and only true love, my sons and nephews, again thank you for this wonderful evening. I believe I can safely say that the females of Houses Je Luneefa, Nui Vent, Pi Zhou and Zhen were surprised and enjoyed the honor of my father's loving tradition. Thank you all."

Alleina quickly added too, "Needless to say, our expectations have again been raised for future surprises!" The females all shouted, "Aye!" in response. The group then started to rise, break into pairs, and leave the hall. Most couples were in very good moods.

"Shall we now take a walk outside?" Nui Jooba asked Je Danei.

"Yes, I would like that," the felf responded. It was early spring, and the night air was still cold. The sky sparkled with many stars. Jooba took his House cape and placed it around Je Danei before leaving the stronghold. They started walking silently towards the easternmost Toronwalein gate.

"You look incredibly beautiful this evening. You are stunning in that dress. I was speechless when I first saw you," Nui Jooba admitted slowly.

"Thank you. You look very handsome in your House uniform," Je Danei said shyly returning an awkward compliment.

"Did you enjoy this evening's events and gifts?" Nui Jooba asked after more aimless, uncomfortable walking in silence.

"Yes, for the most part. But you know I do not enjoy receiving flowers. I have never really cared for them. They are too fragile and do not last long," Je Danei said in a slightly irritated tone.

"Let us return now; it seems to be getting colder," a slightly disappointed Nui Jooba responded after some silent moments. The couple turned around and walked back to the House Je Luneefa stronghold in silence. Upon reaching the door to the stronghold, Je Danei returned Nui Jooba's House cape, thanked him, and nervously bid the melf a good evening. She then turned and went inside.

Saddened, Nui Jooba returned to the House Nui Vent stronghold deep in thought.

Before dawn, Je Danei added more wood to her bedchamber's fireplace. She stoked the fire, rejuvenating its warming flames. After lighting a few candles in her bedchamber, she noticed the fragrance originating from the bouquet of flowers she had received. After finding a small water pitcher, Je Danei unwrapped the flowers and placed them in the pitcher. She then discovered a note from Nui Jooba inside the flowers' wrapping instructing her to check behind the bales of hay next to Starjia's stall for her "real" gift.

The felf dressed quickly to prepare for her customary, early morning ride with Nui Jooba. Je Danei reached the House Je Luneefa's stables hurriedly. Her prized horse, Starjia, was there in her stall waiting anxiously for her rider. Like the days before, the horse would race like the wind again beating all the other horses that would challenge her on this day.

In the stall next to Starjia's, Je Danei looked behind the bales of hay and noticed something covered. Upon removing the blanket, she discovered a fine, custom-made saddle was there. This saddle, like her famous horse, was black and made of fine leather. The saddle's pommel and cantle were noticeably higher than most saddles.

She surmised these features would provide her additional support and capabilities during combat. The felf then recalled the casual conversation she had had with Nui Jooba and Commander Somai two moons ago about wanting a different, more efficient saddle for her horse. When riding on a normal saddle, her archery performance on the shooting range started to decrease when galloping at full speed. Commander Somai had suggested she should try using a saddle like his, one with a higher pommel and cantle. At that time, Nui Jooba seemingly paid little to no attention to the Commander's advice. Je Danei did not realize till now that the young melf had indeed listened very carefully.

Now excited to try using her new gift, Je Danei saddled Starjia quickly and led her to the training ground. There, she mounted her horse and started galloping unto the special shooting range. The felf soon realized she gained more stability and control over her mount with her new saddle. Most importantly, Je Danei now managed to hit six of the eight planted targets while galloping at full speed; and she performed this feat three consecutive times. This was a significant improvement over her past performances. Now, Je Danei was excited to share her new-found capability with Nui Jooba and thank him for his marvelous gift.

Before leaving the training grounds, Commander Somai greeted the first House Je Luneefa daughter. Though a high, commanding House army officer and a highly skilled archer, whether on horseback or standing, Somai also maintained his very strict training regimen. He greeted Je Danei warmly and remarked, "Your new saddle has indeed improved your archery performance while riding at full speed. I knew it would. I do hope you like Nui Jooba's gift. If not, I will suffer more from his pestering. Ha, ha, ha."

Je Danei panted hurriedly through her excitement while responding with a pleasant smile, "Thank you Uncle. I truly do like Jooba's very thoughtful gift. He should indeed no longer annoy you, at least about this particular matter." They both laughed as she departed.

Upon reaching their normal rendezvous place at the easternmost Toronwalein gate, their escort of House soldiers informed her that the House Nui Vent second son had already left and that he was not planning to join her this morning. Puzzled, the felf dismissed the escort and went to the House Nui Vent stronghold to look for Nui Jooba.

Though still early morning, Je Danei entered the Nui Vent stronghold without hesitation nor interference from the posted House guards. Upon reaching the second floor, she was greeted by her younger sister at the top of the stairway. "Good morning," Je Leena said.

"Well met, Sister. Why are you here so early too?" Je Danei asked.

"I came here after dinner to have a discussion with Drachir. We later studied more of the ancient Elvish I was having trouble understanding. It became very late and I decided to stay," Je Leena responded. "But before we speak further, let us go into the sitting room near the dining hall." The daughters of House Je Luneefa descended the staircase and went to a sitting room off the main hallway to have a private conversation. After arriving there and closing the door, Je Leena magically sealed the room to prevent any unwanted eyes and ears from witnessing their upcoming dialogue.

Je Leena started pacing the floor visibly upset. She eventually looked at her older sister, and asked, "Why do you not appreciate Nui Jooba's efforts? Do you know why he was late meeting you at the training grounds two days ago?"

"He said that he was unexpectedly delayed by some earlier errand," responded Je Danei.

Je Leena began a tirade saying, "Yes, he learned the day before that the merchant, bringing the flowers we received last night, had been delayed and would be late arriving in Torondell. Upon learning this, Drachir and Jooba rode through the night to meet the merchant bringing our flowers. Those flowers hold a special meaning: they were the first that Danka, Jooba and Rei had given our aunt on her birthday years ago. That is when they started preparing meals for her and our uncles. It was important to him to give you those flowers too. That was another tradition he wanted to personally uphold. Secondly, he knew you do not like flowers; so, Jooba most likely got you something he deemed *more appropriate* for you did he not?"

Now with tearful eyes, Je Danei said, "Yes, he got me a new saddle to help improve my shooting capabilities from horseback."

"Ah... That seems like something he would do," Je Leena admitted. "Why are there tears in your eyes? Were you not pleased?"

"I remembered scolding him for being late to our training session, because he offered no good explanation in his defense. I was too harsh for something so insignificant. Yes, I like his gift very much. It was very thoughtful. And I had only voiced my dissatisfaction with my shooting performance only once two moons ago. I thought he was not even listening to one of many long rants then," Je Danei commented reflecting back on that discussion.

Je Leena said, "Sister, that melf pays close attention to all that you say and do. Unbeknownst to you, he observes and listens to you very closely. Please do not underestimate nor under-appreciate his devotion and efforts for you. If you still genuinely care for him, go, and find him. Tell him how you really feel. Ask him how he feels. If he feels hurt, I believe you owe him an apology."

Fate's Favors

"What troubles you so?" Je Kei inquired. He, his elder brothers, Ona Drachir and Nui Jooba had all secretly gone to their private sanctuary, a small rooftop garden above the House Nui Vent stronghold. There, the young melfs would sometimes congregate to discuss their most recent frustrations with the Houses' elders or other felfs. In the vast majority of times, their concerns emanated from their respective beloved females. To help them discuss their personal matters and share their irritating issues, they would engage in a knife throwing contest. "All of you are in foul moods; you have been grumbling all afternoon. Speak. Here, you can freely confess your troubles without shame or criticism. Maybe collectively, we can help resolve the issues. Besides, I am about to win this contest since you four cannot properly concentrate.

"Throw Jero; it is now your turn. Do try to at least hit the target's circles. You have missed all on your previous attempts. If you do not, you will again contribute more coins to my coffer! So, concentrate and throw well. 'The eldest should set the example by leading.' Do you not remember your words?"

Frowning, Je Jero responded with unkind words aimed at his annoying youngest brother, "I will say again, that Mother and Father should not have tempted fate after having Tero and myself, her two *perfect* sons. Surely after having Danei, they should have ceased having little ones. You Kei and Leena are most troublesome." Pointing his finger at Je Kei, Je Jero resumed his jealous outpour, lamenting, "You, youngest brother, are just too damn *perfect*; you are most obedient, never cause trouble and are most dutiful, day after day. Have you ever been mischievous?"

"If so, he was not ever caught or witnessed doing some foul deed," Ona Drachir interjected. "And he most likely will not confess now. Why should he?"

Je Kei offered no response other than his innocent, handsome smile. Je Jero, yelling in frustration, screamed, "Argh!"

Continuing, Je Jero proclaimed, "You will even continue to be our parents' *favorite* because you will most likely bless our House with the first granddaughter or grandson!"

"Oh, eldest brother, am I truly the source of your frustration this day or is it the fact that Laehua wants to travel to more of the world's great cities and perform in concerts?" Je Kei challenged.

"Argh! How do you know that secret? Damn you brother; you are also sometimes too smart," Je Jero angrily remarked hesitantly. Je Jero stood alone at the contest's line and threw his long knife at the target, a large wood block on a stand, about fifteen steps away. This target had three concentric circles painted on it. Hitting the innermost circle gained one the most points; hitting the third outermost target gained one the least. Fortunately, Je Jero managed to at least hit the target within the third outermost circle. He still had a chance to recover a small portion of the contest's prerequisite ante. "Finally! Now, I will not be completely embarrassed with my poor performance."

"Hah! Still, if we had to go on a stealth mission, your knife throwing skills would not permit you to join us," Je Tero proclaimed.

"Just throw. You too will soon be contributing coins to the contest winners. And your knife throwing skills are not much better than mine; so, you too would not qualify to be part of that stealth mission," Je Jero retorted angrily.

Je Tero went confidently to the line and threw his long knife. His knife hit the second innermost target. After a long sigh, the second eldest son of House Je Luneefa turned to his brothers and cousins. He sadly said, "Liu wants to study medicine and become a healer. Though she has not finally decided, I believe she is destined to go to the Medical Academy in Rhodell. That is a commitment of ten to fifteen years! We would be separated most of that time. Even if I moved there, her time with me would be little. How can she reasonably expect me to wait for her till she finishes all her studies? Should I even consider waiting for her?"

Throughout most of the time the five melfs had congregated at the small rooftop garden, Nui Jooba had said little. For the past few days, his mood was sullen, and he chose to remain aloof from others most times. However today, he thought he could find some healing remedy by being in the company of the melfs he now considered to be his brothers. Afterall, they all share many good memories. "Why is loving the eldest daughter of House Je Luneefa so painful?" he quietly asked. Nodding his head, he silently urged Ona Drachir to throw next.

Ona Drachir, the usual knife throwing contest winner, went to the line to throw his last knife. Unlike most contests before, he was also very troubled. His performance today placed him third in the current contest's ranking. "The second daughter of House Je Luneefa is also very challenging. She is insecure, immature and wishes to be in control of my life. She even spies upon me. Why?

"She aspires to be so much like first great mother Je Buel, but that comes with time and wisdom. Today, she is not the beloved, first great mother Je Buel!" After walking to the contest line, Ona Drachir moaned loudly, releasing his inner frustration. He then turned his head skyward and momentarily gazed at the brilliant afternoon sun. With an outstretched hand, he commanded, "Ona Tigri Wei, Entelusse." After a few heartbeats, Ona Drachir's shape-shifting shield returned to his patiently waiting hand. "My beloved shield, you have feasted long enough. I forfeit this contest," he last said to the group after retrieving his knives and turning to walk slowly back into the stronghold.

Nui Jooba proclaimed. "Sons of House Je Luneefa, know too that if I could cease loving Je Danei today, I think I would. Fate has been and still is sometimes too unkind. I am tired of love's pain. Also, I too tire of today's contest; so, I forfeit as well." Lastly, he commanded, "Nui Zeinori and Teinori Wei, Entelusse." Obediently, Nui Zeinori and Teinori Wei, his twin, over three fahs long, battleaxes which were also high in the sky, returned to his welcoming, outstretched hands. He also retrieved his knives. Before returning to the stronghold though, he turned and threw one of his battleaxes at another different, smaller stone target thirty steps away. That target was instantly obliterated upon impact, and Nui Jooba simultaneously released a long, pent-up yell of festering frustration. He then silently walked across the garden to the door leading inside the stronghold while his thrown battleaxe again returned to his waiting hand.

Like Ona Drachir and Nui Jooba, Je Jero and Je Tero left next. Today's contest provided no remedy to their sour moods. Je Kei lastly gathered his contest winnings off of a small table. Though feeling some sadness for his brothers and cousins, he then smiled, basking in the afternoon's glorious sunshine and thoughts of his very strong relationship with Je Annaei. He then hurriedly left the garden to find his beloved, seeking to further enhance and strengthen their love like his beloved grandparents had counseled.

The Eagle Talon inn is one of Torondell's most famous hospitality establishments. This inn is truly famous for its superb lodging and meal services. This prestigious recognition is largely due to Master Katsu, an ancient woods elf who is truly a genius of culinary arts and related logistics. Over his lifetime serving in the Canae armies, he had been responsible for the preparation of millions of meals to hundreds of thousands of troops throughout his multi-century military career. He too is another rare individual who had become a living legend.

After leaving the army over one hundred years ago, Master Katsu settled in Torondell and opened the Eagle Talon inn where he himself still prepares meals on a very limited basis. He now works only when he wants to... Other than special occasions or requests, Master Katsu only works from midnight till two hours after sunrise. One of the many attractions the inn offers is that the culinary master will prepare any meal for a customer given adequate time and should the customer provide the main ingredients.

This night was special for a certain, dark-eyed woods felf. Several days ago, arrangements had been finalized with Master Katsu to prepare a special stew for her. The stew, which she had described to Master Katsu in detail a moon ago, consisted of a particular game bird, unique spices, and rare vegetables. The felf had delivered the game bird and the designated vegetables to the inn exactly at midnight. The inn had all the other required ingredients. Master Katsu prepared the stew. Now at the Inn, the lone dark-eyed felf anxiously awaited her meal which was, as she stated, a "treasured memory of her grandmother's cooking."

Like most nights, the inn was busy and still had plenty of patrons who were well into their drinking and conversations. Though past midnight, the mood of the patrons was lively with merriment and mischief, some good and some bad. Good drink and company seemed to have emboldened many patrons tonight. Hopes of good romantic fortune, rising spirits, and/or forgetting sorrowful memories motivated many to continue drinking.

Je Danei sat quietly at a corner table away from the rowdy groups of the drinking hall's patrons. She was there alone hoping to find Nui Jooba who had been avoiding her since their memorial dinner several nights ago. This was a night she thought Nui Jooba would be working at the inn. Je Danei pondered, *"I learned a few* years ago that the sons of House Nui Vent, former homeless refugees, would volunteer four nights a moon cycle at the inn to help in the kitchen. In exchange for their time, Mater Katsu would personally give them cooking lessons and some excess food which the sons would then give to the homeless of the city. Though his brothers had died, Nui Jooba still maintained the tradition he and his brothers started years ago. His helping in the kitchen helped the still grieving melf continue to honor the memories of his brothers."

The House Je Luneefa first daughter still had not seen Nui Jooba at the Eagle Talon. So, she waited there in silence thinking about past events that led to her sullen mood. Her glass of wine was a perfect companion; for it did not speak to her nor did it ask her uncomfortable questions she did not want to answer. After a while, Je Danei slowly sipped away half of the wine in her glass and was growing more and more impatient due to her lack of contact with Nui Jooba. As she continued to ponder her predicament, her moody, self-inflicted silence was immediately violated when she heard an ear-piercing scream from a nearby table.

A few tables away, another lone felf stood staring at a huge man who was now clutching a bloody hand. "You cut off my finger!" he shouted in agony with his face contorted in great pain.

The dark-eyed, felf remained calm with her right hand on the inside of her cape most likely gripping another weapon. Her left hand held a sinister-looking dagger bloodied from severing the finger of the big man's hand. "I only tasted your stew!" the big man yelled.

"Yes, and you only lost a finger for dipping it into *my* stew, my stew that your dirty hand has ruined. Now, if you draw your sword, you will lose more than just a finger this night for your extremely bad manners and stupidity," she said nonchalantly, returning the big man's angry stare. "Fool, that second bowl of delicious stew was meant for me and not meant to be shared!

"If need be, your two friends will die too should they try to help you. So, think carefully. Weigh your options. I urge you not to make another stupid decision whose consequences will surely leave you very much dead." This dark-eyed felf proclaimed the ominous omen of death with such coldness and as an uncaring, simple fact that the big man and his two companions chose not to test their liquor-impaired skills against hers. At least this time... Instead, the half-drunk fools all rose and left grumbling to one another.

After watching the three fellows leave, the dark-eyed felf

turned her attention to Je Danei. Both felfs stared coldly at the other. Still gripping her dagger in her left hand, the dark-eyed felf, a tall, brown hair, lovely woods felf walked slowly towards the House Je Luneefa first daughter. The young felf appeared tense and aggravated, perhaps ready to pounce upon another intended victim... After a few moments, the dark-eyed felf stood directly in front of Je Danei's table and inquired, "You spoke to my server shortly after that altercation began and the server left. What did you say and why?"

Je Danei closely observed the dark blue-eyed felf as she approached. "Her words were curt and deliberate. She did not seem to be the friendly type. Her tone of voice suggested she cared not for frivolous conversation. This felf's eyes and mannerisms perhaps even suggests she might be a leader of merit. The dark-eyed felf too seemed unafraid to fight against foes who may have favorable advantages," Je Danei concluded. "I believe I am staring at another formidable warrior, maybe even an image of myself..."

"I urged your server to quickly go back and get another bowl of that stew for you. I sensed you would still want your precious stew even more so after ending the lives of those ill-mannered fools," Je Danei replied in a calm tone though her left hand was hidden inside her House cape. Ever wary of potential threats, Je Danei too had gripped one of six deadly, concealed blades she carried inside her cape. The felfs continued to stare at each other for a few more tense moments of deadly silence.

The dark-eyed stranger eventually relaxed, smiled, and then said, "Your instincts were correct; I am still quite hungry. Thank you."

"Then please sit and join me. Your table requires cleaning anyways. I too am alone it seems this evening. So, I would welcome the company of another female warrior," Je Danei responded. At that time, the server returned with another bowl of the specially prepared stew and placed it in front of the dark blue-eyed felf. "And there is a cloth for which to clean your blade," Je Danei continued pointing to an extra cloth on the table. "I am Je Danei, the first daughter of noble House Je Luneefa."

"Well met Je Danei, first daughter of noble House Je Luneefa. I am Reza'Di, the first daughter of noble House Norkula of a far distant city. Thank you for sharing your table," the dark blue-eyed felf responded as she sat down. Reza'Di first cleaned her dagger and extended it to Je Danei handle first. Afterwards, she resumed eating her meal.

"How did you know I like blades?" Je Danei asked.

"I saw what I thought was admiration for my fine spider fang dagger. How did you know I was also a warrior?" responded Reza'Di.

"Your stance and hidden right hand foretold your presumed martial arts and fighting skills. If I observed correctly, your stance was the Rocha'Li fifth position. I also assumed your hidden right hand was upon the grip of your hidden weapon, perhaps a short sword or long knife?" noted Je Danei as she closely examined the dagger of Reza'Di who was now fully engaged in devouring the last of her precious stew.

While Reza'Di continued to eat, Je Danei continued her silent inspection of the spider fang dagger, a double-curved, double-edged blade. Its blade length measured about one hand. The dagger's overall length measured less than one fah. The blade itself was of dark steel, dull in color. The dagger's handle was covered in black leather. A glowing, red-eyed tiny spider and its web were finely etched on one side of the blade. The blade's other side just continued the web etching. Both cross-guard and pommel seem to be made of the same dark, dull steel. However, the pommel was shaped like a quarter moon supporting a tiny spider's web. One end of the handle's cross-guard was like a coiled animal's tail and the other end appeared to be a three-pronged flame turned upward towards the blade. Je Danei concluded, "It is an exquisite blade, very well crafted and balanced." Je Danei then placed the blade onto the table and returned it to Reza'Di, handle first. The spider's eyes no longer glowed when the dagger was placed upon the table and taken by the dark blue-eyed felf.

Reza'Di finally looked up at her dinner companion now after her appetite had been finally sated. After a few more moments of quiet observation, Reza'Di said, "First and secondly, 'Thank you.' Your silence while I finished my meal was very much appreciated. I do not enjoy meaningless conversations, especially while I eat.

"My dagger, a family heirloom gifted to me from my grandmother, is very precious. You also have a keen eye, as well as knowledge, of the ancient Elven martial arts. Your House weapons master would be honored. So, tell me, what are your weapons of choice other than the sai swords in your boots?" Reza'Di inquired with a slight smile.

Je Danei responded with a slight, appreciative smile, "We have something else in common; so, it seems. My grandmother gifted me her favorite blades. I also like long knives and scimitars. But my preferred weapons now to deliver death to my enemies are my twin battleaxes, also precious gifts given to me. Unfortunately,

I must leave now to meet someone. Maybe we can meet again to further discuss blades…"

"Or we can discuss perhaps how much you under-appreciate the melf who seems to love you far too much. I do plan to take him from you; so, be forewarned," Reza'Di suddenly spoke again with cold evil eyes. Her once seemingly pleasant mood also shifted, now exuding some hidden evil.

"I think not. How would you possibly know that I under-appreciate by beloved?" Je Danei questioned, after pausing, now annoyed and a bit shocked by such bold statements.

"I have already told you that I do not engage in meaningless conversations. So, I am quite direct and speak honestly. More times than not, *fate favors the bold*. When I accompanied my cousins to the training grounds for a martial arts demonstration by your so-called *beloved* melf, you seemed, hmmm, *uncomfortable* perhaps with the attention he received from the other felfs there. Are you that insecure? Secondly, I was at the same training grounds another time when he apparently arrived late to meet with you. Your small tirade seemed excessive for his late arrival which appeared to be just a small, insignificant annoyance," Reza'Di said with a smug smile.

Displaying a sinister smile, Reza'Di continued, "Your harsh words both times were not truly justified; you wounded him deeply given his reactions. That, all could clearly see. You are still young and quite immature. Do you even know how rare he is and how to fully appreciate him?" Reza'Di scoffed and declared with great confidence, "Truly, you are not worthy of him. Also, you haven't even marked him yet! So, he will be mine!

"Lastly, being so young, immature and of noble birth, I would wager you have only been in just one or two battles at most. Were those even heated battles in which you fought alone against a highly skilled enemy? Have you even killed anyone? I think not. You are pathetic to even think you could defeat me whether we battle with blades or for a melf's heart. You will surely lose in either battle, I assure you!"

With anger growing, Je Danei also smiled menacingly and responded, "This may also be one of those times when *fate unapologetically kills the bold*. Nui Jooba is mine! And like you, I do not share well. Especially in his case, I do not and will not share him at all! So, you be forewarned. Draw your blades if you must. I will gladly give you your life's last lesson by teaching you the seventh Rocha'Li attack."

"Hmmm. I have never killed anyone who wielded battleaxes

nor sai swords; should you be my first victim first daughter of House Je Luneefa? Foolish felf, there are no seven Rocha'Li attacks, only five," evilly protested Reza'Di.

"Ha, ha, ha, your weapons master was then truly not worthy to learn from her master or that master chose not to teach you for some reason. Hmmm... It was most likely the latter in case she needed some advantage to kill you. And should you dare test me now, I will gladly teach you your miserable life's last lesson. I have been in battle! I have killed before and will gladly kill you! Again, you are forewarned," mocked Je Danei menacingly. With that proclamation, Je Danei rose and left the inn.

Not willing to jeopardize the success of her mission now by fighting with Je Danei, Reza'Di just sat at her table in quiet anger, pleased with her verbal victory. Had this been another time, the dark blue-eyed felf would have gladly accepted that challenge and faced Je Danei to a deadly test of Rocha'Li combat. *"Yes, there will be no sharing,"* Reza'Di contemplated as she sat there quietly. Reza'Di had no intention of sharing Nui Jooba either; she wanted the melf to be hers exclusively even if it meant killing the first daughter of House Je Luneefa. However, Reza'Di was totally committed to first accomplishing her mission's objective. *"Fate will always decide who is truly favored and fate truly favors this first daughter of House Norkula!"* she concluded to herself, smiling evilly.

Reza'Di then quietly laughed, feeling confident she would succeed in achieving all her objectives. *"With fate's holy blessings, I may even return one day just to kill you, first daughter of House Je Luneefa,"* she thought, enjoying the silence and the last of her delicious stew.

Scarred Memories

When Je Danei left the Eagle Talon inn, she now desperately wanted to find Nui Jooba. She searched two other inns nearby but still did not find him. As she continued her search, Je Danei fully realized how inconsiderate she had been. The young felf admitted to herself she had become victim to her fears and insecurities again and had inappropriately reacted to her insecurities by lashing out at Nui Jooba without just cause.

"I must find him," she seriously thought. "I need to make things right." After mounting her horse, Je Danei sped toward the House Nui Vent stronghold. "Jooba, where are you? I must see you. I must speak with you. Please answer me," Je Danei pleaded, mentally casting her anguished communication to the young melf. Though the weather was cold and windy, the mental communications she used was most effective. Given the strong blowing winds, no one could hear her even if she shouted at someone just five steps away. However, the great dragon, Ona Kei Kuri Ryuu, had shared her precious blood with the Je Luneefa and Nui Vent family members long ago. So, the magic of the dragon's blood enabled mental communication between these select individuals.

After many long, anxious moments of hearing just the blustering winds, Je Danei finally heard Nui Jooba's voice in her mind's ear. The tormented melf responded, "*Why? Do you wish to berate me further? Wait. Maybe not now since there is no crowd here. Your words were unkind, and you hurt me the last time we spoke."* After more agonizing moments of silence, Nui Jooba continued, *"Again, I ask you why you wish to speak with me? What more do you wish to say now?"*

"I was wrong, very wrong. I desperately want to see you and apologize in person. Please," Je Danei fervently requested.

After more long moments, the sorrowful Nui Jooba said, "Yes, you were wrong. Hah! But how did you come to that revelation? What is so different now than the other day? Has another felt triggered your jealousy again? Be honest. Have I given you cause to ever doubt my loyalty and feelings for you after I declared my love for you at your Day of Adulthood celebration? My patience and my pride do have limits!

"What do you want of me? Can you now honestly tell me if you want me to be more than just your 'friend'? I have now grown weary of your attempts designed not to show affection or emotions toward me. Do not try to find me tonight. I do not wish to see you now. It is best for me to be alone with my thoughts. The memories of the past few days scarred me deeply, bringing much pain. Solitude, lost dreams of shared love and this glass of brandy are now my preferred true companions," proclaimed a sullen Nui Jooba who then abruptly ended the communications.

Silence. Je Danei reined in her horse and Starjia slowly came to a stop. She bowed her head and started weeping upon hearing the jarring truth. Now those same doubts and insecurities flooded her mind more than ever before... For many moments, she was paralyzed, motionless in her saddle.

After recovering a short time later, Je Danei continued her slow ride home. Upon arriving, she went to her younger sister's bedchamber to wait for Je Leena to return. She nervously paced the floor of her sister's dark room as she continued to mull over thoughts regarding her fears and insecurities. Again, the tormented Je Danei mulled over many unanswered questions that continued to plague her including, *"Why would Nui Jooba refuse to see me? Have I finally lost him? Does he still care enough about me to want me? Do I really want him and am willing to fulfill him? Why am I so afraid? When will his patience with my unwillingness to return his affections finally expire? Will I hurt him again? Should I just remain alone and accept my lonesome fate?"*

Je Danei stopped pacing the floor to gaze out the window and looked at the many stars that twinkled throughout the very dark sky. Two particular stars captured her attention. These stars seemed to be close. Unlike many of the other brilliant, seemingly perfect stars, these two stars would "flicker" at times as though they were communicating with each other. This communication continued. One star seemed to flicker; the other would respond. The second star would start flickering and no response was given by the first star. Suddenly, both stars started flickering as though "arguing" perhaps. *"Even the heavens have their share of discord,"* she thought.

Reza'Di's words greatly troubled her too. She had not ever been threatened so boldly before, especially over a melf. No one in her past had ever been so special that she cared about other female competitors. Somehow that was not the case with Nui Jooba. *"Somehow, I really do care about him. Why am I so afraid?"* Je Danei again pondered.

When she returned home, Je Leena magically "searched" the stronghold to locate all her family members. This was a practice learned from her grandmother, the ultimate guardian of House Je Luneefa. Je Leena also found her grandmother's practice useful too when she wanted to avoid certain family members upon returning home... Je Leena smiled, now knowing all seemed well within the House Je Luneefa stronghold.

Je Leena quickly located her sister mentally through the magic of the dragon's blood they both shared. When Je Leena arrived at her bedchamber, she noticed that her sister was there pacing the floor while deep in thought. "Sister, what troubles you so?" Je Leena asked. "What has Jooba done now to upset you?"

Late the next morning, Nui Jooba went to the House of one of Torondell's nobles. There, he was to provide private lessons in certain self-defense techniques to some of the family members. At House Alukron, he was a bit surprised to see some familiar faces from the lessons he demonstrated outside the Warden's stronghold several days before. The same three older felfs had been spectators at the Warden stronghold's training grounds and had shown particular interest in him. Like him, these same three felfs appeared to be in their third century of life. Nui Jooba had been flattered by their attention and small smiles.

Today, he taught four gelfs, all about one hundred fifty years old, the granddaughters of House Alukron, several techniques to equip them for close-quarters combat. Members of their House had been assaulted before on the streets of Torondell; so, the House elders wanted to start preparing their granddaughters for such events should they ever occur again. House soldier escorts alone may not be sufficient protection they found through some unfortunate experiences.

While there, Nui Jooba also learned that the three older felfs were distant family relatives from a city faraway. They were visiting their House Alukron relatives in Torondell. All three felfs were woods elves and lovely. They all seemed brave and courageous given they harbored no fears of travelling long distances alone. Each carried swords and/or long knives at their sides; so, they appeared to be capable fighters. Nui Jooba noticed too that the eldest visiting felf, Reza'Di, paid closer attention to him as he instructed her younger cousins. The other two felfs, Elberithe and Rina, smiled at him often, as well. Rina would also ask several questions while inserting herself physically close to the melf to garner more of his personal attention.

At the conclusion of the lessons, Reza'Di invited Nui Jooba to join her and her other visiting cousins for refreshments in the garden. There, the House Alukron elders thanked the young melf again for his time before they departed to attend an appointment within Torondell's great market.

"Nui Jooba, we brought some water here from a special mountain spring near our home. It has remarkable rejuvenating qualities. After your lessons, I imagine you are still quite thirsty. So, please try some," Reza'Di encouraged. Rina filled the melf's goblet with the special water. After first tasting the water, Nui Jooba found he was indeed still quite thirsty and finished the remainder of his water quickly. After more moments, Nui Jooba smiled at his three hosts as if he were in a drunken stupor.

"How long will it take for the potion to take its full effect?" Rina asked.

Smiling, Elberithe said, "I believe he is almost ready to obey commands." Elberithe then invoked a spell calling forth the magical properties of the "special" water, a mind controlling drug. The battlemage ended her spell with the name "Reza'Di."

"Dear cousin, why did you not give control of him to me? You and Reza'Di have played this game several times in the past. So, it should now be my time. Besides, I really like and want him," Rina complained with a pouting countenance.

"My *dear cousin*, Elberithe knows I would have killed her if she had. This is my victory to fully claim and bring more glory to our House. Learn Rina to not ever get between me and my prize!" Reza'Di proclaimed. "This is your only warning too, *dear cousin*."

"Can I at least test the potion's effect?" Rina requested.

"No, imprudent one," Elberithe warned. "You already know that Reza'Di does not like to share, especially her *prized* possessions."

Reza'Di looked at silent Nui Jooba who appeared outwardly

to be "normal" but was now supposedly mind controlled. She ordered, "Nui Jooba, kiss me passionately now."

Nui Jooba stood, extended his hand to Reza'Di, embraced the felf tightly and passionately kissed her for several long moments.

"Yes, the potion seemed to have again worked quite well," Elberithe declared though a bit disappointed in herself. "Oh cousin, you can stop now. You have enjoyed yourself long enough."

After releasing Nui Jooba from her embrace, the felf was still panting hard. Reza'Di continued to gaze at him silently for several more moments.

"What is she thinking?" Rina asked.

"Elberithe replied, "I am not sure; I am puzzled too. She has not ever had this type of reaction before. Maybe she is falling for him already?"

"I think not. Our cousin is very hard to impress. However, maybe this melf has possibly rekindled her passion?" Rina remarked.

Elberithe smiled evilly and said, "Maybe. We shall indeed see. Like before, the magic of the potion will affect his mind for many days. Our cousin will be able to completely control him indefinitely."

Rina remarked, "Our cousin is, hmmm, most *challenging*; I know her histories with past relationships did not go well, but..."

"But those two fools died well when they wanted much more of me or wanted me to betray my House. Now, I am impressed by this melf before me and will not fall for him. I was just admiring his features." Reza'Di said quickly. "Besides, we must now move on to the next stage of the plan.

"Nui Jooba, listen very carefully and do my bidding. Ignore and forget all thoughts of that felf, Je Danei of House Je Luneefa." Reza'Di then pledged her "love" to the melf and gave him several detailed instructions. "Now go and carryout my orders."

Nui Jooba nodded in acknowledgement and left pleased knowing that his painful scars of love will soon surely heal.

After returning to the House Nui Vent stronghold, Nui Jooba went to his bedchamber quickly avoiding as many individuals as possible. Of everyone he could possibly encounter, he was specifically instructed to avoid his mother, a battlemage herself, who could detect something was amiss with him.

After reaching his bedchamber, Nui Jooba packed some common clothes for travel. He was to bring no weapons or armor. He only needed to leave the required note explaining his departure:

Dearest and beloved Mother,

I have left Torondell for perhaps five days to reevaluate my desperate situation with Je Danei. The weight of my pain is now too great. Decisions about my relationship and future need to be made soon for me to heal the grievous wounds I have suffered.
Nui Kei Dan-Rei Ryuu will accompany me. Please do not look for me.

Nui Jooba

Nui Jooba left the stronghold without encountering his elders or unusual attention. Dan-Rei had first met him when he returned to the stronghold. The young dragon was excited about going on an adventure this late in the day with her rider. So, she would patiently wait for him after his travel preparation. Nui Jooba also insisted, *"Dan-Rei, please do not disclose any information of our departure or adventure to anyone."*
Riding away from Torondell on horseback, a forlorn Nui Jooba left his home without regrets. He thought, "Loving Je Danei has brought me much pain. Reza'Di was right when she told me that he loved the House Je Luneefa first daughter far too much. Did she or can she ever truly love me? All this time of devotion and commitment to Je Danei has been for naught... She does not fully appreciate me; so, leaving all the distractions and any reminders of my home and unrequited love behind for a short while will help me better see and understand my situation. I can then better plan my future accordingly. Further, I have the company and support of new friends who will help me throughout my healing process."
The melf reassured himself he wanted to leave behind painful memories and start healing. He was grateful for Reza'Di and her cousins too. They would be willing to join him as he started his new adventure. The young melf smiled as he rode away pleased that he could start this day recovering from the pain he felt. As Nui Jooba galloped away from Torondell, Dan-Rei flew high overhead. The young dragon was pleased to know that she and her rider would be alone together for several days without that annoying felf, Je Danei.
The next day at the House Nui Vent stronghold, Je Leena was visiting her aunt and uncles in the late morning. The House Je Luneefa second daughter was troubled by a jarring memory she had after accidentally cutting her finger with a dagger. The young felf

sought the elders' knowledge and wisdom for they were all renowned warriors and weapons masters. Further, Nui Honei was also a very knowledgeable and experienced battlemage. Je Leena also invited Ona Drachir to the meeting.

"Beloved elders, I have a mystery that I hope you can help me unravel," Je Leena began after exchanging warm greetings. "Behold. I present to you a weapon I discovered in my grandfather's crypt. Unlike all the others, there was no scroll found that described the history or details of this rare blade." She unwrapped the spider fang dagger and placed it on the table in front of her elders. "This blade is also imbued with magic unlike any other I have read about or encountered before. While examining it again yesterday, I was careless and cut myself. For the next few moments, I immediately had a jarring, frightful memory. I saw my grandmother crying while standing over an infant's crib. Next to her were my grandfather and my mother as a very young gelf. This blade was laying on the floor near my grandmother."

Everyone then examined the blade closely but offered no definitive information. Nui Honei lastly said, "Please leave the blade here. Ona Drachir, please go to our library and see if you can find any information in our family's weapons *Chronicles*. I will try to uncover the blade's magical content. I will also contact Urtha Dal who might be able to share some insight into this matter. Let us meet again tomorrow for further discussions. Leena, also invite your mother and father here too; they may have some knowledge they could share as well."

"I have a personal *Chronicles* detailing certain unusual weapons I have come across during my travels. So, I will do some additional research as well," Ona Noirar offered.

"Our army commanders are well travelled and experienced. I can ask them too if they have any knowledge of such a dagger," Nui Samu added.

Warm goodbyes were then said. Je Leena stayed with her aunt while the others left to perform assigned or other tasks. The young felf said, "Auntie, there is something else you should know. Danei was first to find the blade. When she held it, the eyes of the blade's spider would glow. Today, when others held the dagger, the spider's eyes did not glow."

"That is another mystery to uncover. When we contact Urtha Dal, we will ask her about that too," Nui Honei responded.

On the next day after the evening meal, the same group reassembled. In addition, House Je Luneefa great mother and father, Je Pagi and Je Maron, attended this meeting.

Je Leena welcomed and thanked everyone again for their assistance in helping her in her quest to learn more about the dagger she had taken. "Before we begin our discussions, I wish to point out that Father owes Urtha Dal this season's first bottle of Napa brandy. She said that was her heavily discounted, dear family and friends fee for her consulting services," Je Leena reported.

"Gladly. Fortunately, I have already placed my order for the upcoming season! We have Je Annaei and Kei's wedding celebration to go to in a few moons; so, we will be well prepared," Je Maron said. After some laughter and joyful comments about the upcoming event at the Dwarven stronghold, the mood of the meeting suddenly turned very serious. Everyone had noticed that Nui Honei's eyes were filled with tears. The room became very still with only the soft crackling sounds of the hearth's fire.

Nui Honei said, "Dearest loved ones, I spoke again with Urtha Dal earlier this evening. She sadly shared more information about this infamous dagger laying before you. The great battlemage of Clan Battle Hammer conveyed that this exquisite dagger is a creation of dark elves and used in ritual killings and assassinations most likely.

"Dark elves worshipped an elf-like, female spider. Like all the spiders of the Underworld, the females are the most deadly and terrifying. This deity is referred to as Valdearaneida. Not only is the dagger an assassin's weapon, but it is also used in certain ritual ceremonies. This dagger is also believed to be sentient. The spider at the base of the blade delights, by its glowing eyes, in the touch or tasting the blood of virgins.

"The dark elf Houses will make periodic offerings to their highest deity, Valdearaneida, to garner favor or blessings, as well as submit recompense for their evil requests. Recompense for Valdearaneida's blessings often takes form in ritual sacrifices of the living. Most of these sacrifices are dishonored family members, captured enemies and/or slaves. However, the offering that is most highly valued is the noble House first-born son, especially a virgin. This sacrifice demonstrates the House's most extreme devotion to Valdearaneida. The second highest ranked sacrifice of devotion is the ceremonial killing of the dark elves' historical enemies: woods, rock or sun elves, dwarves, and humans."

Nui Honei then looked at Je Pagi and asked, "What do you know of your younger brother?"

"What? I thought you were an only child," Je Maron exclaimed.

After some moments of inner reflection, Je Pagi recalled a

very old, lost and nearly forgotten memory of a conversation she had had with her mother. "Very long ago, as a very young gelf, I asked my mother if I could have a younger sister or brother to play with. My mother told me that she would discuss the matter with my father. Thereafter, my mother and father would deflect any further questions or requests I would have. As I got older, I made new friends and playmates. Requests for other siblings slowly ceased with time as more playmates were befriended. With time, the thoughts of wanting siblings became lost in memory," Je Pagi sadly remembered.

Nui Honei added, "I learned from Urtha Dal, Je Buel's blood-sister, that House first great mother Je Buel did give birth to a son after Je Pagi. The little brother presumably died after he was stolen shortly after his birth. Urtha Dal described such a dagger used by the dark felf who invaded their House. Urtha Dal described the blade as, 'a double-edged, double curved dagger wid a spider's web etching on bod sides of de blade. Der be a tiny spider too at de base of de blade just befer de guard. Red gems be dis spider's eyes and dey would glow at times.'"

Je Pagi then resumed the gruesome tale, "Still very weak from childbirth, my mother could not kill the thief nor stop her from taking her son. She could only seriously wound the thief who dropped this blade while making her escape. Yes, Je Buel recognized the thief to be female given the thief's evil laughter as she escaped. During that same time period, other young belfs were also abducted from other families. Most of these melfs, if not all, were of noble Houses. Their son's abduction caused the House Je Luneefa first elders great pain. This great pain haunted the House Je Luneefa first elders for a very long time. Even though this grievous event occurred over four centuries ago, Je Buel and Je Taeliel went to great lengths to protect their family members from that time on."

Nui Honei added, "Urtha Dal strongly suspects that the dark felf thief abducted Je Pagi's younger brother to be a sacrificial offering of her House. That year of the abductions was special to dark elves. That was the year they celebrated an event, called 'Abaramerle,' which is a holy celebration culminating with the dark elf House first son's sacrifice to their highest religious deity. The thief's House presumably had no first son of their own to offer; so, they hunted throughout the Aboveworld for the next best thing: virgin, first-born males of their historical enemies, woods elves. Sons of noble Houses were especially a high priority."

Je Maron asked, "Is this year the time for that Abaramerle?"

Before anyone could answer, an enraged, flame-red eyed, Nui Honei looked at Ona Noirar and yelled, "My son will not be sacrificed for some damned, dark elves' purposes! I, great mother Nui Honei of House Nui Vent, declare war upon any House who has stolen my son and Dan-Rei. No mercy will be given; kill all who dares stand in your way. Safely return our family members to me!" Nui Honei picked up the spider fang dagger and then violently stabbed the table where she was sitting. With one vicious blow, the felf buried the blade deep into the table with such force that the table cracked.

"So now, I too owe the House of this dark felf a blood debt which she will pay the full, very painful price," Je Leena said softly.

Luna Fendasse

After traveling two days deep below the Ararateken mountain, certain members of the small party quietly rejoiced when they saw the familiar gate leading to their darkest Underworld, the realm of the dark elves. All the disguised dark elves knew their journey was soon to end. When Reza'Di first saw the great gate leading to the Underworld, she smiled. She knew now that her return journey home was just another short eight days' time given no unfortunate mishaps. The runes on and around the ancient great gate were like a welcome beacon. Despite the evil environment, the felf loved her evil family and great city. She wanted to get home.

The Aboveworld held no joy for dark elves other than to further release their evil and contempt upon any two-legged creature who could enjoyably live under the despicable sun and moon. Despite the darkest days or nights, the light from the sky's sun or moon would still cause any dark elf to feel blinding pain in their unshielded eyes. The Aboveworld's sun, moon, stars or any other "light" in the skies were simply cursed abominations to dark elves.

Reza'Di, a dark felf, reveled in knowing her successful mission was soon to end. Her cousins, Elberithe and Rina, two other disguised dark felfs, had also joined her on the dangerous mission to the Aboveworld. They were returning with a highly valuable prize that would enable their House to triumph against stronger enemies and even achieve greater glory. However, Reza'Di also knew that new perils awaited her and her small party as they continued their journey through the Underworld. This next portion of their journey would prove to be the most dangerous. They were about to enter her world, the most unforgiving, evil and treacherous Underworld, the realm of the dark elves and other dangers untold. A sinister smile came upon the face of Reza'Di as she got closer to the gate. She laughed quietly, incredibly pleased with herself for playing a key role in a plan that would elevate her House in the city's ruling hierarchy. This would lead to more power and glory for House Norkula when her House destroys their archenemy Houses!

Reza'Di was the first daughter of House Norkula of the Underworld city Tol'Tarei. Being the eldest granddaughter, she "ruled" over her younger siblings and cousins in the matriarchal dominant, dark elf society. Her mother and aunts are the second great mothers of House Nokula and second in the power hierarchy within their House to Aysun'Di, the first great mother and tyrannical ruler of House Norkula.

In the dark elf Underground society, the noble House's first great mother is a dictator above all in her family. She holds the lives of many in her hands, including the House army dedicated exclusively to her House. Unlike the Aboveworld, a House army is used to wage war against another House. The House family members and their exclusive House army are all involved in destroying designated enemies through deliberate overt and clandestine actions.

Above the ancient Luna Fendasse gate, the runes read, "Welcome! You are about to enter a new Hell where there will be no return. Pass through these gates to meet your certain death, your final peace. Still, welcome glorious Death!" Other ancient runes were there too, not easily interpreted, but believed to further enhance the gate's ominous warning.

For most inhabitants living in the Underworld, their suffering and misery may not be temporary. Here in this realm, certain death was assured from many different sources. On the other hand, living each day was quite uncertain. To survive in this realm or even to live was arduous. One's life was in constant danger. Here only the strong truly survived or, more accurately, postponed their inevitable fate of welcomed death.

Death too could come from either friend or foe. Hidden jealousy or hatred oftentimes was motive enough for killing. In addition, even family members would assassinate other family members to support one's rise within their own House's power hierarchy.

Ritual killings too were practiced in the Underworld. To

appease the dark elves' religious supreme being, Valdearaneida, it was not uncommon for Houses to sacrifice captured enemies, family members, or slaves to this deity. In fact, to garner favor and blessings from the Valdearaneida, every great House would sacrifice a first son of their House every one hundred years in a special religious event. This event, the Abaramerle, was marked by a spectacular three-day celebration culminating with the Houses' first son sacrifice. This is the year of the Abaramerle.

Here in the Underworld, females were at the top of the societal hierarchy of all creatures. So, a melf, whether dark, rock, sun or woods, were not valued much beyond their fighting, reproductive or special talents or abilities unless the males possessed considerable capabilities in some valued category.

Reza'Di looked at Nui Jooba and said, "Do not fear to boldly enter my world; I will protect you. You are to be an honored guest in my House and city. I will give you all the attention you want and deserve. Most importantly, I will return the love you crave unlike that foolish felf Je Danei who truly did not appreciate you.

"You may find my world, the blessed Underworld, to be far more enjoyable than living under that unpleasant sky with its obnoxious sun, moon, stars, winds and the different despicable seasons. Here, in the glorious dark world, the temperature varies a little. It is pleasantly warm. There are no radical changes in our environment unlike the accursed Aboveworld. Welcome to my world where the dark elves reign supreme!"

In response to her words, Nui Jooba just nodded in quiet, submissive compliance.

Elberithe smiled, pleased too with her accomplishment. She remarked, "Cousins, take heed. His mind is still possessed and controlled."

"Yes, for now. But I will still continue to try to free my rider from Reza'Di's grip," Nui Kei Dan-Rei Ryuu declared.

"Why is your dragon staring at the gate's runes so intently? Is the beast trying to read? Ha, ha, ha. Surely, she cannot know the ancient Elvish language," Reza'Di jested.

Rina said, "She is a beast that just likes the pretty runes and pictures."

Dan-Rei immediately took offense at being implied as "ignorant", turned to face Rina, and opened her fearsome jaws to emit flames. But only an irritating coughing sound came forth. All the felfs laughed.

"Cousin, I believe you offended the young dragon. Fortunately, she still cannot breathe fire; otherwise, you would have been burned to death I believe. Please do not tease our honored traveling companion. She is very important to our House's future; whereas, you are not. So be forewarned," Reza'Di said snickering.

"My dear cousin, it is good to know that you still love me so," Rina remarked sarcastically.

After traveling now for days below the great mountain Ararateken, Nui Jooba still was considerably uncomfortable with the many foreign surroundings. Fortunately, the melf has a special "gift." Through the blessing of dragon's blood that he had received from the great dragon Ona Kei Kuri Ryuu, Nui Jooba could invoke his magical "dragon eyes" that gave him an ability to see objects clearly even in sheer darkness. Yet, dramatically new sights and sounds, even the complete silence at times, continued to unnerve him. Like his adoptive mother, fear of the unknown caused him great anxiety. Yet his fears did not completely overwhelm the young melf; he remained dutiful and obedient to Reza'Di. So, he continued to journey with the disguised dark felf to her home. Nui Jooba's young dragon remained completely loyal to her bonded dragon rider and journeyed alongside him dutifully and peacefully as well. Fortunately, the young dragon could still travel through the mountain's tunnels given her current, relatively "small" size.

Now, four days after passing through the Luna Fendasse, Elberithe found another empty large cave for the traveling party. This cave would provide protective shelter for their one-night stay. Though the cave had a small entrance, it was still large enough to accommodate all the travelers comfortably. Once inside Elberithe, the battlemage, sealed the entrance magically.

"Is a sealed entrance really necessary?" Nui Jooba asked Reza'Di. "I will not leave you."

Elberithe and Rina softly laughed. Reza'Di remarked, "Foolish melf of the Aboveworld, you do not understand the ever-present dangers of this realm. You should be thankful for such a door to guard us against unwanted predators that would gladly slay you for their next meal. Most creatures here are deadly and are a threat to your life. So, you must always be cautious."

All creatures indigenous to the Underworld, required little or no light to clearly see. A moon's light in the above ground world would even be considered too intense for most Underworld creatures. Many low Aboveworld lights would be sufficient to overwhelm the ocular senses of Underworld creatures. Their eyes would require shielding for protection. Additionally, the Underworld creatures' senses were all acute and highly developed over long centuries. Most Underworld creatures could hear the faintest sounds and smell the slightest odors. Some underground beasts even use their inherent sensory capabilities to detect the heat patterns emanating from other creatures.

Many dangers lurked in this vast Underworld. Poisonous gases freely rose from their pools of liquid death. Hideous creatures hide throughout dark crevices in search of unsuspecting prey. Some creatures are small, others large. Unlike many of their Aboveworld counterparts, most of the creatures here are considered "gigantic" in comparison. Some creatures live in water; while most of the Underworld animal populations thrive outside of water in their dens, crevices, or rocky territories. Some transport themselves on just two legs while other creatures make use of their hundred legs.

Still, there are those too that needed to slither their way across the caverns' floors and/or through pools of water. These dreaded basilisks guard and reign over their territories with vicious, unrelenting terror.

Even large, open spaces are not completely safe. The small, bat-like vultures, fleuri, flourished and are winged monsters of death. Their flight is soundless like some of the Aboveworld owls. If their vicious claws did not immediately kill their prey, the toxins delivered through their bites surely would.

Reza'Di knew that even if the melf did leave her, how would he possibly return to his contemptible Aboveworld unharmed? *"Yes, you cannot possibly leave me now if you wished to live,"* she thought, smiling evilly. *"Surely, you know you have passed the point of no return!"*

A Misunderstanding

While Elberithe and Rina built a small fire to prepare their evening meal, Reza'Di, off to the side of their small campsite, stared again at Nui Jooba. Nui Kei Dan-Rei Ryuu, as usual, sat close to her bonded rider. The young dragon was ever watchful and protective of Nui Jooba. As best as she could, Dan-Rei would not let any of the felfs get too close to Nui Jooba without baring her young deadly fangs in warning. Nui Jooba, in response, would attempt to calm the young dragon and reiterate that they were his and her new friends. So, she should act accordingly and not harm the felfs. Dan-Rei, however, was still distrustful and did not easily accept the felfs. *"My dragon's intuition tells me these felfs' true intentions are not truly loving nor honorable,"* Dan-Rei thought.

After their meal, Reza'Di continued to stare at the melf and asked, "Nui Jooba, are you a great warrior? Will you be strong enough to survive the rigors and demands of our House and realm? Will you be loyal to House Norkula? My House first great mother does not value males too highly, but you can become an exception. She may even allow you to become my consort after you have proven yourself worthy. What say you?"

"I am a warrior skilled and experienced with several different deadly weapons. I have killed enemies of my House. But I am not yet *great* but hope to be one day. There is still much to learn. Though now loyal to you and your House, time is still needed for you to evaluate me properly to be considered worthy enough to be your consort," Nui Jooba replied.

"He is both humble and wise unlike the other males of our House. Those are both rare traits in males. You are very different. This Aboveworld melf will surely be challenged by the other males of our House, as well as some of the other female warriors. No males in our House can rise in ranking without thoroughly being tested. Rina, shall we then test him here and now?" Elberithe asked with an evil smile. She then stood and placed her hands upon her weapons, maintaining her evil smile at the melf.

Nui Jooba looked at Reza'Di and simply said, "I did not bring my weapons."

"You favor scimitars do you not? I have two you can use," Reza'Di responded.

Elberithe drew her long sword and long knife. She then walked deeper into the cave. Rina followed quickly, drawing her two short swords. After receiving the weapons Reza'Di retrieved from her pack, Nui Jooba followed the other two felfs deeper into the cave. He walked slowly toward the menacing-looking felfs who now were both ready to do battle.

"Remember cousins, do *not* seriously harm this melf. Our House needs him mostly unharmed, and I want him in very good health. Also, Elbe you cannot use magic," Reza'Di ordered.

"Prizes?" Rina questioned.

"You are so predictable and annoying, Cousin. What do you suggest?" Reza'Di responded in frustration.

"Since I am so predictable and so annoying, you should already know what I want. I want the melf all to myself this night should I win," Rina quickly and boldly replied.

"And you Elbe, what do you *want,* should you win?" an annoyed Reza'Di asked, already anticipating her cousin's answer.

Elberithe quickly replied, "Our young cousin displays wisdom this night. On such a rare occasion, I must concur with her. Exclusive access and use of the melf tonight is what I want should I win."

"And if Nui Jooba wins?" Reza'Di questioned gazing at the melf with slightly parted, luscious lips, longing eyes, and posture signaling to him that she wanted him too completely this night.

Stoically, Nui Jooba thought for a few moments and finally replied, "Each opponent will perform two favors for me since the contest odds of two-to-one are in their favor."

"He is greedy and lustful I see. Oh, I do like him," Rina boasted.

Now greatly annoyed, Reza'Di's demeanor quickly transformed to anger from assumed betrayal by the melf. Even

Dan-Rei released a low growl now, upset with her rider. Both Elberithe and Rina smiled. The competing felfs were now pleased that Nui Jooba was clever enough to want the anticipated pleasures of one or possibly even the two felfs this night. They also found annoying their older cousin was an additional benefit.

After a few more moments of silent recovery, Reza'Di continued, "This is just a *friendly* contest of only weaponry and martial skills. The objective is to claim *first blood*. Nui Jooba must draw blood from both opponents before either of them draws his blood. Only small shallow cuts are to be made without any serious injury. Are all my instructions understood?"

"Yes," Nui Jooba responded.

"Yes," both felfs said in unison as they immediately attacked the melf standing between them just three steps away. Nui Jooba stood still and began defending himself very quickly as both felfs pressed their initial vicious attacks. The blades of all the weapons were of dark, dull-looking steel. And since they were all in the darkest portion of the cave, the blades were all but invisible to "regular" vision. Fortunately, Nui Jooba could still use his dragon eyes magical ability which allowed him to clearly see in total darkness.

Nui Jooba wondered how the felfs could see so well in the Underworld. He did not know that through magic, Reza'Di, Elberithe and Rina had had their eyes altered to allow them see comfortably while they were in the Aboveworld. But now in the Underworld, all three felfs no longer needed such magic.

Nui Jooba had several disadvantages to overcome if he wanted to secure victory. His opponents were skilled with blades and appeared to have fought together in the past. They would not easily allow him to turn his full attention to just one opponent. Secondly, although he moved quickly away from the felfs, they countered his movements by continuing to press and keep him fighting between the two of them.

Bystander Reza'Di began to admire this melf more. He seemed to now display great fighting skills. She now even wanted to test her exemplary fighting talents against his. With her own passion slowly increasing, the party's leader enjoyed watching the near-deadly "dance" of the three combatants. Reza'Di still wondered though, *"Are you Nui Jooba truly a great warrior or could you be? For you to be my potential consort, I need to personally assess all your skills even more thoroughly."*

Now that initial attacks and counterattacks had been completed, Reza'Di found her lust for the melf growing also as she watched Nui Jooba successfully defend himself against two of the better warriors of her House. Battle aroused her primal carnal desires. Elberithe and Rina stopped momentarily and smiled at him acknowledging his skills. Nui Jooba nodded in gratitude.

In the next moment, the felfs' smiles were replaced with sneers of evil. They now began another set of attacks with increased speed and viciousness. Their tactics changed also; one felf would randomly leap onto the cave's wall to launch an attack from high while the other would attack Nui Jooba's lower body. In response, Nui Jooba retreated quickly along with using defensive parries.

After a few more moments of moving and countering the felfs' attacks, Nui Jooba found himself again in the same position where one of the felfs would leap from the side wall to attack high while the other attacked his lower body. This time though, Elberithe attacked his lower body and Rina attacked his upper body after leaping from the side wall. The felfs reversed their previous attack roles. Suddenly, both felfs also threw a blade at Nui Jooba. Fortunately, the melf witnessed this tactic before in his personal intensive training in Torondell. His mother and Je Danei had used this same maneuver against him; so, he was not totally surprised.

Nui Jooba leapt high into the air evading both thrown blades and adversaries. He was also close enough to a cave wall that he used it to launch himself to land behind Rina. He then used his two blades advantage to defeat her one blade and lightly cut her sword hand drawing blood. Thus, Rina was eliminated from the contest. The losing felf yelled in defeated disbelief and frustration.

In the meantime, Elberithe had retrieved her thrown long knife and attacked Nui Jooba. Now only facing one opponent, Nui Jooba increased his own attacks and counterattacks against the lone opponent. After more intense moments of sword fighting, Nui Jooba parried her sword thrust and pinned her blade against the cave's side wall on her left. Pinning her right sword arm left that side of her body exposed since she could not easily use her left hand's long knife hand to defend in time. He then brought his left blade to lightly cut her exposed right leg. Blood began to flow from the wound.

"Stop!" Reza'Di commanded.

Eberlithe complied, took a step backward and saluted the contest victor. She then smiled too with anticipation of the "favors" she was to hopefully fulfill. After sheathing her weapons, she began to slowly unbutton her jacket. Following suit, Rina stepped up to stand by her defeated partner, saluted Nui Jooba and started to slowly unbutton her jacket as well. Both felfs now looked upon Nui

Jooba with great longing for him to fully claim his spoils of victory.

"Argh!" now exclaimed Reza'Di after watching her cousins' shameless provocativeness as they prepared to claim a prize she wanted to completely ravage first. "Now tell us Nui Jooba what *favors* do you now want as the contest winner?" Reza'Di asked with seething anger.

"I do hope you are not exhausted from our contest to claim your well-earned, contest prize *favors*," Elberithe remark lasciviously.

"First of all, thank you for the contest. Secondly, the *favors* I now claim as the contest winner are for Elberithe and Rina to carry the bags that my dragon has been carrying for the next two days. Nui Kei Dan-Rei Ryuu is a most noble creature, a daughter of royalty in the Aboveworld. She is not a lowly beast of burden," Nui Jooba declared. The melf then walked toward Dan-Rei glowing with a dragon's "smile" of victory. He hugged the dragon affectionately as he returned her smile.

Moments later, Nui Jooba could hear the felfs all laughing at themselves over their unfortunate, frustrating misunderstanding. Nui Jooba was truly not a "typical" male like the ones they know or have known.

Secrets Unveiled

On the next day's uneventful journey, the small party passed a lake of fresh water. Presumably, water flowed from some unknown source and collected there. In the far distance, one could even hear the sound of falling water rushing to its unknown destination.

"Let us rest here for a short time while we look for shelter. My cousins do look tired from carrying their extra baggage," Reza'Di jested.

Nui Jooba walked close to the lake and asked Nui Kei Dan-Rei Ryuu that had also followed him, "Is it safe here? Will it be safe enough to hunt for fish?"

The young dragon looked at the melf with puzzlement reflected in her eyes. She still could not understand why Nui Jooba could not still mentally communicate with her. Dan-Rei replied, "*I detect no menacing creatures around and below this water's surface. Before you hunt, do bathe. I too will swim along with you.*"

Looking at Reza'Di, Nui Jooba said, "We will both take time for a short swim. Afterward, I will fish for our evening's meal which I will prepare."

Reza'Di warned "Go then but be careful. Stay close to this side of the lake where I can keep watch. Always remember where you are – in the unforgiving, merciless Underworld."

Some unknown vegetation sparsely located around the lake and on the walls of the cavern slightly illuminated the lake area. Nui Jooba found some nearby large rocks behind which he started to undress. After stripping down to his under garment, he plunged into the cool water. The melf was quickly followed by Dan-Rei. After a short time, the two returned to the shore. As Nui Jooba emerged from the water along with Dan-Rei, he noticed that all three felfs were now lounging against the rocks where he had left his clothes. Nui Jooba started to feel embarrassment as he got closer to the rocks. The weight of the felfs' collective gazes upon his near nakedness made him quite uncomfortable. All three felfs just smiled at him.

"Slowly Cousin. Slowly," Elberithe remarked. Instead of handing Nui Jooba all of his clothes, Rina intentionally returned his garments slowly, one piece at a time. She of course was delaying the covering of his well-developed, muscular body which the felfs all seem to admire.

After dressing, the melf turned his attention to fishing. He luckily caught five large fish, three of which he immediately gave to Dan-Rei. Without hesitation, the young dragon devoured the welcomed delicacy quickly. She had become bored with her previous repeated meals of just deer meat.

Reza'Di showed Nui Jooba and Dan-Rei the way to a new cave her cousins had found. Rina had already started a small fire in waiting for the melf and his catch. Elberithe magically sealed the cave's entrance.

After retrieving all the ingredients for their evening meal, Nui Jooba prepared a small feast. Their meal featured Aboveworld vegetables, fruits, cheese and bread – rare items Reza'Di had procured knowing they would not have them again for a very long time. After the final meal preparations, he called the small party over to the blanket near the fire. There the felfs were first greeted by the delicious aromas of the food. Reza'Di also brought along a bottle of wine.

"He doesn't talk much, listens well, and has a strong muscular body," Rina observed.

Elberithe rudely interjected, "He also fights very well, and he cooks well too judging by just my eyes and nose!"

Rina concluded, "Nui Jooba may just be perfect! What more could a felf possibly want from a consort?" Rina exclaimed with prolonged admiration.

"Please, I am not even close to being perfect nor can I ever be," Nui Jooba quietly confessed with great humility. "I still have much to learn."

Reza'Di added, "Yes, you truly are not *perfect*; you are no dark elf!" All the felfs then chuckled. "By the way, where is your dragon's meal?" Is she not dining with us this evening?"

With a puzzled look, Nui Jooba replied, "Of course, I prepared Dan-Rei's meal first and gave it to her."

Based upon what appeared to be slight annoyance and/or anger with Nui Jooba's response, Reza'Di frowned at the melf. Rina wanted to now deflect her leader's attention and said, "You are truly amazing Nui Jooba. You will be a welcomed addition to our great noble House!"

"Cousin, you are young and inexperienced. There are still some things we should first know about this melf. We must also learn about his skills in other very important areas too," Elberithe quickly remarked as she assessed the food before her. "Let us all now enjoy the meal Nui Jooba has prepared."

Reza'Di quietly observed the melf during the meal without engaging in much of the conversations between her three companions. Nui Jooba too was silent most of the time. Even when he was asked questions, his answers were short and a bit evasive. He tried to avoid sharing information about himself, his family, and his past. The felf leader was pleased with his responses; she only cared about the present and the future. Nui Jooba's past meant little to her. Reza'Di silently contemplated to herself, "*How can I take future power and glory for House Norkula with the assistance of this melf? Nothing else matters now!*"

"Nui Jooba, who are 'Taeliel, Maron and Noirar'? I do not know those names. Why do you call those names in your sleep?" Reza'Di asked suddenly.

The melf hesitated for a few moments but continued slowly eating his evening meal. After a short time, he responded, "They are the elders of my House. I owe them much."

"How could you possibly continue to think about them, especially when you were in my arms the other night? You called out their names then too," Rina boldly confessed.

"My dear young cousin, do you not know that our leader here was also frustrated with the same reaction when she attempted to seduce this melf last evening? He too whispered those same names thwarting her amorous attempts," Elberithe joyfully reported. "Like her, you and I were both completely unsuccessful in getting this melf's full, undivided attention."

"Remind me to kill you both after we return home," Reza'Di said. All three felfs again quietly laughed at each other for their total combined defeat.

For the second time on this journey, Dan-Rei "smiled" too, but just to herself. "I was keenly aware of the felfs' silent movements during the nights when you tried to steal another "victory" from me. Though Nui Jooba's mind was still controlled by Reza'Di who did not allow him to dwell upon his former beloved Je Danei, I could still secretly flood his mind with thoughts of the three elder melfs whom he admires most in this world. These three House elders' love for their respective "ones" is unbreakable. Regardless of your attempts, dark felfs, his body would just not respond to your charms. I will continue to protect my rider from you vile unworthy females!" Dan-Rei thought.

"Nui Jooba, you are no longer a son of the Aboveworld's noble House Nui Vent but a soon to be favored son of the Underworld's great noble House Norkula," the felf leader announced. "Cousins, let us show him the true wonders of our world." Reza'Di stood still gazing at the melf. The other two felfs stood and joined their leader who stood behind the fire opposite Nui Jooba. Elberithe waved her hands in front of them dispelling the magical disguises they all wore. Now all three disguised woods felfs appeared as they truly are, dark elves of the Underworld. All had their same original facial and bodily features except now their hair was completely white and their skin color was dark blue.

"He does not seem surprised," Elberithe announced somewhat puzzled.

"Why should I be? Your skin color are not important; your beauty still remains; it transcends your race and color; that will not ever change," Nui Jooba observed out loud.

"Remember cousins, I was first to say that Nui Jooba may be the *perfect* melf!" Rina said flattered by the melf's simply said, matter-of-fact comment.

"Nui Jooba, tomorrow we will rendezvous with other members of our House at a secret location. The following day we will all travel together and bring you and your dragon into our city through a secret passageway. You and your dragon must remain our secret known only to certain elders and soldiers of our House," Reza'Di said. "My cousins and I will always be by your side till we are safely within our House stronghold." In acknowledgement, Nui Jooba just nodded.

The next day, the small party rose, ate a light meal, and quickly continued their journey to the secret rendezvous destination. After walking silently most of the day, now guided by Elberithe, the battlemage signaled for her party to halt.

Further ahead, about one hundred steps away, there was a sharp bend in the large tunnel. Now wary of the familiar surroundings which could hide many threats from other competing

Houses, her "senses" alerted her to be even more cautious. Her senses foretold something or someone dangerous were very close. The battlemage reached into one of the small bags around her waist and retrieved a flying insect. After citing an incantation, she released the insect that then flew around the bend. The insect was tiny in size and made no sound while flying. Like most creatures of the Underworld, its vision was exceptional. Through magic, Elberithe controlled the insect that now rapidly flew high and beyond the turn in the tunnel trying to detect potential threats. The battlemage used the multi-faceted eyes of the scouting insect and could see what lay ahead of them.

"Daughter and nieces, welcome back," a familiar voice called out.

Through the eyes of her scouting insect, Elberithe could now see the other warriors of her House, including her father. These members of the House Norkula army came to rendezvous with the Reza'Di party and to safely escort them to the House stronghold. Eight House soldiers had come. Elberithe signaled to her group that it was safe to proceed forward.

As the returning party turned the corner and saw the approaching House soldiers, Dan-Rei looked up toward the cavern's high, about one hundred steps, ceiling and noticed movement in the utter darkness. Nui Jooba noticed that Dan-Rei's attention was focused above; so, he too started scanning the upper region of the cavern.

"Ambush!" Nui Jooba yelled as he pushed the escort leader aside before an arrow shot high from above could hit him. "There are at least four archers hiding on the ceiling." Elberithe immediately cast a spell to place a shield above their small group.

Nui Jooba drew his borrowed scimitars and took a defensive position next to Dan-Rei committed to defending his dragon. In kind, the young dragon barred her deadly fangs and foreclaws. She too was now ready to fight. Unfortunately, the young dragon still could not breathe fire, but her foreclaws, teeth and tail are all formidable.

Within a short time, Elberithe, her father, another battlemage, and two House Norkula archers quickly killed the enemy archers high above with well-aimed fireballs and arrows. Meanwhile, more enemy troops emerged from another tunnel and attacked. Though the enemy had a greater number of soldiers, perhaps twenty, the House Norkula soldiers fought well. The enemy soldiers attempted several times to press their way to Nui Jooba and Dan-Rei. These non-dark elves had become the enemies' primary targets for unknown reasons. Undaunted by the superior enemy numbers, the three felfs who travelled with Nui Jooba and his dragon fought ferociously by their sides. During the peak of the battle, Nui Jooba saved Rina from sudden death after an enemy had viciously kicked her breathless to the ground.

Nui Jooba and Dan-Rei had also fought together during many training exercises too. Today that extensive training resulted in dead enemy soldiers who challenged them.

After a short time, House Norkula soldiers claimed this battle's victory. Amongst the victors, there were no deaths and only a few wounded. As a symbol of their victory, some of the House Norkula soldiers beheaded all the enemy soldiers and placed severed heads upon the enemy swords or spears.

"Uncle, shall you leave our message or Elberithe?" Reza'Di asked.

"Elberithe has the honor," the senior battlemage replied. After bowing to her father, the felf battlemage magically drew the blood of the fallen enemies and used it to inscribe a message of death on the cavern's wall overlooking the spiked, severed heads:

> Here lie the fallen enemies of House Norkula.
> They all died foolishly. Enemies beware.
> You will find no glory in attacking our great House.
> Only your final peace awaits you!

"So, this *final peace* is a message or warning of death?" Nui Jooba inquired.

"And smart too. You still amaze me Nui Jooba, my near-perfect melf!" Rina said smiling.

After she had completed inscribing the message, Elberithe recited another spell to make the blood glow softly. "This gravesite is now finished," she then said.

"Then let us go quickly," Reza'Di ordered, smiling and quite pleased that House Norkula defeated another enemy attack.

For the next few leagues, the senior battlemage led the group through a series of tunnels some of which were protective with presumably magical wards only House Norkula soldiers knew how to bypass. They travelled silently and with haste. Eventually, they emerged from a tunnel connected to a large cavern. Close to the tunnel's exit was a large, covered wagon. Standing guard around the wagon was another group of House Norkula soldiers.

The senior battlemage stopped the group short of exiting the tunnel. He then nodded to Reza'Di after speaking privately with the soldiers' commander at the front of the tunnel.

Reza'Di looked at Nui Jooba and said, "You and your dragon must enter that wagon. Please do so silently." Obediently, Nui Jooba complied, and Dan-Rei did so as well. The wagon was thereafter closed and sealed magically several times with different protective wards to completely conceal the wagon's contents. Afterwards, the entire group made its way to the House Norkula stronghold.

When the wagon finally stopped and the doors opened, Nui Jooba looked out and saw that they had been taken to an enclosed building that resembled a barn. Reza'Di, Elberithe and Rina were all there to greet him and Dan-Rei.

"Welcome to House Norkula, your new home," Reza'Di said warmly. "We will escort you to your quarters, but we must do so with secrecy. Before you even ask, I will tell you that certain secrets within our House are very, very guarded. You and your dragon will be treated as such until our House first great mother orders otherwise. Please be silent and follow me." Reza'Di led her guests to another room after a short walk. "Please go in, clean yourself and rest awhile. I will return later to take you and your dragon to meet our House first great mother."

Nui Jooba and Dan-Rei went into their room and closed the door. The four guards outside the room were given strict orders that no one was to be admitted into the room until she returned. Nui Jooba cleaned Dan-Rei first and then himself. The melf found clean clothes placed there for him. Afterwards, they both settled into the room which was comfortable and well-appointed but not lavish.

Sometime later, Reza'Di returned. The felf led Nui Jooba and Dan-Rei and the four guards to a large room also protected by six other guards outside the room's large doors. At the front of the room was a dais with seven beautifully carved chairs. The center chair was larger and on it sat an ancient, stern-looking felf, presumably the House Norkula first great mother. She was flanked by six other felfs sitting on the dais as well. In front of the room, standing before the dais, but off to the sides, were Elberithe, Rina, the escort commander and two other melfs. Twelve other soldiers were also in the room along the exterior of the room. All the soldiers, Nui Jooba noticed, were fully armed and wearing full body armor. *"Meeting a dragon for the first-time warrants precautions perhaps,"* he thought.

Reza'Di led Nui Jooba and Dan-Rei to stand about eight steps from the center of the dais. As soon as he entered the throne room-like hall, he immediately felt uncomfortable. Most on the dais seemed to not only scrutinize him, but their disdainful looks conveyed underlying reasons for their anger and dislike. Yet the House Norkula first great mother just stared at him with cold emotionless eyes.

After a few moments, the elder felf seated on the throne-like chair lightly tapped her tall walking stick on the floor. The already uncomfortable silence became frightfully more silent. Reza'Di then began introductions, "House Norkula first great mother and elders, I present to you Jooba, formerly of the Aboveworld's House Nui Vent, and his dragon, Kei Dan-Rei Ryuu, also formerly of same House." Both Nui Jooba and Dan-Rei bowed to the House elders.

With a malevolent voice, the House Norkula first great mother Aysun'Di said, "Jooba and Dan-Rei, I wish to first welcome you to our House. Secondly, I want to express our sincere gratitude. I have heard accounts of your great fighting skills and bravery from my granddaughters. Your feats were also confirmed by the House escort commander, as well. Further, you saved the lives of our House soldiers, including my favorite son-in-law. Neither of you shirked away when the battle ensued against enemies with superior numbers. Our House values such skills and courage. Additionally, I hear you have exemplary culinary skills too. Those too are valued by the ruling mothers of this House.

"Have your dragon stand by the side of the room." Nui Jooba looked at Dan-Rei and nodded, requesting her to go to the side of the hall. The dragon complied, walking slowly to the side of the room about twenty steps away. She was, rightfully so, wary of these dark elves. These unknown surroundings and elves made the dragon quite anxious. What disturbed the dragon most was her rider's inability to mentally communicate with her. Dan-Rei turned around facing her bonded rider still standing in front of the dais. "Now command her to stay there regardless of what happens to you."

"Dan-Rei, I love you. Stay there. Should I meet death this night, kill them all. Die nobly befitting the honor of House Nui Vent," Nui Jooba requested while returning the cold stare of the House first great mother.

Aysun'Di then commanded, "Admit our gladiators." The hall's doors were opened and in walked four warriors carrying weapons, mostly swords and shields. One warrior carried a spear. All were males: two dark elves, one human and a woods elf. They all stopped ten steps behind Nui Jooba. They all then bowed and saluted the House Norkula first great mother.

"Grandmother?" Reza'Di questioned.

"Silence!" Aysun'Di commanded with cold evil. "You and your cousins move now to the side of the room." Looking to her left and right, the House first great mother commanded those on the dais to move away as well. She was now alone on the dais; Nui Jooba stood eight steps away facing Aysun'Di, and the four gladiators stood beyond the lone melf. "Give Jooba weapons," Aysun'Di further commanded. Reza'Di took the sword belt holding two scimitars and gave it to Nui Jooba.

"Give me your long knives too," he requested. The felf also handed him her two long knives which he placed in his boots. Reza'Di then returned to her place along the wall.

Aysun'Di stood with the assistance of her long cane and addressed the assembly in the hall, "These gladiators of House Norkula have been sentenced to find their final peace in the infamous Tol'Tarei Coliseum tomorrow. There they will bring glory to our House through their last, final battle. Now looking directly at the gladiators, the House first great mother continued, "Gladiators, you can gain your freedom this day if you can kill me. You only need to first pass through this melf protecting me and standing in front of you."

Without any forewarning, the gladiators immediately charged and attacked Nui Jooba. Instantly, he drew the twin scimitars and started defending himself. Unable to keep all his opponents in front of him, the lone melf moved quickly about the front of the room not allowing any of the gladiators to get closer to the House first great mother. A stoic Aysun'Di sat motionless in her chair and just watched the fine battle unfolding before her.

Nui Jooba's greatest fear was the one gladiator who used the spear and shield. He knew he could not afford ever letting this warrior get behind him while facing the other three warriors in front. Nui Jooba also knew he could not afford to be bashed by multiple shields repeatedly. So, he had to constantly move, defending himself and counterattacking when opportunities afforded themselves. Fortunately, he had also learned that patience is a warrior's asset despite superior numbers. Most fortunately perhaps too, these warriors were not a well-coordinated, experienced fighting unit.

After isolating the spear-wielding gladiator for a few moments, Nui Jooba shattered the unprotected knee with a kick during one of his counterattacks. As that gladiator winced from the excruciating pain, Nui Jooba seized his spear and dealt him a killing blow with his scimitar.

In the next instant after he parried an attack, Nui Jooba threw a scimitar at the exposed head of one of the remaining gladiators. He then used the spear to stab that warrior's leg. Fortunately, the other two gladiators did not try to protect their fellow warrior who had to block the thrown scimitar. Nui Jooba twisted the spear causing more pain and that gladiator lowered his shield for a moment which was sufficient for Nui Jooba to deliver another killing strike to the gladiator's neck.

Now, there were only two gladiators remaining. After saluting each other, they looked at Nui Jooba, screamed their last war cry, and charged at him. With their shields forward, they hoped to bash the melf who served as an unsuspecting pawn in the evil gambit of Aysun'Di. While one gladiator fully intended to engage Nui Jooba, the other feinted an attack, but then darted toward the House great mother hoping to deal her his final blow before he died. In a set of powerful sword attacks, Nui Jooba defeated the third gladiator with a sword thrust to his opponent's briefly exposed chest. Nui Jooba threw his long knife at the fourth gladiator's exposed head, killing him instantly. This last foe died two steps away from Aysun'Di who still seemed emotionally unaffected by the last gladiator's failed attempt.

Aysun'Di clapped her hands congratulating the melf for his victory. Aysun'Di rose from her chair and issued orders to remove the dead gladiators' bodies. "Jooba, return your weapons and kneel before me." With cold, unforgiving evil in her eyes, Aysun'Di stood and slowly approached the bloodied warrior who had skillfully and marvelously defended her. *"I am indeed puzzled as to why he would do such a thing knowing I may kill him and his dragon. Why?"* Aysun'Di pondered. The House first great mother walked slowly towards the kneeling melf. She tapped her walking stick again and it transformed into her deadly naginata. Aysun'Di then smiled, acknowledging that Nui Jooba's furious battle had also reawakened her own battle rage and lust. Further, she was reminded of something she had seen long, long ago.

"Jooba, tell me what fighting style did you use and who taught you?" a curious Aysun'Di inquired.

Jooba lifted his head and replied proudly, "My fighting style is of the ancient elven martial art Nur'Pontic taught by my House great mother. As you may know, Nur'Pontic was a dark felf master." Several quiet gasps were released throughout the room. "I also combined the Nur'Pontic form with two secret Rocha'Li, another ancient dark felf master, attacks rarely taught."

Pleasantly surprised, Aysun'Di then announced, "Jooba,

again you have proven yourself to be wise, as well as a fine warrior. Thank you. Other than your freedom, what gift may I bestow upon you?"

After thinking carefully, Nui Jooba said, "May I have your ring with the red and black stone then?"

Still puzzled and nonetheless amazed, Aysun'Di gladly complied and gave her ring, an old inexpensive trinket, to the melf. "Though unimportant, this ring, like other taken trinkets, still reminds me of my glorious and adventurous youth. But why would this Aboveworlder request it?" Aysun'Di thought.

Looking at her personal attendant, Aysun'Di ordered, "Go and bring me my lava stone box." Obediently, the attendant did as ordered and returned carrying a small black stone box. Though it was plain-looking and made of ordinary stone, the great mother of House Norkula held and caressed the box as if it contained great wealth or wonderous power. After removing the lid, Aysun'di retrieved a folded piece of paper from the box. She carefully unfolded the paper and studied what appeared to be two ancient markings. Looking at the abducted melf, she asked, "Do you know these strange runes? Have you ever seen such glyphs before?" She then held the precious paper before Nui Jooba to see her important, cherished missive.

The young melf studied the runes for a short time, looked up at Aysun'Di and replied, "I have seen this type of special parchment before. It is commonly used by seers. I believe these runes foretold your future. These runes are the ancient Elvish words, 'karae uyduae' which means 'black moon'."

With his response, Aysun'Di smiled. "Again, young one, you amaze me. You are quite knowledgeable of the language of the First Elves. You are also correct in that this paper was given to me many, many years ago by a great seer who foretold a day when another *black moon* would come and save me.

"I received this fortune long ago just before one of my last missions to your accursed Aboveworld. On my eighth mission there, I witnessed what I thought was a 'black moon'. Aboveworlders refer to it as a lunar eclipse which is a very rare occurrence I have been told. My band was escaping through an orc burial site which is sacred ground protected by very mystical magic. Before we reached our destination, which was a cave entrance in the Iinkyyu mountain, my sister pointed skyward and exclaimed, 'A black moon approaches!' Indeed, it was not. It was just a dragon, a black dragon, with folded wings, traveling through the skies towards us. The massive beast blocked the moon as it hurtled towards us. That dragon hurled fireballs at a group of orcs laying in ambush near the cave's entrance. That dragon saved us for unknown reasons.

"That seer surely prophesied correctly as you can now witness," Aysun'Di said, proudly displaying her sickly, but excited self. "You, Nui Jooba and Dan-Rei, I believe, are mow my *black moon* as the seer foretold!"

She next said, "I now wish to call upon another talent you may possess. Unbeknownst to most of my family, I have been poisoned. I am not ready to meet my final peace; so, what can you do to possibly prolong my life if not heal me?"

Still breathing heavily from his battle, Nui Jooba looked at the ancient felf with some sympathy. He then asked Dan-Rei to rejoin him by his side. Nui Jooba also requested her wine cup and another knife. Aysun'Di handed a hidden knife, handle first, to Nui Jooba as well as her wine cup. After the young dragon joined Nui Jooba, he spoke privately to her in the ancient Elvish language requesting the drawing of her dragon's blood and a single Massicenae blessing of her blood. He then lifted one of the dragon's scales and made a tiny incision drawing some blood upon the knife.

He presented the bloodied knife to Dan-Rei and bowed. Dan-Rei then made some deep guttural sounds citing an ancient Elvish incantation that bestowed her blessing upon the freely given blood. Nui Jooba then let a few drops of blood fall into the cup. Next, Nui Jooba returned the knife to the House great mother handle first. While bowing again, the cup was extended to the first great mother of House Norkula.

Nui Jooba explained, "Dragons are creatures of great magic. Black dragons especially possess the most powerful magic of any creature in the Aboveworld. I have also seen with my own eyes the healing powers of a black dragon's blood. So, please accept my token of a hopeful remedy to the poison."

"First great mother, hold! Let me first examine it to ensure it is not harmful," the nearby Kelvae warned as he quickly approached to stand in front of his House first great mother.

Aysun'Di looked at her devoted son-in-law and hesitated a moment before signaling him to come forward. Kelvae took the cup from Nui Jooba and peered closely at its contents. He whispered several incantations. Afterwards, he then extended the cup to Aysun'Di, saying, "House first great mother, I detected no harmful components within the dragon blood wine.

Aysun'Di took the cup, looked at its contents and said, "I too see no discernible differences either. However, I do 'feel' something is now very different about my drink." She studied Nui Jooba standing before her for several long moments. Aysun'Di stopped swirling the cup's shimmering contents and drank half of the hopefully miraculous new potion. She closed her eyes to perform a self-assessment of the potion's effects. After more moments of silence, Aysun'Di opened her eyes and declared to all, "I now feel much better. The lingering debilitating pain has left me. Jooba, welcome to House Norkula; you and Dan-Rei are my most honored guests!"

Cheers went up from around the room. None were more pleased with Nui Jooba's acceptance than the three felfs who had travelled with him to his new House in Tol'Tarei. Reza'Di, Elberithe and Rina were all overjoyed that Jooba had survived his deadly tests, at least this day... They knew their grandmother well; more of her evil yet awaited him and his dragon.

Even though House Norkula had fewer battlemages, their House army's primary, core strength was grounded in their battlemage ranks. Until they could increase their battlemage ranks, protecting their current resources was an extremely important House priority. A multitude of history's greatest battles have proven battlemages can be worth many regular soldiers in battles. Secondly, increasing their current battlemages' capabilities and power could be accomplished by utilizing the blood of the world's most powerful magical creature, a black dragon.

After hearing several smugglers' stories long ago about the magical creatures called "dragons," Reza'Di had become intrigued. She had learned that their blood was a source of great magical energy, unlike anything in the Underworld. After learning that some young dragons had recently hatched, the bold felf thought it would even be possible to somehow steal a young one and bring it to the Underworld where her House could benefit from harvesting the dragon's blood.

Reza'Di first discussed her unprecedented ideas with her cousin, Elberithe, a mage and daughter of House Norkula's most powerful battlemage. The two felfs then developed and first proposed a daring plan to Elberithe's father. With his approval and support, the felfs then proposed their plan to the House first great mother. Their plan aimed to rapidly enhance their House's battlemages' capabilities significantly. The few, select House elders, informed of the plan, were all enthusiastic and supportive. House first great mother Aysun'Di was especially supportive of the plan to abduct a young dragon when she learned of the dragon's blood healing properties. After again studying the seer's strange missive she had received, Aysun'Di finally decided to take great risks to save the lives of herself and, through extension, her House.

Today, the House Norkula first great mother is very pleased. Greater honor and glory still await her House! Further, she could now seek revenge upon those who had somehow secretly poisoned her. *"Yes, today is a glorious day indeed,"* she thought, reveling in knowing she could still unleash her total merciless evil and destruction upon her enemies.

Hell Hath Much Fury

"I do not care whom you must torture or kill. Bring back my son and Nui Kei Dan-Rei Ryuu!" the House Nui Vent great mother vehemently ordered. "No one, I mean no one's life there in that accursed Underworld city is more important. Kill them all if you must to rescue and safely return my son and Dan-Rei! Kill any, ancient or infant, who might defy you! Show no mercy!" The assembled group remained deathly quiet as she spoke. Nui Honei was angry, very angry. She also had shaved her head; only two, front to back, bands of short red and black hair remained. This was a sure indication the House Nui Vent great mother was ready and about to wage battle. Fortunately, her enemies were not close for they would surely die horrific deaths from the enraged House Nui Vent first great mother.

Nui Honei had declared war upon an unknown House. Though very pregnant with two elves, Nui Honei wore some newly adjusted armor. She carried her two scimitars now on her back; long knives were on her sides. Despite her late stage of pregnancy, Nui Honei's presence was intensely frightening.

"And you, my dear beloved. You are the one who impregnated me at this inopportune time. I should be going to war, not delivering infants at this time! Do not ever think of impregnating me ever again!" Nui Honei ranted; her frustration was again solely aimed at Ona Noirar. "I must be ready at all times, at any time to take war to our enemies! Stop! Do not even think you can console me now. I do not want any consolation. Only the safe return of my son and Dan-Rei could possibly console me now!" The brave Ona Noirar had taken a silent step towards his beloved but wisely retreated where he had been standing given her unwelcoming hostile temperament.

Nui Honei's unbridled fury continued seething through her words as she spoke with intense anger, "Nui Jooba left Torondell days ago and had not returned as his note indicated after his five days' absence." His mother was also angry with herself too for not finding Nui Jooba's note days sooner. Given her late stage of pregnancy, Nui Honei had other health-related concerns at the forefront of her mind other than to worry about her very capable warrior son. *"I have already lost two other sons; I do not intend to lose another!"* Nui Honei screamed into all the assembled minds since they all shared the blood of Ona Kei Kuri Ryuu. All displayed shocked expressions; some even slightly cowered in fear at Nui Honei's sudden burst of outrage.

Ona Kei Kuri Ryuu is also present at this combined families' meeting. She, like Nui Honei, was in a very foul mood. The great dragon would periodically release small bursts of flames and smoke as she and Nui Honei walked about the House Nui Vent stronghold's garden.

"Why am I so pregnant now? I need to lead this mission. I need to kill the unknown enemies of my House!" she thought aloud. "Keiku, you know my rage best. Represent me and show the enemy my fury and hell! I want you to annihilate all those involved in this crime against our family. I only trust you to completely represent me in this matter. The others would give mercy, while I would not. No other here fully understands our pain more than we. Mercy is not to be given to these enemies! Kill them all! Razed their strongholds! Leave nothing behind but ashes! Leave nothing of the enemies to even bury!"

Keiku added angrily through mental communications with all there in the assembly, "I too will remind the world why one should not ever be the target of a dragon's rage and revenge. A never-before-seen hell, my hell, will fall down upon our enemies!"

Both dragon and House great mother were enraged unlike any time before. Both Keiku and Nui Honei were alike in thought: many will die; merciless hell's fury will rain down upon those who harmed their family. Nui Honei then released a terrifying scream, frightening all in the assembly. In acknowledgement and agreement, Keiku reared back on just her rear legs and tail and unleashed a mighty, grotesque roar that startled the assembled group. They all had heard Keiku's great roar before, but something eviler and more sinister was now heard. This time, a mighty dragon's full, unbridled terror will be unleashed upon an enemy. There is no doubt in anyone's mind there that Ona Kei Kuri Ryuu, the mightiest dragon the world has known, will not relent and mercilessly kill all who wronged her family.

After Nui Honei had earlier obliterated an innocent tree with a magical lightning bolt, no one dared to speak. Respectfully, the members of House Je Luneefa and Nui Vent remained silent and waited for the House great mother to continue leading the discussions to recover their two abducted family members. Keiku and Nui Honei ended their brief walk by taking their places again in front of the assembled House Je Luneefa and House Nui Vent families.

Now a bit calmer, Nui Honei looked upon her loved ones there, collected her thoughts and calmly said, "We are again at war and have been called once again to wage battle. However, we are not completely certain who our true enemies are this time. What we do know is this:

"While waiting to meet Nui Jooba at the Eagle's Talon Inn seven nights ago, Je Danei met a felf, Reza'Di of House Norkula. This felf and her House are unknown to us. This Reza'Di carried a spider fang dagger that resembles, if not mirrors, the one on this table. This same felf told Je Danei that she intended to take my son away from her.

"Centuries ago, Je Pagi's infant brother was abducted from the House Je Luneefa shortly after House great mother Je Buel gave birth. The House great mother tried but could not kill the thief, a dark felf. This thief dropped that dagger while making her escape. Other male first-borns were also abducted from other noble House families during that same timeframe.

"That particular year, dark elves celebrated a centennial devotion to their religious supreme being, Valdearaneida, in a three-day event called the Abaramerle. This celebration culminates with each city great House sacrificing its first son. Should no first son be available, House enemies and slaves would be offered as substitutes. These sacrifices are made to garner favor from their deity. Rock, sun and woods elves, especially first-born, male virgins of noble Houses, are the most highly prized sacrifices. This year is another year of the Abaramerle.

"Dan-Rei, Keiku's precious daughter, too was a victim of this Nui Jooba's abduction. Of course, she would follow her bonded rider to the ends of the world if need be. She too would be a highly valued prize if for nothing else than her powerful, magic-enriched blood. It would not surprise me to later uncover that abducting Dan-Rei, not Nui Jooba, was truly the thieves' intended objective. Given her relative small size now, the young dragon could now travel easily underground through many tunnels.

"Six days ago, Nui Jooba had an appointment at the House Alukron where he gave the young felfs of that House some private, self-defense lessons. That same late afternoon, my son left Torondell with Dan-Rei. He only left a note to me describing how he needed time to think and start healing from the pain he was suffering from his relationship with Je Danei. Nui Jooba left without taking any of his weapons, armor, and dragon-blood potions. He was supposed to return within five days.

"Being concerned mothers, Keiku and I asked Je Danei, Je Leena and Ona Drachir to visit House Alukron and inquire about Nui Jooba's visit there. That was a few days ago. There were three other, older felfs who were distant relatives visiting House Alukron when my son was there. One of the visitors was Reza'Di. All three visiting felfs left Torondell that same night Nui Jooba supposedly left. Je Leena tested the entire House Alukron family without their knowledge. House Alukron still stands today because the House elders were found to be ignorant of their visiting relatives' true objectives. Had House Alukron been willing accomplices in this abduction scheme, that entire family would have been killed per my orders.

"Also, four days ago, Keiku took flight to look for clues. Dan-Rei, like her mother, is very intelligent and left us a very special trail to follow. Dragon dung is unique. Keiku was able to find her daughter's marked trail which seemed to be leading somewhere south of Rhodell. Our guess is they are going to the Ararateken mountain where there is a known tunnel leading to the Underworld.

"Fortunately living with us, we have someone who has knowledge of the tunnels below that particular great mountain. Centuries ago, when Duenor Heartstone was a young engineer, he accompanied his grandfather on an expedition to search for a new mountain stronghold for their clan. Ararateken mountain had been explored. Its tunnels had been greatly detailed. The dwarves ruled out the possibility of establishing a stronghold there due to the existence of a dormant volcano deep within the same mountain. Je Kei's book, *The Mathematics of Tunneling,* is based upon the early maps Duenor Heartstone developed from that mountain's tunnel system. Je Kei still has these early maps.

"Again, let me repeat that you are to bring back our family members. Kill all who oppose you without hesitation and without mercy. Make them all pay heavily for this heinous crime against our families. Lastly, none of you are to die while on this quest! All of *you* are to return home safely, as well. Now go and prepare yourselves. You leave from here tomorrow at dawn," Nui Honei lastly commanded.

Ona Noirar moved to the front of the group and announced, "Some of you might be wondering *where* we are actually bound in the Underworld. It is a vast realm and mostly unknown to us Aboveworlders. At this time, our specific destination is unknown. We are still identifying clues, but we do have Dan-Rei's trail to follow." Several long sighs and other quiet conversations started amongst the House Je Luneefa family members, Nui Samu and the leaders of House army. As expected, Ona Noirar sensed various levels of fear and doubt permeating throughout the assembled group.

Now turning towards Alleina, Nui Honei repeated her plea for an impossible miracle, "Can you transfer my unborn infants to Ona Noirar and restore me to my warrior form? You are the greatest healer in this world. You have performed miracles before. Now perform another, please. I beseech you now more than ever!"

Alleina noticed that the House Nui Vent great mother was again looking at her with pleading eyes. Unafraid of Nui Honei's violent temper, the annoyed healer responded, "I already researched that anticipated request, again. I have even consulted again with highly regarded colleagues and renowned mages, and we have all arrived at the same conclusion: males are not equipped physically nor emotionally to handle such pain. Most likely, he would die.

"And no. No! No! No! The answer is still 'No!' You are in no condition to leave here to lead any part of this mission. You must stay here in my care now more than ever. You are already under great stress with your pregnancy and worries about our missing family members. Your time of delivery will come sooner given the current, extraordinarily strenuous circumstances.

"As you have ordered, Ona Noirar will lead the Houses' daughters, sons, and army on this mission. Keiku will accompany them to the mountain's entrance and wait there with Commander Somai's soldiers. You will also be able to scry with Leena everyday too. You formulated the battle and rescue strategy. After more details of Nui Jooba and Dan-Rei's situation are gathered, a tactical rescue plan will then be formulated and executed. Enemies will die terrible deaths, and all will return home safely with Nui Jooba and Dan-Rei.

"There is nothing more for you to do but stay here and deliver your unborn elves in good health. That is your duty, your only responsibility now. House Nui Vent must flourish as our beloved House elders wished! So, calm yourself dear Sister for your unborn infants."

"If Je Buel and Je Taeliel were still here, no doubt Je Buel would truly lead this mission. My true mother...," Nui Honei started.

Alleina boldly interrupted, "Yet, Ona Noirar will have much on his mind as he traverses the deadly Underworld and infiltrates the enemy city and House. Do you want him to also worry more than he should about you and your soon-to-be-born infants?" Alleina took Nui Honei's hands to further comfort her and continued, "Ease his and the families' burdens by taking good care of yourself and help your elves enter this world without additional issues you might cause. Please dear Sister, heed my words." Nui Honei's frustration and anger subsided slowly; she knew Alleina's words were true and sincere.

"Can I at least destroy another tree to release more of my anger and frustration?" the House Nui Vent great mother quietly asked.

"No! You already destroyed one innocent tree here in this once beautiful garden; that is enough. Have Keiku destroy some trees while on her flight," Alleina replied quickly. "If you like, let us go inside where you can knead some dough for our evening meal's bread. But please do control your rage." Nui Honei, Alleina and Je Pagi looked at each other and all started laughing. They each recalled a very recent memory of Nui Honei's merciless bread dough kneading that resulted in her breaking a second table.

Je Kei, who had been studying his maps during the meeting, approached the great dragon and asked, "How powerful is the fireball and flame you can bring forth? How much devastation can you create with them?"

Keiku raised her head slightly, acknowledging she had not ever been asked such questions before, the great dragon mentally replied, *"Let us walk together for a while and discuss my answers."*

Je Pagi called her daughters to her and Nui Honei. The elders wanted to have a private conversation with the young felfs. Before speaking, the House Je Luneefa great mother took a deep calming breath to steady herself. Still, after many years of silent grief, tears formed in the corners of her eyes. Je Pagi looked at her daughters and said, "I have a hidden family secret to share." Tears started to fall from Je Pagi's eyes. "As your aunt mentioned, I had a younger brother." Je Danei and Je Leena both remained silent; only their eyes reflected their surprise at not ever knowing anything about that uncle whom Nui Honei had mentioned earlier. "Though they did not ever speak of my brother's abduction and assumed sacrifice by the dark elves, your grandparents secretly mourned his death for a very, very long time.

"They were greatly affected by that evil event and hid their grief well. My parents' grief was further magnified when they did not have another infant after that horrific tragedy. That tragedy and other atrocities taking place in Rhodell led your grandparents, I believe, to become obsessed with protecting their remaining family henceforth.

"My parents killed any, without hesitation or mercy, who threatened me or any member of their extended family. Even when they could or should not act directly against a known threat, your aunt Nui Honei, a trained assassin, would secretly act as their angel of death.

"I believe we fled here to Torondell afterwards to lessen your grandparents' grief. Here, in Torondell, your grandparents were able to build a formidable stronghold and protective wall constructed to further shield us.

"Though you and your brothers sometimes complained about certain decisions restricting your freedom or contrary to your youthful ambitions, understand your grandparents were overly protective of all within their House. Despite many noble woods elf families *frowning* upon my parents' adoption of non-woods elves, like Nui Honei, Nui Samu, Ona Noirar and the extraordinary healer, Diazae Alleina Isabella, their protection extended to these family members and even to our House soldiers and servants as well."

Je Leena then looked at Nui Honei and inquired, "When Alleina was at the Academy, she was harassed by certain classmates for being 'more brilliant and talented' than them. She is a sun elf of peasant blood, a shunned war orphan who later became a ward of House Je Luneefa. Yet, she outperformed all of her noble-born classmates and even most of those already years of training ahead of her. She became renowned as a medical prodigy unlike ever seen before. According to the tales, even her professors were astounded by her medical genius. As I recall, after several years, Alleina displaced a son of House Gevaruk as the reigning top, promising medical student at the Rhodell Medical Academy even though he was ten years her senior."

"The fool assaulted Alleina twice; he chose not to heed my warning thinking his status and family would protect him," Nui

Honei confessed.

"But his death was ruled an 'accident'," Je Danei added. "No evidence of foul play was ever found."

Stoically, Nui Honei remarked, "Yes, it was an *accident*. That fool did *accidently* kill himself when I chose not to save him from falling to his death on my third *warning* visit. My two previous warnings should have been sufficient. He was indeed a very foolish and obstinate male.

"And before you even ask, I will tell you that I have killed others on behalf of our families. On some occasions, I was asked to kill enemies of our Houses by the Je Luneefa first elders. And I even killed some when I thought they seriously threatened any member of Houses Je Luneefa, Nui Vent or Ona Feiir. Know that I will kill again, if need be, to protect our families. I believe I am most like your grandmother's evil side; whereas your mother and Alleina mostly reflect her good side. I still struggle to be more like my dear sisters."

After a few moments of quiet inner-reflection, Nui Honei's mood became very dark and evil again. She remarked, "It is perhaps due to fate's great fortune I am not leading this rescue mission for I would kill all in the enemy House and anyone else who would dare stand in my way without mercy and any remorse. My rage sometimes even frightens me. Dear beloved nieces, know that I am first, an elite warrior devoted to our families. Secondly, I am a skilled assassin trained by a master of assassin arts. I am also evil and can inflict my great evil upon others.

"With that devoted purpose, I am bound to our families with unconditional loyalty and love. Like the House Je Luneefa first elders, I will protect our Houses till I draw my last breath. You two must return to fulfill your House responsibilities; do not make me go there to rescue either of you!"

"So, dear Leena, *return* this spider fang dagger to the House first great mother who killed my brother, Je Gerard. Help her feel some of the pain we had to grievously endure for many years before Death takes her," Je Pagi ended.

Nui Honei looked solemnly at Je Danei and said, "And you my precious, beloved goddaughter and niece, take the head of that damn felf who stole my son and Dan-Rei from us." Both daughters of House Je Luneefa just nodded their heads in silent acknowledgement that they would do their duties as ordered.

Later that evening, Je Pagi wanted to have another scrying session with the great Dwarven, battlemage Urtha Dal, Nui Honei and Je Leena. Ona Noirar also joined them to hear more about the

Underworld and dark elf customs. They also discussed how best to confer with the sentient being within the spider fang dagger.

After erecting protective wards around the blade, Je Leena again "spoke" with the dagger's sentient being. She learned the history and purpose of the blade. Of most interest was the fact that the blade had been recklessly abandoned by the felf thief. Dilara, the spider fang dagger, felt grievously betrayed. She greatly mourned the centuries-long separation from her twin sister dagger and was extremely angry with the thief who had not returned to take her back home. Dilara conveyed in a tiny, whispering voice, "My anger burns like the fires of hell, and I seek revenge!"

"So, if I were to return you to your sister, would you be appreciative and how would you show your gratitude for my efforts?" Je Leena inquired.

After some quiet moments, the blade's sentient being spoke again to Je Leena, "I was born of the Underworld's merciless and evil hell. In return for your efforts, I will help you. Also, you can use me to remind that thief of hell's revenge whose wrath and destructive fury have no limits."

After further negotiations, Je Leena reached an agreement with Dilara.

"I greatly wish to be with my sister, never to be separated again. She is the joy of my heart. I will help you on your quest to the Underworld, to my home in Tol'Tarei where my sister should still be. There, unleash my revenge upon the House Norkula thief Aysun'Di," Dilara lastly conveyed within an angered whisper.

Ona Noirar declared, "So, we are now bound to go to House Norkula, a dark elf noble House of the Underworld city, Tol'Tarei. This is our destination; this is where we hope to find Nui Jooba and Dan-Rei."

After the meeting, Ona Noirar asked Nui Honei and Je Leena to meet him in his private study. When the felfs arrived, Ona Noirar was already there standing next to his desk. Ona Noirar greeted his beloved and niece; then he pointed to the weapons displayed on his desk. "Leena, your role on this mission is the most dangerous; you alone will most likely need to enter an unknown enemy's stronghold where more unseen dangers will await you. I expect there you will encounter several magical, protective wards and obstacles. Even some you may need to kill will also be protected by certain magical shrouds. These displayed weapons are the assassin's perfect tools for they are designed to detect and defeat magical wards that may enshroud an enemy; so, you can still eliminate that targeted soul. As you might suspect, they are made powerful through with enhancement of dragon's blood, Keiku's most powerful blood.

"Leena, you favor short swords and long knives. Before you lay my prized black dragon short swords, long knives and daggers. They were all forged in dragon's fire and made of dull, diachrom-infused black steel. These blades are extraordinarily and forever sharp, indestructible and invisible in darkness. No protective armor nor magical ward has ever safeguarded my intended victim when I wielded these weapons. If you like, I will *loan* my mighty weapons to you should you want any of them for this mission. If so, your aunt will perform the necessary blood-magic ritual releasing them from me and binding the chosen weapons to you."

Je Leena started to closely examine the fine, exquisitely crafted blades. All the blades are similar in design, all being forged by the renowned master bladesmith, Master Nimru. Each short sword was identical, like the long knives and daggers. The short sword and long knife blades are single-edged and slightly curved. But the daggers are all double-edged, straight blades. The two short sword blades are two fahs in length. Each of the two long knife blades is just a fah in length. Each of the four daggers has a blade length a bit longer than half a fah. All weapons' hilts were covered in black leather and about half a fah in length. The pommels resembled Keiku's head. The cross-guard resembled the great dragon's wings.

The young felf picked up each blade to test its weight and balance. For the next few moments, she used the short swords to slash and stab several imagined enemies around the study. She next expertly performed another difficult attack form, the tuxa-effreine, death by a hundred cuts, with the long knives. This unique attack was used only to inflict the most excruciating pain, more like horrific torture, onto a truly hated enemy before the victim died.

A small smile appeared upon Ona Noirar's face as he quietly admired Je Leena's demonstration of the complex tuxa-effreine attacks. Je Leena was truly a reflection of Je Buel, the first great mother of House Je Luneefa and a mighty warrior. Other than Nui Honei and Nui Samu, both elite warriors, Ona Noirar had only witnessed Je Buel perform the complete, "perfect" tuxa-effreine attacks.

Lastly, she picked up the four daggers and threw them at a target ten steps away. All daggers hit the target's center within eight heartbeats' time of her throwing the deadly blades. Quite pleased, Je Leena smiled at her elders and said, "Dear Uncle, thank you for this great honor; I want to them all. So, I *will* return all these magnificent weapons to you after completing the mission." After taking a long, calming breath, she continued, "Uncle, thank you again for this rare, great privilege. Dear Auntie, please officiate the blood-magic, release and bond ritual now. Our enemies will soon learn that they will not be protected from the hell I will unleash."

"Ah, this is my dear and beloved niece who reflects my evil!" Nui Honei proudly declared as she also threw her four hidden long knives at the same target's center within six heartbeats' time.

Blood-magic is an ancient and powerful form of sorcery used to lock or unlock a designated enchantment. Unlike other enchantments or spells, one's blood, which is unique, must be used in the original casting of the enchantment, as well as each casting thereafter to effectuate the magic. Certain weapons can be bound to an individual by blood-magic such that only that person can access and use the weapon's special powers or capabilities through that blood and person's voice. On the weapon, there is a "blood point," a place where one can prick her/himself to draw blood which the weapon will absorb to activate the designated weapon's capabilities when the incantation is evoked.

Nui Honei took a ceremonial dagger, cut the palms of Ona Noirar's hands, and thereafter placed a dragon sword into each bloodied hand. Ona Noirar then spoke the ritual incantation ending with, "Canela voi drago Ona Solganli and Solganlae Wei. I release you now to my niece, Je Leena." Nui Honei then cut the outstretched palms of her niece and placed the swords, Ona Solganli and Ona Solganlae Wei, upon Je Leena's bloodied palms. The swords began to glow and magically absorbed the blood from Je Leena's palms. Nui Honei continued by cutting Ona Noirar's already-healed palms again. He then raised the dragon long knives with both hands. "Canela voi drago Ona Didvaki and Ona Didvakae Wei. I release you now to my niece, Je Leena." After again cutting the palms of Je Leena's hands, Ona Noirar handed her the long knives which also began to glow, as well as absorb Je Leena's spilled blood from her hands. Both weapons, Ona Didvaki Wei, and Ona Didvakae Wei, ceased glowing after absorbing the blood of Je Leena. This same ritual was also repeated for the four dragon daggers.

Ona Noirar announced, "My dragon-blade weapons are now bonded to you. This bond cannot be broken and only you can take advantage of the weapons' special powers. Also, now only you can further release and bond these weapons to someone else in the future. Specifically, when you return, you will need to release and bond my weapons back to me.

"Know too that when you make your final preparations for battle, you will again drink your fully blessed dragon's blood Keiku bestowed upon each member of our families. You will thereafter let your weapons feast upon your drawn blood that would then be mixed with that of a black dragon, nature's most powerful source of magical energy. Then your weapons' might well be unequaled and completely devastating. "

"Take these scrolls, go and learn how to better use these weapons," Nui Honei then said. Je Leena hugged and thanked each of her elders again and then silently left her uncle's study feeling more confident with her role on the mission.

After magically sealing the room, Nui Honei kissed Ona Noirar. "On behalf of all the House elders, we thank you for bolstering Je Leena's courage and confidence with the loan of your mighty blades. We all appreciate your profound generosity. Thank you again.

"Beloved, I do deeply and truly love you. Despite my many contrary words and actions, you have been and are my *one*! There will never be another I could ever love as much as I love you. So, your courage and confidence should also be greatly bolstered knowing my love makes you greater. For no one nor any creature there in that accursed Underworld or even here in the Aboveworld realm can kill you. That is my great honor alone!" Nui Honei lovingly and lastly declared; she then kissed the scowling Ona Noirar again.

After leaving her aunt and uncle, Je Leena returned to the House Je Luneefa stronghold with her uncle's weapons and the scrolls detailing their blood-magic properties. She was both excited and filled with much anxiety. The new weapons now in her possession were highly prized by her uncle, an elite warrior of the Canae kingdom and perhaps the world. Ona Noirar did not "loan" any of his weapons to her knowledge; so, she felt very honored and very privileged to wield them. The stories of his famed dragon blades had always fascinated her. She had even already memorized some of the weapons' blood-magic incantations she had learned from his stories. Now that the time had come for her to prepare to wield such powerful weapons, she felt overwhelmed and unworthy.

Many thoughts raced through Je Leena's mind as she left the House Nui Vent stronghold, "My grave concerns with my mission role are to possibly infiltrate the enemy stronghold. What unknown magical alarms and traps will I encounter? How many guards? My success is highly dependent upon the words of a betrayed sentient being whose memories of that stronghold are centuries old.

Further, I will be completely alone there. Will I be able to return from that enemy stronghold after completing my objective?"

However, other than her aunt, no other House Je Luneefa battlemage had the skills and knowledge to possibly defeat all the potential, protective magical wards she expected to encounter. For one moment, Je Leena felt her grandmother's last dying gift of her magical essence and knowledge would be a curse. Now, the young felf praised her grandmother very quickly again for her wisdom and such a wondrous gift she would always cherish.

Just before leaving the House Nui Vent stronghold, Je Leena reached out mentally to Ona Drachir and asked him to join her in the second training room at her House. Sensing the concern in her voice, Ona Drachir simply responded, *"I will meet you there soon."*

"Please come wearing your armor and covered in your magical, protective wards. Know that I want to perform the close quarters combat training drills like we are in the halls or rooms of the enemy's stronghold," Je Leena additionally requested. Other than her elders, Je Leena knew Ona Drachir was the next most formidable warrior in their extended family. This night's training would help her learn more about the new weapons she now carried. She simply just needed to kill him before he defeated her in their upcoming deadly training exercise.

After reaching her home, the felf went to her bedchamber and donned her armor and House cape. She magically cut her hair such that there were only two long bands of short, black and red hair atop her now bald head. Houses Je Luneefa, Nui Vent and Ona Feiir are now at war. She then placed her borrowed weapons into sheaths at her sides, back, boots and inside her cape. Lastly, she cast several protective magical wards upon herself.

Now prepared, Je Leena silently went to the stronghold's second training room, a large fifty-step by fifty-step space with a six-step high ceiling. This room could be magically reconfigured for different training purposes.

Je Leena sensed Ona Drachir had already preceded her and changed the last known layout of the room. Before entering the completely dark training hall, Je Leena could sense she was not completely alone. For one instant, Je Leena sensed Ona Drachir was still there too. He had then completely veiled himself invisible and undetectable; he now is hidden somewhere in the darkness. Je Leena closed the training room's door behind her and magically sealed it. She too then veiled herself invisible and undetectable. Even after calling upon her dragon eyes' vision and quickly scanning the hallway before her, Je Leena could not detect the melf's presence anywhere within the training hall. She now began to silently stalk her prey.

Je Leena drew her short swords and started cautiously walking down a newly configured hallway within the training room. Her eyes constantly scanned the hallway and each room she passed. The complete darkness and silence began to spread fear and doubt within her. Again, nothing could be seen, nor could any sound be heard. Je Leena could not even detect the melf's faintest heartbeat or scent. Of all the daughters and sons of their Houses, she secretly feared Ona Drachir the most. He is not only a great warrior, but he was also becoming a formidable assassin. More fear started to slowly take hold of the young felf.

After a few more long moments of sheer unnerving silence, Je Leena questioned if Ona Drachir is even still in the training facility. Suddenly, she heard the very low twang sound of released tiny bow strings. Evidently, Ona Drachir had chosen this night to use small hand crossbows, a favored weapon of dark elves.

With the aid of her magical House cape, Je Leena immediately reacted by quickly levitating upwards and to her left. She then detected one small arrow, whose tip was most likely dipped in a paralyzing agent, had missed her as it flew past. The second arrow missed her but did hit her cape. She also discerned that those arrows were shot from behind. Somehow Ona Drachir had already managed to slip behind her. *"How could that be?"* she thought quickly. She had now become his prey. With ever rising fear, she quickly dodged away knowing her pounding heartbeat could be heard by the melf's dragon-sensitive hearing. Je Leena also moved away again not wanting to remain stationary for too long.

Alarmed, but calming herself, Je Leena quickly made her way into another room off the hallway. This room resembled a bedchamber. There, on the bed she detected some small movements and the appearance of a covered sleeping figure. As she slowly and silently creeped towards the bed, about four steps away, her dragon-sensitive hearing detected minute sounds behind her. She turned in time to parry a deadly sword thrust aimed at her. The initial attack was quickly followed by an immediate second sword thrust.

Both attacks Je Leena successfully parried and viciously counterattacked. Instinctively, Je Leena had switched to a different, magically enhanced variant of her dragon eyes which now allowed her to see the heated outline of her adversary. Fortunately too, she had also reverted to using her dragon-sensitive hearing earlier.

Other than her uncles and aunt, Ona Drachir was the most formidable swordsman she knew. Defeating him would be very difficult, if not impossible. Je Leena and Ona Drachir battled around the room for a long while in nearly complete darkness. Most terrifying was that no noise emanated from the clashing of their blades. That was one magical feature of the dragon blades, an assassin's perfect weapons. The silence of their battle unsettled Je Leena for it was a new frightening experience.

Je Leena knew too that she could not "out-duel" this melf; so, she called upon her magic as a sinister smile formed on her face. At that same moment, Ona Drachir recognized that foreshadowing, and quickly disengaged from their duel by running through the wall's secret door. Je Leena quickly followed him, now far more prepared to deal with her formidable quarry. Sensing his presence above the hidden door, Je Leena threw herself through the door but in a prone position facing upwards. As expected, Ona Drachir instantly pounced upon her from above the door as she came through the hidden passageway. They again engaged in another deadly duel.

This time however, Je Leena called upon more magic of the dragon blades that continued the duel with Ona Drachir "for her." One blood-magic capability of the dragon blades is that they learned and adopted the fighting skills and prowess of the one who was most proficient in using them. The dragon blades "learned" how to duel from Ona Noirar. "Defend me Ona Solganli and Solganlae Wei," she instructed her blades. Both blades, possessed with the fighting skill and prowess of Ona Noirar and henceforth skillfully protected the felf from all Ona Drachir's attacks. Je Leena then was free to quickly cast another spell that paralyzed the melf and pinned him against the wall.

"I win this contest," Je Leena proclaimed proudly.

"Yes, congratulations. It is your first, well-earned victory against me," Ona Drachir responded with a curt dry voice.

"Thank you. It is the first of more victories to come, I hope," Je Leena said smiling, reveling in her great victory. Her mood then changed to become more serious. "You have been avoiding me lately. Why? Will you stay with me tonight? I..." Je Leena hesitantly asked.

"No, I think not," the melf immediately replied. "Please release me."

"No, I think not. If I do, you will just walk away," she

sarcastically responded, very annoyed with his fast, seemingly selfish response. "Are you still angry with me over my words spoken yesterday?"

Silence. After several long moments, Ona Drachir asked, "Did you assault Tamara last moon after Jooba and I left the inn? She just wanted to dance with me. Direct your anger properly."

Je Leena stood before him in a bit of a shock; she thought she had cleverly disguised herself as a burly, seafaring rogue melf with a Rhodell accent, such that no one would ever know her true identity.

"Given the surprised look upon your face and silence, I will assume I am correct," Ona Drachir continued. "Your words afterwards to me were very unkind, as well as malicious."

Je Leena's eyes filled with tears as she hung her head from the weight of guilt. "Did you also cause Tahtali's horse to throw her?" Ona Drachir further inquired as he recalled this last incident.

Silence. Je Leena had been down that street and hidden from their sight. So, she thought and now thinking, *"How did he possibly see me?"* She eventually replied after a sorrowful sigh, "She scorned me days earlier by insinuating she planned to win your heart back. When I saw her talking to you yesterday for a while, I became angry. I made her horse buck. And I aimed some hurtful words towards you later. I am sorry for my words; please forgive me."

"Please release me," Ona Drachir requested again.

"If I do, will you stay, comfort me by reassuring me your heart is still only mine or will you silently just leave angry again?" Je Leena asked. Before he could answer, Je Leena released him from her paralysis spell.

Silently, he sheathed his weapons and stretched himself to finally recover from the temporary paralysis. Ona Drachir then looked at the felf with an indifferent gaze for several long moments. He then turned away and started to leave the room.

Je Leena yelled, "Wait! Why must you leave this way? Can you not discuss your current feelings with me now? Do you not want to try to resolve our issues now?"

In great anger, Je Leena suddenly summoned and silently cast all the Nimru dragon daggers and long knives at the melf. All the blades stopped just before hitting him. Like before, Je Leena paralyzed or froze each blade in flight. They now were all suspended just outside his heart, less than a fah away...

Ona Drachir had taken several long steps towards the room's door then stopped. Tears formed in his eyes as he recalled the previous days' painful memories she caused. Without turning, he simply said, "Your words did hurt me. Why do you doubt my loyalty? What have I done or said for you to have such insecurities?

"Why do you feel the need to control everything at all times? You are so very much like your grandmother and our auntie. They knew practically everything about our Houses, even the secrets we tried to conceal. Those House elders were and are extraordinary. You too one day will lead a great noble House by becoming its ruling great mother. I have no doubt about that. Yet, you still lack the House elders' great wisdom, wisdom partially developed through self-onfidence.

"So, aim your frustration at your heart's real enemy – yourself. It is true we are not each other's first love. That is our past and should no longer be important. We are, I hope, each other's last love. Fight to make that so now, not decades later. But, if that is not your true desire, then stop your senseless charade.

"Lastly, did your blades come closer to striking my heart this time?" Ona Drachir sorrowfully asked. He then continued his silent departure from the training room and House Je Luneefa.

Je Leena fell to her knees as tears silently fell.

One Hundred Daughters and Sons

With the aid of the magical and powerful blood of the great dragon Ona Kei Kuri Ryuu, Ona Noirar quickly led his war group of Houses Je Luneefa, Nui Vent and Ona Feiir soldiers to the great Ararateken mountain of the southern plains. From Rhodell, this group only needed four days, instead of the normal six days, to make the trek.

While the small war group rested late that fourth day, Ona Noirar received a message from Keiku, happily declaring, "Rejoice! I have explored the mountain's top and found one of the large tunnels detailed on the maps that Je Kei has. Let us pray I too can take my battle to the enemy!"

Ona Noirar smiled, pleased with Keiku's news; he thought, "Keiku will be the undeniably greatest ally in any battle we have. Truly the great dragon will unleash a fury, her and Honei's hellish fury, unlike ever seen in the Underworld."

After setting up camp late afternoon outside the mountain's entrance, the small, united army settled into an anxious repose. The next day, a smaller group would enter the mountain and journey further into the dark, mysterious underground.

While most of the small army, about three hundred soldiers, would stay encamped outside the mountain, another group of one hundred soldiers would escort Ona Noirar and a handful of others deeper into the mountain to the anticipated, infamous Luna Fendasse gate, the known gateway to the Underworld. Journeying still deeper below the mountain, Ona Noirar would continue to follow the clever trail Nui Kei Dan-Rei Ryuu left.

At the army's base campsite, outside the mountain that night, an impatient Keiku wanted to meet to finalize the plans of their mission's next phase. Like most Aboveworlders, the dragon was very anxious about journeying into an unknown world, the highly feared, lightless Underworld. Keiku nervously paced about in front of the small war group for a short while. When she stopped, she rose to her full, majestic height and mentally asked all in the assembled group, *"Who plans to journey to the Underworld city, destination now believed to be Tol'Tarei, a great city of dark elves? I understand Ona Noirar you must go since you are the leader and you have dealt with dark elves before in your past, but who else will accompany you on your perilous mission?"*

Ona Noirar then addressed the group, interjecting his thoughts to force his soldiers' deep and truthful contemplation, "Before any of you volunteer to further journey with me into the Underworld, know that it is a realm unlike any other you may have encountered. Most of the time, we will travel fast in deathly silence and be in complete overwhelming darkness or have very little illumination around us. The realm's silence, unfamiliar surroundings and the deathly darkness will make you uncomfortable, very uncomfortable. Fortunately, your senses will be greatly enhanced by the taking of dragon's blood. This will provide you with some comfort. The dragon's blood will also help counter the many tricks your mind will play given the utter darkness of the Underworld. Still, unknown creatures and dangers abound in this realm too. The Underworld has also been known to drive weak-minded Aboveworlders to near madness.

"Now, I hope you can appreciate why much of your battle training was conducted at night or in the stronghold's training rooms where you were immersed in complete darkness many times. Never had we ever thought your training would ever be for a battle waged in the dreaded Underworld. But here we stand and there we will go! That day of using all that training is now upon us. Fear, unlike any other time, will tightly grip you, if not choke you mercilessly. You must steel yourself, focus, be brave and trust your training and those fellow soldiers around you.

"I am sure you all have heard the rumors; it is widely known throughout the Aboveworld that no one who lives under the sun would willingly venture into the dark Underworld. Truly, it is where a multitude of untold dangers infest that realm. Before unseen creatures, dark elves, gnomes, and other two-legged kind are all there too. These inhabitants of the Underworld consider us to be their enemies or their next meal. So, attempting to kill us will be most like a normal, reflexive action for them. You must be even more wary and vigilant at all times.

"Lastly, the Underworld is home to the dark elves, masters of darkness. Even though few dark elves ever venture to the Aboveworld, fewer remain and live in our world. Dark elves are born, live and thrive in darkness. They will most likely die in darkness, as well. Dark elves natural physiology is well-designed for life in their lightless, ominous dark realm. In the Underworld where there is little to no light, these elves can still see clearly. Like practically all of the creatures that inhabit the Underworld, dark elves' keen vision is best in darkness. Unlike us Aboveworlders, even candlelight brightness can overwhelm the ocular senses of the Underworld creatures. So, dark elves hate the Aboveworld's sun, moon and stars and detest those who dwell under these heavenly bodies. To dark elves, those heavenly bodies are all heinous abominations.

"So, who now wants to join me on this most perilous journey?"

For some silent moments, each member of the small army let the war group leader's words force them to take full measure of themselves. Ona Noirar knew most were now trapped deep in paralyzing thought and fear. Yet, he hoped their loyalty and love for their families and Houses would be far greater and that their loyalty and love would overcome their fears.

"I shall go as well. My bow may be needed, as well as my blessed Ona Tigri shield," said Ona Drachir, volunteering first to break the group's silence. Though still quite a young melf of two hundred twenty-three years, he is a highly skilled and courageous warrior. Like his family and ancestors, Ona Drachir was trained to be a warrior since he could walk. He had already thought and concluded, *"Nui Jooba has become closer to me over the last few years. The bond between us is fiercely strong and true. So, I have an extreme family obligation to help rescue the one I consider to be my only brother. Further, Dan-Rei is the offspring of Keiku and the eldest of Ona Tae Kuri Ryuu and Je Ri Kuri Ryuu. For the sake of Taeku, my bonded dragon, I am also compelled to help rescue Taeku's sister, another precious member of my extended family."*

"As will I too. Most likely, the talents of a battlemage will also be required," Je Leena quickly added with confidence. *"Plus, I have a blood debt to repay to the House great mother responsible for the murder of our uncle,"* the young felf thought to herself as she tightly regripped the spider fang dagger, recommitting herself to her sworn duty.

"I too must go to take the head of that felf who first dared to commit the crime against our families! My primary responsibility as well is to take back what was stolen from our Houses!" Je Danei bravely declared.

Other courageous souls also volunteered to go on into the Underworld city, but Ona Noirar finally decided that just a very small deadly and highly skilled group would have the best chances of infiltrating the city and enemy House undetected, rescue their family captives and safely escape. So, he finally decided that only he, Je Danei, Je Leena and Ona Drachir would only go on to Tol'Tarei, leaving about one hundred soldiers by the Underworld's Luna Fendasse gate, their next immediate destination. Ona Noirar again pondered heavily, *"How we will successfully recover Nui Jooba and Dan-Rei is still very much undetermined."*

Later that night, Keiku directed Je Leena to draw some of her dragon's blood. After Keiku fully blessed her blood, three drops were distributed to each of the designated one hundred soldiers who would journey further into the Underworld's depths below the Ararateken mountain. One drop of dragon's blood when taken would again greatly enhance the soldier's senses, strength and stamina for an extended period of time. Dragon's blood would also serve as a wondrous healing agent. Extra dragon's blood was lastly given to the designated four Houses' members who would continue to journey further to the suspected enemy's city.

Keiku blessed the war group in the ancient Elvish language. She then told the group, "Let me reassure you that I too will try to enter the great cavern where Tol'Tarei is located. I will kill many enemies when I unleash Nui Honei and my fury upon that city! Those of you who will enter the mountain the next dawn, go with honor and duty to the great noble Houses of Ona Feiir, Nui Vent and Je Luneefa." Keiku then suddenly left the camp to again explore the tunnels she had found at the mountaintop.

Afterwards, Ona Noirar, Ona Drachir, Je Danei and Je Leena quietly met to further prepare themselves. Ona Noirar instructed his nieces and nephew, "Go. Let your blood-magic weapons feast upon your and Keiku's powerful blood. In addition, Je Leena please also prepare an elixir with the great dragon's blood and distribute it to the one hundred soldiers entering the mountain."

After leaving the meeting, Je Leena quickly prepared the healing elixir. Later, she returned to the assembled one hundred House soldiers who would safely escort the chosen four to their mission's next Underworld destination. When Je Leena handed the elixir to Ona Drachir with tear-filled, pleading eyes, he just took his vial from her hands and walked silently away.

The brooding Ona Drachir returned to his tent again and sat alone in the chilled darkness where he found some solace in his foul mood. He examined the small vial he had just received, knowing the contained elixir would combat poison and other mind- and body-numbing agents dark elves commonly cover on their weapons to wield against their enemies. While slowly moving the vial in his hand, he further wondered, *"If only you could heal the pain in my heart... Leena, why do you trouble me so? Why did you unleash a barrage of unkind words upon me before we left Torondell? Do you now realize I had to distance myself from you over the past several days in order to not let my anger further frustrate me?"*

Now on a mission, Ona Drachir welcomed distractions and other priorities that first concerned him. However, throughout the journey there to the Ararateken Mountain, he had again reflected upon his troubled thoughts, *"In the back of my mind and deep within my heart, I am plagued with the longing to fully restore my good relationship with you Je Leena again and increase the loving bond between us. I still desire and hope you will be very much a part of the future I want to create for myself. Sadly, I do not know how I can mend my emotional turmoil. That is still my great mystery."* So, Ona Drachir sat alone again questioning his uncertain love and wrestling with his thoughts about his uncertain future.

No light was needed to illuminate his tent's dark interior for his dragon eyes' vision continued to serve him well. The young melf felt truly blessed to be a good friend of a great dragon. Keiku had long ago first blessed him and a very select few others with her powerful, magical blood that greatly enhances his senses, strength and stamina. Even his health had been greatly fortified against illnesses.

Though unsettled with many thoughts, he immediately remedied his discomforting thoughts as he soon embraced another most welcomed distraction. Ona Drachir returned his attention to that which is ever steadfast and very certain – his weapons. As Ona Drachir gazed upon his beloved weapons, he felt assured they would all serve him well on this mission like other missions before.

After taking a drop of the dragon's blood that he had just received, Ona Drachir took each weapon, pricked his finger upon the weapon's blood-point and cited the weapon-specific incantation to allow the weapon to absorb his dragon-enriched blood. "Now I, and only I, can draw upon the weapon's special and unique capabilities," he again quietly reminded himself.

Ona Drachir next slowly touched his full-body, form-fitting, flexible armor clothing. He then smiled, thinking, "It is made of dragon cloth, a cloth integrated with ground dragon scales. This material is superior to chain mail not only in protective properties, but also in weight. In addition, this dragon cloth is infused with diachrom, the most precious and hardest metal in existence. Lastly, it was also enhanced with dragon's blood. Never has an enemy blade, magic-enhanced or not, ever pierced my precious armor clothing nor my outer armor - a breastplate, bracers, and greaves. These too were also constructed of diachrom infused, dull black leather."

"The helm of my House is like that of the visored bascinet style. The one-piece, protective covering has one narrow opening across the front permitting clear, unobstructive vision. Three different, distinct and fierce looking, small dragons crown my helmet. Even my outer leather armor breastplate, bracers and greaves also bear small, sketched images of the same three House dragons."

The young melf smiled to himself so pleased that he could don all of his magnificent armor in less than twelve heartbeats' time with the aid of magic. He again silently thanked Nui Honei for all the wonderful, magical enhancements she had bestowed upon his armor and weapons that Ona Noirar had given him long ago.

Ona Drachir next examined his shapeshifting, great recurve bow, Ona Alada-Kizil Wei, the only heirloom he received from his deceased father. Primarily made of the finest Nubian ash wood and reinforced with steel, this bow's size could be magically altered from small to great depending upon the present need. Beside his bow, lay the magically enhanced, ever-full quiver of arrows, Ona Alada-Gurte Wei.

Ona Teva Wei and Ona Geva Wei, his twin scimitars, were always close and lay before him. His scimitars, like all of his other blades, were forged from dull black steel infused with diachrom. Through blood-magic, all his blades were bonded to him; they would never break and would retain their extraordinarily sharp edges till he died. And only he could ever call upon their unique, intrinsic magical properties.

Smiling, Ona Drachir thought, "My shape-shifting shield, Ona Tigri Wei, is here. This shield, also forged from dull black steel infused with diachrom, is another fine, blood-magic weapon. This mighty shield has protected me from many attacks; yet it still remains unscratched, like it was still just newly forged. With the incantation of a certain Ra'Aure spell, I can call upon this shield to emit the stored, blinding sunrays which could prove invaluable in the Underworld, a realm of near to total complete, ever frightening darkness."

His two short swords, four long knives and four daggers which he also seemed to favor on clandestine missions, lay quietly there. Ona Drachir "felt" all of his beloved weapons silently hailing and encouraging him; they were again ready and seemingly eager to serve. From some deep place within his mind, he sometimes thought he could hear his weapons chanting his war song. As he imagined his weapons singing the House Ona Feiir war song, the young melf quietly started singing along with them. All were eager, but patiently waited. Like him, his weapons all are courageous and will do their duty without fail and hesitation. His mighty weapons reassured him, as well as reinforced his will and devout dedication to his assigned purpose: rescue Nui Jooba and Nui Kei Dan-Rei Ryuu, mercilessly kill any who might oppose me and safely return home.

Lastly, his neatly folded, black House cape lay before him too. He affectionately rubbed his hand across his House heraldic sigil, three vertically aligned, black dragons in front of a blood-red moon. His great grandfather created this sigil long ago. Each dragon represented his great grandfather's noble two daughters and son, all fierce warriors. This was another prized possession for it was made of dragon's cloth and could conceal his other weapons and magical contents. *"With my House cape, I can even levitate through magic too,"* he concluded, silently praising Nui Honei again.

Other than the short, three bands of black and red short curly hair upon his head, the young melf's head was bald. Ona Drachir was ready to wage war. His terrible rage and fury will again be unleashed. Ona Drachir quieted his mind and slowed his breathing, searching to find more inner peace.

Slightly trembling, he acknowledged to himself, "I am afraid. Fighting in the Underworld, a realm of near complete to total darkness and against an enemy I had not ever encountered before. This causes me to have great concern."

Though relatively young of age, Ona Drachir possessed a wealth of fighting history, knowledge, experience and skills he could call upon. After sighing heavily, he acquiesced, calmly thinking, *"I will not let fear defeat me! Yet though afraid, I am ready to face the upcoming dangerous challenges. Like my courageous House elders, I too must find courage originating from my family's long history of bravery and accomplishing nearly impossible deeds."* Soon, he found needed inner peace.

"Most of my family have died in battle as warriors, fighting for the glory of the Canae kingdom or House Ona Feiir. Some died in battle fighting against marauding Houses or orc tribes of the northern frontier. Like those before me, I will die fighting till I draw my last breath!" the melf whispered reverently. Ona Drachir closed his eyes and stretched out his hands before his weapons and whispered a prayer in ancient Elvish, "Ancestors of House Ona Feiir, I beseech thee. Please protect me as I take war to the enemies of Houses Nui Vent and Je Luneefa. Calm my fears. Fortify my courage. Lend me your courage and strength once again. Should I fall, let me do so with the blood of my enemies upon my hands and with my death song upon my lips as I bravely welcome my final peace. Ancestors, please then welcome me home. May thy holy blessings continue to be upon me."

Ona Drachir considered himself blessed even when about to encounter many unknowns in the enemy's home realm. The young melf then quietly slipped into a peaceful meditation after concluding the preparation of his weapons and remembering his family's history. He knew his weapons would never fail him despite his personal fears and uncertainties. He knew his heritage would sustain him through the upcoming terrifying ordeals.

While deep within the comfort of his warrior's meditation, taught by Ona Noirar, he heard a familiar, disturbing soft voice call out to him, "Last son of House Ona Feiir, may we enter?"

"Je Leena and, most likely, Je Danei, are both here; but why?" he wondered. After a few silent moments to allow his conflicting, meditative rage to settle, Ona Drachir finally replied, "Yes, please do."

The House Je Luneefa daughters entered the tent silently. Ona Drachir, Ona Noirar's nephew, is the last of his noble House Ona Feiir; and though not of their blood, both felfs looked at the melf who too seemed more like another dear loved one of their noble House.

Both felfs too admired this melf for his steadfast discipline, limitless courage and his quiet, mysterious, yet unfaltering nature. Like their adopted uncle, Ona Noirar, Ona Drachir did not seek fame and riches, but only a peaceful life. Like his uncle, Ona Drachir is a quiet, stay-in-the-shadows melf whose love and loyalty to family and friends are profound and unwavering. Like their real brothers, Je Danei and Je Leena had come to truly love their extended family young cousins Nui Jooba and Ona Drachir.

Je Leena remarked, "See Danei; I told you Drachir would be here quietly inspecting his exquisite, perfectly forged weapons. Though nothing has changed since he examined them last, he still needed to inspect them again. Such is his way, dictated by his family-forged warrior's discipline. I also believe this is his way of preparing for war or a dangerous mission. Interestingly enough, this may also be his way of calming himself when he is deeply troubled. Life holds many uncertainties, but his weapons are ever constant and give him great comfort for they have not ever disappointed him."

"Yes, I understand. I too have a similar ritual. But, more importantly now, you two need to discuss and resolve your issues as best as you can," Je Danei said quickly and pushed her younger sister towards the melf who caught the surprised, stumbling Je Leena with a welcoming arm. "Recently, you both have been uncommonly distant from each other. Avoiding your issues will not solve them. We are on a very dangerous mission; we could die. There should be no personal distractions. Now, you still have some time and can hopefully repair, or at least, start to repair what may be broken in your relationship. Please learn from my mistakes. So, talk and listen with honesty; you first Leena. Like his beloved weapons, show him you too are another precious constant in his life, a constant who will not disappoint him" Je Danei insisted sternly.

After some silent moments and a sorrowful sigh, Je Leena sadly said, "I apologize for my hurtful words and behavior. I confess jealousy had overtaken me more than once recently. Please forgive me."

Ona Drachir smiled slightly at Je Danei knowing how much she cared for her sister. Je Danei said earnestly, "I am very concerned that Je Leena is the only one planned to infiltrate the enemy's stronghold. I want you Sister to be at your *best* and having any personal issues that could affect your abilities could be disastrous, if not fatal." Je Danei also feared any personal concerns worrying or distracting her sister could be detrimental to their mission's complete success.

Feeling very grateful, Ona Drachir conjectured, "The eldest daughter of House Je Luneefa has surely become wiser to recognize her sister's dilemma and distance from me, the one melf Leena truly cares for the most. Danei took the difficult steps to help her sister overcome the agonizing distance Leena has with me. You gave needed words to my thoughts when I could not. Thank you Danei, thank you."

Ona Drachir looked at Je Leena for several long moments.

He did not have the right words to say. So, he just slightly smiled and opened his arms to chance embracing the one felf he truly loved. Je Leena entered his embrace with tearful eyes sincerely apologizing again and promising to become more worthy of him. Concluding, she solemnly pledged, "Drachir, know that I truly love you, though my poor actions recently demonstrated otherwise. I will become better and show that I will become another of your precious life's constants."

"Drachir, you should smile more often. You are more handsome when you do, and you will frighten little ones less with your scowls," the eldest Je Luneefa daughter said, hoping to lighten their moods. Je Danei smiled at them both and reminded them, "Your love is precious. Do not yield to relationship-crippling fears and doubts. Time too is very precious; time should not be misused, taken for granted nor expended unwisely."

Je Leena hugged her sister tightly as tears fell from their eyes. Ona Drachir said, "Danei, thank you for your wisdom and taking these difficult actions. But do I really scowl often? Do I really frighten others, especially young ones?" Ona Drachir suddenly inquired after some inner reflection upon Je Danei's words.

"Yes!" both Je Danei and Je Leena immediately exclaimed in unison.

"And now, please do not withdraw from us in your quiet, isolated contemplation. Though inherent to your mysterious nature, that appears to be quite selfish," Je Danei said, reminding the melf again of his known behavior. "Please know we also love you and your scowls, especially Leena who loves you more than you know. And thankfully, my sister does not easily lose her *focus* by your charm too often, like Annaei does over Kei."

"So, my scowls are charming then?" Ona Drachir sincerely asked.

"Not quite, beloved; though at times, maybe. They are just characteristic of you, my mysterious one," Je Leena replied. "Uncle Noirar scowls often too; so, it may just be another family trait."

After some laughter, the three companions quietly discussed their mission roles and how they might find and rescue the abducted Nui Jooba and Dan-Rei. In a short while, their earlier melancholy spirits were greatly lifted.

Now pleased with her accomplishment, the eldest House Je Luneefa daughter turned her attention to another mysterious topic of great interest to her. Je Danei inquired, "From time to time, I have had chances to scrutinize the blades and other fine weapons Uncle Noirar has gifted members of our family. Even some of the ones still remaining in his private study seem to also bear similar qualities and traits to those he first gifted us long ago. Why is that? "Each group of blades are usually different with each new forging. However, all your blades seem similar too, like those Uncle has given us. I am very curious why so many blades have these same unique qualities. "Do you know any of the history of the exquisitely crafted blades Uncle Ona Noirar gifted you and to us?"

Ona Drachir reflected inwardly for a few moments after closing his eyes. When he opened them, he saw that the felfs were still patiently waiting for a response. Now unfortunately, he knew he could not easily escape anticipated, upcoming uncomfortable discussions... The young melf said, "Yes, I do. Our uncle, as you know, cares little for fame, riches and power. Beyond his beloved felf, Nui Honei, his beloved great dragon, Ona Kei Kuri Ryuu, his beloved family and very few beloved friends, he was only obsessed with one other thing he loved: finding and wielding the *perfect* blade.

"Long ago, disguised as a commoner, Uncle embarked upon an adventure to the Underworld to find a certain bladesmith renowned for his craft amongst the world's masters. He learned that this master of master bladesmiths was an exiled dark elf elder of the noble House Nimru, of the Underworld city Tol'Tarei. House Nimru found fault with this elder after he refused to share his unique, blade-smithing secrets with his two elder brothers. These were family members the Master deemed 'unworthy' since they only sought to just gain more wealth through his knowledge and skills. The two elder Nimru brothers, who were good bladesmiths, but inferior to the Master, had initially funded their younger brother, Master Nimru Janvier, to start his own trade business. Even after repaying his elder brothers handsomely for their initial investment, those elder brothers still did not truly respect and honor the craft.

"In time, Master Nimru Janvier was exalted far above his elder brothers. As Master Nimru's fame and business success grew, so did the hatred and jealousy of his elder brothers. The elder Nimru brothers first threatened the Master. One elder brother wanted to break each finger of Nimru Janvier's hands. The other elder brother wanted to simply sever both hands of the Master. These and other extreme threats aimed at Nimru Janvier still were not enough for him to divulge his craft and forging secrets.

A few hostile conflicts had even occurred within House Nimru amongst these brothers. "To reduce the increasing tension within House Nimru, the ruling House great mother decided to expel Nimru Janvier from the family for his on-going, deliberate rebellion against her orders to share his knowledge with his elder brothers. With no House and family protection nor resources, it was expected the gifted master would soon perish by becoming another pitiful family outcast and fatality of the Underworld's dark elf society.

"However, the elder Nimru brothers also wanted to deny the world of any possible future, Nimru Janvier blades since they could not profit from the Janvier's knowledge. Fearing for his life, Nimru Janvier quickly and surreptitiously fled from the Underworld city Tol'Tarei without a determined destination. When the elder brothers failed to find their younger brother after several moons of searching, these evil and revengeful two elder brothers soon murdered the master's son, Master Nimru's last living offspring. Master Nimru foolishly thought his son was a favored grandson of his House and his mother, a powerful House second great mother, would protect him from his revengeful uncles. Nimru Janvier was gravely wrong.

"As fate would have it, Uncle Noirar encountered and rescued Master Nimru from certain death as four assassins attempted to kill Master Nimru on his exile from Tol'Tarei. In return, Master Nimru, now destitute, gave Uncle his last valuable possession, a long knife, as recompense for saving his life and the meal Uncle prepared for him.

"After carefully examining and testing the fine, exquisitely crafted weapon, Uncle returned the long knife to Master Nimru. Uncle then pledged to safely escort Master Nimru to the Underworld city Alaca where he could start anew within another noble House, well known to Uncle. Uncle had befriended certain elders of a prestigious, Alaca noble House, House Korogulu, after providing vital assistance to them in a House war many years before then. During their travel to the new city, Uncle befriended the Master.

"Master Nimru did find sanctuary in Alaca and his new House. Master Nimru also accepted the new name bestowed upon him by the House Alaca ruling great mother. Master Nimru became Elder Kylian of House Korogulu. Before departing, Uncle gave Kylian one hundred gold coins to help him restart his trade business. Uncle also gave that same amount to House Alaca for their generosity in welcoming the Master into their House and maintaining Master Nimru's new identity.

"Master Nimru's fine blades were quite expensive and commanded ten silver coins for just a mere long knife. As you know, a good long knife should normally cost only two to four silver.

Uncle's generous gift would pay for two hundred long knives. Overwhelmed with gratitude, Kylian promised to make Uncle one hundred blades of his choice, one for each gold coin he had received. Uncle needed to only supply the critical resources: diachrom, steel and the very rare fire source needed to forge his most unique blades. Fortunately, Tol'Tarei was located near a volcano; so, that primordial heat source was used by the Master and other highly skilled workers for certain metalworking.

"However, the master was also still concerned for his safety and more attacks by his revengeful family. So, Kylian pleaded to seek another secret place where he could hide for a time. He also did not want to risk House Korogulu's safety.

"Uncle and Kylian left Alaca, bound to another destination that only Uncle knew of. They returned to a secret location within the Aboveworld's Taurus Mountain where Uncle and I had made a home after the House Ona Feiir stronghold had been destroyed. There, Kylian could be sequestered from the Underworld and well protected from his hateful family. Also, more importantly, Kylian would have a forge fired by one of the two flames that can melt diachrom: dragon's flames."

"So, the great dragon, Ona Kei Kuri Ryuu, also met and helped Kylian," Je Leena remarked.

"Yes," Ona Drachir confirmed. "She too became fond of the old master as did our aunt and your House elders. Thereafter, over the next few years, Uncle had many sets of weapons made at the secret forge within Taurus Mountain. As promised, Kylian forged one hundred blades for Uncle consisting of eight pairs of scimitars, two pairs of dragon short swords, two pairs of dragon long knives, eight dragon daggers, sixteen pairs of long knives, sixteen spears, sixteen shields, two battleaxes, and two flanged battle maces."

"Your recall of the Master Nimru's work seems to have a peculiar elegance, does it not Leena?" Je Danei inquired. The captivated Je Leena did not reply, but only continued to just lovingly gaze at Ona Drachir.

"Thank you," Ona Drachir hesitantly replied, unwilling to release the reassuring gaze of Je Leena. "I try to pay the Master the highest honor he is due in my recalling of his blades' histories.

"Soon after meeting the Master, the ever-vain great dragon wanted her likeness to also be captured and memorialized on some of the blades. The dragon argued that without her flames, there would be no famed blades at all forged at Taurus Mountain. Kylian and Uncle agreed quickly for neither wanted to debate with Keiku. Thereafter, all our long knives, his and Auntie's scimitars and

Uncle's infamous, prized dragon blades were initially forged. Further, the pattern of each of the first one hundred blades forged bears some features of the great dragon. Of course, Keiku's request that *some* of the blades should bear her likeness truly meant *all*."

Ona Drachir paused, recalling that fond memory. With a small smile, he continued, "Many highly regarded Damascus sword and knife blade patterns reflect the banding and mottling of flowing water. All the one hundred blades Master Nimru first forged for Uncle are truly unique, characterized by the distinctive patterns of different dragon features, such as Keiku's eyes, horns, fangs, wings, scales, talons and tail. All of Keiku's physical features are incredibly unique. She might even say they are all 'perfect.'"

"Truly, she would not say 'might' at all, I assure you," Je Leena quipped.

"Agreed. Keiku would attest all her dragon features are perfect!" Je Danei offered with quiet laughter.

Ona Drachir further remarked, "Accurately capturing these seven different dragon features in the blades' patterns was difficult. Some blades reflect the great dragon's eyes while others reflect her talons. Some blades' patterns capture the likeness of her horns while others reflect the patterns in her fangs and tail. Capturing and reflecting these dragon features were a daunting new challenge for the Master; yet it was a challenge he gladly welcomed. In a few blades' patterns, even Keiku's distinctive blue flames have been captured and memorialized. Keiku, as you might expect, had to inspect and approve all finished work. She found Master Nimru's work to be exceptional. The great dragon was very impressed and pleased.

"When he finally fulfilled his pledge, Kylian was overjoyed knowing that his new weapons would be in very worthy hands, hands that truly appreciate and honor his craft."

"Drachir, how do you know all of this?" Je Leena quietly inquired.

"And, most importantly, what more can you tell us? Please withhold no details," Je Danei impatiently inquired, observing that Ona Drachir had paused again in his recalling of the blades' histories.

First responding initially with a small scowl, Ona Drachir hesitantly continued, "Each blade holds a secret, a testimony of endearing and unconditional love, a great love that captures and holds hearts together. All of Kylian's exquisitely crafted first one hundred weapons were also completed with one drop of his blood. For many years, Kylian greatly mourned the loss of his son and only descendant.

"Uncle's one hundred weapons became most precious to Kylian; such that they became his new, beloved *young ones*. Kylian affectionately named each of the blades also. Each weapon has its name etched at the base of the blade, on the sun side. Kylian had ceased etching his own personal symbol on his blades to remain hidden from his family. However, I maintained a scroll documenting all of Kylian's *daughters and sons for the sake of posterity*."

"Drachir, you are a gifted storyteller; I am mesmerized. You continue to fascinate me with your hidden talents," Je Leena remarked lovingly. "I did not know all the blades' historical details either. Those details were not captured on any of the scrolls I received from Uncle."

"Nor would he have documented such personal details. Uncle only shared those very personal details with our Houses' elders and me," Ona Drachir remarked.

A less mesmerized Je Danei inquired, "Are Auntie's scimitars, Nui Aeijo and Nui Aeignor, Master Nimru's blades that Uncle gifted to her?"

Ona Drachir replied, "Yes, those blades are the Master's *eldest daughter and son,* being the very first forged by Master Nimru for Uncle. Like the Master, Uncle too cherished each of the Master's blades as if they were also his progeny. At that time, Uncle had already pledged himself only to Nui Honei. As you may also know, Nui Honei would not marry him then since she thought she had been irreparably *damaged* by dark magic of the first great mother Si Cairyn of House Si Moina. That magic was presumed to prevent Nui Honei from ever bearing young ones. So, those particular weapons acquired a deeper, new meaning for Uncle. Uncle somehow took some of our Auntie's blood secretly from a battle training exercise. He gifted Nui Aeijo and Nui Aeignor to her as though they were their beloved offspring since both blades were also completed with a drop of Auntie and Uncle's blood. Nui Yilkimsei and Nui Yilkimzwei are the two matching long knives he also first gifted her along with those scimitars and they were also completed with the blood of our uncle and aunt."

Ona Drachir scowled remembering the tale of that time when his uncle first presented the scimitars to Nui Honei. "Auntie refused to accept the gifted scimitars' names. To this day, she still just calls them her Sun and Moon," Ona Drachir concluded.

"Know too that Uncle and Auntie's four dragon short swords, four dragon long knives and eight dragon daggers were also completed with a drop of their blood. These are the last blades that have that particular, very unique distinction."

"Why are the melfs of House Ona Feiir so mysterious, yet so romantic?" Je Leena softly asked, looking lasciviously at the melf as she lovingly caressed his hands.

"Clearly, that is another, inherent family trait and part of our endearing charm," Ona Drachir quietly replied.

"Leena, please focus! Seduce him later after the mission's completion," a slightly annoyed Je Danei insisted, wanting now to know all, if more remained, of the Master Nimru blades' histories. "What else can you share about Uncle's gifts?"

After taking another deep calming breath, Ona Drachir reluctantly released Je Leena's hands while pulling away from her hypnotic gaze to regain his focus. Slowly, he resumed his tale, recalling, "All of the first, one hundred superbly crafted weapons are made of diachrom-infused black steel. Each blade also holds a drop of Uncle's blood too. Some of the weapons were further enhanced through blood-magic by a powerful mage, either Grandmother Je Buel or our Aunt Nui Honei.

"Uncle first gifted our Houses' elders with fine weapons long ago. Other than my bow, all my cherished weapons too were gifts from Uncle. They were all forged by Kylian. Later, each of the House Je Luneefa daughters and sons, Nui Jooba and myself too have received a pair of long knives from Uncle's famed Nimru collection of the first one hundred blades. So, cherish his gifts; they are all extraordinary and given with great affection from Uncle's heart, noble pride and warrior's essence."

Unconsciously, both House Je Luneefa daughters then drew their hidden Nimru long knives and reexamined them again; but their scrutiny is now different, knowing some of their blades' precious, previously unknown histories. Greater reverence and affection are now attached to their blades.

The melf remarked, "Look at the blades' names etched at its base, on the sun side. Danei, you hold 'Uzunyirmi' and 'Uzunyirmibi.' Leena, your long knives are 'Uzunserive' and 'Uzunseribe.' All of Uncle's gifted long knives that are of the first one hundred blades reflect the unique patterns contained in Keiku's deadly fangs."

Ona Drachir concluded, "After fulfilling his pledge, Kylian returned to House Korogulu in Alaca where he still lives quietly and peacefully. The jealous House Nimru elder brothers ceased being a threat to Kylian since Auntie joined Uncle and Kylian on their last return to the Underworld's Alaca city. Nui Honei assisted Uncle on a mission to help those House Nimru elder brothers find their final peace through some *unfortunate accidents*. The Master also finally found lasting solace knowing that his bladed *daughters and sons* helped avenge their murdered elder brother and would continue to greatly honor him."

After some long moments of silence to reflect upon their very limited knowledge of their uncle's past, Je Danei quietly asked, "Did Master Nimru or Kylian also forge my battleaxes?"

"Yes," Ona Drachir reluctantly replied. "The Master did return, from time to time, over the last century to do additional work for Uncle. For example, Kylian forged other weapons too, like some bracers and greaves. Know too that Jooba and I also helped the Master as he made your battleaxes," Ona Drachir proudly recalled. Suddenly scowling again, Ona Drachir added, "But the Master would only allow us to watch and hand him the needed tools or materials. He would never allow us to use his very special hammers. That was indeed quite disappointing."

Je Danei paused, now thinking deeply and recalling an old mystery of her highly prized, beloved weapons. "Over the years, I have studied many of Master Nimru's original one hundred blades Uncle gifted to our families. But, the patterns in my battleaxes do not seem to reflect any of Keiku's features like the Master's first forged one hundred blades. Why is that?" Je Danei inquired.

"But I thought you knew…" Je Leena quietly interjected.

"Leena, shhh… I felt Jooba nor you ever revealed the entire truth to my unanswered question. So, please let Drachir reveal the *complete* truth to that long-standing mystery; so, he should continue his tale," Je Danei earnestly requested. Je Danei then returned her full, weighted attention to the melf.

Ona Drachir paused, thinking silently, "As before, Je Danei waits patiently for my response. In the past, delaying my response at critical moments would often give me a chance to divert the impatient Je Danei's attention and sometimes create a possible escape route away from a potentially uncomfortable discussion. Unfortunately now, the eldest House Je Luneefa daughter silently holds her steadfast gaze upon me and waits."

Je Danei said, "I am determined to now know all there is to know about my gifted blades that still hold mysterious patterns not dragon-kind."

"This is true; the patterns captured throughout your battleaxes purposely do not reflect any features of the great dragon. Those patterns secretly reflect the distinctive and exquisite eyes, ears, fangs and claws of the deceased Je Onyxia Ryoshi, your beloved, great black panther," Ona Drachir finally replied. "Nui Jooba had made this request of Master Nimru." Now shocked by Nui Jooba's great thoughtfulness, tears immediately formed in Je Danei's eyes and started falling.

"And?" Je Danei whispered, choked with emotions.

"Jooba also somehow managed to secretly obtain some of your blood, through battle training, and he later added drops of your and his blood as the Master completed work on your battleaxes. Please understand Jooba's gifts to you, your precious battleaxes meant much more to him than just another different and unique, bladed gift he thought you would like. At your Day of Adulthood celebration, had he lost your elders' blessing to formally court you, he still wanted to secretly remain very close to you through his beloved gifts. Cherish your gifted battleaxes like he cherishes you above anyone else.

"Please understand too that the love Nui Jooba bears for you is like what Je Taeliel had for Je Buel, Je Maron has for Je Pagi and Ona Noirar has for Nui Honei. Each of those House elders profoundly exemplified or exemplifies that the love of their respective *one* makes them all much stronger and powerful. I believe any of our elders could move mountains or do what may seem impossible with such love. So, do not ever doubt nor fear that power. Rather, be so very thankful to accept and embrace it if he is truly your *one*."

Je Leena's eyes filled with tears as she soon realized that Ona Drachir's words were aimed at her as much as her sister. Knowing she had acted so foolishly in the recent past caused her guilty tears to slowly fall again.

Tears fell from Je Danei's eyes too as she stared at all of Ona Drachir's displayed weapons. Slowly, she declared, "I too love blades, all types of blades. And I want more than ever now to have additional blades forged by the Master with my and Jooba's blood."

A great stillness then fell upon Je Danei and Je Leena as both felfs reflected upon their own personal, inner thoughts. For many long moments, the two daughters of House Je Luneefa and the son of House Ona Feiir just stared at the ground, each shrouded in the darkness and heavily weighted silence of their respective, riveting, personal thoughts.

Finally, Je Leena broke their silence, proclaiming, "Know that more descendants of the Master will surely be forged," she solemnly committed. Taking Ona Drachir's hands again in hers, Je Leena looked deeply into the melf's eyes and also declared, "Truly more blades will be forged by the Master. Drachir and I must also have our own blessed, bladed descendants as well. Do you not agree, my beloved?" The melf, now a bit overwhelmed, just smiled in silent agreement.

Eventually, a more gripping, fearful silence returned as each became consumed with divertive thoughts of their mission's many risks and unknowns. Ona Drachir broke their silence. "Leena, I also know your role in this rescue mission is extremely dangerous; only you right now will venture into the enemy's stronghold. Know that I will come rescue you if need be and kill everyone in my path who might oppose me," Ona Drachir pledged solemnly. "I will not leave you there alone. Should fate have it so, know that I will die there with you, by your side."

"Nor would I ever leave you alone dear sister," Je Danei added. "We *all* came here, and we shall *all* leave there together after rescuing Nui Jooba and Dan-Rei. I also agree with Drachir. Your mission's role is the most perilous; so, you must be very careful. Sister, please do not take any unnecessary chances. Being a great mage, only you can best enter and leave that stronghold undetected. You will be alone there but fear not. We will boldly go through the stronghold's front gates, brandishing our Houses' colors, and kill all to rescue you if need be. This I too promise."

The youngest House Je Luneefa daughter quietly confessed, "I was also disturbed that Drachir and I had not really spoken much to each other since leaving Torondell. We were emotionally distant from each other due to our weakened relationship for reasons I foolishly caused. That greatly troubled me. Know too that I know I do not fight as well as either of you; so, I truly do not yet possess the great confidence either of you have in my own fighting abilities. However, I find great comfort in your words though I still harbor certain fears as well.

"I will soon bravely go into a foreign unknown environment, fighting against Underworld unknowns, unknown magic, and in complete darkness. Reliance upon Dilara, a sentient blade's centuries old memory unnerves me too. Yet, I did find strength in Ona Drachir's embrace when he opened his arms wide to welcome me again, despite my recent unkind behavior. Though frightened, my courage is bolstered by you dear sister and beloved Ona Drachir; your presence and words mean very much to me. I sincerely thank you."

"None of us should be nor feel alone on this eve of the next phase of our dangerous journey. Let us all renew our strength and courage through our collective presence and unified spirits. So, we shall all sleep here in your tent assuming you have no objections,"

Je Danei announced after some reassuring confidence returned, desperately hoping the melf would still welcome Je Leena to quell her lingering fears.

"None," Ona Drachir responded after a few moments. "Let us then rest; tomorrow will start the beginning of our journey into the underground realm of dark elves."

After the felfs settled themselves in the tent, some less serious conversation amongst the three continued. Shortly afterwards, Je Danei retired. A smiling Je Leena soon fell asleep too, wrapped tightly in Ona Drachir's warm and reassuring arms while he quietly whispered to the second daughter of House Je Luneefa why and how much he loved her. Soon, his words of love were enhanced by his gentle, one hundred strokes of her long auburn hair.

Je Danei listened carefully to all his words and reflected upon her own true feelings again for the second son of House Nui Vent. Before finally falling asleep, Je Danei vowed to herself, *"I also will confess my true feelings to you, Nui Jooba, before I die. Fate must favor me till I confess!"*

Tol'Tarei

At the next dawn, Keiku, in her frightful majesty, addressed the smaller group entering the mountain before they left, "After reviewing and discussing the maps of this mountain's tunnel system with the House Je Luneefa youngest son, I too plan to join you after you enter the city. If I truly can is still uncertain, but I will most assuredly try. I too have loved ones there being held against their will. Many will surely die because of the crime committed against our Houses. Remember too that none of you should die on this mission! Return safely!"

After the great dragon's blessing, the select one hundred soldiers quickly made their way to their next objective, the Luna Fendasse gate, below the great Ararateken mountain. Even Keiku was able to march along given the large tunnel's size. From there, only Ona Noirar, Ona Drachir, Je Danei, and Je Leena would venture on continuing to follow Dan-Rei's unique trail. This much smaller group, now disguised as noble dark elves with dark bluish skin color and white hair, hoped to slip unnoticed into the destination underground city.

Without encountering any mishap, the four companions should arrive at the outskirts of Tol'Tarei in five days, not the normal eight given the aid of the wonderous, magical dragon's blood. Before departing through the gate, the four companions had taken an extra portion of dragon's blood to heighten their normal physical and mental capabilities later.

Despite being far underground, Je Leena was still able to

mentally communicate with Keiku magically. Je Leena did so each day, giving the dragon the four companions' journey updates. Keiku, in turn, would communicate with another battlemage in Commander Somai's battle group. Lastly, Commander Somai's battlemage would scry the expedition's overall progress and status information to the anxious House Nui Vent great mother and other House elders.

Tol'Tarei, the enemy's lair, is a great city of the dark Underworld. It had been initially constructed deep below the great mountain of Ararateken. In this particularly enormous cavern, Tol'Tarei was founded and rose from the dirt floor millennia ago. Though there were many gigantic stalactites suspended from the cavern's high ceiling, there too were many gigantic stalagmites rising from the dirt floor trying to meet their inverted counterparts. These rock formations were sparsely covered with various types of Kackar, a moss-like vegetation that emitted different shades of low light. The light shades signified the season in the dark Underworld. The very low, golden light now emanating from the Kackar would correspond to the Aboveworld's Autumn season.

Eight unusually enormous pillars of stone supported the ceiling high above Tol'Tarei. Legends claim that these pillars collectively were considered to be a holy symbol from the dark felf-spider deity, Valdearaneida. Around these eight magnificent pillars, a great Underworld city was founded. These pillars also displayed millennia of dark elf history. Each pillar was adorned with carvings and paintings capturing historical events of the city and the respective great noble House claiming ownership of the pillar. Now, these pillars serve as monuments to each great House ruling the city. Each ruling House built and/or claimed, through House wars, its stronghold around the base of one of the monumental pillars.

Tol'Tarei is home to just over three hundred thousand dark elves and other creatures. Like other great dark elf cities of the Underworld, this city is ruled by the leaders of the eight noble, most powerful Houses. Each House is ruled by a great mother whose power over her House is absolute. These eight ruling House first great mothers are members of the City Council and delicately share the City's governing powers. Together these eight powerful, tyrannical matriarchs direct and oversee the operations of the city.

In the dark elf society, the House ranking normally represents its position of power. Lesser houses, outside of the ruling eight great Houses, are considered insignificant. These lesser houses, should they hope to advance within the city's ranking of power, a higher-ranking House must first fall and be completely displaced through a House war. Like in the Aboveworld, a House war requires the complete annihilation of all blood and extended family members of the conquered House unwilling to swear allegiance to the conquering House. Failure to completely destroy a defeated House would justify the non-warring, ruling Houses to unite and "thoroughly punish" the aggressors for their failed contemptible attempt. The dark elf's resolution of a "thorough punishment" requires death...

All ruling Houses had to be cautious at all times. It was not uncommon for a non-warring House to prey upon a suspected weakened House that emerged victorious after a House war. Houses that achieved complete victories were highly respected, praised and glorified. Weak, defeated Houses or even individuals received no pity nor mercy. It was believed to be their fate or their Valdearaneida's supreme will for the weak individuals' detestable positions. Weakness is abhorred in the Underworld.

Even the lower, insignificant Houses needed to remain vigilant lest it could possibly fall prey to opportunistic Houses just seeking to capture treasure, glory or even additional important resources to bolster the aggressor's House.

For dark elves, friendships, like alliances, formed today can be easily nullified or forgotten tomorrow in selfish quests seeking more fame and glory for oneself or one's House. Dark elves, though considered evil by nature, were very proud of their culture. Even within a House structure, family ties and bonds were formed more likely through fear or mutual benefits than love. Here in Tol'Tarei, like the other great cities of the dark Underworld, many dark elves lived fully representing and even exalting their dark elven culture.

Ona Noirar led his group close to Tol'Tarei by following the trail Dan-Rei had left. However, after encountering magically warded tunnels and hidden traps, detours were taken when necessary. Fortunately, the maps from Je Kei proved useful in aiding them to find another, safer route to the great city. Now by the eastern entrance of Tol'Tarei, the four companions, without difficulties, blended in amongst the other unremarkable-looking travelers going into and out of the city.

It was considered midafternoon in Underworld's terms. Ona Noirar led his group to an inn where they could find food, lodging and some potentially useful information. He also mentally reminded his companions that the Underworld is very different than their home world. *"It is best to 'kill first' any potential threat. Kindness and courtesy are often rewarded with the first swift, merciless blade thrust. Here, if anyone senses you are weak, they will most likely target you as prey. So beware,"* Ona Noirar told them.

During their late afternoon meal, the four companions continued to speak little "aloud" fearing other unwanted ears may overhear their conversations. So, all the "important" discussions took place exclusively through private mental communications just amongst them. The dragon blood of Ona Kei Kuri Ryuu, they all shared, was truly an extraordinary blessing.

"I will leave here after our meal to find the House Norkula stronghold. Our family members most likely will be held there," Ona Noirar said.

"Shall we then explore the city for a short time to learn what we can about this city and the best escape route?" Je Danei asked.

"That would be wise. Stay together. Learn what you can and let us meet back here for a late evening meal," Ona Noirar ordered. "One last note from my beloved: she said if, by chance, you encounter a fortune teller in the Tauru marketplace, by the name of Suphan, say to her that 'Pyrene, her third misguided love, sends her best regards and warns, you should leave the city immediately!' Lastly, give the renowned seer three gold coins." Afterwards, he left the inn to find and secretly reconnoiter the House Norkula stronghold.

Like Ona Noirar, Je Danei, Je Leena and Ona Drachir had all been disguised magically as dark elves before passing through the Luna Fendasse. The three young companions, like their uncle, did not want to draw any unnecessary attention to themselves as they wandered throughout the Underworld city.

No heraldic sigils were to be displayed on their House capes until battle when rescuing their family members. Ona Noirar had also required them to attire themselves as nobles but not lavishly, bearing only dark clothing with no House distinction. Only light armor was to be worn, as well, under their outer cloaks. If required to disclose their identity and business in Tol'Tarei, he instructed them to share that, "We are members of noble House Korogulu from the distant Underworld city Alaca. We are here seeking to buy certain rare goods."

The three young elves too were all fully armed with some weapons magically concealed within their House capes. A few weapons, like their swords, duly hung at their sides, projecting the image they would not be "easy" prey.

The three companions took several carriage rides and walked around Tol'Tarei. They soon learned that there were four main entrances into and out of the city. Two were in the east; one was in the south; and the last was in the north. All had strong gates and guards were posted at all of them. However, there seemed to be little scrutiny paid to the comings and goings of travelers. Fortunately for the four companions, the city's security was not regarded as a high priority.

They also noted that each gate of Tol'Tarei was guarded by different soldiers belonging to one of the city's ruling Houses. Ona Noirar had told them on their journey there, "The eight ruling Houses *cooperated* and shared certain city administrative duties that mutually benefited all the ruling Houses. Guarding the city against an outside threat was just not believed to be crucial. Afterall, who would dare attack a great city, a most feared city of the Underworld and home to the fierce, evil dark elves?"

Later that day, the three young, disguised Aboveworlders eventually found the Tauru marketplace. Like any other great city's market, it was crowded with a diverse population of citizens: commoner and noble, rich and poor, free and slaves, thieves and the laws' conservators. As expected, the citizenry of the great Underworld city was predominantly dark elves. However, there were some gnomes, rock elves and a few humans there too. Unlike the Aboveworld, most, if not all, of the Underworld's citizens proudly brandished a variety of weapons. But like many Aboveworlders, some weapons were definitely concealed.

The air in and around the Tauru marketplace was filled with many distinct pungent odors and chaotic mixtures of customers and merchants' voices haggling over prices and wares. A few fights even erupted to settle heated disputes. The Aboveworlders also observed that even individuals from different Houses would engage in unprovoked battles.

Different languages could also be heard. Amidst it all, there was still an air of calm uneasiness; death and evil still prevailed even in this place of a normal day's routines. The crowd, in constant movement, seemed unconcerned and unaffected by all the chaos of the market and the daily life seemingly difficult patterns and ordeals.

It was perhaps Ona Drachir who first noticed a dark felf who handed a seemingly destitute, ancient-looking, blind beggar some silver coins. *"I did not expect to see such uncommon kind and generous behavior in the Underworld,"* he pondered to himself.

"May Valdearaneida's blessings be upon you dear Suphan. Again, you have saved an ancient from death by starvation this day. Thank you. But why not just kill me and save your coins?" The beggar sincerely petitioned the felf.

"Ah, dear friend Zelsongl, you are still my small guiding flame of hope in this dark, foul city. Your sage words often comfort me. Know that you will not die by my hand this day. You are still precious to me. Death will not find you this day either. So, be well," Suphan quietly remarked. The felf then walked away meandering through the crowd. Soon after Suphan walked away from Zelsongl, Suphan drew the attention of two other dark elves who mysteriously started stalking the seer from a respectable distance. The two followers were soon slowly joined by others who also seemed to have some interest in the seer. After walking about one hundred steps through the crowded streets, Ona Drachir noted six others were now following Suphan.

"Drachir, why are you so interested in that felf?" Je Leena inquired.

"I believe I have discovered our aunt's friend. Follow me," Ona Drachir replied. The felfs accompanied him when he also started following the suspected Suphan from an undetectable distance.

Suphan finally headed towards a small shop amongst many buildings on a side street, unlocked the door and went in. Four of the seer's stalkers went to the back of her shop's building; the other two went to the shop's front street door and guarded the entrance. Shortly thereafter, three well-dressed, assumed nobles approached the shop and boldly entered without speaking to the guards.

Moments later, Ona Drachir approached the front of Suphan's shop while his felf companions went unnoticed to the back of the building. Ona Drachir casually walked past several shops before arriving at the seer's plain, unremarkable shop's entrance. Since no signs denoted the businesses along the street, Ona Drachir innocently asked the two guards outside the seer's shop, "Tell me if you know where I may find the renowned seer of this street. I desperately need her counsel and pay the tribute my brother owes her for his unusual good fortune."

The first guard did not reply; she only regripped her sword and looked menacingly at Ona Drachir. The second guard, perhaps tempted by the opportunity to profit by robbing a presumed stranger to that part of the city, attempted to draw his sword. Before the guard could clear his weapon from its sheath, Ona Drachir fatally stabbed each guard with his long knives. Before promptly dispatching the guards, he had called upon the magic of his blades to leave his victims paralyzed in place. The victims' outer neck wounds were also immediately sealed; so, no blood would flow outwardly. Again, this was another important feature of his magic-infused blades. To any casual onlooker, the guards would still seem alive and dutiful at their designated posts. Yet the guards died from profuse internal bleeding. The Aboveworld melf then silently entered the seer's shop.

Typically, the Underworld is immersed in darkness; however, the shop's outer room was dimly lit, barely illuminated by a few braziers' fire stones. Ona Drachir noted that the seer appeared to be a commoner, about four centuries of age, of medium height and build. Suphan too, like most dark elves, has dark blue eyes, blue skin and long, flowing white hair. Other than her piercing intelligent eyes, she has no other unique distinguishing features.

Suphan is seated behind a large table facing the three nobles who had drawn their swords. The seer seemed unafraid, perhaps knowing she could save herself from her dire position, like times before perhaps... No one appeared to have noticed the Aboveworld melf's stealthy entrance nor presence. Ona Drachir, now standing about fifteen steps behind the nobles, still held a deadly long knife in each of his hands.

"Pray and then cast your runes for the last time mighty Seer. You will have no other chance; for today, you will find your final peace," declared the noble standing in the middle.

The seer moved her lips silently giving quiet thanks to an old, dear friend who had taught her how to use a blade. *"Those lessons saved my life before and will again save my life this day too,"* she thought and sadly hoped. Even though she faced three blades determined to end her life, Suphan courageously displayed no fear.

Suphan scoffed. "Why have you come here? To kill me because you fools *twisted* my reading of the runes at the House Nemrutae second great mother's celebration, or because I know the truth of your foul, supposedly secret deeds committed for House Karasa. Ha! I pity you; for I will not die this day either, fools!" Suphan defiantly yelled back at her assailants. The center noble then noticed that his comrades were motionless and had no life in their expressionless faces. When he returned his eyes to Suphan, the seer was now armed with a short sword she had silently retrieved from a hidden location under her table. Suphan continued to smile defiantly and waited patiently for her now lone assailant to make his next, perhaps fatal and last move. "Where is your haughty arrogance now, fool? Your odds of killing me now are no longer favorable. In fact, those odds have now dwindled by two-thirds. And you alone cannot defeat me!"

"There are still six more guards outside who will come to end your life should I fail," the last noble fearfully said.

"I think not. They are all now dead also," Ona Drachir quietly announced. Upon hearing that news emanating from an unknown voice behind him, the noble's arrogant composure quickly drained away as his eyes filled with great fear. The noble then regained some courage and sheathed his sword, acknowledging and yielding to his new-found, very unfortunate position.

"Oh, how the table has now turned. It seems that you are now currently very alone and in a desperate situation," Suphan said, laughing mockingly. Now smiling with an evil countenance, Suphan declared, "Now you wish to bargain for your life? Is this not now ironic?" Without moving her eyes from her assailant, the seer cast a single rune and prophesized, "I now think *you* will not live beyond this day. Welcome *your* final peace like your worthless noble brothers, all fools who died a fool's death!" Suphan nodded to Ona Drachir who was now standing silently a few steps behind the last noble. In the next moment, two daggers hit the noble facing the still seated seer. Like Ona Drachir's long knives, these blades made no sound too. Both daggers buried deep into the chest of the last assailant who then collapsed to the floor lifeless.

Smiling evilly, Suphan gazed at Ona Drachir and asked, "Who are you and your friends behind me? Why would you assist me? Were you also ordered to kill me? Nonetheless, thank you. Should you kill me, at least I will die by the hands of a skillful and handsome assassin and not by these inept, hideous, wretched and incompetent creatures lying dead on my shop's floor."

After pausing for a few moments to study Ona Drachir, Suphan surmised, saying, "Hmmm... I think not. You do not look like you want to kill me. Or am I wrong?" Doubtful, but still wary, Suphan regripped her sword.

Je Danei and Je Leena emerged from the darkness of another room behind the seer. They walked silently around the table and stood beside Ona Drachir after retrieving and cleaning their daggers. Standing to properly greet the three young protectors, Suphan sheathed her sword and said, "Well met my lovely and handsome saviors. Your intervention was much appreciated. The issue with those dead fools has been finally resolved and you also perhaps helped me make some extra coins when I take these dead fools' purses. Then I should easily be able to pay my next rent on time."

Judging by the puzzled expression of Je Danei's face, Suphan explained, "Ah... You do look like real visitors; so, you must not know how things work in this part of the city. The Tauru market beggar, Zelsongl, the ancient felf beggar is the secret leader of one of the city's largest gangs. All the shop owners on this street pay *rent* to her; it is basically her extortion fee for her gang's protection services."

"So, why were Zelsongl's gang not protecting you today?" Ona Drachir stoically inquired.

"I was late with my last rent payment and, most likely, these dead fools paid more coin to have those services *temporarily* suspended," Suphan replied, laughing quietly. Ona Drachir slightly frowned.

"In truth, we are here to deliver an ominous message from an old friend of yours," an impatient Je Danei remarked. "'Greetings from Pyrene, your third misguided love. She sends her best regards and warns you to leave this city immediately.'"

Shocked to hear the name and dire message of her only and long-lost friend, Suphan slumped back into her chair. For several long moments, the seer could not speak; she just seemed to silently reflect upon many old personal memories. Soon, Suphan recovered and asked, "Why must I leave?"

A more impatient Je Leena replied angrily, "Merciless Hell has now come to Tol'Tarei to wreak a great vengeance unlike ever seen before! You should leave now if you wish to live!" The second daughter of House Je Luneefa then gave the seer three gold coins.

"Truly Pyrene has sent that message of impending doom," Suphan acknowledged, rising from her chair. She then walked to and quickly peered out of the front window. "There are more soldiers from the assailants' House now stationed across the busy street. Our escape path will be blocked," Suphan announced as she drew her short sword and a long knife.

"I think not," Je Leena calmly declared, walking away. The second daughter of House Je Luneefa next cited an incantation over a nearby brazier. She then went to the shop's stone side wall and cited a second incantation which created an opening in the wall. "Make haste and follow me," Je Leena ordered. She then led her group through the opening leading to an empty room in the adjacent building. After everyone had passed through the opening, Je Leena quickly closed the aperture.

After secretly passing through to the fifth adjoined building, a loud explosion could be heard as a great fire erupted from Suphan's former shop. All those standing within or dangerously close by the seer's shop were instantly killed from the fiery blast. Within a few moments of the explosion, horrific flames completely engulfed the shop's building.

A now disguised Suphan looked at the three Aboveworlders and quietly said, "Thank you again. Blessings be upon you, friends of Pyrene." She and the Aboveworlders parted ways as they emerged from that last building's front door into the chaos and panic overwhelming the crowded streets.

While walking along another street, populated with many different noble and commoner elves and varied merchant stands, the three Aboveworld companions noticed that there was an unusal excitement emanating from the citizens. "Today is the first day of Abaramerle, a high and holy holiday for us dark elves," one shouted gloriously.

"Yes," others excited individuals responded loudly. "Third day's events at the famed Tol'Tarei Coliseum should be the most exciting! Many deadly contests will take place there for our entertainment. I do hope to see new types of death matches unlike we have witnessed before."

Another exuberant Tol'Tarei citizen contributed, gladly announcing "Creatures from both the Aboveworld and Underworld had been pitted against each other in those matches; so, I want to see what new surprises the City Council has planned to pay homage to our Valdearaneida!" Unlike most of Tol'Tarei's citizens, the three Aboveworld companions were sullen, still not knowing how they could rescue their abducted family members.

After spending most of the afternoon and early evening going around the city and observing the sights, citizens, and several unseen-before creatures attached to leashes, Je Danei, Je Leena and Ona Drachir decided to return to their inn. On three occasions, they saw groups of House soldiers escorting presumed House elders throughout the crowded streets. They had discovered little other than some information about potential escape routes they had assessed. So, they were all frustrated, not gaining any significant information that would help them better formulate a rescue plan for Nui Jooba and Dan-Rei.

Before turning onto the street leading to their inn, Je Danei, Je Leena and Ona Drachir noticed a commotion in the distance. A melf and a felf were having a disagreement with another felf who appeared to be calm despite her counterparts who had drawn swords and clearly were angry. As the onlookers moved away from the potential combatants, the melf yelled and lunged at the calm felf. The calm one remained unflustered as she threw a hidden long knife at the melf who died after taking one step toward his intended victim. Her long knife was similar to those of the Aboveworld: a double-edged, straight blade about a fah length of dark steel with a cross guard and leather-wrapped handle. Unlike many long knives, her blade had no distinctive pommel.

The melf's assumed partner now charged the still calm felf. The intended victim parried the sword strike with another revealed long knife and spun into her attacker clearly surprising the attacking felf. The attacker's assumed sword advantage did not have its desired effect. The calm one's demeanor rapidly changed from prey to a vicious predator as she produced a third hidden long knife and kissed the surprised felf as she fatally stabbed the attacking felf. Within another few moments, both initial assailants lay dead in the street. After retrieving and cleaning her knives, the felf, a skilled warrior, reached into the jacket pockets of her victims and removed bags of coins. She then left, regaining her calm, quiet demeanor.

The onlookers seemed not affected, nor cared, by the two dead bodies lying in the street. The crowd seemed most annoyed with having to either walk around or step over the new obstacles impeding their travel. Now that the brief entertainment had concluded, the regular noises of the street and crowd returned. Like the crowd who witnessed the deadly encounter, the three Aboveworld companions resumed their silent walk back to the inn as though nothing extraordinary had happened but ever wary of their evil and dangerous surroundings.

After returning to the inn, Je Danei, Ona Drachir and Je Leena found an isolated, unadorned table in a back corner of the inn's large drinking hall. Many tables were placed in the hall, probably enough to accommodate just over one hundred seated patrons comfortably. The inn, like most dwellings in the Underworld, was shrouded in near complete darkness. Even the inn's décor was also a constant reminder that glorified the Underworld, the home realm of dark elves and vicious creatures. The little light that emanated from the hall's great hearth and the few firestone lamps was still sufficient to provide adequate lighting for the dark elves to view everything clearly.

Still after traveling in the dark Underworld for days, Je Danei, Je Leena and Ona Drachir, Aboveworld's woods felfs and rock melf, were very much unsettled. Instinctively, they all regripped their hidden weapons reminding themselves they were far unground, in the realm of the dark elves. Here in the Underworld, death and chaos were life's constants lurking behind corners, even staring unabashedly in front of you, walking through the crowded streets, high in the caverns and even in one's own

House.—Yet the three companions pushed aside their fears of the unfamiliar ever-deadly surroundings and recommitted themselves to their rescue mission despite their great discomfort.

All three Aboveworlders entered the hall unnoticed as magically disguised dark elves. Other than their moderately lavish clothing, they all presented and bore the distinction of being noble born; yet they all displayed no House sigil.

Each table in the inn is unique, with different distinctive patterns and made from giant petrificd mushrooms. The tables are under three and a half fahs in height. The mushroom's volva had been cut in order to form each table's large and sturdy base. Like the volva, each mushroom had its spherical cap cut, resulting in a flat tabletop. After careful inspection, Je Leena quietly conveyed to her companions, "The table's petrified state had been rapidly facilitated through magic that allowed the wielder to also capture and preserve unique designs highlighting folk tales, sacred carvings and/or any other significant memorabilia. These intricate, artistic patterns were created with many tiny, multicolored stones infused within the tables' tops and stems.

"Many tables memorialized presumably the names and sigils of famous dark elves and noble Houses of Tol'Tarei. Many tables bore depictions of the dark felf-spider deity Valdearaneida, the dark elves' highest and most holy god. The tables bearing certain noble House markings also carried an unspoken warning for those who were bold enough to violate the sanctity of these prestigious tables: Unprovoked and deadly altercations could erupt just by one's sitting at the 'wrong' table."

From that moderately defensible location in the hall's corner, Je Danei, Je Leena and Ona Drachir could observe most of the patrons and activities taking place around them. They quietly discussed what they had learned from their earlier observations. Shortly thereafter, they ordered their meals while still waiting anxiously for Ona Noirar to return.

More patrons entered the inn's hall and started drinking. Soon afterwards, six musicians, playing different string and drum instruments, started entertaining the hall's customers. The musicians played some lively tunes. More fire stones were added to the inn's hall great hearth to slowly increase the room's temperature. As more rowdy patrons congregated in the popular inn's drinking hall, the patrons' clamor increased significantly as well. More food was served. More drink was served as well to continually fuel conversations and even more hopeful adventures. In turn, the inn made more coins.

It is now well into the evening. Je Danei also observed that most of the patrons there now are female and appeared to be warriors. All seemed armed with seen and unseen weapons. Many wore light armor and dressed boldly displaying their House colors and sigils; others chose to just wear plain dark clothing with no distinguishing House allegiance markings.

Before the rescue war group departed from Torondell, Nui Honei had warned them all that many dark elves, especially nobles, protected themselves with magical shrouds too. Afterall, death was ever close and present in the Underworld. Should any of the Aboveworld companions needed to kill, they had no doubts that their fine, dragon blood-enhanced weapons would pierce through any would-be protection whatever the foe might have. Je Danei pondered with great confidence that any enemy here of Houses Nui Vent and Je Luneefa, whether shrouded in the finest armor and/or magical wards, would surely die. And when the time came to kill, Ona Noirar, Ona Drachir, Je Danei and Je Leena would all kill swiftly and mercilessly.

Other than the disguised Aboveworlders, all there were dark elves. Their fine elf features were highlighted with their distinctive and unique, dark blue skin color and long white hair. Most of the patrons too seemed to be of noble Houses too. Many patrons seemed uncharacteristically boisterous, reflecting the drinks' desired effects. Many others were just quietly watching while they ate or drank.

Ever wary of their unfamiliar surroundings, Je Danei also pondered, with great concern, the current conditions of Nui Jooba and Dan-Rei, their abducted family members. Again, the felf scolded herself for her past foolish actions. After watching Je Leena and Ona Drachir gaze affectionately at each other while presumably holding hands under the table, Je Danei recounted the past times she had scorned Nui Jooba without just cause. Now, Je Danei wanted to desperately release her anger. While looking around the hall hoping to discover a doomed soul, she thought, *"If only a member of House Norkula is here to kill, especially that damned Reza'Di..."*

Je Leena, sensing her sister's mounting anger and frustration, reached out and touched her hand hoping to calm some of her elder sister's inner emotional storm. *"Sister, calm yourself. Please do not release your anger upon anyone here through an unprovoked attack. Now is not yet the time,"* Je Leena wisely counseled mentally through the magic of the great dragon's blood they shared. In response, Je Danei closed her eyes and took a deep breath. Looking at her younger sister, Je Danei just nodded her head in gratitude.

A short while later, the noise from the patrons slowly decreased as a lovely felf, dressed in fine robes of different lavender shades, started walking towards the front of the hall. She stopped near the musicians and talked with them for a few moments. Afterward, she turned and silently walked to the hall's front center. The finely dressed dark felf gazed across the hall, drawing everyone's attention to her. She is beautiful by dark elf standards. Her fine exotic features were highlighted by her rare, lavender-colored eyes. Shortly thereafter, the musicians resumed playing, but a different song.

The hall is now crowded as though the felf had attracted even more patrons just to see or hear her. This new song is slow, haunting and melodious. All conversations ceased too as this felf commanded everyone's attention when she began to sing. Her persona seemed to also hold many mysteries. Her voice is distinct, strong, dark, and captivating. At the same time, she sang an aria with great sensual power:

> Know your wonders; embrace your powers.
> Know her pleasures; delight her body and mind.
> Master your treasures; know your wonders.
> Discover all her pleasures; deeply love her body and mind.
> Be forewarned. Escape her loving, deadly embrace.

After just hearing the song's first verse, Je Danei could not take her eyes away from the songstress. The song touched Je Danei's inner being as the songstress continued singing her song glorifying the dark felfs who, some say, are the world's fiercest warriors. Something very mysterious about the singer's sultry voice, slow deliberate movements and song captured Je Danei and many others in the singer's relentless, musical, hypnotic trance. The songstress' ode, her looks and her movements aroused one's inner being and awaken one's deep desires. Somehow the dark felf songstress made such musical "magic" that made you desperately want her...

Armed with an exquisitely painted fan, the dark felf songstress gracefully danced a traditional Kabuki across the front of the hall while the musicians continued to build an atmosphere incenting the patrons to "want more." As *more* lustful memories returned, *more* wanton desires grew, *more* passion-filled unadorned hopes now defied sound reason, and like many of the patrons ensnared by the song's hypnosis, Je Danei's inner being ignited unfamiliar feelings…

The second verse was sung with greater power, passion and majesty building upon the "magic" the songstress had already created:

> She is filled with mysteries unknown.
> She is the epitome of evils untold.
> She is grace, beauty, and hell's fury embodied.
> Beware not to lose your heart to a dark felf.
> Beware not to yield your mind to a dark felf.

"Very clever," Je Leena quietly remarked. "The tavern's owner over there is also a mage," Je Leena discerned. "She controlled the hearth's glowing firestones through magic. As the hearth's heat increases, the heat from their table, and maybe others, also intensifies. The patrons will spend more on drinks to cool themselves in turn. The hearth and all the tables were connected through magic. Very clever indeed," Je Leena proclaimed her last statement aloud for her companions to hear and then she explained her discovery to the others. She also discerned that many of the table stems throughout the hall resonated with the sounds of the drums too. The amplified beats also contributed significantly to increasing the patrons' desires.

Suddenly, Je Danei slowly realized that the songstress and the "calm" warrior felf she saw earlier that afternoon are the same. At this time too, Je Danei, like so many other patrons felt her passion rise steadily keeping pace with the sensual music and songstress' hypnotic song's next verse:

> She is the favored daughter of Valdearaneida.
> Her sultry evil ways have no bounds.
> Once embraced, there is only one escape.
> Beware not to lose your heart to a dark felf.
> Love but hate the beautiful, marvelous, perfectly made dark felf.

The songstress resumed dancing slowly across the small stage area while the musicians continued playing the melody of their wonderous and beautiful song. Je Danei could not help but think, *"Can I truly love someone and still become a great warrior?"* She then replayed the songstress's battle in her mind and assessed she is definitely a skilled warrior. *"She was fearless. Does this warrior-songstress also deeply love someone? If so, her warrior's abilities nor spirit seemed diminished. How is that so?"* Je Danei's mind raised other unanswered questions as she continued to watch the songstress dance.

The musicians consisted of daiko drummers, koto, shamisen and flute players. While the koto and flute players would drive the melody, the daiko and shamisen players engaged in a musical "battle" accenting the song. They were all skillful as they demonstrated mastery of their chosen instruments to compliment the singing and dancing of the songstress. The music and dance increasingly built upon the inherent passions of the many patrons.

Now very much surprised, Je Danei listened more closely to the song of this intriguing, mysterious warrior songstress:

> Know your mysteries; know your rage.
> Learn her mysteries; fear her rage.
> Love with passion; love fiercely without care.
> Love her completely without boundaries.
> Love but hate the beautiful, marvelous, perfectly made dark felf.

The last line of the verse was repeated a few times deliberately concluding the song's passionate paradoxical message. The song not only praised the dark felf, but it also carried an important message to those who dared love whom many believe to be the evilest females in the known world.

When the songstress finally finished singing the ode to the dark felf, thunderous cheers erupted throughout the hall. The roar of the patrons was long and loud as though some great epic battle had just been won. Many toasts were made to the glory of dark felfs, past and present. The dark felf songstress expertly manipulated the passionate delivery of her song. In a few cases, some patrons whose unbridled passions, hate and/or fears were driven to extremes, erupted in deadly fights. A few of these battles finally ended with long passionate kisses. For other lascivious patrons, their desperately charged passions erupted in public display of more intense affection. Still, some just left quietly to release their wanton carnal desires in private.

Je Leena looked at Ona Drachir who also returned her lust-filled gaze. No words had to be spoken either aloud or mentally. Knowing either or both could die on this rescue mission reignited their love and desires for each other. That song of the dark felf repaired any final lingering, last wounds they may have had in their relationship.

Je Danei, like most other patrons, was greatly moved by the song. But unlike the other patrons who only gave the songstress copper coins or sometimes a silver coin when the songstress walked around collecting tribute for her rare talents, Je Danei gave the felf a gold coin and a sincere "Thank you."

The lovely, enchanting songstress evilly smiled at the disguised House Je Luneefa first daughter. The songstress next quietly and seductively inquired, "Most patrons only pay me five coppers; a few who truly appreciated my vocal talents might give me a silver coin; and then too there are those very select few who highly *value* all my other many talents and might pay me five silver. Your gold is worth several days of my full, dedicated attention and your unbridled feasting upon all my other *many talents*. Either you are most generous or maybe you might be just paying me in advance for more of my talents perhaps?"

Now a bit unnerved by the songstress's close presence, hypnotic scent, voluptuous lips, sensual radiation and seductive gaze, a flustered Je Danei returned the evil smile. Je Danei, still wary and gripping her hidden sai sword, quietly replied, "No, but thank you again. Your battle this afternoon and your song tonight helped me make a very important decision."

"Really? Are you quite sure I cannot aid you further then? I could even just sing for you privately if you wish," the warrior songstress pressed, hoping this extremely rare opportunity could easily earn her more gold.

"Again, thank you... but I still must decline your offer," Je Danei slowly stammered, still flustered by the songstress' proximity and her own unfamiliar heightened desires.

"If not you then, maybe I could bestow my gifts upon your friends. Like you, they also are also gripping hidden weapons I suspect. And your beautiful felf friend is also firmly gripping her handsome melf's most private *weapon* too, I had noticed." The songstress declared her last observation with her evil smile as she then lasciviously gazed upon Ona Drachir and Je Leena. "What say you, my handsome, mysterious looking melf? Would you and your beautiful felf care to feast upon my other many talents?"

Flattered by the unwelcome attention, Ona Drachir just nodded his head in gratitude, frowned and stoically remarked, "Like your amazing song, I too offer you sage advice and a warning: First, strengthen your right hand. I also witnessed your battle this afternoon. You favor your left hand too often. Consider investing some time learning close-quarters martial arts of Zhang Chu.

Lastly, I am already thoroughly marked by *my* 'beautiful, marvelous, perfectly made dark felf' here beside me. She is also the very jealous type and would kill you by her seventh attack move. So, I too will decline your generous offer, but please accept my sincere thanks instead."

Je Leena, regripped her borrowed Nimru dragon long knife, then smiled with evil intention at the songstress and simply said, "I too was there today and witnessed your battle. Seven attacks surely would not be needed. Know that you would be dead by my fifth attack move. Also, know that my handsome lover here is neither greedy nor unfulfilled. Like you, I too have *many talents* which he thoroughly enjoys. You have all our most sincere, as well as most generous, *golden* thanks for your glorious song. But now, please begone."

The songstress smiled warmly, nodded in gratitude, and continued collecting coins from the other patrons in the drinking hall. After the songstress left their table, Je Danei turned and saw that Je Leena and Ona Drachir were looking at her with the serious visage of assumingly wanting to know the details of her "very important decision."

"Later," Je Danei only said. "I do not want to lose focus to discuss a possible distracting personal matter." Thereafter, very little else was spoken between the three of them while they waited anxiously for their uncle's return. They just watched and listened to the other patrons while maintaining constant vigilance.

When Ona Noirar finally did return, it was very late that evening. While eating his meal, he mentally communicated with his companions, explaining, *"I was able to gain an audience with two of the second great mothers of Houses Zafet'Hu and Elra'Ki. Both great Houses are the two highest ranking of the city's ruling hierarchy. Known only as Turgutae in the dark elven circles, I reestablished contact with my old connections in an Underworld's smuggler's ring. Through these connections and a generous gift, Turgutae met with both Houses' great mothers who seemed eager to hear my story of great importance and potential threats to their Houses.*

"After leaving the secret audience, I could only hope that the ambition of the Houses' second great mothers would encourage them, through their respective Houses' first great mothers, to act quickly against House Norkula's Aysun'Di. For one House, especially an ambitious third ranking House, to possess a significant amount of an extremely, powerful magical agent, like dragon's blood, would upset the balance of power that is carefully managed by the current eight great noble Houses ruling Tol'Tarei. Noble Houses Zafet'Hu and Elra'Ki, with the most wealth and power at risk, would surely view House Norkula's recent acquisition as a great threat to their respective power.

"This new threat also creates great new fears - great fear of this unknown, powerful magical dragon's blood. This should force the Houses Zafet'Hu and Elra'Ki ruling great mothers to act, but not start a war against House Norkula. Those fears should mitigate the risks of war.

"I also confirmed, as suspected, neither House Zafet'Hu nor House Elra'Ki wanted another House to challenge their positions in the city's ruling hierarchy. These two great Houses have many shared benefits they greatly enjoy. And Turgutae's smuggling associates also did not want any disruption to their highly lucrative business that potential House wars could devastate.

"Much is at risk. Would the Houses' second great mothers believe my claims? Would these same Houses' elders be bold enough to act alone or together act directly against House Norkula? Would either rival House attempt themselves to take possession of the highly valued dragon? Would House Norkula first great mother Aysun'Di just kill the dragon and Nui Jooba if they suddenly came under attack?

"Before going on this expedition, all of your Houses' elders and Keiku reviewed and weighed many questions and their potential answers. None of us slept well during those immeasurable anxious nights. We often discussed and wrestled with a variety of options and possible outcomes. I also reminded them that the dark elf Houses were very vicious and extremely competitive. No one House or two Houses would dare to attack House Norkula for fear of House Norkula, greatly enhanced mages' powers through dragon's blood they may have already harvested and used. House Norkula would most likely kill their captives before sharing their highest valued prize, the blood of Dan-Rei. So, Nui Honei, Keiku and I concluded that they had to again gamble upon fickle, precarious fate."

That night, Je Danei could not find sleep easily again. Her fears increased with each day since departing Torondell. Most of her tormenting fears were related to Nui Jooba and Dan-Rei. The felf's mind wrestle incessantly with many unanswered questions, *"Were Nui Jooba and Dan-Rei even still alive? Were they in any pain? Where are they now? What were the real plans of their dark elf captors? How will we find and rescue them?"* A few fears were now related to just her and seemingly insignificant compared to others... She started pacing the cold, dark room's floor again hoping to calm herself.

Je Danei attempted to again reach out to Nui Jooba mentally; but again, she received no response. Her attempts to mentally communicate with Dan-Rei were also in vain. She realized then that her relationship with the young dragon had not been well developed. Their relationship was unfortunately "poor" or "weak" at best. So, mental communications between the young dragon and the felf could not take place over assumed long distances.

Je Danei stopped pacing around the room and re-examined all her weapons and the other items she carried. Before her lay her twin scimitars, two long knives, eight daggers and two short swords. Her grandmother's gifted sai swords remained still in her boots, always, always very close to her. Lastly, she reexamined her battleaxes, now her second most prized weapons. For some unknown reason, her gifted battleaxes have now become much more important to her...

After turning her battleaxes upside down, she laid them next to each other. Je Danei scrutinized the blades' patterns again with her eyes and touch. For the first time, she could now see and feel the subtle features of her deceased Je Onyxia Ryoshi emerge. Indeed, Nui Jooba had Master Nimru cleverly hide her panther's likeness within the blades' patterns. She briefly recalled the memory of Nui Jooba gifting her the fine weapons...

"Why do you love me so Nui Jooba? Why? I do not deserve such affection..." she repeatedly thought. Finally, Je Danei smiled again, steadfastly resolved that she would not die before she reclaimed what is rightfully hers and killing anyone who would dare oppose her! The ode to the dark felf revealed much to her, helping the House Je Luneefa eldest daughter resolve certain inner conflicts. *"I will find and save you Jooba and Dan-Rei. And I promise to retake your heart too Jooba,"* Je Danei, now calmer, vowed solemnly to herself. While recalling the words of the ode to the dark felf, Je Danei fell asleep.

Choices for Death

"Praise Valdearaneida!" Aysun'Di declared loudly with a victorious voice. As she gazed upon her mirror's regal image, the House Norkula first great mother again reflected upon her sacred duty to her House, *"I am a House first great mother of a great noble House. As the sole ruler, I must lead my House through warranted violence, cunning unmatched intelligence, fear and evil. I am the only one responsible for leading my House to greater glory and power!*

"By nature, all House first great mothers are cunning, evil, strong and merciless. Most are also very intelligent; otherwise, they would soon die from, most likely, internal family conflicts. I epitomize all these qualities to lead my House! I have victoriously survived many conflicts.

"Threats to my House are ever present without, as well as within this House. The right to rule a House, through an overt challenge by a House second mother or even a granddaughter, means killing me. But today is not my day to die! Still, I am House Norkula's first great mother and must remain wary of even covert threats, such as being poisoned by one's own family member... Such is the chaotic, evil life and society of the dark elves!"

Again, Aysun'Di shouted, "Praise Valdearaneida!" After taking a long, calming breath, Aysun'Di continued admiring herself in the large mirror with renewed high spirits. She resumed contemplating the fate of her House, *"Noble House Norkula currently holds the ranking of the third great noble House, a ruling* council House, of Tol'Tarei. *In our dark elf society, eight noble Houses rule a great Underworld city. In terms of power, including dedicated military resources, wealth, financial and political influence, the first five ranking, noble Houses are considered 'significant.' House Norkula is not only significant, but much, much more now..."*

She then quietly laughed, remembering her glorious evil past, "About four hundred years ago, House Norkula was only ranked seventh and considered "lowly" and insignificant by the high-ranking ruling Houses. Yet I, a House Norkula second great mother, was very ambitious then and had the necessary evil intentions and resources to lead my House to greater glory and power! I then bravely dared to tempt Fate!

"It was and still is common for the Underworld's great noble Houses to wage war upon one another in their quests to gain more riches and power. Long ago, I devised the plan to propel my House into the upper rankings of the city. With long, careful planning, secret alliances, timely betrayals and deadly emotional manipulations, I eventually controlled the fate of House Norkula. In addition, I garnered extraordinary favor from our god Valdearaneida as a result of my House's exemplary devotion and sacrifices to Valdearaneida, the dark elves highest deity,

"After annihilating the ruling third House of Tol'Tarei, House Norkula became the third ruling House of the city, but at a great cost. Through that one particular House war with the then doomed third House, noted battlemages of House Norkula had been killed. This deficit severely weakened my great House; yet I successfully led my promoted House in defending its city's highly ranked position in several House wars thereafter. With each successful war outcome, House Norkula acquired vital resources from the vanquished House. All others remaining who would not pledge loyalty to my conquering House were just simply put to death. Praise Valdearaneida!"

Her deliberate slow walk around her bedchamber temporarily stopped as she gazed upon certain relics sitting upon a a small table. These tokens, some very valuable to plain and ordinary, all reminded her of the significant, risk-filled, actions she took in her past. These relics glorified her past and daring accomplishments that very few knew completely, and most would never know.

In near complete darkness, Aysun'Di could also clearly see the minute details of a small black orb. The spherically shaped, black stone reflected its irregular crevices within its surface as her bedchamber's firestone lamps illuminated the room with its darkened red glow. After picking up the stone, she again thanked Valdearaneida for her fortuitous blessing her stone, her most highly prized *black moon*, represented. She smiled evilly, returning the stone to the table and acknowledging to herself, *"There is still space on my table of glorious monuments! Praise Valdearaneida!"*

The House Norkula ruling great mother took a long calming breath before resuming her slow stroll within her large, spacious bedchamber and thought, *"House Norkula's growth in power and fighting forces was steady over the last three centuries. However, any newly acquired resources are still insufficient today to challenge House Elra'Ki, the second highest ranked House and House of my most hated nemesis, first great mother Halime, my older cousin. Halime and all within her accursed House will now surely die soon!"* Aysun'Di drew another long, calming breath.

Lastly, she pondered, "Now that another hundred years have passed, I knew that another great sacrifice, like none other before, would be required to garner more favor from Valdearaneida. I am still voraciously committed to taking more glory and power for my blessed House before I embrace my final peace. So again, I bravely dared to tempt fate! Praise Valdearaneida!"

Unlike before, the House Norkula first great mother planned to arrive early at the City Council meeting chamber. Aysun'Di proudly still is *the* ruling matriarch of Tol'Tarei's third most powerful noble House. Aysun'Di, despite her ancient, near six hundred years of life, felt extremely healthy and vigorous again since taking her new-found potion. This defiant felf and House ruler had suffered physically for a considerable amount of time; but now, she has recovered. Aysun'Di also re-discovered her passion for attaining more power and glory for her beloved House. Her enemies thought she would die soon from the poison she had received. That vile act of her poisoning became a blood-debt which she intended to repay in full. The ruling, first great mother of House Norkula now wanted her enemies, known and unknown, to recognize full well that the aftermath of the attempted murder will surely bring death. She planned to destroy the House of the would-be assassin.

While again admiring her lovely mirror's reflection, Aysun'Di continued thinking, "Afterall, I am a glorious, female dark elf, an evil and powerful House first great mother, raised, surviving and prospering in the Underworld, the world's most deadly and chaotic realm! So, my enemies need to see the healthy, rejuvenated first great mother of House Norkula in all her fine evil glory. With my recovery, righteous revenge and death will be mercilessly inflicted upon those who dared to harm me."

Today, she adorned herself in her fine black and shimmering gold robes. Aysun'Di also donned several highly valuable and distinguished jewelry pieces reflecting her position and wealth. The ever-cautious, House Norkula first great mother also rechecked her concealed weapons, safely stowed away in her House cape. Lastly, she verified her protective magical wards are fully intact. The City Council meeting is supposed to be a peaceful gathering of the city's ruling House great mothers. However, with long-standing, covert hatred and jealousy, war amongst the Tol'Tarei's most evil and powerful House great mothers could erupt at any moment during the meeting. So, Aysun'Di again solemnly repeated her vow that she would not ever be the first to die within that revered meeting hall should war ever start there.

"I want, no, demand my enemies to fear and respect my mighty wrath and power! Today is going to be a welcomed glorious day," Aysun'Di continued thinking. "Even at my age, my beauty remains. Oh, I still yearn for life's delights! Ha, I am so very pleased that I have aged very well. I am still lithe, graceful and retain a young, attractive, three hundred years old figure. Females and males even still desire me!"

Most importantly, she presented herself well as a distinguished, powerful, ruling House great mother, a highly coveted and praise-worthy position. In her dark elven society, Aysun'Di knew many felfs dream of becoming a House ruling matriarch, but fewer dared to take the necessary steps to become one and successfully retain such power. She declared loudly in her mind, *"Yes, within House Norkula, I am still the sole and absolute ruler!"*

With renewed voracious cravings, Aysun'Di wants more of life! "That new potion is indeed marvelous," she said, reflecting upon her lovely, aged features in the mirror. She then laughed quietly knowing that her rejuvenated life's cravings extended well beyond her next repast...

When she heard a soft knock upon her bedchamber door, the House Norkula first great mother admired her mirrored image one last time before turning toward the door. She knew her three, highly favored granddaughters, who had successfully abducted and returned with the most valuable prize her House had ever claimed, now wanted her decision regarding the future of the abducted, young melf. Though they were all there to also escort her personally to the City Council meeting, she knew they cared more about this melf's position within their House than her personal protection today.

A sinister smile formed on her aged, slightly wrinkled face as she thought about her true, secret plans for this melf, not caring too much for her granddaughters' so-called "happiness." *"Foolish young females. Why should I not take the melf just for myself?"* she wondered. *"Or could we all share him? He could be desirable breeding stock which my granddaughters seem to want. And he would not be anyone's exclusive consort. Fewer resulting conflicts perhaps? Would that please them?"*

She turned toward her bedchamber's door and said, "Enter." After her guards opened the doors, there she could see her three precious, eldest granddaughters eager to hear her decision. Aysun'Di placed a fake smile upon her face to warmly greet the three young felfs. The young ones in response reflected their grandmother's demeanor with insincere smiles of their own. They all knew that the House first great mother would make important decisions that gained their House the most benefit. Individual benefits were not ever her priority.

"Grandmother, you look exceptionally well today," Reza'Di said, first greeting their House Norkula's elder.

"Good morning, Grandmother," Elberithe and Rina said, also greeting their elder.

"My beloved eldest granddaughters, you are the pride and glorious future of House Norkula. You are indeed my most cherished granddaughters! Well met!" Aysun'Di responded, exemplifying her good spirits. "I do feel quite well today, the best I have felt in many days. I strongly suspect that the new potion I took helped improve my condition immensely. Our House physician concluded that the potion truly did counteract the poison's effect. I will fully recover! As another precaution, more of that potion will be taken each day in the foreseeable future. I will not die soon contrary to the hopes of my enemies! Before we leave, let us first go to our chapel; I wish to speak with all my daughters."

Aysun'Di left her bedchamber followed by her granddaughters. As recent as two days before, the House Norkula experienced pain with walking and could only maintain a slow pace. Now, her pace was again "normal" if not even a bit faster, statelier and far more purposeful.

As expected, Aysun'Di found all her eight daughters, the second great mothers of House Norkula, had congregated in the House chapel where they had just finished their morning devotional prayers. Several of the House's second great fathers and consorts were there too. Only female mages, as dictated by the *Chronicles of Valdearaneida*, were permitted to do so. Their deity cherished and valued her female devotees far more than any male.

Elberithe's father, Kelvae, the senior mage of House Norkula, still could not preside over the daily religious services. Kelvae was also the only exclusive husband taken by a second great mother of House Norkula. This distinction alone caused much jealousy and some anger. Despite his wishes, Eylaenora, his wife, did not heed his advice to divorce him or take other consorts. Eylaenora seemed to be pleased and enjoyed having only the one, very close male companion. This felf was even more secretly elated that all her four descendants were female, for none had to be ever sacrificed during the Abaramerle, the dark elves' holiest celebration. Aysun'Di's second eldest daughter, Eylaenora, also enjoyed reminding her sisters that she *knew* the father of all her daughters. This fact also seemed to please Eylaenora but greatly irritated some of her siblings. Only two of Eylaenora's sisters had come close to death when they threatened to kill Kelvae.

Aysun'Di proceeded directly to the front of the chapel. There she surveyed the fine room and scrutinized the faces of her daughters, the second most powerful matriarchs of House Norkula. She then announced, "Elders of House Norkula, today is a blessed day! As you can see for yourselves, I am in much better health. The new potion I tried has greatly improved my condition. So, rejoice; I shall not die soon! I will be able to continue leading this House to greater glory! Though this news may disappoint a few of you, I know most of you share my joy. Thank you. For those who are disappointed by my not reaching my final peace soon, challenge me openly. Do not lurk in shadows, hiding behind cowardly acts of poison. Find the courage to face me directly in combat for the right to lead this great House! I promise you a swift and merciless death!" No one spoke nor accepted her challenge. Asyun'Di stared at her daughters again with cold, evil eyes.

Asyun'Di finally announced vehemently, "Granddaughters, let us go now before I kill them all!" The House Norkula first great mother looked at her daughters with contempt and then left as abruptly as she had arrived. Her mood now was even more uplifted after delivering her challenge again. She knew the evil ways of dark elves all too well. Aysun'Di knew the responsibilities of being a noble House first great mother and wanted to carry that wonderfully painful burden for many more years.

Aysun'Di left the House Norkula stronghold escorted by two units of House soldiers in addition to her eldest granddaughters, also fine warriors. These twenty-four elite soldiers were some of her House's finest warriors. Hidden amid these troops were three of the House's sixteen, most highly prized battlemages. Since battlemages often could greatly influence the outcome of battles, these resources were extremely valuable and first targeted by enemies. As a routine countermeasure, Kelvae would magically change the facial appearance of the battlemages to confuse enemies spying upon them. Additionally, Kelvae's routine "presented" a greater number of deadly magical resources than the House really had. Deceiving enemies was a very common "game" the senior House battlemage greatly enjoyed just after killing his House enemies.

Though few, these battlemages were all accomplished, loyal, fearless, and powerful wielders of magic. However, Aysun'Di knew that many battles were still won based upon sheer numbers along with no or few capable battlemages. She, as well as the other great mothers of her House, knew they desperately needed to increase this highly valued capability of their House as quickly as possible. An attack upon House Norkula or any other noble House was a real threat and a looming present danger.

Respectively, House Zafet'Hu and House Elra'Ki are the two highest ranking Houses of Tol'Tarei and they have more battlemages and warriors than House Norkula. Neither of these higher-ranking Houses would chance engaging House Norkula in a House war out of fear that the other non-attacking House would just attack the surviving House with its depleted resources. However, tension between the three highest ranking Houses of the city continued to rise with each new decade. War was coming; it was inevitable. Afterall, death and chaos were the only certainties for a dark elf of the Underworld.

Aysun'Di arrived first at the meeting chamber of the Tol'Tarei City Council. She wanted all, especially her enemies, to witness her new, greatly improved health and vitality. Before long, the other seven Houses' first great mothers arrived. They too were clad in their fine robes displaying their status, rank and wealth. All were very much vain and enjoyed displaying an Aboveworld kingdom's highest-ranking, ruling female persona, a queen. As in war, outperforming one's enemies in politics was a key objective in the Council meetings too. So, Aysun'Di was well prepared to demonstrate her newfound health, energy and strength to successfully deal with the issues brought forth in recent earlier meetings.

Most importantly, today's meeting aimed to finalize the

ending ceremonies of the three-day Abaramerle celebration for the public of the city. For this general population of Tol'Tarei, grand spectacles have been presented in the past. The City Council's efforts to glorify Valdearaneida had been nothing less than magnificent. Sacrifices to their supreme god, on behalf of the city, will again be made. Thereafter, each great House would conduct their own sacrificial offerings in the privacy of their respective stronghold.

As usual, the ruling matriarch Council members of the five lower ranking Houses were next to enter the meeting chamber. Neylan of House Zafet'Hu and Halime of House Elra'Ki made their grand entrance together. These last House great mothers knew no City Council meeting could start until they arrived. Both Neylan and Halime deliberately made and took every opportunity to remind the other House great mothers that they ruled the highest ranking, most powerful Houses of Tol'Tarei. No one dared criticize either Neylan or Halime, because the consequences of such offenses were often fatal. So, their entrances were purposely delayed till the very last moment, just before the scheduled meeting time.

House first great mothers Neylan and Halime were both ancient felfs, like Aysun'Di. Both were intelligent, cunning, evil, and ruthless. Like all House first great mothers, increasing one's House power and wealth were important priorities. Annihilating enemies along the way to attaining more glory, wealth, and power for one's House was also a sacred duty which all ruling House mothers totally embraced and, by nature, greatly enjoyed.

On this second day of the Abaramerle, House Zafet'Hu first great mother Neylan wore fine black robes with several images of the Underworld's most ferocious spider, the female phonelentari, embroidered in solid gold thread. House Elra'Ki first great mother Halime also wore robes of shimmering blackness. Her outermost robe featured an image of the same deadly spider resting upon its web embroidered in solid silver thread across the entire garment. Two red jewels served as eyes for the deified felf-arachnid. The remaining City Council's members consisted of the first great mothers of noble Houses Arayi, Yildize, Nimru, Erciyes and Karasa. These House first great mothers were also attired in their fine black robes with different images of a dark felf-spider honoring Valdearaneida.

After the last House great mothers entered the council meeting chamber, the stationed guards closed the doors. House Zafet'Hu first great mother Neylan magically sealed the room. Insincere salutations were spoken by most of the council members and all the council members then took their designated seats.

The council members sat at a large, circular, spiderweb-like, designed table. At each end of the spiderweb's eight spokes, there is a large ornate chair supplied by each House represented there. Each chair was fashioned befitting the tyrannical ruler of her powerful, noble House.

Neylan slowly looked around the chamber with cold, piercing eyes and then stood. There were many reasons why her House ranked first amongst the great noble Houses of Tol'Tarei. Many of those same reasons this House great mother totally personified. She is powerful in will, exemplifies unmatched evil and ruthlessness when needed, and places her House's glory and well-being higher than anything else. This House first great mother survived several assassination attempts against her, external House wars and even two internal House wars when two of her daughters attempted to usurp her power and position. As the victor in all these past conflicts, Neylan quickly annihilated her adversaries without mercy or remorse. This House first great mother is still determined and committed to achieving other lofty objectives that remained her secret. So, she is not yet ready nor willing to accept her final peace or relinquish her House's ruling position.

No one ever knew when Neylan of House Zafet'Hu is angry or not, for she seemed to always hold the same cold, emotionless facial expression. However today, her overall demeanor foretold she is quite displeased about something or someone. Someone in the council chamber might even die by her hand today. Though "officially" unauthorized, all the other council members carried hidden weapons and they silently gripped them. Neylan started slowly speaking with her eerie voice, "Glorious ruling House mothers and esteemed members of the City Council, greetings. This is another blessed day. We have guided Tol'Tarei for well over two centuries. During this time, most of our great Houses have flourished. Three new great Houses emerged; three were eradicated from the *Chronicles of Tol'Tarei's Great Noble Houses*. This has been and is the nature of our glorious dark elf culture, pervasive with death and chaos.

"A delicate balance of power was created during the last century and has been maintained by the great noble Houses represented here. Our leadership and cooperation of our great Houses benefit us all. However, it has come to my attention that our tenacious efforts to maintain this delicate and complex balance is now greatly threatened by one of our Houses." Neylan then scrutinized each of her fellow council members silently. *"Should I* now just kill the one House first great mother whose House perpetrated this heinous offense? Or should I just kill all these annoying wretches in front of me?" she again considered, thinking to herself.

In response to her last proclamation and momentary private reflections, several quiet conversations broke the silence across the room. Aysun'Di, on the other hand, just sat quietly, indifferent to the other council member's comments. Aysun'Di knew all the appropriate and many security measures had been taken to secretly bring a dragon, an unfathomable powerful creature into the city. No one outside of her most trusted family elders, her three eldest granddaughters and a select few House warriors knew of their highly confidential, clandestine mission. Aysun'Di reassured herself thinking, *"I personally had checked, double-checked and checked again all the secret mission plans and critical preparations."* So, she was still unconcerned. However, she trusted no one in the Council and was ever wary of the dreaded House Zafet'Hu first great mother. Aysun'Di also instinctively gripped her poison-enhanced, hidden long knife and Kama sickle.

Though unspoken, Neylan knew the other Council members' were rightfully intimidated as their festering trepidation grew. After a few more tense, silent moments, the House Zafet'Hu first great mother and Tol'Tarei City Council leader resumed voicing her ominous concerns, "As leaders of our great city, we have decisions to make to possibly thwart unnecessary new House wars. However, should House wars be, declare so now! My House stands ready to destroy any or all of you if need be!"

"House Zafet'Hu first great mother, please share your knowledge of the offense which has been committed. We all then would be better prepared to deal with this new situation," requested Aysa, first great mother of House Arayi, the fifth highest ranking House of Tol'Tarei. House Arayi is secretly an ally of House Zafet'Hu. Where House Zafet'Hu enjoyed the largest dedicated fighting force in Tol'Tarei, House Arayi's might is anchored by its core of many unknown, elite assassins and battlemages. House Arayi had thwarted several House wars by skillfully eliminating enemy opposition leaders with preemptive secret attacks.

Though unspoken openly, Neylan of House Zafet'Hu coveted certain resources of this lesser House and wanted them for her own direct control. *"One day soon, House Arayi will be mine! But not this day,"* Neylan reminded herself.

"House Norkula first great mother Aysun'Di, you seem much healthier now. What has happened to you since last we met?"

Neylan suddenly queried with her cold, menacing stare. Aysun'Di knew lying to Neylan would not be tolerated; in fact, it would trigger a deadly response or assumed punishment from the House Zafet'Hu first great mother. This ancient felf was like a coiled arachnaloco, the Underworld's deadliest serpent, always ready to strike unexpectedly.

"I have just started taking a new healing tonic which has greatly revitalized me. Thank you," Aysun'Di artfully responded with the truth, but without revealing her House's secret.

"Ah, I see. Is it true then that your House performed a clandestine operation to abduct and bring a dragon here, just yesterday? Is your new tonic based upon its blood, a most powerful energy source for magic?" Neylan pressed immediately, wanting to uncover the truth quickly; and if need be, kill Aysun'Di for any further attempt to try her very limited patience.

Several gasps could be heard across the meeting chamber. In addition, Neylan's demeanor became a bit more relaxed; this was a sure sign that she wanted to give her enemies a false sense of security.

"This is one of Neylan's tactics of deception," Aysun'Di remembered. "Further, Neylan is ready to kill with any of several weapons she conceals. She would strike immediately without mercy should I hesitate or offer any inappropriate response. Only the complete truth would postpone any killing attempt of the House Norkula first great mother, at least till another day."

"Think carefully before you respond. Your very life now depends upon only the complete, unadorned truth you speak henceforth," Neylan warned with the sure coldness of being a harbinger of certain death.

Though surprised, the shocked Aysun'Di returned the cold stare of Neylan with equal intensity, anger, and hate. Aysun'Di then calmly told the Council that her House had abducted a young dragon and secretly brought it into the city. "The dragon's blood was used to help heal me since I had been poisoned," Aysun'Di reported. With that short, truthful confession, Neylan retook her seat, staring at Aysun'Di as if still trying to decide if she should just kill the defiant House Norkula first great mother for such boldness.

"Aysun'Di, you are truly a ruling House first great mother for your unforeseen daring move; it is indeed praiseworthy! It also justifies your death. However, is there some way my House could possibly benefit from this situation?" Neylan seriously contemplated. "Should I kill all but Aysun'Di now or just the four wretched, annoying hags? What a glorious aftermath this would cause..."

"Are you mad? Can this dragon breathe fire or spew forth horrible, frigid ice shards or acidic water? Are you not concerned about the possible destruction it could wreak upon your own House?" House Yildize first great mother Oyku quickly asked with sheer amazement.

"No, it is still too young to bring forth deadly fire, ice or water," Aysun'Di responded.

"From what little knowledge I have of dragons, it is bonded to its rider at birth. So, for you to have enough control over this beast to bring it here safely alive, you must have also abducted its rider who travelled here willingly. Is this correct? Who is this dragon's rider and of what race is she or he?" Fatima of House Erciyes questioned hurriedly.

Aysun'Di calmly replied again, "Yes, the dragon's rider was first mind-controlled, also abducted, and willingly came here. His dragon through its bond willingly accompanied its rider. The rider is a young melf supposedly of mixed dark and rock elf origins."

A barrage of angry questions followed from other council members. It was evident, overwhelming great fear now possessed most council members. Neylan of House Zafet'Hu and one other sat quietly through the entire harsh inquisition. Though Aysun'Di was in dire need of a remedy to her poisoned condition, the Council is far more concerned with the fact that an unknown and possibly an inordinate amount of magical energy is now within their city. This power too is now solely controlled by House Norkula. This last fact also mostly unsettled the other ruling House first great mothers. House Norkula could not only disrupt but totally destroy the balance of power the eight ruling Houses of Tol'Tarei shared.

Neylan would not release her threatening stare from Aysun'Di. "House Norkula has to pay dearly for this transgression. Aysun'Di had greatly overstepped her authority by bringing such a dangerous beast into our city. Had House Norkula made a very dangerous move to enhance its power while attempting to save its first great mother? Which motive might be a ruse?" Neylan pondered as she continued to weigh all her options and their very deadly consequences.

"So *dear* Cousin, how much blood did you take from this dragon, what did you do with it and where is the remainder currently?" Halime of House Elra'Ki inquired lastly with renewed hate. Like a few others, Halime too wanted to take the head of Aysun'Di now more than ever. Halime and her younger cousin, Aysun'Di, hated each other. Halime knew that a war between her

House and House Norkula would surely come one day. She also secretly realized that war could not start today; her House was not quite ready. The House Elra'Ki first great mother had to ensure her House would surely survive any attack from another opportunistic House after she first destroyed House Norkula. Halime concluded, thinking to herself, *"Yes, today is still not the right time, not yet. But soon, very soon, I will destroy all within House Norkula."* This powerful felf too had sat silently during the inquisition till this point. Now, her anger overflowed into the tone of her aged voice as she asked her most important questions.

Now, Aysun'Di of House Norkula had become greatly irritated and angry from the rapid bombardment of questions. She should not be treated as some lowly commoner; after all, she ruled the third ranked House of Tol'Tarei! Aysun'Di made mental notes of those House great mothers upon which she would take revenge. Disrespecting her would not be tolerated! She still calmly replied in her stoic voice, "Only enough drops were initially taken to fill a small vial. The blood was mixed with a wine potion thereafter only for me. Only a few drops remain in the vial. Again, this blood is intended to be mixed with my wine potion and taken today and the next two days. No other blood has been drawn from the dragon since the initial meeting and there is no other dragon blood remaining beyond what is in this vial."

Though she knew discovery of the abducted dragon would cause much concern and discord amongst the great Houses, Aysun'Di also knew the other House first great mothers would secretly acknowledge and admire her boldness for taking such a daring initiative. Gaining such an overwhelming advantage would potentially incite war and temporary chaos. She then contemplated, *"If only her secret had not been discovered so quickly. Someone within House Norkula will surely pay for divulging my House's most highly confidential information. However, leaving the council meeting chamber alive is still my immediate concern."*

Aysun'Di released a long, calming sigh. Now it seemed the worst of the inquisition had passed. Neylan, the first great mother of House Zafet'Hu and City Council leader, tapped her walking stick twice on the floor. This was her signal for the council members to stop talking since no additional significant information was to be gained from further insignificant bantering. Neylan coldly remarked, "Decisions now need to be made." An uncomfortable, deadly silence again settled over the meeting chamber. Neylan closed her eyes momentarily as she reanalyzed all that she had heard.

Culminating her last thoughts, Neylan considered, "Should I kill all here within this council meeting chamber? House Zafet'Hu could then claim House Norkula's most valuable prized possession... Before attending today's Council meeting, I ordered my House to secretly prepare for war; this was a necessary precaution. No doubt Halime placed House Elra'Ki on high alert, as well. Now the only question is which House, Norkula or Elra'Ki, should I destroy this day?"

On a different occasion, Neylan had closed her eyes and reopened them to start killing two other Council members who had foolishly threatened her House in an evil jest. Those two House first great mothers learned their last life's lesson in pitiful humiliation. Though the target in today's meeting should solely be Aysun'Di of House Norkula, all the other House first great mothers of Tol'Tarei's ruling council regripped their hidden weapons. Unlike before, Neylan also heavily weighed the possibility that another opportunistic council member might even come to the aid of Aysun'Di. Alliances in the Underworld were indeed tenuous since most were based upon certain and unknown fears...

Aysun'Di, still feeling the ominous pressure and deadly stare of Neylan, contemplated, "Which fears do you now harbor most, and which fears carry the most weight and dire consequences? Now Neylan, you choose very, very carefully. Though I may still die and not leave this Council chamber, praise blessed Valdearaneida for this most unique and unrivaled chaos and great fear I instilled on this day! So Neylan, what options and consequences do you choose and accept now?"

The other House first great mothers peered at each other with some reserved evil and hatred. When Halime gazed at the House Norkula first great mother, Aysun'Di quietly responded with her small, devious smile of peaceful evil. *"Yes, I will most assuredly kill you first should war erupt here!"* Aysun'Di conveyed emphatically with her persona.

After a few more moments, Neylan opened her eyes and continued her menacing gaze upon the House Norkula first great mother. Neylan remarked stoically, "You spoke truthfully; so, I did not immediately kill you. Also, we need not punish your House just yet for your intrepid decision. Fortunately, only you have received the benefit of the dragon's blood. Given the severe decline in your health, we, the ruling City Council and leaders of our noble Houses, understand how desperate your situation was. You needed to take desperate actions to save yourself and perhaps indirectly, your

House too. We can all only surmise that this dragon's blood has significantly improved your health given your present appearance and condition. For that, we are grateful. You are still a valued leader of your House and this great city.

"However, we also understand that this dragon and perhaps its rider absolutely cannot remain alive here. Your imported, newfound, unknown, powerful, magical energy source greatly disrupts the balance of power our great noble Houses share. So, how do we best dispose of this dragon and rider?"

"Must we too kill the dragon rider? Might he be useful in any other ways?" first great mother Akara of House Nimru asked.

"He is a fine warrior. I have actually tested his skills against four of our gladiators and the rider survived," Aysun'Di offered.

"If this dragon rider vanquished your gladiators fighting one at a time, that is not impressive at all. Was that your simple test?" Oyku of House Yildize arrogantly asked.

Filled with disdain by Oyku's example of a "simple" test, Aysun'Di scoffed, replying, "Of course not. Standards of my House are much higher. *My* test compelled him to fight against all four gladiators concurrently."

"Surely, both dragon and dragon rider must die. Leaving the rider alive may invite unnecessary future plots of revenge. So, none of House Norkula's new *pets* should remain alive," Halime offered.

Akara asked, "Is this melf dragon rider, by chance, a first son?"

Fatima and Oyku quickly asked a few more petty questions and Aysun'Di offered more truthful answers.

Finally, the silent Halime, the first great mother of House Elra'Ki spoke again, "Let the dragon and rider both die for the glory of Valdearaneida tomorrow, the last day of the Abaramerle celebration. This sacrifice will be unlike any other our great city has offered to our supreme god. Valdearaneida will be pleased to have the highly prized Aboveworld beast and the mighty warrior and dragon rider as a sacrifice, a highly valued sacrifice that that will surely garner favor for each of us! Our citizens too should enjoy this never-before-seen spectacle. What say you Council?"

Except for Aysun'Di, approval came quickly from the council members after the City Council leader concurred. Response to the new threat was immediate, absolute and thoroughly resolved. The Council would gain praise from the Tol'Tarei citizens for many years to come. The balance of power shared by the Tol'Tarei great Houses would rightfully be maintained.

"Somehow, I do not think the dragon and its rider would be

willing sacrifices," Fatima of House Erciyes said. "How should we kill them then in a worthy manner that honors and glorifies Valdearaneida?"

With an evil smile, Halime quickly replied, "In battle against my famed House's velociraptors. House Norkula's *pet* dragon and rider can battle against my House pets. We can ensure the dragon cannot fly and it does not yet breathe fire; so, the battle should end quickly in savage glory. The dragon and its rider will get their final peace by the claws and teeth of one of the Underworld's most vicious creatures, one of Valdearaneida's most esteemed creatures. Besides, my pets have never tasted dragon flesh before; so, they too will benefit from this battle. Council, what say you?" Halime returned her evil smile to Aysun'Di thinking, *"Yes, dear Cousin, I still long for the day when I can unleash my pets even within House Norkula! One day soon, I will destroy you and your loathsome House!"*

Nods of approval were quickly given by most of the council members. Lastly, the Council's leader said, "A glorious sacrifice it will be! A rare, bloody and vicious spectacle, truly worthy of Valdearaneida on the last day of our Abaramerle celebration. What say you Aysun'Di? Even your bold, daring, very unique and somewhat justified actions have dire consequences. Your actions result in the aftermath of your choosing who will now surely die: this dragon and its rider or your entire House of four hundred ninety-four members? What say you first great mother of House Norkula?

"Choose!"

Meeting Death

Upon leaving the City Council meeting chamber, Aysun'Di was infuriated. With several turbulent thoughts raging in her mind, including killing all in the Council meeting chamber, Aysun'Di maintained her regal composure. Blood rage was starting to overwhelm her; she now wanted to kill her enemies.

The incensed Aysun'Di left first followed the first great mothers of the five lesser Houses. Aysun'Di, the House first great mother, is the sole dictatorial ruler of House Norkula, the third ruling, noble House of Tol'Tarei, a dark elf city of the dreaded Underworld. Only two other felfs, Neylan of House Zafet'Hu and Halime of House Elra'Ki respectively, wielded more power than her in Tol'Tarei, the epitome of the dark elven matriarchal society.

Neylan and Halime lingered in the chamber when their council meeting concluded. Halime could be heard laughing just before the doors were closed again. Aysun'Di knew Halime's laughter was deliberate, wanting her archenemy to hear the celebratory gesture before Neylan resealed the room again magically against outside ears and eyes.

Had not first great mother Neylan of House Zafet'Hu attended today's council meeting, Aysun'Di would have attacked Halime for poisoning her. Though Aysun'Di did not yet have solid evidence to identify the guilty party, none was needed for her to kill her long-time nemesis for any provocation, justified or not, new or even centuries old. In the dark elven realm, little reason was ever needed to kill an enemy.

Halime's mocking laughter further angered the already enraged Aysun'Di because the House Norkula ruling matriarch was shamed in the Council's meeting. Additionally, the secret prize, or rather an expected new weapon, of House Norkula had been mysteriously discovered and very soon to be "sacrificed," more like slaughtered by the incredibly vicious "pets" of House Elra'Ki. Halime's unadorned message of foreboding was abundantly clear: House Elra'Ki patiently still hungers and waits to mercilessly annihilate House Norkula.

"Despised Asyun'Di, I revel in my great victory of today! I do hope my celebratory laughter angers you even more! I also know what you, the first great mother of House Norkula, must do next: try to identify and kill the House member who supposedly divulged the extremely confidential information about the Aboveworld's abducted dragon and its rider! I am again overjoyed that the source of that revealed secret, and its vital confirmation, came from an unimaginable, extremely well-hidden source still unknown to you, dear Aysun'Di, my most hated enemy. Yet Aysun'Di, you must spend time and energy to uncover how the two highest ruling council members knew of House Norkula's most extremely confidential secret, a secret whose assumed planning and execution took well over three years! Now, your highly guarded secret and related unknown strategy have been countered in less than a day's time! Fool!" Halime contemplated, as she continued her evil laughter of glorious victory.

The House Elra'Ki first great mother knew all of Aysun'Di's attempts to uncover who divulged House Norkula's secrets would be in vain. Aysun'Di may even kill a few family members during her ensuing House internal investigation. Whatever damage and/or whoever died resulting from the House Norkula first great mother's investigation mattered not to Halime. Not uncovering the identity of the conspirator would greatly irritate Aysun'Di and that lack of knowledge greatly pleased Halime. After four hundred years, Aysun'Di still had not yet found the House Elra'Ki very well-hidden spy.

Just before the City Council meeting ended, Council leader Neylan gave Aysun'Di very specific orders that were to be executed immediately:

Whatever drawn dragon's blood remained had to be destroyed.

No additional dragon's blood was to be taken.

The dragon and its rider were to be taken to the Tol'Tarei Coliseum this day and locked in an honored warrior's cell until tomorrow's last event of the City's Abaramerle celebration.

Inform the dragon rider to allow the Coliseum's attendants to secure the young dragon's wings by tomorrow's last event so it cannot fly.

"Failure to delay or not completely comply with any of these orders will lead to your House's utter destruction," Neylan lastly added.

Three City Council members were appointed to also accompany Aysun'Di on her return to the House Norkula stronghold. House Arayi first great mother Aysa, House Yildize first great mother Oyku, and House Erciyes first great mother Fatima were appointed to oversee the execution of the City Council's orders. The first great mother Akara of House Nimru also joined them, claiming she had never seen a dragon before and was quite "curious." The other House ruling great mothers knew this was not her true reason. Neylan trusted very few. She did trust her secret ally, Akara who would be her real "eyes and ears" as she overwatched the other House great mothers.

The ever cautious and calculating House first great mother Zehra of House Karasa chose not to go to House Norkula after the Council meeting. She instead returned to the security of her stronghold and the fourth ruling House of Tol'Tarei. The conservative Zehra was wary that some great mishap could occur at House Norkula, and many possibly could die in the ensuing mayhem, including the visiting House first great mothers.

Zehra reasoned with herself, "There is always an ever-present level of 'tension' amongst the eight ruling noble Houses of any Underworld dark elf city. All dark elf noble Houses incessantly sought more power and glory. To gain more power and glory, lower Houses need only displace, through annihilation, a higher-ranking noble House within the city. Such is the way of the dark Elvish society within the Underworld realm, a realm of chaos, danger and evil. Even so-called 'friendly' House visits can lead to one's untimely and misfortunate death.

"There is some safety in numbers, especially when those 'numbers' include the powerful City Council members; still Neylan nor Halime chose to go to House Norkula. Why? What if Aysun'Di plans to kill all the visiting Council members? Also, might not the doomed dragon and dragon rider choose to kill as many of their captors as possible instead of dying in our famed Coliseum?"

The first great mother Zehra of House Karasa had no intention of dying this day; so, Zehra chose not to go to House Norkula. She further thought, *"After all, I have seen a dragon once before many years ago and killed many rock elves in my past too. So, this day holds no special opportunity for me, at least not enough to needlessly gamble with Fate. No, I will surely wait while secretly preparing for war! I would rather be opportunistic and reap the benefits of the potential mayhem that could very well occur. Fools! I do hope the Aboveworlder and his dragon kill them all!"*

After returning to her House stronghold, Aysun'Di started giving orders immediately to various attendants. The House first great mother's tone and demeanor both demanded one's utmost swift, silent attention and obedience. Thay all knew any response less than that would lead to one's immediate death.

Fortunately, Elberithe had been able to magically scry a very brief message to her father when she first saw her grandmother emerge from the city council meeting chamber. The young felf could read her grandmother's countenance well and knew something had gone terribly wrong in the meeting. As expected, Kelvae immediately placed House Norkula on high alert and had all House elders assemble in the House Norkula chapel.

Upon arrival at the House Norkula stronghold, the visiting Houses' first great mothers were escorted to the chapel while Aysun'Di went to her private bedchamber to change. She removed her fine elegant robes and changed into warrior's garb of dark leather and light chain mail. She retrieved her famed naginata and long knives. She then went to the chapel where she knew all her House elders would have congregated and would be waiting. Aysun'Di knew betrayal of House secrets was an unforgivable crime. Punishment must be final and swift, reminding all the penalty for such an unforgivable transgression.

The first great mother of House Norkula silently went to the front of the House chapel and stood alone in the center of the dais. In front of the assembly, the visiting City Council members stood, all bearing evil smiles. House first great mothers Akara, Aysa, Oyku and Fatima also knew what the first great mother of House Norkula must do and anxiously waited to witness Aysun'Di's evil justice. The visiting House great mothers all reveled in the soon-to-be demonstrated power and glory of the House first great mother. The swift and merciless killing of a House traitor would remind all of the power wielded by a House ruling great mother.

After introducing the visiting House first great mothers, Aysun'Di quickly told the House elders what had transpired at the City Council meeting earlier that day. "Now, one of you elders of House Norkula, maybe even all, will die a dishonorable death," declared Aysun'Di who projected her majestic, most evil and merciless persona.

Most of the elders appeared shocked with the news; some remained fearfully quiet and just observed. Some cowered in fear; a few smiled evilly thinking or hoping that a member or members of their family, potential rivals, were about to die.

The House Norkula first great mother is obviously furious as she quietly paces the floor in front of the assembly. With the aid of Kelvae, her House's senior battlemage, House Erciyes first great mother Fatima, and first great mother Akara of House Nimru, Aysun'Di first subjected each House elder and soldier close to the clandestine operation to an intense mental interrogation. She then subjected all the other House elders to the same interrogation. To the House Norkula first great mother's great dismay, she found no hidden betrayal within the minds of those assembled House Norkula members.

Postponing the execution of anyone who betrayed a House secret further frustrated the already enraged Aysun'Di. "Bring me the three House gladiators who are to fight in the Coliseum," she ordered. As ordered by the House first great mother, the three great gladiators, two dark and one rock elves, were brought before Aysun'Di. "Kneel to receive my blessings." After each gladiator knelt before Aysun'Di with bowed heads, Aysun'Di released a battle cry and beheaded all the gladiators with two blindly swift strokes of her naginata. Attempting to sate her immediate need for revenge, Aysun'Di executed the House gladiators. Without any remorse, she coldly announced, "The wretched souls just received my blessing of an early death instead of dying in the Coliseum."

With no appropriate target left to further unleash her anger upon, Aysun'Di regained a calmer demeanor. None of her House members spoke out of fear that the House first great mother might again resume her former killing rage. The visiting House first great mothers just looked on approvingly at Aysun'Di's outrage. They all silently, with just small smiles seething their collective evil, applauded the House Norkula's merciless actions.

Aysun'Di ordered the chapel to be cleared of the dead bodies and debris. Afterwards, she ordered more chairs to be placed on the chapel's center dais next to her chair. Next, she also ordered the remaining potion, the abducted Aboveworld melf and his young dragon should be brought before her and placed ten steps away from the dais. Lastly, Aysun'Di took the center ornate chair on the dais and invited the visiting House first great mothers to join her there.

Aysun'Di's private attendant returned with the vial of the remaining potion. The visiting House first great mothers verified that Aysun'Di spoke truthfully that the vial before them was the only and last. House Erciyes first great mother Fatima took the potion vial and threw it into one of the burning fires in the House chapel. Moments later, Nui Jooba and his young dragon were escorted into the chapel by twelve House Norkula soldiers. Aysun'Di wanted to ensure the safety of the visiting House first great mothers. So, these extra guards were also posted about three steps away behind and on the sides of Nui Jooba and Nui Kei Dan-Rei Ryuu.

Aysun'Di introduced her noble guests, the visiting House first great mothers. Nui Jooba and Nui Kei Dan-Rei Ryuu both bowed deeply. "Well met House Norkula first great mother. Well met esteemed, great mothers of the noble Houses of Tol'Tarei," greeted the young melf.

"He is well mannered for an Aboveworld dweller," first great mother Akara of House Nimru skeptically remarked.

"And he does not speak much. That is another good male quality," first great mother Fatima of House Erciyes added. "How old are you?"

"Only two hundred thirty years," Nui Jooba answered.

Intrigued, House Arayi first great mother Aysa taunted the foreign visitors, "As you can see lowly, unfortunate melf, there are now twelve additional guards surrounding you and your dragon. Also, three guards from each of our noble Houses are here to protect us from you and your dragon should you dare decide to attack any of us. Please be foolish enough and do so; we all would enjoy seeing you killed this night." It was clearly displayed on the House Arayi first great mother's face that she enjoyed her evil taunt. Wisely, Nui Jooba just remained silent, appearing indifferent to the House Arayi first great mother's words.

House Erciyes first great mother Fatima next remarked, "The guards from our Houses are some of our finest warriors, unlike those doomed, pitiful House Norkula's gladiators you fought." Like before, Nui Jooba was unmoved by Fatima's words. He continued to remain silent, standing still without displaying any emotion. Unsatisfied, Fatima pressed and further inquired, "However, what would you do if our Houses' guards are truly here to assassinate

House Norkula great mother Aysun'Di?" Fatima was secretly hoping to embarrass and unnerve the House Norkula first great mother.

"I would kill as many guards as I could trying to protect the House Norkula first great mother," replied Nui Jooba with a calm, matter-of-fact tone. "I have already noticed two of the visiting House escort soldiers walk with a limp; three seem to have already had strong drink this day and suffering from its effects. I believe Dan-Rei and I could kill four of them before any harm befalls the first great matriarch of House Norkula. The House Norkula first great mother's naginata is close and she too is a famed warrior. She will not die easily. My sacrifice should provide enough time for the other House Norkula members to rally and further defend their House first great mother before we first died."

"You are confident, perhaps a bit too confident for one so young. You are also apparently very loyal to this House and its first great mother. Why? Do you already know and accept your fate? Or are you just another damned fool who would die protecting the House that abducted you away from your hideous Aboveworld?" The first great mother Aysa of House Arayi questioned angrily.

"Shall we just execute him now? He still does not realize nor seem to respect enough the power of the first House mothers sitting before him. This young fool is still too calm and arrogant," provoked an agitated House Arayi first great mother Aysa. Unexpectedly, the doomed Aboveworlder still did not cower in fear before the powerful leaders of Tol'Tarei.

"Dear Arayi, killing him matters not to this fool standing before us. He apparently knows he will surely die soon. Strange, but it seems he has already quietly accepted his pitiful fate. He is unlike any Aboveworlder I have ever encountered here in our glorious, blessed Underworld. Those fools all cling to life far too much." Now, turning her hateful attention to Nui Jooba, House Yildize first great mother Oyku continued, "However, what if we, the visiting House first great mothers, are here to fatally punish Aysun'Di for the crime of her attempting to greatly disrupt the balance of power our Houses share and maintain?" House Yildize first great mother Oyku derided Nui Jooba with a sinister smile. Her voice was filled with much malice and arrogance given her secret alliance with House Elra'Ki. She desperately wanted her sixth ranked House Yildize to displace House Norkula in the city's noble House hierarchy. "*If only I had been given the privilege to end this hag's life tonight,*" she thought.

"I will still protect the House Norkula first great mother.

The only difference in your scenario is that I would kill you first being the closest to her should you try to attack the House Norkula first great mother," Nui Jooba again responded calmly and indifferently. Three House Yildize guards immediately drew their weapons and stood ready to attack the stoic Nui Jooba.

Reza'Di, Elberithe and Rina, Aysun'Di's eldest granddaughters who had abducted the Aboveworld melf and his dragon, were all standing near the front and side of the chapel's dais. In response, Rina quickly drew her swords and started to boldly step forward in response to confront the House Yildize soldiers. Wisely, Elberithe extended her arm to restrain her younger rash cousin. Elberithe also quietly ordered, "Not now. Calm yourself."

In that same moment, Oyku quickly stood and held up her hand to stop her guards. Clearly, the House Yildize first great mother was now enraged. With hate glaring from her eyes, the House Yildize first great mother thought, *"How dare this fool insult me! I cannot believe anyone, other than a higher-ranking House first great mother, would openly threaten and disrespect me with such calm boldness. No melf, especially an Aboveworld melf, should live after what he said."*

"You are indeed fortunate that you *must* die in the Tol'Tarei Coliseum tomorrow. There your death will be swift. You and your beast will be viciously torn apart by some of the Underworld's deadliest predators. You will die horrifically. You will have no honor when those beasts rip you and your dragon apart and then devour you. However, if I had my way, you would slowly die over days by the excruciating pain I would inflict upon you," the first great mother of House Yildize said vehemently.

First great mother Akara of House Nimru quickly interjected, "Have you forgotten *where* you are, Oyku?" Akara's sudden warning reminded the House Yildize first great mother she too still may not leave House Norkula alive. Disrespecting a House, like threatening to kill or killing a House's honored guest, such as Nui Jooba or Dan-Rei, would justify that hosting House first great mother ordering the immediate death of the assailant. In this case, Oyku could be justifiably killed by House Norkula for her contemptuous verbal assaults without any regard of repercussion from the Tol'Tarei's ruling Council. House Elra'Ki surely could not protect the foolish House Yildize first great mother Oyku while within House Norkula. Just as important, none of the other visiting House first great mothers would possibly come to Oyku's aid.

In that next moment, Oyku quickly glanced at Aysun'Di who

displayed an equally or much more evil smile upon her face. Aysun'Di, the first great mother of House Norkula, was ready and appeared to gladly welcome the opportunity to kill Oyku herself should she proceed with any more verbal assaults against her House's honored guests. Instead, Oyku released her rage and just slightly nodded her head towards Aysun'Di, acknowledging an apology for overstepping boundaries. In response, Aysun'Di removed her hands from her long knives...

"Enough!" Aysun'Di commanded, interrupting and ending the near hostile verbal exchange. The House Norkula first great mother nodded to an attendant and refreshments were brought into the chapel and served to the Houses' first great mothers. Tempers and egos settled, becoming less incensed with the serving of excellent wine. The House Yildize first great mother though was still furious by the insolence of the Aboveworld melf. She wanted his head at her feet now!

Now studying Nui Jooba's face, Aysun'Di asked, "Do you wish to speak?"

Nui Jooba replied, "Yes, if I may please. I would like to bestow small gifts unto several of these distinguished House first great mothers."

"Gifts? What worthy gifts could you possibly give us, accursed Aboveworlders?" A surprised and dismayed Fatima of House Erciyes responded. "Surely, you will not commit suicide now? That would only be gifts of great disappointment and of little worth."

Nui Jooba remained still and expressionless with his eyes still fixed upon Aysun'Di. Astonished again by the young, calm, surprisingly mature and well-disciplined young melf, the House Norkula first great mother nodded in approval.

Nui Jooba then directed his attention to the House Nimru first great mother, smiled, bowed again and said in his best ancient Elvish, "Blessings be upon you and your House." He then reverted to his Aboveworld's common language, "Under different circumstances, my father would send his greetings and sincerest thanks. He claims your House has the world's finest bladesmiths. My father is proud to own a blade made by a House Nimru great master." Nui Jooba bowed again and said in ancient Elvish, "Thank you."

Aysun'Di straightened herself a bit and displayed a small smile aimed at Nui Jooba. Though not very skilled in communicating with "superiors," she appreciated that he could honor her distinguished guests by communicating in the ancient

Elvish language, the recognized most honorable and respectful language. *"Indeed, this Aboveworlder is truly fascinating,"* she thought. *"His compliment now also diverted the visiting House mothers' attention and hopefully further eased some of their anger."*

The first great mother Akara of House Nimru smiled slightly and nodded in gratitude. She added, "I am proud to know that my family's highly renowned craft is even greatly recognized, valued and appreciated in the Aboveworld so far away."

Next bowing to the House Arayi first great mother, Nui Jooba smiled and remarked, again in his best ancient Elvish, "Blessings be upon you and your House." Reverting to the common language, he continued, "House Arayi first great mother, your spear and shield attack forms are indeed legendary throughout the Aboveworld. Even many of your battle formations are taught at our military Academies. Your spear and shield attack formations and tactics are considered to be the finest. They are taught in my House as well. Thank you." Pleased and proud, Aysa also nodded in appreciation.

"Which attacks do you favor?" Fatima of House Erciyes questioned, now a bit more curious about this strange Aboveworlder.

"Fool! Why must you continue to test my guest? Do you really think you can unnerve him now by possibly revealing some ignorance? Curse you, Fatima! Why must you continue annoyingly provoke me?" Aysun'Di wondered.

Nui Jooba contemplated for a few moments and said, "The Sweeping Wind attacks suit me well. But the advanced attacks of your Crashing Waters form are extraordinary and are most lethal given their versatility, I believe. But I am still a student of your deadly art and have insufficient knowledge and experience to fully evaluate your gifts to the world."

A very small smile appeared upon Aysun'Di's face as she looked at the humble Nui Jooba, secretly wishing his fate was not so dire. *"Oh, how I would gladly trade the lives of all my eight grandsons for just this one melf's life standing before me!"* she thought.

"True, since neither the fourth and fifth advanced attacks can be successfully countered when executed properly," Aysa proudly stated. This last remark was purposely aimed at the other great mothers whom she may need to kill at some point in the future. Intimidation was another deadly weapon and artform all House first great mothers learned to wield very early with great skill.

With a slight scowling countenance, Nui Jooba respectfully remarked, "But my uncle, our House weapons master, has solved those great mysteries and taught us his counters. For example, the Crashing Waters fifth attack's second movement provides an opportunity to..."

Now enraged, the House Arayi first great mother stood and ordered with contempt heavy in her voice, "Silence! Show me now how you would counter that attack!" Nui Jooba immediately stopped talking, took a calming breath and bowed to House Arayi first great mother Aysa. Aysa was now infuriated. No one in her past had ever survived that famed attack, especially when she executed it with deadly purpose and was engulfed in battle rage. Two of her beloved elder sisters, both famed warriors, perished by her devastating Crashing Waters attacks when they challenged her for the right to rule their House. Now, her pride could not allow this Aboveworld, insignificant melf's words go unchallenged. House Arayi first great mother Aysa held great pride in her House's famed spear and shield attacks; it is a revered honor and exalted responsibility she proudly and dutifully carried from her elders.

Aysun'Di noticed that Oyku and Fatima were now smiling with pleased evil. Aysun'Di surmised, "You wretches still want my abducted prized melf to pay heavily for his previous disrespect, behavior and usually remarkable loyalty to House Norkula. You are indeed jealous! You also correctly assumed I would not intervene in Aysa's challenge to Jooba's response. One day, I will take both of your heads!"

"Commander Benoit, *properly* teach this young fool our Crashing Waters fourth and fifth attacks, but do not kill him." The House Arayi escort commander looked at a House Norkula attendant and nodded. With an approving wave of Aysun'Di's hand, the attendant immediately left and returned shortly with his long spear and a large round shield, the favored weapons of House Arayi soldiers. The House Norkula attendant handed these weapons to the House Arayi escort commander.

A large space had already been cleared around the soon to be combatants who moved further away from the front of the spacious chapel. Commander Benoit saluted his House first great mother as did Nui Jooba saluted Aysun'Di. The combatants then saluted each other. Commander Benoit immediately attacked Nui.

In response, Nui Jooba reflexively started moving defensively across the floor as his opponent was attacking him using the House Arayi infamous spear and shield, Crashing Waters attacks, a set of deadly, comprehensive attacks and counterattacks in which both spear and shield are used for lethal purpose. For many moments, Nui Jooba moved his hands and feet quickly and perfectly during the near deadly battle under the severe scrutiny of the House Arayi first great mother, the renowned, strict weapons master of her House.

Though ordered not to kill the Aboveworlder, Commander Benoit fought like his life depended upon his winning the battle. The commander knew he could die by the hands of the abducted Aboveworlder or by the hands of his House first great mother for his "poor" instruction. Mercy was not expected nor would be given by the House Arayi first great mother.

At the critical, designated moment, Nui Jooba secured his opponent's spear within his tight grip. Now inside Benoit's spear-length and just avoiding a sweeping shield attack, Nui Jooba savagely kicked his opponent, sending him crashing into a nearby wall. Benoit was rendered unconscious from the blow, falling heavily to the floor. Nui Jooba dropped the tightly gripped spear, stopped his movements and calmed himself.

Soon, he returned to the front of the dais and bowed again to the House Arayi first great mother. Next, he then explained Nui Samu's solutions to the unique and very deadly, Crashing Waters fourth and fifth attacks. Afterwards, he bowed again to the House Arayi first great mother and stood silently before her, awaiting her evaluation.

More silent, intense scrutiny followed as Aysa listened to the explanation and replayed Nui Jooba's movements in her mind. Finally, the House Arayi first great mother said, "I applaud your uncle for his unique creativity. Using a foot or knee attack at my Crashing Waters attack's eight-two movement is brilliant and unquestionably, a superb counter. I also applaud you Jooba for being such a good student. Thank you."

Nui Jooba bowed to the House Arayi first great mother and simply said in ancient Elvish, "Thank you again on behalf of my uncle and myself for blessing us with your gifts."

Two of the other visiting House mothers now seemed more impressed with the Aboveworld melf. However, House Yildize first great mother Oyku was still quietly angry and maintained her contemptuous glare upon the accursed Aboveworlder. On the other hand, Aysun'Di smiled slightly that her House had such a capable guest. Another House great mother's ego decreased a bit more thanks to House Norkula!

"Aboveworlder, have you accepted your fate that you will die soon? Tell us why you are so calm knowing your very short future?" Oyku questioned still wanting to unsettle the unusual, Aboveworld young melf.

Nui Jooba replied, "Dan-Rei and I understand our living here could greatly change the balance of power amongst the ruling Houses of Tol'Tarei. We understand that we must die and are both pleased to die like warriors."

Aysa of House Arayi, remarked, "You are also insightful for one so young."

Nui Jooba bowed to the first great mother of House Arayi and continued, "Despite our fates, Dan-Rei and I must continue to honor our House by acting nobly till we draw our last breaths."

House Yildize first great mother Oyku just scoffed at the Aboverworlder who again defeated her attempt to displace his calm noble demeanor with fear. On the other hand, Aysa, Akara and Aysun'Di displayed small smiles with the young melf's response. Fatima's visage remained stoic.

"And what might your Aboveworld say about Houses Norkula, Erciyes and Yildize then since the others here seem to be well known?" Fatima asked. Though still annoyed with her repeated failed attempts to unsettle the young melf, Aysun'Di, as well as all the visiting House mothers, were quite interested in now hearing the Aboveworlder's response to the House Erciyes first great mother's arcane question.

After taking and releasing a deep calming breath, Nui Jooba slowly replied, "During the few times, I have over heard conversations of strange or mysterious deaths, dark elves were also often mentioned. The Aboveworld greatly respects and fears the dark elves of the Underworld.

"Though your noble Houses may not be widely known in my former realm, I believe that is of your deliberate doing. You wish not to be known in the Aboveworld by the many; only the very few know of your Houses. For example, I believe Houses Norkula, Erciyes and Yildize have all committed 'perfect' assassinations for your secret allies in the Aboveworld."

"And how would you know this?" Fatima further questioned vehemently.

"I was fortunate enough to start studying the *Chronicles of Tol'Tarei* this morning. My focus was initially upon my new House, House Norkula; but later, I reviewed the history of each of the other seven ruling Houses. As you know, each House's heraldic sigil is documented along with the House's unique famed expertise. All great Houses are noted for their great skills in the art of killing enemies, overtly and covertly. I believe some of the Aboveworld's most infamous and mysterious deaths came about by the most feared and skilled assassins of Houses Norkula, Erciyes and Yildize given no evidence was ever found.

"Though the deaths of the six Kenmerae and four Kayseri nobles occurred many years ago, they are still great mysteries to this day. And those deaths are reviewed, discussed and debated within our Military and Science Academies where the assassins' arts are taught."

"If there was no evidence found, how can you claim these Houses were allegedly involved?" Oyku asserted, now intrigued.

"I surmised this conclusion given the ways in which those mysterious deaths occurred and your Houses' unique killing expertise and sigils. In a few cases, strange unknown markings were left behind at the scenes of the crimes – your disguised House sigils. And my mother claimed, 'Those mysterious deaths were perfect assassinations, only committed by dark elves, the world's perfect assassins.' Though Houses Norkula, Erciyes and Yildize remain mostly unknown in the Aboveworld, your expertise is still also paramount, admired and celebrated," Nui Jooba concluded, bowing deeply to the visiting House great mothers.

Aysun'Di slightly nodded, choosing to just display her evil countenance. Fatima momentarily relaxed after receiving a small bit of praise. Oyku remained angry, stoic and glared more intensely at the young melf.

Aysa of House Arayi first broke the tense, stifling silence, saying, "Again young one, you have pleasantly surprised me, but now with your knowledge and reasoning skills. And yes, we too congratulated Houses Erciyes and Yildize for their infamous, perfectly executed assignments. No doubt they earned much coin afterwards."

Fatima laughed evilly, remembering some of her Houses most challenging and highly profitable missions. Oyku just scoffed in response.

"You are wise, very wise Nui Jooba; you finally found a way to compliment those wretched Fatima and Oyku. Thank you," Aysun'Di thought. "Are all your family members warriors like you?" Aysun'Di inquired after her noble guests had resettled a bit and were talking quietly amongst themselves. She hoped her serving the exquisite wine and question would further diffuse any lingering tension amongst the visiting House great mothers.

"Yes. Yet, I am the least proficient. My brother is a superb swordsman. He can equally kill with either of his hands. He is also a very fine bowman. My uncle is our House weapons master. He is an elite warrior, extremely skilled and has great knowledge of different weapons and fighting tactics. Whether armed or unarmed, he is a master of inflicting death upon enemies. My father too is a famed warrior of extraordinary skill. He too can deliver death with either hand, empty or not. But the finest warriors in my family are my mother and aunt," Nui Jooba proudly stated, declaring the last fact with a bit more pride. The young melf stood a bit straighter too with that proclamation. He closed his eyes reflecting upon thoughts of his House elders. When he opened his eyes again, a tear fell. "You are indeed fortunate that Dan-Rei and I will die very soon without them knowing how to find you."

Puzzled, Aysun'Di inquired, "And why is that?"

With a small smile, Nui Jooba stoically replied, "They would kill you all. My mother's deadly skills and rage are unmatched and unlike I have ever seen. My aunt can be even more terrifying. I am my aunt's favorite nephew." Jooba smiled quietly knowing that his investment in the times he pampered the great dragon, Ona Kei Kuri Ryuu, had indeed earned him some "extra" favor periodically.

Nui Jooba further declared, "My mother and aunt greatly love us both. They would tear down any stronghold trying to find us. They would even die, should fate have it so, to save the young ones of our House. Without any hesitation, they would mercilessly kill all in their paths. Like you, great House mothers, they bear the full weight of leading our House nobly, proudly and mercilessly. Like you, they know full well how to deal with enemies. So, they would completely annihilate this great House and any others that would dare oppose them.

"My mother and aunt's battle rage and fighting skills too are unequaled. Even with all your entire House army forces against them, my mother and aunt would certainly destroy you all. House Norkula would be no more after they left. Pray that they never find their way here; for if they do, they will surely bring and inflict their most terrifying, merciless hell upon you."

"From your proclamation, you have great respect as well as revere these female elders of your House. That is good. But what makes them such formidable warriors?" asked House Arayi first great mother Aysa, a famed warrior of reputed great skill. She herself has vanquished many distinguished enemies and fears no one.

Nui Jooba continued, "My mother and aunt are like Valdearaneida's twin daughters, Peaeste and Traeste whose skills and fury are unmatched and have no limits. Of her eight daughters,

Valdearaneida's twins are her finest warriors."

Several gasps were released by the noble House first great mothers and several others in the chapel. "How do you know of our god?" an astonished Oyku of House Yildize queried.

Nui Jooba replied, "My family equally values all knowledge as much as martial skills. Centuries ago, my mother was a devoted student of the dark elf master Quan'Be. My mother, in turn, shared her knowledge and skills with her family.

"Though the exiled Quan'Be left the Underworld and journeyed to your Aboveworld in her last years of life, she mattered little. However, I like your mother and aunt. Maybe we should go and kill them too," House Yildize first great mother Oyku remarked.

"Try if you must, but your attempt would surely fail. Even if you five powerful, House first great mothers were to challenge just my mother alone, she would take all your heads first. Such is my mother's great fighting skill and battle prowess," Nui Jooba professed with esteemed pride and subtle defiance.

"Are you ready to meet your final peace, lowly melf? For tomorrow by this time, you will be dead," First great mother Oyku of House Yildize asked, still hoping to unnerve the defiant, and calm Aboveworld melf.

Nui Jooba closed his eyes momentarily and thought about his deceased brothers who had died before him in battle, chanting their death songs, and with smiles upon their faces. The melf then reopened his eyes and met the questioning elder's disdainful eyes with his peaceful indifferent countenance. Nui Jooba replied, "I will then embrace my final peace nobly with the blood of enemies upon my hands. I will also chant my death song till I take my last breath and with a welcoming smile upon my face."

Turning to the House Norkula first great mother, he bowed deeply and continued, "Thank you first great mother of House Norkula for the opportunity to die in battle; for that is how I wish to meet my final peace." In ancient Elvish, he concluded, "Thank you for this great honor." Nui Jooba and Dan-Rei bowed deeply again.

A so moved Aysun'Di rose from her throne-like chair and looked around the room at the House Norkula elders, young ones, and soldiers. Looking lastly at Nui Jooba, Aysun'Di thought, "*If only you had remained a hidden secret of House Norkula. You would be my finest grandson! My granddaughters who abducted you and your dragon first told me you are rare. They all said you are unlike any melf they had ever known or knew. They all covet you and each surreptitiously came to me seeking my approval for you to be her consort if not husband. Though you have only known them for a very short time, yet somehow you have greatly impressed them. In fact, one is willing to even share you with her cousins if I had approved to prevent future conflicts. I saw with my own eyes how you alone vanquished four opponents and even protected me when one attempted to attack me. Other family members and House soldiers were also saved by your great fighting skills and bravery when enemies attacked your returning party.*

"Now, you even thank me for sending you to your certain death? You do not beg for mercy. You do not pity yourself. You are not even angry about your dire misfortune. How can this be? I do not understand how you can remain so calm and noble still under these conditions. Had I not witnessed all these things with my own eyes and ears, I would not believe anyone, especially an Aboveworld melf so young, would be this way. You are indeed truly unique Nui Jooba of House Nui Vent."

Aysun'Di looked up from the lone melf standing before her and then scrutinized the faces of the House Norkula members there in the chapel. The House Norkula first great mother declared, "House Norkula, we have in our midst a most noble warrior who chooses to welcome his final peace with calmness and honor. Take note all of you for he will glorify this House even though he is not of our blood. All of you should be more like him! Praise Valdearaneida for bringing Nui Jooba to us. I believe she will be most pleased with our sacrifice on the last day of our Abaramerle!

"I have lived well over five centuries now and have had very few regrets. Today, however, I do regret not being able to have Nui Jooba become a highly valued and favored son of this House.

"Granddaughters, escort Nui Jooba to the famed Tol'Tarei Coliseum where he and his dragon are to be locked in an honored warrior's cell. Tend to all his needs this night, for it is his last."

Reza'Di, Elberithe and Rina moved to the front of the chapel, bowed to their House elder and then to the visiting elders. Thereafter, the felf cousins led Nui Jooba and Dan-Rei out of the House Norkula chapel and into the stronghold's courtyard where they again boarded the same covered wagon used to secretly bring them into the city. They now waited for the visiting House first great mothers and their guards to escort the doomed melf and dragon across the city, to the Coliseum.

Before the wagon's doors were closed, Aysun'Di walked out to personally escort her departing noble guests. The House Norkula first great mother's heart was filled with great pride and sorrow.

She walked to the back of the wagon and looked in at the melf and his dragon. A tear fell from her eye. "Nui Jooba and Nui Kei Dan-Rei Ryuu of House Nui Vent, will you receive my blessings though I am not of your House nor of your world?" a truly sad Aysun'Di requested.

"Yes, gladly. Thank you," an appreciative Nui Jooba replied. He and Dan-Rei got down from the wagon and knelt before Aysun'Di.

Aysun'Di placed a hand upon each of their heads, closed her eyes, and whispered an old, warrior's prayer in ancient Elvish. She then looked at the melf and dragon and blessed them ending with, "You made your family and this old House matriarch proud this night. Die well tomorrow! Now go and meet your deaths with honor."

Aysun'Di turned around and bid the visiting House first great mothers a good evening. Lastly, she aimed a faint smile at House Yildize first great mother Oyku before returning inside her stronghold with a heavy heart. Revenge now would be the only balm to heal her wounds. Aysun'Di would now start planning the annihilation of the House Yildize first great mother Oyku and the others who betrayed her House's secret.

The House Norkula first great mother contemplated, "Nui Jooba's response to Oyku's supposedly poor attempt at humor was deadly serious. Without hesitation, a despicable, Aboveworld lowly melf disrespected a ruling House first great mother. Under normal circumstances, I would have preferred a less truthful direct response; but these are not normal times, and the doomed Nui Jooba is still very young.

"Ha! Unknowingly, the melf did send a very clear message to that puppet of my most hated enemy, Halime. It was a message I greatly enjoyed: House Norkula will not be defeated easily. When the inevitable House wars come, House Norkula's blood-cost will be great indeed. Oyku and her pitiful House Yildize will be the first eradicated!" Aysun'Di concluded her thoughts with an evil smile.

The Tol'Tarei Coliseum commanders had received messages earlier that day from the City Council that honored, but very dangerous "guests" would be arriving there later in the day; so, needed preparations had been made. After arriving at the Coliseum, the large, multi-House, escort entourage made their way to an inner area much like a large training ground. The Coliseum commanders formally greeted the noble Houses' first great mothers and escorted them to a pavilion overlooking the training area. Many fully armed, coliseum guards were already posted on the perimeter of the training facility.

The wagon doors were opened, and Nui Jooba and his young dragon quietly left the vehicle. He was pleased to see that Reza'Di, Elberithe and Rina were still there. Nui Jooba aimed a small warm smile at the felfs hoping to lift their sullen moods. As the wagon departed the training area, the House Norkula guards who were part of the combined escort entourage left too. Afterwards the House soldiers of House Arayi departed next followed by the House soldiers of Houses Erciyes and Nimru. The House Yildize soldiers purposely delayed their departure.

"Prepare for battle!" Nui Jooba suddenly ordered, commanding the House Norkula full attention. Though surprised, the House Norkula cousins heeded his warning and came to acknowledge the looming threat before them, just ten steps away.

Just before the gates to the training area were closed and locked, all the House Yildize guard escorts had quickly moved into an attack formation. No other House Norkula escort soldier realized the new threat in time before they were locked out. Despite their repeated, heated requests, the House Norkula soldiers remained locked out from the training area. Now in front of Nui Jooba, Nui Kei Dan-Rei Ryuu, Reza'Di, Elberithe and Rina were the sixteen House Yildize escort soldiers.

Above in the distance, the House Yildize first great mother Oyku ordered, "My escorts require more training; see to it now!" Oyku stood, gave the Coliseum Third Commander a bag of coins, and departed, leading the other Houses' first great mothers away.

"Do you want any weapons, accursed Aboveworlder?" the Coliseum commander asked.

"Yes, two of your finest spears, scimitars and long knives," Nui Jooba replied.

Then turning to the House Yildize soldiers, Nui Jooba addressed the assumed commander standing in front, "I suspect your task now is to kill us for the presumed disrespect I displayed towards your House first great mother? So, we are to die here tonight instead of tomorrow? If so, need we all die? Can you and I just settle this matter ourselves? I and Dan-Rei have already accepted our fates and are prepared to meet our deaths. At the least, I committed the transgression; these felfs were not involved at all. Why should they battle your soldiers? What say you Commander?"

The House Yildize escort commander just scoffed at his appointed, doomed enemies but did not reply.

The Coliseum attendant brought all the weapons Nui Jooba requested. After inspecting the weapons, he put on the sword belt and placed the long knives into his boots. He then grabbed a spear in each hand. The Coliseum attendant left hurriedly. Nui Jooba again turned to the House Yildize escort commander and repeated his question regarding omitting the House Norkula felfs from the imminent battle.

"For your foolish honesty and direct truthfulness, I am honor bound to kill you for that disrespect you displayed to our House first great mother. The felfs will meet their deaths too because..."

Before the commander could utter another word, Nui Jooba hurled both spears very quickly with such extreme force killing the House Yildize escort commander, the assumed second escort commander next to him, and the two unfortunate soldiers standing directly behind the First and Second Escort Commanders.

The second son of House Nui Vent then drew the scimitars and quietly waited for the other soldiers to attack. Dan-Rei roared, crouched, and barred her deadly fangs and claws. The three House Norkula felfs too had already drawn their weapons upon hearing Nui Jooba's earlier warning. They too were ready for battle.

Elberithe immediately paralyzed the three assumed, House Yildize battlemages who foolishly stood next to each other. She then quickly called upon a Ure or fire spell that encapsulated the House Yildize battlemages who died quickly in the inferno. Unexpected to engage in battle this night, Elberithe did not carry all of her magical energy crystals. Though she depleted all of the energy in the crystals she did carry, she still looked formidable, like her cousins.

Reza'Di then loudly declared, "Cousins, Jooba and Dan-Rei, none of us will die here; only those fools of House Yildize will embrace their final peace this night!

Now unsettled by the rapid, unexpected, ferocious initial attacks of the Aboveworld melf and the unsuspected House Norkula battlemage, the House Yildize soldiers were no longer so confident with their superior numbers. The remaining House Yildize escorts were also without leadership and battlemage support.

"Soldiers of House Yildize, steady yourselves! Attack!" one soldier cried out. Calling upon whatever House pride remained and summoning their battle rage, the House Yildize soldiers yelled battle cries and charged the small House Norkula group.

Dan-Rei charged too, seeking an advantage that the lightly armored House Yildize soldiers had not ever battled an enraged, mighty young dragon. Nui-Jooba charged too, wanting to take the fight to the dazed, enemy House soldiers. He also would not ever let Dan-Rei fight alone in a battle he caused. In his own way, he felt responsible for his misbehavior and wanted to protect his felf captors. Moments later, the daughters of House Norkula joined the raging battle.

Fighting side by side, Nui Jooba and Dan-Rei killed enemies with deadly slashes and thrusts. It became evident within a very short time that the Aboveworld creatures had indeed fought very well together before.

The House Yildize soldiers' uncoordinated attacks further proved to be a great disadvantage. Their expected deadly "training" did not go as hoped by the House Yildize first great mother Oyku. All her House Yildize escorts found their final peace, now lying dead upon the coliseum's gore- and blood-soaked ground after their final "training" session.

None of the House Norkula contingency suffered any serious wounds. After the heated battle, Nui Jooba could hear a distant yell of frustration emanating from some faraway dark corner of the grand Coliseum. While in another, far away deep corner, evil laughter could be heard.

The Coliseum commanders all stood and saluted the House Norkula party in appreciation of their displayed deadly fighting skills.

The same Coliseum attendant returned and retrieved all the weapons he had given Nui Jooba. He then led the House Norkula party into the interior of the famed Coliseum and to a cell designated for an honored warrior. It is a well-appointed cell, more like a luxurious room one would find at a high-quality inn. Instead of staying in the lavish, comfortable cell, Nui Jooba requested to stay in a much larger, plain cell where he and Dan-Rei could stay together comfortably. Appropriate furnishings were then relocated to that cell. Fine weapons had also been placed in the plain cell.

Rina with tearful great appreciation said, "You saved my life again tonight. Thank you. Please, may I stay here with you on your last night? I could attend to your wounds, bathe, and comfort you. I want..."

Before the melf could answer, a heavily panting Elberithe pulled her younger cousin away and said looking deeply into the eyes of the melf, "Another time, perhaps even another place and I would have made you completely all mine Nui Jooba! My blood now boils unlike any other time; I want you now too. Take me!" Elberithe declared quietly.

"Only if I had not succeeded in making him mine first," Rina countered, determined not to ever lose to either of her older cousins whether fighting with words or not. "Afterall, I loved him first!"

Reza'Di just scoffed at her shameless cousins. She said, "Again, battle has ignited their lust. Forgive them. I had hoped our grandmother would have blessed your becoming *my* consort, if not *my* husband. Again, she surprised me with her decisions. Our House will now only be further glorified by your deaths, not through your lives devoted to serving our noble House. For this, I am truly sorry.

"Somehow those accursed Houses Zafet'Hu and Elra'Ki discovered that you and your dragon managed to surreptitiously enter our city. Our plans of accelerating the rebuilding of our House's fighting capabilities have been countered with this discovery. You and your dragon do not deserve a death sentence; but maintaining the balance of power Houses Zafet'Hu, Elra'Ki and the others demand will avoid the complete destruction of House Norkula. Please understand, you and your dragon will be the greatest sacrifice our House can make on the third day of the Abaramerle. Not even eight sacrificial, virgin first sons could compare to your value. May Valdearaneida find our great sacrifice unequaled and worthy. May Valdearaneida blless House Norkula accordingly."

"Grandmother will also be pleased when she learns of our deadly *training* we gave the House Yildize escorts. Oyku's failed, indirect attempt at revenge left her more frustrated and angrier," Rina said somberly.

Elberithe still focused on the quiet, aloof Nui Jooba who just continued preparing his weapons for the upcoming battle, his expected last battle. "Cousin, your words still do not provide him with any comfort; whereas I will gladly give you, Nui Jooba, delights and comfort like no other felf you have ever experienced. Will you again deny yourself the pleasures and wonders of this dark felf?" Elberithe inquired, completely disregarding her eldest cousin's rising anger.

Reza'Di gazed provocatively at Nui Jooba and inquired, "This is your last night of life; so, why should you and I not fully celebrate this time?"

A small smile came upon the melf's face. Despite the felfs' multiple attempts to seduce him, he had not yet succumbed. The memories of the three melfs he most admired and their respective relationships with their 'ones' were his unbreakable shield. For unknown reasons, he still could not respond to the felfs' wanton desires.

"Why will he still not yield to *my* wishes and desires?"

Reza'Di demanded, looking angrily at her battlemage cousin whose father had designed the mind-controlling potion. "Thoughts of his former love should have been eradicated and replaced with me."

"Apparently controlling his mind was not enough to completely control his body or his heart. He is strange, very different from all the males we know. Must he truly *love* someone before fulfilling lustful, physical desires? Nui Jooba is unlike any other melf we know. I do not understand this at all," Elberithe confessed with some ironic disappointment.

Nui Jooba, who had been quietly preparing his weapons for his upcoming battle looked at the three felfs and smiled. "Thank you for your companionship and hospitality while on our journey and here in Tol'Tarei. Though our future is bleak and coming to an end very soon, Nui Kei Dan-Rei Ryuu and I do appreciate the opportunity to die like warriors. Should fate have it so, we both will die gloriously with the blood of enemies on our hands and claws. So, do not mourn us; for we all must die one day. We are prepared to meet our fates like warriors, with honor and peace. Please give our thanks again to House Nokula first great mother Aysun'Di," Nui Jooba said.

Rina started crying softly, so moved by the melf's noble, dignified and quiet spirit, knowing he had just one more day of life remaining. Likewise, a few tears started forming in Elberithe's eyes. Reza'Di remained ever stoic, untouched by Nui Jooba's words and demeanor. Instead, anger briefly flashed across her face. "Is there anything you want?" Reza'Di angrily asked.

After a few moments of thought, "Yes. Could you possibly tell us who or what we will face in battle tomorrow? Afterwards, please leave. Dan-Rei and I wish to be alone this our last night to prepare to meet our deaths," Nui Jooba asked.

After leaving Nui Jooba's cell, the three felfs departed in frustrated, angry, still violent moods. Blood-rage from another pitched battle had ignited their wanton passions. All three felfs desperately desired the dragon rider. Like her cousins, Reza'Di too had been engulfed with the fury of a desperate battle and wanted Nui Jooba to quiet the raging, passionate storm within her. She, like her cousins, had been rejected again by the melf for some mysterious reasons unknown to her. No other melf had ever repeatedly resisted her, let alone her attractive cousins too, like Nui Jooba.

Elberithe caught the eyes of Reza'Di, scorning her with anger and hatred. "Do not test me, Cousin; for I will surely kill you," Elberithe warned, knowing the festering frustration and evil temper of her eldest cousin. Elberithe continued, "I relented to you, the ruling granddaughter, many times in the past, but not this time!" Elberithe's defiance reflected her darkest and most evil mood the young felf now projected without fear. Nui Jooba, the abducted young melf was truly a prize she coveted greatly and would fight for, even kill her cousin if need be. Like her cousins, Elberithe was angry too and very frustrated with unsated passions. Her feelings towards Nui Jooba had become remarkably intense unlike she had ever felt for any melf before.

After rejoining with their House escorts just beyond the training area's reopened gates, they all departed the Coliseum quickly to return to their House. Upon their arrival at the House Norkula stronghold, they were greeted by a House attendant who told Reza'Di, Elberithe and Rina they were to go immediately to the House chapel.

Aysun'Di and her House elders were all there in the chapel meeting to discuss next actions by their House when the three young felfs entered the chapel. Upon seeing her granddaughters covered in blood, the House first great mother dropped her wine glass and stood, visibly angry again. Her countenance portrayed her as being vehemently furious; she now needed to anxiously wait a few moments to learn why.

"Are we now at war?" the House Norkula first great mother asked.

"I would think not unless House Yildize deems losing all their escort soldiers this night now warrants a House war. The fools died in battle seeking revenge against Nui Jooba for his daring and foolish, but truthful words towards House Yildize first great mother Oyku," Reza'Di reported. She and her cousins then gave a summary of the events that took place at the Coliseum.

With a long evil laugh, Aysun'Di said joyously, "Praise Valdearaneida! Oyku is far too arrogant. Of course, House Elra'Ki first great mother Halime sanctioned the attack. Further, House Yildize first great mother Oyku will claim her escort commander acted on his own. She would not openly defy the Council's orders by attempting to kill Nui Jooba and Nui Kei Dan-Rei Ryuu tonight. Praise Valdearaneida; she still blesses House Norkula!"

After another long, evil laugh, Aysun'Di continued, "Sixteen House Yildize soldiers fought against the five of you! Again, this Nui Jooba is so very clever; he killed four of their soldiers early with his surprise, preemptive strike. No doubt the House Yildize soldiers never expected such a dark elf tactic from a lowly Aboveworlder. Ha, ha, ha. Fools! And you, Elberithe, seized the opportunity to first kill their mages who were stupid enough to band together and not suspect a skilled, enemy battlemage was in their presence. No doubt Reza'Di and Rina you too fought bravely and fearlessly again. Bless you all granddaughters!

"And, this Nui Jooba would have willingly fought all of them by himself had the House Yildize Commander not threatened you, daughters of House Norkula." More amazed, Aysun'Di said, "Still, why is he even so protective of you? What makes him so loyal to this House that caused his House great pain? I still do not understand.

"Regardless, know that all House Norkula rejoices; for you granddaughters all returned without serious injuries. We are honored by your actions tonight. Well done," House great mother Aysun'Di announced proudly as she laughed again with much evil and pride in her voice. "Let House Yildize and the others now fear our *thorough* training methods too! Fools!

Kelvae and Eylaenora still looked upon their daughter with pride and great admiration. However, now an enraged, Eylaenora said, "Mother, House Yildize would not have killed the Aboveworlder and his dragon, only these daughters of our House. Oyku would not defy the Council's orders; she only wanted to defy you for the humiliation she suffered earlier! Let us plan to destroy that despicable House!"

Aysun'Di looked evilly at Kelvae who then returned her stare with his most terrifying countenance and acknowledged, "House Yildize unprovoked attack must be answered with all of their blood!" Kelvae vehemently declared. Concurring comments erupted across the chapel as Aysun'Di quietly listened and contemplated.

Soon, Aysun'Di, also enraged, commanded, "Silence! Calm yourselves. Know that war is surely coming, and House Yildize will be destroyed. However, let us all first praise Valdearaneida!"

In response, everyone in the chapel shouted, "Praise Valdearaneida!"

"Elders, please leave. I now wish to speak with my beloved granddaughters in private."

As ordered, the House Norkula elders all departed from the House chapel quietly praising the three honored felfs as they left. After all the elders had left and the chapel doors were closed again, Aysun'Di frowned upon her granddaughters and issued a stern order saying, "Under no circumstances are any of you to try to save Nui Jooba and his dragon from their unfortunate fate. House Norkula must obey the orders of the City Council. Nui Jooba and his dragon must die in the Coliseum tomorrow; otherwise, all the other great Houses will rise up to destroy us."

Puzzled, Aysun'Di inquired, "Why did *all* of you return? Why did he reject all of you again?" The House Norkula first great mother again scrutinized her granddaughters in quiet disbelief. After long moments of silence, Aysun'Di said, "Surely his former Aboveworld lover cannot compare with you, my most beloved granddaughters. No other female has greater sexual prowess than a dark felf. Is he such a complete idiot to disregard and forgo the pleasures of you fine dark felfs on the eve of his last day of life? This Nui Jooba continues to fascinate and confuse me. He is very rare indeed."

The House Norkula first great mother sighed heavily and continued with great empathy, "So, do not hang your heads in frustration; you are all still quite young and yet have much more to learn about your glorious female powers. Find some comfort in knowing that he rejected *all* of you and not just one or two. If he had not, you would be fighting amongst yourselves. So, do not fight amongst yourselves either for your collective failures. You precious granddaughters are far more important to this House than this one Aboveworld melf!

"Praise Valdearaneida too; you all survived another great battle, though perhaps seriously frustrated with more unfulfilled desires. This too I understand," Aysun'Di quietly remarked with a smile as she reflected upon some old memories. "Also, do not leave this stronghold tonight either. House Yildize will seize any opportunity to kill you should they find you outside our stronghold's walls."

"Grandmother, I beseech you! Will you bless me tomorrow so that I may then die with the blood of House Yildize on my hands? I almost died again this night had it not been for Nui Jooba. I want to avenge their attack upon us! His dragon also saved the lives of Reza'Di and Elberithe too. House Yildize must account for their treacherous actions. I alone stand ready to challenge them all!" an emotional Rina emphatically pleaded.

The House Norkula first great mother studied her third eldest granddaughter for many moments. Though quite proud of Rina for her warrior's skills, exemplary loyalty to House Norkula and noble pride, Aysun'Di knew Rina's death would not accomplish anything significant for House Nokula. Rina's words did however cause the House Norkula first great mother's blood-rage to heighten; she too now wanted to kill enemies of her House, starting with House Yildize.

The young felf's request also made Aysun'Di reflect upon her own daring challenge of an entire House who had assassinated her favorite aunt long, long ago. Then, the very young and brash Aysun'Di challenged an entire enemy family to single combat. Aysun'Di killed four of the enemy House elders and a granddaughter just before her House finally rallied around her. Had she died then, her death would have still served an important purpose for her House. *"However, Rina's death, even after killing some House Yildize family members, would not greatly benefit House Norkula,"* Aysun'Di had finally concluded.

Coldly, Aysun'Di remarked "My brave, but foolish granddaughter, know that House Yildize will surely pay for their actions this night. Oyku's head will be mine! But my first concern is to learn how Neylan of House Zafet'Hu and Halime of House Elra'Ki discovered our secret of bringing Nui Jooba and his dragon into this House. I must uncover the truth to this very bewildering and serious mystery. Somehow House Norkula is still at grave risk of having family secrets exposed to enemies. So, until I solve this mystery, stay your hand and still your passionate rage till I command you otherwise. So, you will not receive my blessing to die just yet. Now go and clean yourselves. Do *not* disobey any of my orders tonight! Know too that your grandmother is immensely proud of each of you. You have again honored our great House tonight! I again praise Valdearaneida for having such skilled warriors and dutiful granddaughters!"

Elberithe boldly asked, "If by some miracle Nui Jooba survives his battle tomorrow, might it be a fortuitous sign from Valdearaneida that he should live to serve our great House?"

Now greatly annoyed and angry, Aysun'Di loudly remarked, "I will say this one *last* time; Nui Jooba and his dragon must battle in the Coliseum tomorrow as the City Council ordered. He and his dragon must face the most terrifying and undefeated Coliseum champions who will mercilessly kill them. Do not question or doubt their fates. This matter is closed. I will not repeat my words again!"

After some long, silent moments and a little less angry, Aysun'Di said with a comforting voice, "Now go. I need to now be alone to think." The three granddaughters, heaped in frustration and anger, bowed to their grandmother and silently left the House chapel.

Now alone with just that last riveting thought, Aysun'Di started pacing the chapel floor, daring to search for a possible answer to Elberithe's unimaginable question. *"Indeed, what should House Norkula do should Valdearaneida spare the lives of the*

Aboveworlders? What if Nui Jooba alone survives the horrors of the Coliseum? *Would this again truly be another blessing from Valdearaneida bestowed upon House Norkula?*" Aysun'Di solemnly pondered.

More agonizing thoughts then entered her already tortured mind, "Indeed, how should House Norkula respond if the Aboveworlders do survive the Coliseum? How will the other ruling Houses of Tol'Tarei respond in kind? How will House Norkula survive the follow-on House wars initiated by opportunistic or predatory Houses?" Additional unanswered questions savagely erupted; these too required difficult immediate answers.

With only her festering anger and frustration to keep her company in the dark House chapel, Aysun'Di continued slowly pacing the floor. Never in her lifetime had she ever known a melf, let alone a young Aboveworld melf, like Nui Jooba who was so extraordinary. No one else had ever moved her three, most precious granddaughters like this Aboveworlder. "I too am greatly impressed by this dragon rider," the first great mother of House Norkula even acknowledged quietly.

Aysun'Di stopped in front of the ornate altar where several first sons of her House had been sacrificed to Valdearaneida. She fell to her knees, raised her hands and silently thanked Valdearaneida for blessing her House again with the brief time Nui Jooba and his young dragon, Nui Kei Dan-Rei Ryuu, were there. The Aboveworlders brought a blessed healing to her personally. She was made whole again and *that* renewed her fighting spirit to claim more glory for her House!

Aysun'Di contemplated, "Though no one or creature had ever survived a battle against the famed House Elra'Ki velociraptors, these Aboveworlders already survived three great battles in which they were greatly outnumbered. How can this be? Has Valdearaneida already blessed them? Has Valdearaneida again greatly blessed House Norkula with these Aboveworlders?" Yet, Elberithe's last question this night mostly troubled the House Norkula's first great mother. Her agony compounded as she continued to weigh, "What indeed should she and House Norkula do should Valdearaneida spare the lives of the Aboveworlders?"

Falling prostrate onto the floor in front of the altar devoted to Valdearaneida, Aysun'Di silently prayed fervently again for guidance.

In another, seldom used, secluded corner of the House Norkula chapel, a special scrying bowl rests upon a small table. There were a few other items placed there for devotional services purposes, but only the bowl was significant for it was of magic. This bowl started bellowing small clouds of purple smoke. These clouds were a signal only to the House first great mother; someone of great importance was trying to contact her through this exclusive, secret channel. This bowl of communication worked through magic and only for Aysun'Di.

After locking the chapel doors, Aysun'Di walked quickly to the scrying bowl. She then cited an incantation to seal her small corner of the chapel from unwanted outside sight and hearing. Another magical incantation was then cast to activate the scrying bowl's special properties. Within moments, the purple smoke slowly swirled till she could clearly see the visage of an old friend, Neylan, the first great mother of House Zafet'Hu.

"Greetings, *my dear friend*. Ah, you too cannot easily find sleep this night?" Neylan said. "Centuries ago, when we were both at the Academy, life was so much simpler then. Then, we could easily recognize our enemies and friends. Then we just simply killed our enemies and continued living in this ever deadly and chaotic realm of dark elves. Then, we could limit our battles between us to a mere game of chess, in which lives were not at stake. Now, we both lead noble Houses and have much more of life's complexities to deal with. Entire Houses and many lives can be extinguished by the decisions we make. The weight of House leadership grows heavier with each decade. Oh, to be that young felf again."

"Blessings be upon you and your House, *my dear friend*," Aysun'Di responded. "Indeed, those days of our simple lives have long passed. Rejoice Neylan, we were born to lead great Houses to great glory. This day may even be a sign of a fortuitous future. Praise Valdearaneida for the glorious chaos and opportunities she has blessed and bestowed upon us!"

Neylan quietly inquired, "How so?"

"As you have already seen, my health has greatly improved after taking the new potion that was mainly based upon dragon's blood. Surely, you have already received reports from Aysa, Fatima and Akara about the day's events. This Aboveworlder is truly unique and worth more than three of my daughters!"

Neylan gasped in amazement. The daughters of a noble House are highly prized; and in this case, Aysun'Di's daughters are the esteemed second great mothers of House Norkula. High praise for a male is typically equated to just one daughter or granddaughter. Aysun'Di's praise was extraordinary and very uncommon to bestow upon a male, especially a commoner or non-dark elf. "Yes, indeed. This young Aboveworlder is rare. I secretly witnessed Oyku's escort soldiers' so-called *training* this night. He and his dragon fought bravely and courageously. For one so young, his fighting skills are exemplary. You should also be proud of your granddaughters; they too are very skilled warriors. The Aboveworlders and your granddaughters brought much glory to your House!"

"Thank you," Aysun'Di responded also with a slight nod, acknowledging her gratitude.

"That fool Oyku's training surely did not go as she had hoped," Neylan said quietly laughing.

"Indeed," Aysun'Di responded with her own supporting, quiet evil laughter.

Neylan's visage quickly transformed from the current uncharacteristic warm, pleasant and social felf to the all-powerful, cold, stoic and evil first great mother of House Zafet'Hu. She said, "We have something of great import to discuss." For several long, uncomfortable moments of silence, Neylan just stared coldly at Aysun'Di. Eventually, Neylan asked, "Is Tol'Tarei great enough for us to share just between us?

"Should, by some miracle, the Aboveworlders be fated to survive tomorrow's ordeal in the Coliseum, would that be a sign of great fortune from Valdearaneida that they should be spared? Could we then go to war against House Elra'Ki and House Yildize? The combined Houses Zafe'Hu and Norkula armies could then easily defeat the armies of House Elra'Ki and House Yildize in a great House war unlike any other. After we destroy those two despicable Houses, our Houses could rule for several more centuries without Halime's insatiable greed for power. What say you Aysun'Di?"

"Please answer this question first – why are you making this offering?" a shocked Aysun'Di inquired.

Neylan slowly admitted, "As you may or may not know, my daughters have started the deadly *purge* within my House; there is incessant hostilities amongst them. For some reason, the fools think I may find *my* final peace soon. They are fighting internally and covertly trying to eliminate their so-called *unworthy* competitors from having the honor of becoming the next House Zafet'Hu first great mother. In fact, my favored two daughters and three granddaughters have already been poisoned. I want to save these highly favored females. In doing so, I will also truly safeguard the future of my House.

"I witnessed firsthand your healing; so, I hope a similar

potion derived from dragon's blood will also heal my daughters and granddaughters. Destroying the annoying Houses Elra'Ki and Yildize would just happen sooner than planned."

Aysun'Di reasoned, "It would not surprise me to discover later that Halime instigated some of your House's inner turmoil. She fears you and your House. So, she will take advantage of opportunities to weaken you and House Zafet'Hu anytime she secretly can.

"Surely, Akara and House Nimru would ally with us. The pitiful Zehra of House Karasa would take her usual cautious, predatory position and wait, hoping her House could survive the wars of others. Aysa of House Arayi and Fatima of House Erciyes are both far too reasonable to forgo gaining a significant advantage at the expense of another great House. Houses Arayi and Erciyes would certainly join us when they see our victory is ensured," Neylan added.

Aysun'Di raised an eyebrow signifying she was truly intrigued by the offer. She then heavily weighed several, once-in-her-lifetime opportunities, *"Should Nui Jooba and Dan-Rei survive the near-impossible feat of defeating the House Elra'Ki undefeated velociraptors, Valdearaneida truly has blessed and favored House Norkula!"* she now finally accepted. *"And Neylan's present communications confirms this blessing!"*

"House Norkula will gain another mighty warrior and a magical power source unlike any other. And if the information I purchased long ago was true, my House mages would no longer be solely dependent upon their power crystals with their inherent disadvantages. And there may be even greater, dragon-blood based power yet to be discovered and derived. Most importantly, I will still control this most valuable asset!

"House Norkula will gain a highly prized grandson, unequaled by any in Tol'Tarei. Lastly and just as important, Houses Elra'Ki and Yildize will thereafter be annihilated which would greatly satisfy my immediate need for revenge against my most hated enemies."

Suddenly, Aysun'Di turned frightfully cold and cast her most evil and dark visage upon the image of Neylan above the scrying bowl. "Tell me now who within my House has betrayed me? I led the inquisition myself and found no one here to be traitorous. So, how did you and Halime learn of my House bringing a dragon rider and his dragon secretly here?" an enraged Aysun'Di vehemently demanded.

"It is good that we are meeting this way. Otherwise, I would have responded with killing you for the disrespect you just displayed. You must always remember; your actions have consequences," Neylan evilly responded. Neylan took and released a deep breath slowly. She then calmly replied, "Halime informed me the night before our Council meeting that she had first received word from one of her daughters that House Norkula had just received a 'source of immense magical power.' Halime later confirmed that fact with her 'well hidden' spy within your House. I still do not have any knowledge of her spy within House Norkula. So, you must remain vigilant and wary of everyone."

After many long silent moments, Aysun'Di finally regained her composure, accepting the words from Neylan as true.

Neylan responded in kind by relaxing her cold, evil and stoic visage. She then asked again, "Is Tol'Tarei great enough for us to share just between us?"

After more silent moments, Aysun'Di simply replied with an evil smile, acknowledging her agreement. She then said, "Should we not be prepared for the *unexpected* then by having additional units of escorts accompany us to and from the Coliseum tomorrow?"

"Agreed," Neylan concurred with an evil smile. "Two last points to finalize our agreement and bind our Houses' together. And in the spirit of sharing, I want this Aboveworlder, Nui Jooba, to be a consort of my most favored granddaughters, like your granddaughters. I also want half of the dragon's blood we will draw before it dies. Blessings be upon you and your House, dear friend."

"Let us discuss these new matters again after tomorrow's last Abaramerle celebration event. Given our desired hopeful outcome, we will have much to discuss," Aysun'Di replied. After ending the scrying session, Aysun'Di knelt and fervently prayed again to Valdearaneida. The first great mother of House Norkula sought much more guidance.

Afterwards, Aysun'Di was again enraged. She stretched out her hand, calling for her famed weapon. With her formidable naginata in hand, the incensed first great mother of House Norkula destroyed several chapel pews as she pondered Neylan's deviously clever, last request. Calmer, Aysun'Di acknowledged, *"Neylan, my dear friend, you are truly the exemplary House first great mother! But why must you now seek your death too?"*

A short time later, Aysun'Di went to the dais and sat on her chair, *her* coveted throne of House Norkula. She now wondered, "Could House Norkula truly become much more than I ever imagined?" Aysun'Di still had much to consider, knowing she would not find sleep this night...

Reunion in Death

"Soldier! Identify yourself now!" a House Norkula guard ordered and immediately attacked the soldier who had somehow gained unauthorized entry to the House soldier's guarded post.

    Je Leena turned toward the House Norkula soldier and quickly cast a spell upon the House guard paralyzing her instantly. The disguised Aboveworld felf walked up to the guard, realized she was alone, and pushed her toward the wall of the hallway. Je Leena evoked another spell that allowed her to dispose of the soon-to-be dead body within the thick wall. Within moments, there was no evidence left that the guard had ever been there. The guard died entombed in the stone wall.

    Je Leena continued her slow, determined walk further into the interior of the House Norkula stronghold. Though she now veiled herself invisible, that was not an adequate counter to defeat the various magical wards protecting the inner private chambers of the House elders. So, the Aboveworld battlemage, with the aid of Dilara, made her way steadily toward the level where she should find the House Norkula first great mother.

    According to Dilara, the sentient being within the spider fang dagger Je Leena carried, the bed chamber of the House first great mother was located on the third level of the House stronghold. Je Leena took perhaps an unusual route to get to this level of the stronghold. She first levitated high above the House Norkula stronghold and then descended to the outside of the fourth level. With the magic of her House cape, Je Leena had levitated from the heights of the cavern ceiling cloaked with an invisibility veil. Though the magical wards protecting the exterior of the House stronghold were powerful, Je Leena's dragon blood-enhanced magic and having the magical essence and knowledge of her grandmother made the young felf more powerful. She was able to bypass the House Norkula's magical alarms without difficulty.

Je Leena then used the Dwarven magic spells she learned from Urtha Dal to "bend" stone and earth walls of the stronghold exterior to allow her to easily pass through. After gaining entrance to the stronghold's interior, Dilara guided the felf to the room above the bedchamber of the House Norkula first great mother.

Je Leena conjured another spell and learned that the bedchamber below was empty; so, she proceeded entering the bedchamber through its high, thick ceiling after defeating the few magical wards of protection. Once there, Dilara quickly located her twin sister, Dimara, and directed Je Leena to her twin's exact location within the room. Je Leena picked up the second dagger and waited.

"Finally, my long-lost sister has returned! You have brought immeasurable joy to our hearts. Thank you," rejoiced both daggers' sentient beings. Dilara and Dimara immediately started chatting with faint voices slightly above a quiet whisper. After a short while, Dimara asked, "Felf, while we wait, do you wish to hear an old tale of great importance?"

After hearing Dimara's story, Je Leena cast another spell of silence upon the sentient blades as a precaution and continued to patiently wait.

Later that evening, Aysun'Di returned to her bedchamber. Moments after entering her bedchamber, Aysun'Di "felt" something is not quite right. She stretched out her hand and her naginata came to her obediently. She then crouched and scanned the darkened chamber. "Who else is here?" the House Norkula first great mother called out.

"One who is here to return something of yours you lost many years ago," replied a cold and sinister voice. Je Leena cast her voice too to make it sound as though it originated from several different places in her bedchamber. "Do not try to call your guards. All entrances and exits have been sealed, even your secret ones."

"Do you plan to kill me?" Aysun'Di asked. "If so, please identify yourself and tell me of my offense against you. Afterwards, you can then foolishly try to kill me!"

"Who I am is your *angel of death*. Many years ago, you abducted and killed one of my family members; so, I am here now to repay that debt of blood in full," Je Leena replied.

"Then show yourself and let us fight to see who will die this night!" Aysun'Di yelled back defiantly while standing in the middle of her bedchamber. The House Norkula first great mother stood tall with her naginata in her hands. If she were to die, she wanted her assailant to know how defiant, formidable, and noble the first great mother of House Norkula can be. *"I shall not die easily!"* she vowed to herself. *"Afterall, I have survived several murder attempts and many battles in my lifetime!"*

In the near complete darkness of the bedchamber, a few lines of smoke started to swirl four steps away from Aysun'Di. Suddenly the ancient felf attacked the center, left and finally right of the swirling smoke, hoping to kill the would-be assassin before she could completely materialize before her. The attack form used by Asyun'Di looked familiar to the young felf assassin. Indeed, it was the famed mantis attack Uncle Samu's grandmother had taught him. He in turn, conveyed that knowledge in his many lessons to the daughters and sons of Houses Je Luneefa, Nui Vent and Ona Feiir. Nui Samu had also taught his nieces and nephews effective counters to the ancient attack.

The swirling smoke Je Leena conjured was an intended feint. As soon as Aysun'Di attacked the "mirage" of an assassin, Je Leena descended silently from the high ceiling behind the House Norkula first great mother. Within two heartbeats' time, Je Leena stabbed Aysun'Di in four critical areas that completely immobilized her. As a result, the ancient felf dropped her weapon and became deathly still. The ancient felf's fine armor nor her magical wards protected her from the young felf's deadly assault by her dragon blood-enhanced blades. These infamous dragon long knives had been purposely loaned to Je Leena. Somehow, Ona Noirar instinctively knew they would prove to be of great assistance to Je Leena.

Je Leena then moved to face the first great mother of House Norkula. Peering into the ancient felf's cold, near lifeless eyes, her angel of death said, "I am here to kill you, not to fight you. You do not deserve the honor of a fair battle for the sacrificial killing of my uncle!"

The ancient felf slowly moved her lips in vain trying to voice some last, dying words. Aysun'Di finally mouthed, "I have killed many enemies throughout my life. Whose revenge must you take?"

An evil smile appeared upon Je Leena' face as she then removed a belt worn by Aysun'Di. This ordinary-looking adornment secretly hid the crystals used to supply the elder felf's magical energy. "I want you to feel some of the excruciating pain you caused before you die," Je Leena whispered. Je Leena then cast two spells; the first would defeat the elder felf's remaining, protective magical wards. The second spell eliminated Aysun'Di armor's protective properties. Je Leena finally replied, "I will now take revenge for the one who was very young and completely unable to defend himself."

Je Leena then screamed, "Now die!" Taking both spider fang daggers, she deeply slashed both sides of the neck of Aysun'Di. Suddenly, Je Buel's many years of silent suffering and grief flooded an enraged maniacal Je Leena just before she stabbed Aysun'Di deeply in her heart with both daggers. The twin sister daggers, reunited there together, finally extracted their revenge upon the one who had caused them centuries of great pain. Dilara and Dimara rejoiced again, now finally giving Aysun'Di her final peace, a just betrayer's reward.

Like before, Je Leena buried the dead body along with the daggers in the thick stone of the bedchamber's wall. She also buried all the spilled blood within the stone floor.

After centuries of separation, both sister daggers were overjoyed to now be reunited with each other. When she listened very, very carefully with her dragon hearing, Je Leena could hear the eerie voices of Dilara and Dimara whispering very faintly to each other for there was much for them to tell each other given their lonely, miserable separation of over four centuries. Her dragon blood-enhanced hearing served her again so very well.

Je Leena lastly heard the now happy sister daggers softly say, "Thank you again, great warrior. You have our ever-lasting thanks." Lastly, Dimara pleaded to the felf as she ascended through the ceiling, "Please, now finish what you started. No word of you, your actions and my sister's return will be conveyed to my tormentor, regardless of the pain she might inflict upon me."

After ascending to the rooftop of the House Norkula stronghold, Je Leena stopped to rethink all that the sentient blades Dimara and Dilara had told her. Though the felf now had more questions, the twin sister blades shared their history with her while she had waited for the doomed House Norkula first great mother.

Dimara recalled, "As young felfs, Aysun'Di of House Alada and Halime of House Elra'Ki were cousins, unusually good friends, even blood-sisters. They were inseparable during their early years. They were also the first daughters of their respective, great noble Houses. As such, they "ruled" over their siblings. As appropriate, they disciplined their siblings too per the right and privilege of being the eldest female sibling of their respective families. Their family love for each other dramatically changed after they entered the Military Academy of Tol'Tarei.

"During their required time at the Academy, they secretly assassinated other young felfs and melfs of noble families by the orders of their most evil grandmother, Mahya, first great mother of House Elra'Ki. Since Academy discipline and training exercises were and are oftentimes fatal, the intended assassinations could easily be masked without connecting House Elra'Ki to the fatal incidents.

"Like many young elves experiencing an independent life on their own, Halime and Aysun'Di continued behaviors first learned at her House. Both dominated the younger and weaker Academy students. Mahya directed them, 'Consider the Academy as a six-year training ground to learn many things, including how to become a successful leader.'

"The first great mother of House Elra'Ki groomed her granddaughters to become leaders of their own Houses. Since Halime and Aysun'Di were her favorites, Mahya's oversight was extreme. The House first great mother had lofty plans of marrying her favored granddaughters into other noble families that could help propel the lesser House Elra'Ki into the ruling hierarchy of Tol'Tarei. Knowing that young ones do not always follow their elders' plans, Mahya also formulated contingency plans.

"Many centuries ago, the first great mother of House Elra'Ki developed an extraordinary plan to offer a great, unique sacrifice at the upcoming Abaramerle. Halime and Aysun'Di were to lead a small group of their House soldiers to the Aboveworld and abduct at least eight virgin, first sons of noble families. This operation was targeted to take place in Rhodell, the capital of the Canae kingdom where House Elra'Ki *allies* resided. These allies, a melf and felf of noble House Rho, also had ambitious plans of taking more glory and wealth for their House. House Rho had used the deadly resources of House Elra'Ki before. Now, it was time to reciprocate with the locations of the desired target noble Houses. Since the dark elves had secretly killed his older brother for him, the new King John and Queen Jiedae of House Rho gladly provided locations of sixteen first-born sons of Rhodell's noble families. These sons were of other noble families the King Rho John and Queen Rho Jiedae disliked or viewed as potential future threats.

"After the Abaramerle that year, Aysun'Di was to marry the second son of House Norkula, the seventh Tol'Tarei ruling House. This marriage was not what Aysun'Di wanted. The heart of

Aysun'Di had other plans at that time. When Aysun'Di had become attracted to another Academy student, one whose family elders "looked down" upon House Elra'Ki as being too 'lowly and insignificant.' Regardless, Aysun'Di's attraction grew stronger with time; and later led to love, the truly maddening, you are my only 'one' kind of love. Aysun'Di and her lover secretly planned to run away to another Underworld city after graduation, but they were not able to do so. They were betrayed by a most envious and jealous Halime whose cold wicked heart could not bear her dear cousin's joy.

"House Elra'Ki first great mother Mahya was furious when she confronted Aysun'Di, her family's pride and joy, one of her two favorite granddaughters, and learned the whole truth. 'Love was a luxury a rising House cannot afford,' Mahya vehemently declared. For her disobedience, Aysun'Di was banished from House Elra'Ki, but that was after her lover had an unfortunate *accident* while on patrol duty with his fellow Academy's soldiers. Halime first told her cousin the news. When tears fell from the eyes of Aysun'Di, Halime just laughed and called her 'foolish' repeating their grandmother's distaste for love. It was learned later that Halime had indeed engineered and secretly executed that deadly accident.

"A forlorn Aysun'Di decided to marry the second son of House Norkula and took her husband's House name. She abandoned House Elra'Ki taking with her eight of the abducted, Aboveworld sons. She surreptitiously stole again what she believed to be the most noble first-born sons. Her offered dowry of the intended sacrifice had been gladly accepted by the House Norkula elders.

"Leaving the other eight abducted sons alive was a mistake Aysun'Di made and learned to regret. House Elra'Ki still sacrificed the remaining eight noble first sons at the end of the Abaramerle. Valdearaneida bestowed much favor upon House Elra'Ki and Halime. Halime, now seemingly blessed by their supreme deity, went mad with new-found power. She first killed her grandmother, mother, and any other House Elra'Ki second mothers who would not swear allegiance to her as the new ruling mother of House Elra'Ki. After annihilating the then sixth House, House Elra'Ki rose steadily to their current second rank over the past four centuries."

Dilara then requested after Dimara finished recounting the history of Halime and Aysun'Di, "Help me and my sister one last time. My sister and I, as you might suspect, are conjoined magically. Though Dimara had been gifted to Halime and I to Aysun'Di, Halime had first magically enslaved our souls to her will before I was given to Aysun'Di. I became an unwilling spy for Halime. Whatever I saw or heard through the dagger's spider while with Aysun'Di, Dimara had to relay that information to Halime. Otherwise, the first great mother of House Elra'Ki would torture my dear sister. That is how Halime learned that the Aboveworld melf and his dragon had been secretly brought into the city.

"Mighty warrior, I just need two small things from you. First, please give my blade's spider a tiny drop of your dragon's blood you must surely carry; it should greatly strengthen my blade's spider for what it will need to do. Secondly, get my blade's spider close to that evil wretched Halime who tormented my sister for centuries. It will wreak my merciless fury and revenge upon her. My sister cannot be completely free from Halime's grip until that most evil felf is dead. In exchange for this last kindness, I will share with you another long-kept secret of unimaginable great importance to you."

Je Leena had looked at the small black spider that had crawled from the Dilara dagger onto her hand. There, it had drunk the dragon's blood Je Leena had placed onto the tip of the blade. The felf had made her fateful decision. Je Leena knew had anyone ever tormented her sister, she too would seek deadly merciless vengeance.

While gazing out at the soft glowing lights around Tol'Tarei, she called out to Ona Drachir mentally, "Where are you beloved? Return to the inn and wait for me there. I need to help kill someone else before I return. The furor of a sister's vengeance is yet to be sated."

Dimara had also informed Je Leena that the bond with the House Elra'Ki first great mother was bilateral. The blade's sentient being easily located Halime and conveyed that information to Dilara. Dilara, in turn, told Je Leena how to get close to her intended victim. All Je Leena needed to do was just shoot an arrow from her hand crossbow onto a building above the street where the House Elra'Ki first great mother's litter would pass underneath. Upon that crossbow's arrow would be the Dilara blade's spider.

When the lavishly appointed personnel litter of the second ranked House Elra'Ki first great mother passed, no one saw the tiny spider descend onto the litter and disappear inside. Since Dilara's spider was not a living being and originally of House Elra'Ki, it would easily pass through any magical wards Halime may have erected to protect her.

"Thank you again, great warrior," Dilara's spider last said as the litter passed into the House Elra'Ki stronghold.

Later that night, long horrifying screams could be heard emanating from the House Elra'Ki first great mother's bedchamber. The tiny Dilara spider had silently crawled into the bed of Halime. After managing to find a place next to the bare skin of the House Elra'Ki first great mother, Dilara's spider first bit Halime, paralyzing the felf. The spider next cited an incantation, drawing upon the power of the dragon's blood. That magical spell caused the spider to revert to its original, former self, a full size, adult phonelentari, the Underworld's deadliest spider. Dilara's spider then crawled across the hopeless body of Halime to peer into the House Elra'Ki first great mother's eyes. Fear like no other time was portrayed upon Halime's tortured face. She somehow knew merciless certain Death now stared back at her.

A female adult phoneletari weighed about a quarter of a stone and it could grow to a full length of about two fahs. Phoneletari were master assassins of the Underworld, alpha predators and feared no other beasts. Its venomous bite injects neurotoxins that caused the victim to experience torturous pain emanating from the bite wound. To magnify the felf's fateful agony, the Dilara spider bit Halime three additional times across her naked body. Dilara had thought, *"A bite for each century of torment Halime inflicted upon my sister would be a fitting evil end to the House Elra'Ki first great mother."*

When Halime's screams finally stopped, the eyes of the Dimara blade's spider turned a dull, lifeless gray too indicating she was no longer enslaved to the hideous Halime of House Elra'Ki. Sister blades Dimara and Dilara quietly rejoiced for now both souls could finally rest in peace together forever.

Blessings and Forgiveness

Late that same night, Je Leena returned to the inn. There she met Ona Drachir, Je Danei and Ona Noirar. They each shared, through private mental communications, information they had gathered.

Je Danei remarked, "Jooba and Dan-Rei are no longer held at the House Norkula stronghold. Instead, an 'encouraged,' drunken House Zafet'Hu escort soldier told me that the 'Aboveworld abominations' had already been taken to the Coliseum. They were to be confined there till their death match against the House Elra'Ki velociraptors. Extra coliseum guards, two hundred fifty-six total, had been posted to thwart any potential rescue or escape. Further, should any escape or rescue be attempted, a magical trap would be tripped killing the captives."

Ona Drachir confirmed Je Danei's comments noting, "I saw a large multi-House group of soldiers escort a covered wagon to the Coliseum. Being suspicious, I followed the strange entourage for it was quite uncommon for soldiers of different Houses to march together. My suspicions were rewarded when I saw a small pile of dragon dung was thrown from the back of the wagon."

Je Leena told the group about all her activities. She told them too all the information she learned from Dilara and Dimara. Je Leena also reported, *"Both first great mothers Aysun'Di of House Norkula and Halime of House Elra'Ki died earlier that evening."*

"Uncle, you have said these particular Houses are archenemies. What if they start their long overdue war this night?

What if House Elra'Ki also attempt to kill Nui Jooba and Nui Kei Dan-Rei Ryuu this night? What if..." an exasperated Je Danei suddenly questioned as tears fell from her eyes.

"Calm yourself Danei," a scowling Ona Noirar replied with his stern mental voice. With a soothing quiet voice, he continued, "Should war start between those two hated enemy Houses, it is good fortune then that Jooba and Dan-Rei have already been moved to the Coliseum where they are heavily protected. Further, both Jooba and Dan-Rei are protected by the City Council which includes the leaders of Tol'Tarei's six other most powerful Houses. Surely House Elra'Ki will not defy the Council's edict and wage war against all those Houses unified against a common enemy. Leena also said she entombed the dead body of the House Norkula first great mother within her bedchamber's thick stone walls and hid all traces of the assassination with magic, a powerful magic that will not disclose its secrets easily. Well-done, well-done Leena. Your aunt will surely be pleased with her student."

Ona Noirar also confirmed that Nui Jooba and Nui Kei Dan-Rei Ryuu were to be sacrificed the next evening at the Coliseum on the last day of the Abaramerle celebration. Ona Noirar explained, "*Jooba and Dan-Rei are to fight against vicious Underworld creatures called velociraptors, vicious dinosaur-like predators. This event is to glorify the dark elves' supreme being, as well as provide a spectacular ending to the City's Abaramerle celebration for the entertainment of its citizens.*"

"Why is it referred to as a 'sacrifice' if Jooba and Dan-Rei will be fighting against those beasts?" Je Danei asked.

Ona Noirar maintained his deep serious scowl, reflecting his dark mood. He then said, "In the Tol'Tarei Coliseum, these beasts have never been defeated. So, the expected slaughter of our family members will be considered a 'sacrifice' by these dark elves."

New rescue plan options were formulated and discussed. Also, knowledge of a potential escape route was again reviewed. The aloof second daughter of House Je Luneefa pledged that two others had to die for their roles in their uncle's death upon her return home.

Plans had to be finalized for the daring rescue of their family members now on the eve of their planned deaths. All the information shared had been done mentally by the magic of Ona Kei Kuri Ryuu's blood they all shared. Ona Noirar, his nieces and nephew were all in foul moods as they grudgingly continued their discussions. So, little was ever said openly aloud as they slowly ate their late evening meal.

The next morning, before any Abaramerle celebration events started, the anxious Nui Jooba and Nui Kei Dan-Rei Ryuu were able to walk alone upon the sands of the Coliseum. Neither the young melf nor dragon said much as they walked silently around the main arena floor which was about six hundred steps in diameter of unremarkable, loosely packed sand. A high, thirty fah tall wall enclosed the sand floor. Painted on the wall were many gruesome pictures memorializing glorious past battles and famous gladiators of the famed Tol'Tarei Coliseum's renowned past. Upon closer inspection, Nui Jooba discerned many of the gruesome wall paintings contained grotesque, dead body parts of the vanquished that had been entombed magically.

High above the coliseum were unique, Underworld vegetation-covered stalactites that cast a soft, gray-green luminescence upon the sands. This low, eerie light was more than sufficient for the coliseum spectators to clearly see the expected, horrific battles. Further, each noble House giant pillar's writings and drawings were magically glowing, not only to provide some illumination in the near total darkness but to also remind everyone of the power and glory of that designated House.

After returning from their walk, Nui Jooba and Dan-Rei slept for the remainder of the day.

Mudui Este or "final peace" was the well-appointed name for Tol'Tarei's infamous coliseum where many different creatures had perished. The Coliseum was a circular monument of dark elves' glory. Battles, all for deadly, sadistic entertainment, were waged in this place. The citizenry of Tol'Tarei enjoyed their bloody contests; so, these events were always well attended. Here, upon the sands of the great coliseum, combat was always to the death. Mercy was not ever expected nor given.

Eight magnificent pavilions were erected long ago, one for each great ruling House of the city. All of these pavilions were equally spaced apart and located on the coliseum seating tier that provided the best view of all the activities taking place on the coliseum's sands. Each pavilion had also been erected as a monument magnifying that esteemed noble House's glory.

"Are you ready, daughter of the great dragon Ona Kei Kuri Ryuu?" Nui Jooba asked.

"*Yes, let us meet our fates together,*" Nui Kei Dan-Rei Ryuu responded proudly and boldly. "*Let us kill them all before we die!*" Dan-Rei stood tall towering just over her bonded rider. Although still a very young dragon at less than one year of age, she stood twelve fahs tall, muscular, and well proportioned. Like a much smaller version of her most noble mother, Dan-Rei was a striking mirrored-resemblance of the great dragon, Ona Kei Kuri Ryuu. Like her mother, the young dragon is fearless and noble. She knew her mother would remember her with great pride and joy, knowing that her daughter, her first offspring, died honorably and with the blood of her enemies on her claws. *"I am honored to die by your side, great warrior,"* Dan-Rei said bowing to the melf. *"Please honor me too with a death mask like yours."*

"So, you too want a death mask? So be it; I will gladly paint yours too," remarked Nui Jooba smiling. "I am honored to die by your side. I too am so very proud of you, like your mother. You greatly honor her, our family and House Nui Vent." Dan-Rei then knelt, and Nui Jooba used the red paint he had received to decorate the face of the young dragon like his. Using his hand, Nui Jooba painted the sigil of House Nui Vent, three red, left to right, diagonal lines, onto the face of the dragon. The masks will let their enemies know that they do not fear death and that both will welcome death should fate have it so.

"Will you grant me two final requests?" Dan-Rei asked.

"If I can," Nui Jooba responded solemnly.

Dan-Rei pleaded, "Please forgive yourself. Your mind was controlled by that dark felf, Reza'Di, who used you to capture and control me. I have deduced that I was her real objective, not you. These dark elves wanted my blood to greatly enhance their magic. House Norkula had been weakened and they sought the benefits of my blood to help them capture new glory and status. You truly did not abandon nor betray your House, mother, and family. Rightfully so, you did leave Je Danei who did not fully appreciate you nor your love for her."

With tears in his eyes, Nui Jooba begged, "Please forgive me too. I was foolish and did not want to cause you any harm."

"I forgave you days ago before arriving at this accursed place. The look on your face then convinced me that all that had happened was truly not your doing. You did not act of your own free will," Dan-Rei said.

"Before leaving Torondell, I was shackled and lost in despair," Nui Jooba said as he cupped the kneeling dragon's muzzle in his hands and kissed her affectionately upon her head. "And your other request?"

"Give me your blessings that I die honorably, worthy of my famed mother and our proud and noble lineage," Dan-Rei humbly requested.

"Most assuredly you have my blessings," Nui Jooba said

with sadness knowing that his last battle is truly forthcoming. He knew there would be no escape from this place. Yet, he vowed to himself that he will kill as many of his enemies as possible before taking his last breath.

Dan-Rei responded, "And you, my noble warrior and rider, have my blessings. May you die well with the blood of our enemies upon your hands." Dan-Rei reared back onto her hind legs, extended her left forearm, and said, "To the end!"

Nui Jooba extended his right arm holding the blade he had received and touched the young dragon's claw. "To the end," he quietly said, releasing a long desperately frustrating sigh.

The coliseum's large gong was then struck. The ominous sound echoed throughout the coliseum and the preparation cells below. This sound indicated that the evening's final event was about to start. This day's last event was to be another death match pitting the undefeated velociraptors of House Elra'Ki against Nui Jooba and Dan-Rei of House Nui Vent.

Velociraptors were some of the most vicious creatures of the Underworld. These dinosaur-like predators were large, standing a bit taller than eight fahs, muscular, and usually weighed between one hundred fifty to two hundred stones after reaching adulthood. They were bipedal with deadly claws used for slashing their prey. Like many creatures of the Underworld, these carnivores could see very well in very low/no light conditions and had extraordinary senses of hearing and smell. The relatively long head featured a mouth filled with finger-length, razor-sharp teeth. Its long, thick tail provided balance as it chased its victims or was used for bashing prey.

In the past, House Elra'Ki only allowed up to four of the ferocious beasts to fight in a match. Tonight's match is to be different, very different. House Elra'Ki chose to send all their velociraptors into the famed Coliseum to fight. The seven beasts versus two opponents sent a clear message: the dragon and its rider will die horrific deaths! Clearly, this was not to be a "fair" fight. House Elra'Ki wanted nothing left to chance; so, all their House "pets" will participate in the intended "sacrificial" slaughter. To the glory of Valdearaneida, the dragon and its rider are to be sacrificed on this last day of the Abaramerle. House Elra'Ki first great mother Halime wanted to send a message too to her nemesis: *House Norkula will be destroyed just as easily!*

Nui Jooba also knew no other ruling noble House would allow the dragon to live under the control of a single rival House. So, their deaths were assured regardless of some unexpected miracle, should he and Dan-Rei defeat the House Elra'Ki beasts. *"It is far better to die in battle than to live in bondage to any House of Tol'Tarei,"* he had thought and bravely accepted days ago.

To lift their spirits, Dan-Rei started chanting an ancient war song she had learned from the House Nui Vent great father Nui Samu:

> We will die with blood of enemies upon our hands.
> We die protecting our House and our lands.
> May our black dragons fly us home.
> May our ancestors welcome us home.
>
> Yes, my sons and daughters,
> You will die with blood of enemies upon your hands.
> I know this will be your final stand.
> Die well my sons and daughters for our black dragons to carry you home.
> Die well for our ancestors to welcome you home.

The warrior's pride swelled within Nui Jooba who joined in singing the chant along with the young dragon. Both performed an ancient Haka as they chanted their song of death.

The Eighth Hell

As the heavy gate to their staging area slowly opened, a loud "pffttt" sound erupted inside their tunnel as an invisible arrow slowly materialized above Nui Jooba's head. The arrow had struck the inside of the tunnel, on the wall above where he and Nui Kei Dan-Rei Ryuu were standing. The arrow looked familiar as it softly glowed while buried deep in the tunnel's wall. Near the end of the arrow, just before the fletching, there was a small vial and a note. The vial had his personal heraldic sigil of House Ona Feiir emblazoned upon it. Now filled with hopeful anticipation, Nui Jooba immediately drank the entire contents of the vial after reciting the incantation that would evoke the magical capabilities of the contents. As greatly hoped, the potion's healing properties started to take immediate effect. His mind's shackles were finally removed.

The melf released a deafening battle cry for his new-found freedom. Nui Jooba hugged his dragon tightly thereafter. In response to the melf's war cry, echoing laughter emanated deep within the famed Coliseum's hallways. "Another doomed soul will meet his death soon; so, he is preparing himself," someone said mockingly. "Rejoice fool; today, your miserable life will end."

An encouraged and revitalized Nui Jooba scoffed at the unknown speaker and then read the note tied to the arrow. The note simply read: *You are not alone.* Smiling at Dan-Rei, Nui-Jooba said, "I believe Ona Drachir is now here!"

"There is indeed hope then. Perhaps we may yet escape this

accursed place alive," an encouraged Dan-Rei remarked.

As the tunnel gate slowly continued to open, Nui Jooba checked the weapons he had been given. He now had a fine spear, shield, two scimitars and two long knives. He sorely missed his own weapons and briefly mourned the fact that he did not have his beloved battleaxes.

He also mourned the fact that Nui Kei Dan-Rei Ryuu's wings had been shackled so that she could not take flight. The special harness his captors placed upon her wings could not be easily cut with the weapons he had. Surely, the authors of their match wanted their deaths assured without hope of any possible escape. When the gate finally opened completely, he and Dan-Rei calmly marched to the center of the arena as they both sang their death song.

Few cheers rose from the coliseum stands. Whatever cheers they did hear were most likely chants of praise for their upcoming sacrifices to their deity. Some derisive laughing voices could be heard from the spectators. Very few, if any, of the Tol'Tarei citizens had ever seen a dragon before. The citizens knew the Aboveworld creatures had no hope of defeating the undefeated House Elra'Ki velociraptors. As another gate across the coliseum started to open, cheers erupted from the spectators. The long-standing, reigning champions of creature battles were about to enter.

Nui Jooba said to Dan Rei, attempting to inject some humor into their most dire situation, "If what the House Norkula felfs told us is true, we can expect four of the House Elra'Ki beasts to fight. You kill two and I will kill two. That seems fair. Remember too they might be bigger and stronger than you; so, beware. Lastly, be wary of their tails. Maybe, you should kill three and I will kill one.

"Wait. I now see seven beasts have walked onto the sands of the coliseum. I estimate these beasts ranged in height from seven to nine fah and weigh about fourteen hundred to sixteen hundred stones. They all have long tails and vicious looking claws. But their foreclaws are quite short compared to their hind claws and bodies. So, you should kill five and I will kill two.". Nui Jooba and Dan-Rei resumed singing their death chant.

"Why are you two singing a death song? Did the House Nui Vent great mother give either of you permission to die this day? I think not," a familiar voice rang in the minds of Nui Jooba and Dan-Rei. "Besides, your family is here and there are only, I believe, ten, maybe fifteen thousand or so enemies we may need to kill to escape this place. Are you ready to show these fools the might of Houses Nui Vent, Je Luneefa and Ona Feiir?" Ona Drachir triumphantly declared, encouraging his family members.

"I am currently high above you, cloaked invisible and hiding amongst the stalactites. I promise you will escape this place on this day! Our escape route will be through the northern tunnel leading from the city. There, other family members guard our escape path."

The arena's large gong was then struck. This signaled to the crowd that silence was now required for the forthcoming last, climatic event announcement. The first great mother Neylan of House Zafet'Hu stood and with a magically enhanced voice said for all to hear, "Citizens of Tol'Rarei, welcome to the final event of our great city's Abaramerle celebration. To the glory of Valdearaneida, we bring to you two of the Aboveworld's mightiest creatures, a powerful young dragon, a winged beast of extraordinary magical power and a mighty warrior melf. Both will fight against our Tol'Tarei coliseum champions, our fearless, undefeated velociraptors of House Elra'Ki! Praise Valdearaneida!"

A thunderous noise of cheers then erupted across the coliseum stands as seven velociraptors slowly walked further onto the coliseum's sands. They all had been there before and instinctively knew what they must do - whatever else was on the coliseum sands was to become their next meal. Afterall, the pets of House Elra'Ki had not eaten in two days, and they were now all extremely ravenous and ready to kill.

The velociraptors, though mighty beasts of the Underworld, were still a bit cautious. They fanned out when they noticed a lone melf and some other unknown creature in the distance. There were many steps of open space between the velociraptors and their intended prey.

The dinosaur-like beasts started to walk a bit faster toward Nui Jooba and Dan-Rei. The carnivores also knew stealth was not required on open sand; so, their pace toward their next meal quickened. Concurrently, the cheers from the crowd increased with the anticipation of the upcoming slaughter.

When the velociraptors were about four hundred steps away from their intended prey, the lead beast suddenly fell to the sands. The other six beasts stopped. After the remaining six examined the fallen beast and found it dead, they all started tearing it apart to appease their immediate, acute hunger. To the bewilderment of the crowd in the stands, the death of the first velociraptor was a complete mystery. Had they been able to see the two initially invisible arrows materialize, they would have known. But these very deadly, dragon blood-enhanced missiles were now covered in sand, blood, and gore.

In the frenzy of their tearing apart the first fallen

velociraptor, Ona Drachir killed another of the remaining six during their feeding frenzy. Just as he released his second arrow, four fire bolts of magic had been hurled at him from two different locations in the coliseum seating tiers. The would-be rescuer had been discovered. Somehow the battlemages from Houses Elra'Ki and Zafet'Hu could perhaps "see" the invisibly cloaked Ona Drachir who had to now quickly move to another location in the ceiling above the coliseum. For the time being, he had to stay hidden behind other stalactites, for he was now being hunted.

More random fire bolts were aimed again at hopeful targets. Battlemages and archers from the other noble Houses also hunted the beasts' assassin. A new wave of cheers erupted from the citizens seated in the coliseum as the ground started to shake. Like the fire bolts hurled at the ceiling, the spectators thought the shaking ground was more theatrics for the Abaramerle celebration. The minor tremble did not last long and did little to dampen the festive, sadistic spirits of the Tol'Tarei citizens in the coliseum.

Only five velociraptors now remained. After feeding upon two of their own, the still ravenous velociraptors, with their voracious hunger, now turned back toward the melf and the dragon. The new leader of the dinosaur pack roared some commands and the beasts started running toward the melf and the unknown creature standing next to him. The velociraptors were fearless, ferocious, and alpha predators of the Underworld; so, they had no fear of the two assumed insignificant creatures who were destined to become their next meal.

Meanwhile, two battlemages of House Elra'Ki stood lifeless in the coliseum as a disguised House Elra'Ki soldier stealthily moved away from the death scene. After taking five more steps into the crowded stands, the disguised Je Leena knew both battlemages, the two who had first cast fire bolts at the hidden archer above, would collapse and finally fall to the coliseum stand's floor.

Though her House pavilion chair was empty, the ornate, throne-like chair of the House Norkula first great mother suddenly burst into fire for an unknown reason. A group of disguised soldiers of House Elra'Ki suddenly attacked the elders sitting in the House Norkula pavilion. Fighting immediately broke out in the stands between these two factions.

Earlier, word had spread that the first great mother of House Elra'Ki had been killed during the night by a phonelentari. "Is not House Norkula famed for its training and use of these spiders? Is not House Norkula the archenemies of our House?" a disguised Je Leena vehemently asked those at the House Elra'Ki pavilion. Somehow, a well-regarded House Elra'Ki elder had already spread rumors that House Norkula was responsible for their House first great mother's death. Je Leena, disguised as an enraged soldier of House Elra'Ki, led some blood-thirsty soldiers towards the House Norkula pavilion to seek immediate revenge. The disguised House Elra'Ki soldier, after inciting House Elra'Ki to respond with the taking of their presumed enemies' blood, melted back unnoticed into the now frantic, coliseum spectators as a commoner rushing to leave the stands to let the warring Houses continue their enraged, frantic fight. However, there were still many sadistic souls who remained to watch the upcoming battles continue to unfold in the coliseum stands and upon the sands.

The ground shook again. This time, the ground shaking was longer and severe enough that one part of the coliseum outer wall collapsed. To increase further panic and chaos in the stands, Ona Drachir would move and shoot invisible arrows at the remaining soldiers of the non-warring Houses. Several soldiers of Houses House Arayi, Erciyes and Karasa were killed.

Unmoved by the chaos in the stands, the velociraptors were still quite hungry and were still charging toward their next intended prey.

House Zafet'Hu first great mother Neylan kept her House forces close around her and had communicated to the non-warring Houses' first great mothers to remain in their pavilions. Neylan, through magic, emphatically ordered them, "Stay calm! We are all needed to collectively destroy anyone trying to rescue our intended sacrifice. At all costs, the first great mothers of the Tol'Tarei ruling Houses must ensure that the dragon and its rider are sacrificed to the glory of Valdearaneida! This must be our unwavering and zealous duty to Valdearaneida!"

Four more arrows were shot at the soldiers guarding the House Zafet'Hu pavilion. Two fell dead. Though more fire bolts were fired at the unknown assailant, the battlemages and archers in the stands only had a momentary, magical glimpse of an invisibly veiled figure moving between the stalactites. More invisible arrows would still rain down from above, randomly killing soldiers of the non-warring Houses. In response, the battlemages and archers also increased shooting fire bolts and arrows at random targets in the ceiling.

More violent tremors shook the ground.

After a barrage of fire bolts and arrows hit different areas in the ceiling above the coliseum, a lifeless figure clutching a long bow fell onto the coliseum sands. The archers and battlemages yet alive in the stands cheered now that they had presumably killed the unknown assailant. The clever Ona Drachir had taken the dead body of a soldier he had killed to the heights of the ceiling. At an appropriate time, he released the corpse and let it fall onto the sands. The last son of House Ona Feiir laughed quietly thinking, "Rejoice enemies. Now claim your false hope."

With eyes refocused on the sands again, the coliseum spectators could all see that the remaining velociraptors were closing in on the dragon and its rider. As a declaration of presumed victory of winning their next meal, the dinosaurs stopped their advance and roared, hoping to paralyze their intended prey that had chosen not to flee. Instead, two more velociraptors fell dead to the ground. One could see invisible arrows materialize in the back of one. The other velociraptor suffered a very large cut as it toppled over from some horrendous blow to its throat.

More House battlemages collapsed in death from an unknown assassin moving stealthily throughout the stands of chaotic spectators. Whether using poisoned darts or magic, her dragon blood enhanced weapons proved to be far more powerful than the magical wards protecting the doomed, targeted mages.

More invisible arrows were shot from the ceiling killing more random House soldiers. More arrows and fire bolts were aimed at the ceiling again; they all missed the target who continued to move throughout the ceiling. Again, preoccupied with an invisibly cloaked archer high above the coliseum, the remaining soldiers of the different Houses started panicking. The soldiers knew, with ever-rising fear, death was still above and amongst them in the stands. They also knew any of their remaining battlemages yet alive could not adequately shield them from the assailant's powerful arrows which would pierce any magical shield the battlemages conjured.

With a magically enhanced voice that she had learned from Dimara and that only the phonelentari would hear, seven more great fires exploded at the other Houses' pavilions adding to the growing chaos in the stands. All six remaining House first great mothers in the stands were instantly killed. Each fire had been caused by a tiny phonelentari hidden underneath each House first great mother's pavilion throne. Each phonelentari had eaten the dragon's blood offered by Je Leena. After Je Leena freed these tiny spiders from captivity, Dilara commanded her family to repay a final debt so they too could all embrace their final peace together. Je Leena invoked a magical spell that allowed each hidden phonelentari to become a firebomb whose destructive force was greatly magnified by the dragon's blood. Like before, the last six House pavilions were totally destroyed by a terrifying inferno and killed those unfortunate souls close in proximity to each pavilion.

All this additional mayhem was created as a diversion to allow another invisibly cloaked figure to run upon the sands of the coliseum unnoticed.

"*Well met Je Danei,*" Dan-Rei greeted the felf as she joined Dan-Rei and Nui Jooba. The felf became visible beside them holding a bloodied battleaxe.

Before any further conversations could take place, the last three velociraptors were now within attacking distance of their intended prey. Even though it was just fifteen steps away, one velociraptor managed to sidestep the spear powerfully hurled at it. A second velociraptor managed to dodge both battleaxes thrown at it. When Je Danei, invisibly cloaked again, ran away from her group, one of the dinosaurs immediately followed her. The Aboveworld folk then surmised that the beasts could recognize the heat signatures of their prey and not depend upon visual recognition.

The velociraptor that engaged Nui Jooba attempted to bite his shield to rip it from his arm, but it missed. It was rewarded with a vicious scimitar cut across its snout. In response, the beast roared in pain and swiftly swung its tail around launching the melf into the air and away from the unknown creature. Nui Jooba lay upon the sands as though dead.

The wounded velociraptor turned its attention to the dragon who was a much larger meal reward. Dan-Rei kept its immediate foe, the third velociraptor, at bay with her own sharp claws and teeth. But now she had to fight two adversaries, two formidable beasts. Either could deliver death to her with their claws or teeth. Dan-Rei had not ever faced such mighty opponents as these. For the first time in her young life, she was very frightened. Death now confronted her; she was terrified. She screamed loudly to Nui Jooba pleading for help!

When she tried to counterattack one of the velociraptors, the other would try to attack her blind side. These velociraptors had hunted prey together many times in the past; they instinctively knew their pack killing tactics well. The beasts somehow conveyed a message that a killing blow would be delivered soon by one of them. So, the velociraptors patiently stalked the dragon who continued to slowly move away from them.

Boom! An explosion could be heard high above, in the ceiling, as some stalactites started to crash down upon the coliseum floor. At the next moment, both velociraptors attacked Dan-Rei. The dragon counterattacked one slashing it across its shoulder with her deadly foreclaw. The second velociraptor missed a vicious bite to Dan-Rei's hind leg to disable the dragon. However, it was not a complete miss. The shallow bite still caused Dan-Rei to roar in great pain. The first velociraptor had recovered by this time and swung its tail around and hit the dragon in its chest knocking it over breathless.

At that next moment, another extremely loud explosion occurred above in the distance. Using her blue flame, her most powerful flame of power and destruction, the great dragon Ona Kei Kuri Ryuu had blasted through the great cavern's ceiling high above the coliseum.

The two velociraptors now cautiously approached the downed dragon. They hoped to finally kill this new prey and then finish their well-deserved meal. Though only five steps away from their next meal, one of the velociraptors dropped dead from a vicious cut to its throat. When the last dinosaur turned its head seeking a new threat, it saw a lone felf walking towards it with one battleaxe in hand. The velociraptor roared and charged at the felf, the last impediment to its meal of dragon flesh. When it got twenty steps away from the felf, her second battleaxe returned to her outstretched hand as she bravely awaited the terrifying charging velociraptor.

Roar! A new, mighty roar then sounded behind the velociraptor. This roar was different, very different and it came from the recovered, bleeding Dan-Rei who was now back on her feet running toward the beast who had terrorized and wounded her earlier. The young dragon ferociously declared she was not finished! She yet wanted to do battle! Though wounded, Dan-Rei's roar was that of a challenge! *"No one interferes; I must finish what I started with this foul creature,"* the young dragon demanded.

"Are you sure? You still bleed," a recovered and worried Nui Jooba asked.

"And that makes me all the more dangerous! I must finish this fight alone!" Dan-Rei declared vehemently.

Upon hearing the call to challenge, the primal instincts of the velociraptor felt compelled to answer. It knew the dragon was bleeding; it was blood it drew earlier; and it was a different kind of blood it had not ever tasted before. Raging bloodlust too excited the velociraptor as it now charged roaring back at the wounded dragon. It would answer the challenge by viciously killing its wounded prey. That was its purpose, its nature, and its duty as an alpha predator of the Underworld!

Unfortunately for the velociraptor, it was about to learn its final lesson of life: This Aboveworld, unknown creature is a mighty black dragon; and black dragons breathe fire! When the velociraptor was just about six steps away from Dan-Rei, she was able to summon and unleash dragon fire for the first time. Being frightened and wounded caused her to evoke her inner rage, a dragon's mighty rage unlike ever before. Facing death and hurting from a serious wound greatly enraged the young dragon. She was determined not to die this day, at least not by this foul beast that tormented her. The young dragon unleased her first red flame inferno upon the velociraptor which was incinerated. Dan-Rei reared back upon her hind legs, roared again, and emitted another mighty burst of red flame.

Keiku arrived invisibly cloaked and flew directly to her wounded daughter standing across the coliseum. Hell incarnate has just arrived in Tol'Tarei! Keiku landed next to Dan-Rei, applied healing magic to her daughter's wound and said, *"Well done, Daughter. Well done. Now, it is my turn to unleash Nui Honei and my rage upon this accursed city! Witness my fury!"* Keiku then took flight.

"Make haste all of you; go to the north tunnel leading away from this city. It is your escape route. Ona Noirar, Ona Drachir and Je Leena should be on their way there too. Go quickly now!" Keiku commanded.

After taking off, Keiku flew around the city once, announcing herself with terrifying roars and hellish dragon flames. Several large buildings exploded after being struck by Keiku's devastating blue flame-balls. Many horrifying screams could be heard all around. Keiku proclaimed angrily, *"Citizens of Tol'Tarei bear witness to the wrath of one very enraged dragon, a very angry aunt and mother who has come to protect her offspring and family! I too have come to reclaim what is mine! The abduction of my precious daughter and nephew for House Norkula's evil purposes requires a deadly response just as evil! Witness a mighty dragon's horrific revenge!"*

For a moment, Nui Jooba shuddered in unmatched fear for Tol'Tarei, knowing that the great dragon would be utterly merciless. Many would suffer the consequences of the crime committed against her and House Nui Vent. Further, he thought, *"Keiku surely will represent my mother's fury as well and will unleash such devastation upon this city unlike ever imagined possible in the Underworld."* Tears fell from his eyes as he momentarily pitied the many innocent lives that would soon be extinguished.

Jolting himself away from the many cries for help and the horrific sounds of destruction, Nui Jooba walked over to Dan-Rei and hugged her affectionately. "I thought you wanted to fight that last velociraptor," he said.

"I did, but I never said it would be a fair fight!" responded the young dragon proudly.

More tremors shook the ground. Flames and lava erupted high into the air from several fissures.

"I would suggest we leave this place now!" Je Danei yelled.

"Who are you and why are you here?" a seemingly confused Nui Jooba questioned.

"I... I...," a shocked Je Danei responded slowly, uncertain of what to say.

Before she could utter another word, Nui Jooba pulled her close and kissed her.

"I most definitely know who you are and why you are here. You need not speak now. Let us first escape this accursed place," Nui Jooba said, smiling at his beloved.

"Take your things first," Je Danei responded, pleased now that Nui Jooba definitely recognized her. Nui Jooba threw away all the borrowed weapons he received. He quickly removed his outer clothing and magically donned his armor after citing an enchantment. When she turned around, the melf started taking his weapons from her back harness, moving his hands across the felf's lovely body, reveling in touching her body.

"Again, your touch was uninvited; however, this time, I welcome and will cherish it more now than ever before," Je Danei quietly promised.

"Even with enemies all around us and the threat of death hanging over and below us, I want you to know I still love you," Nui Jooba responded. The felf smiled knowing he was still *her* beloved Nui Jooba. He placed one of his battleaxes onto his back and his long knives into his boots. He also donned his House cape. With his dragon blood enhanced battleaxe, Nui Jooba quickly broke the harness that shackled Dan-Rei's wings. They all then started running towards the north end of the vacant coliseum.

Shortly after Je Danei, Nui Jooba and Dan-Rei entered the northern tunnel exiting the coliseum, a different enraged voice yelled out far behind them, "Je Danei, stop and face me now!" Reza'Di stopped running and slowly walked towards her nemesis.

Now about a half league away from the doomed city, some small tremors could be felt underground. Fortunately, the tremors had not yet reached their peak there in that northern area beyond Tol'Tarei. Still the small tremors reminded all that a great disaster was still forthcoming.

Unphased by the looming and very imminent danger, Je Danei then said to Nui Jooba and Dan-Rei, "Ona Drachir has already left; now, you go. I will follow you soon. I too must now finish something and teach that fool her life's last lesson! I promise it will not take long." Before either could respond, Je Danei turned to face Reza'Di who was now just a few hundred steps away.

Je Danei looked around quickly to assess that part of Tol'Tarei's northern tunnel. The main tunnel here measured about twenty steps high and thirty steps wide. The ground was mostly level, and the path was clear of large rocks. *"This will be a good battleground,"* Je Danei thought. Je Danei smiled as she waited patiently, seeing that Reza'Di was approaching her death with determination and purpose. Je Danei sonfidently pondered, *"I truly hope this dark felf will be a worthy opponent..."*

The first daughter of House Je Luneefa spun her battleaxes a few times. Reflecting back upon her request to Nui Honei prior to departing on their quest, her prized weapons had been enhanced with three-fah length shafts. Her battleaxes, with their full-length shafts, were much better suited for killing beasts and fighting enemies with anticipated long swords.

Je Danei had also magically shaved her head, replacing her head full of long white, luxurious hair with only a single, short band of black and red hair, running from the front to the back of her head. Her form-fitting armor was dull black in color. Though she had already removed her sword belt holding her scimitars, Je Danei still carried several other blades – her two Nimru long knives, four Nimru daggers and her ever-close two sai swords. Blood and gore from slain enemies covered her body, projecting an ominous image of a beautiful, merciless death angel. Je Danei smiled evilly, reveling in her gruesome incarnation.

Despite the new fiery destruction approaching the great Underworld city, Reza'Di was calm, walking quickly and assuredly toward the Aboveworld felf she planned to kill. Her purpose was clear: kill the ones who had dared to attack House Norkula. Just as important, her nemesis had even dared to take back from her the only melf she thought she could ever truly love. After many years of disappointing, loveless relationships, Reza'Di was not yet willing to release what she knew was now the only melf she desired madly. And she recognized that the unknown feeling was madness beyond reason. Love, true love, had finally possessed, if not overwhelmed her. Hatred now continued to propel her to kill and finally rid herself of an obstacle to her true and only heart's desire.

"Welcome first daughter of House Je Luneefa. Even disguised, only you would be stupid enough to journey here. Why have you entered my hell? Are you truly that mad?" Reza'Di shouted as she got closer to seeing Je Danei's rage in her eyes. "Wait! Before I kill you, I must first kill another enemy! Renal of House Elra'Ki, stop lurking behind me and come forth!"

Maintaining her eyes fixed upon the Aboveworld felf, Reza'Di drew a Katar dagger from within her House cape and waited for the ill-fated House Elra'Ki melf to attack. She also drew her short sword quickly. Reza'Di drew both weapons skillfully such that her undisturbed cape shielded her movements.

Moments later, another small tremor shook the ground. At that same time, a hidden warrior emerged from behind a large boulder and attacked Reza'Di. The Elra'Ki warrior Renal wielded a long sword and shield. He immediately first attacked with his shield, hoping to catch a stumbling Reza'Di off-guard. His feint was quickly followed by his real attack, a fatal slash with his sword.

Je Danei quickly discerned the melf's actions as the battle began. "But the impetuous fool may have made a mistake by not anticipating her particular blocking tactic and counterattack..." she thought.

In the next moment, Reza'Di quickly dipped low, avoiding the shield strike and parried the anticipated sword thrust with her short sword. When the melf attempted a knee attack, he again missed his fast-moving enemy. Reza'Di rewarded the impatient Renal with a kick which he blocked with his shield. Now three steps apart, Reza'Di evilly smiled and said, "Fool! Leave now while you can. Know that I did love you once... but that time has long passed. Free yourself of your meaningless emotions and your desire for revenge for my betrayal. If not, I will surely kill you. I now love another much, much more; so, go before you die an unfortunate, miserable death. This is my last warning." Raising her Katar dagger close to her face, she kissed her blade and saluted the melf. Renal, in response, just scoffed disdainfully.

Breathing heavily with immense anger, Renal released a mighty battle cry that echoed loudly throughout the tunnel while a small tremor shook the ground again. Renal charged with his shield forward, to hide his sword. In response, Reza'Di released her own terrifying battle growl and charged, again avoiding the shield bash and parrying the sword strike. Reza'Di turned around after running past her foe and again smiled evilly at her enemy who now stood motionless, paralyzed in place.

When she stood just behind Renal, Reza'Di, with a hideous sneer, looked at Je Danei as she raised the Katar dagger and released the dagger's two other blades. Mercilessly, Reza'Di plunged the dagger's three blades deeply into the back of the melf. Reza'Di then yelled vehemently, "Fool!" as she walked past the dying melf who collapsed painfully to the ground, tightly held in Death's unforgiving grasp.

"So, you pulled a hidden dart from your Katar dagger, blew and hit the melf's exposed neck with it when you ran past. Shameful for a so-called warrior to resort to such a low, ignoble tactic," Je Danei acknowledged, disappointedly.

Reza'Di smiled and then scoffed, "Were you really hoping he would kill me? Yet, the fool is still dying miserably by the blade he once gifted me after he tried to kill me with it. Instead of dealing him an immediate fatal blow, Renal dies slowly and painfully, learning from his last mistakes while I am very much alive to still kill you."

Je Danei scoffed. "You will not kill me this day! And I told you before at the inn, 'I do not share well.' I came here to take back what is rightfully mine and only mine! Now, taking your head before I leave will be an added joy," Je Danei shouted in response.

"Then, you should also be wearing a death mask. But no matter, I plan to carve one on your pretty face before I finally kill you," Reza'Di vehemently responded. The dark felf drew her long sword, smiled and saluted her Aboveworld nemesis. "Fool! Welcome to my hell. Here, you will stay by losing your pitiful life. Like many other fools, you will die here in an unmarked grave. Your loss will not be mourned but rather rejoiced. You are indeed an insane, foolish and pitiful felf! You should know too that I have killed three warriors wielding battleaxes since we last met," Reza'Di proudly gloated.

"That is indeed good news; you have had some meaningful practice then. I truly did not want to take full advantage of such an ignorant, unskilled warrior. But that will not be sufficient as I teach you your life's very last lesson," Je Danei bitterly remarked.

"I too also brought some *hell* with me. Dark elves believe in seven hells, do you not? Well, an eighth hell has now been unleashed upon your doomed city. Today is your last day of life and your city will be repaid a great debt of blood!" Je Danei declared. "By abducting Nui Jooba, you also abducted the daughter of a mighty dragon, a very incensed mother dragon who is now here in the Underworld, your hell! You will not live long enough to bear witness to the hellish power and fury of Ona Kei Kuri Ryuu! House Norkula is already destroyed and Tol'Tarei will be no more after this day! You have little time left; so, let us begin our battle now," Je Danei said, returning the salute of Reza'Di with her twin battleaxes.

Both felfs stood still, looking at each other with unbridled hatred. This will be a battle to the death! Both instinctively knew no mercy would be given nor requested. Only the other's death would sate one's rage. For a few more moments, both felfs stood stationary, allowing her respective battle rage to build. Both knew one, maybe both, would soon die.

In the next moment, Elberithe and Rina silently joined Reza'Di and stood by her side with drawn weapons.

Rina scoffed and asked, "Is she the one Nui Jooba loved? How disappointing, she is not that pretty. Where is Jooba? Did he allow you to return by yourself? If so, you are indeed a great fool."

Je Danei scoffed in response, then smiled confidently and said, "He has wounds suffered from battling the raptors and he is not needed. And Nui Jooba also still loves me very much, fool!"

Next, Je Danei said, "Reza'Di, I did not think you would be cowardly enough to rely upon others to help you in a very personal battle. I am again disappointed. Still, it matters not if I first kill you and them next or I battle the three of you at the same time." Anticipating fighting all three dark felfs, Je Danei instinctively changed her stance to the Sun'Chi fourth defense that Nui Honei had taught her. During her last movement, Je Danei continued smiling confidently.

Responding with her own confident, but very evil smile, Reza'Di remarked, "You are indeed an arrogantly confident wench. I will greatly enjoy killing you and ridding this world of your pompous, insignificant presence."

The Aboveworld felf lastly taunted, "Ha, ha, ha. Before I kill you, tell me truthfully Reza'Di, were you or any of you dark felfs ever successful in marking my beloved? I think not! Nui Jooba helplessly and unconditionally only loves *this* beautiful, marvelous, perfectly made Aboveworld felf! And yes, I know of the famous warrior-songstress Aliyya's song, paying high tribute to the dark felfs. You are indeed unfortunate misguided fools! I did not need to mark him to make him completely mine! However, upon our return to our House, know that I will mark him deeply, very deeply. Such is the wonder and might of my great love and prowess!"

A bit of shock was displayed on the dark felfs' faces as Je Danei recalled a line from the infamous dark felfs' tribute ode. A new respect for the Aboveworld felf was silently acknowledged by

Elberithe and Rina when they both slightly nodded their heads.

Not far behind the three dark felfs, two other House Elra'Ki soldiers emerged from one of several, side secondary tunnels and silently approached the unsuspecting and completely preoccupied Elberithe and Rina. These House Elra'Ki soldiers, with weapons drawn, displayed sinister smiles, hoping to deliver death blows soon to their hated enemies of House Norkula. Killing an unaware or unsuspecting enemy was considered a "poor fool's death," a true delight relished in the Underworld.

Reza'Di had already resumed slowly approaching Je Danei, standing now about twenty steps away, and was completely focused upon her upcoming battle to the death.

Rina started to move forward instinctively too with her eldest cousin, but Elberithe held her back. Elberithe quietly said, "This is far too personal; let them fight without our interference."

Reza'Di arrogantly proclaimed, "Meet my cousins, Elberithe and Rina, who both helped me abduct Nui Jooba and his dragon. They will ensure you will die."

"I think not," declared a familiar voice behind Je Danei. When Ona Drachir removed his spell of invisibility, he stood four steps to the right side of Je Danei with bow in hand. In the next four heartbeats' time, he drew and released two arrows that blazingly flew past Elberithe and Rina, killing the two approaching House Elra'Ki soldiers.

"Fool, you missed!" shouted an angry Rina.

"I think not," Ona Drachir responded. Rina then turned after suddenly hearing bodies falling heavily to the ground. The two House Elra'Ki soldiers now lay dead upon the ground. She returned her gaze upon the Aboveworld melf who, like the Aboveworld felf, was also wearing dull black leather armor. After removing his helm, Rina smiled at her unexpected savior, a melf with a single band of short black and red hair. Ona Drachir then laid aside his helm, bow and quiver of arrows. After removing his House cape, Ona Drachir drew his scimitars and waited patiently to engage the two felfs in deadly combat should they try to intervene in the battle between Je Danei and Reza'Di. Instead, Elberithe and Rina then sheathed their swords.

A now mesmerized Rina asked, "Oh. Like Nui Jooba, you saved me too for no good reason. Why? I still do not understand this Aboveworld behavior. Are you Jooba's brother, the one called Ona Drachir?" The melf only slightly nodded in response. For several long moments, Rina just observed the Aboveworlder and quietly remarked, "Like Jooba, you do not speak much. I do understand this behavior and like this family trait very much."

"Elbe, remember your promise!" Rina then said sternly. Returning her most seductive gaze to Ona Drachir, Rina continued, "Thank you. Well met Ona Drachir. I am Rina, the third daughter of House Norkula. I am also your destiny and your future wife."

Still oblivious to other present dangers and those around them, Je Danei and Reza'Di maintained their cold stares of hate as they continued slowly approaching each other. One, maybe both would die; yet neither cared as long as her opponent died first!

Keeping her eyes fixed upon her opponent, Je Danei relaxed a moment and requested of Ona Drachir, "Count?"

Ona Drachir frowned, but hesitantly responded, "Your best so far has only been eight; so, I will wager seven since you are now much more *motivated* it seems."

"Only seven, not six? Ha! So be it then!" Je Danei defiantly declared.

Puzzled, an impulsively rash Rina asked Ona Drachir, "Beloved, what does this 'count' mean?"

Je Danei smiled and promptly interjected, "We just wagered on how many strikes I would need to kill this wretched fool approaching me. Reza'Di, know that you will die within seven strikes. And your death gains me only one copper from my wager. You are indeed an unimportant and worthless hag."

When only five steps apart, both warring felfs became deathly quiet and seemed to summon and draw upon more of their respective battle rage. Reza'Di and Je Danei both released war cries and charged. An insulted and enraged Reza'Di attacked first, hoping to gain an initial advantage. Reza'Di confidently assumed, *"I know my deadly sword movements will be much faster than Je Danei's battleaxes! This I have already proven against those battleaxe-wielding fools I killed."*

Though heavier than swords, Je Danei battleaxes had been specially crafted and customized for the House Je Luneefa first daughter. She could move her weapons as quickly, if not faster than Reza'Di. Hard, long training with her prized gifted weapons, under the tutelage of renowned weapons master, Nui Samu, also contributed immensely to her superb weapons and fighting skills. Hence, Je Danei blocked all four first attacks of her enemy. Reza'Di altered her next attack, a deviation of the Rocha'Li fourth attack that left a small cut upon Je Danei's cheek. Je Danei disengaged from their battle, recognized her small wound and saluted her enemy. "Impressive. You improvised a Rocha'Li attack. Good. Know that will be the first and last time you will ever cut me," Je

Danei said, scoffing at her hated enemy.

Reza'Di smirked and retorted, "Ha! Then you will truly appreciate my next attack, an improvised Rocha'Li fifth attack. Pay attention. It *will* be the death of you!"

Je Danei scoffed in response and remarked, "I really doubt it and you still do not know the most highly advanced Rocha'Li sixth and seventh attacks which I have mastered."

Rina declared, "There are only five Rocha'Li attacks!"

"No. There are truly seven. The last two were hidden, only taught in secrecy and only shared with a very select few, worthy students. Our aunt was one of those highly privileged few. She, in turn, shared her knowledge with us," Ona Drachir admitted quietly.

Rina gasped and then asked of Ona Drachir, "Will you teach me those secret Rocha'Li attacks? Will you also train me on how to use a bow? What else can you share? Are you a fine cook also, like your brother? Are you the elder or younger brother?"

"Silence!" a frustrated and very annoyed Reza'Di ordered. "Fool, I will kill you next if you do not remain quiet!" Rina just scoffed in disbelief but ceased her questioning which she deemed far more relevant and interesting than Reza'Di's very personal feud.

Je Danei smiled mockingly, "And I hope you were not relying upon any poison or other debilitating agent you may have placed on your blades. That will not be sufficient insurance either from your meeting Death this day by my hand.

"Surely, I need no other help than my blades to kill you! You are indeed the most arrogant, loathsome and despised wretch of the Aboveworld. Killing you will bring great joy and some peace to your world," chided Reza'Di.

Reza'Di released another enraged, terrifying battle cry and charged again at Je Danei, unleashing a flurry of blinding fast attacks. The ground trembled again from the catastrophe occurring above and below the distant Tol'Tarei. In that same moment, Je Danei slipped and Reza'Di landed a vicious cut across Je Danei's momentarily exposed torso. Reza'Di screamed in frustration when she realized her blow had not even left a scratch upon her enemy's outer leather armor, let alone dealing a possible death or crippling blow with her short sword.

"Damn good armor," an amazed Rina observed, acknowledging loudly.

The ever vigilant and stoic Ona Drachir just frowned, thinking, *"You have no idea..."*

The very personal war between Je Danei and Reza'Di waged on with great fury. Throughout the felfs' battle, Rina remained unconcerned and detached; her focus was solely upon the Aboveworld melf. As she lasciviously studied him, she quietly asked Elberithe, "Do you think this Aboveworld melf is handsome? Nui Jooba has already professed his brother is an excellent swordsman. He even returned here to battle us if need be. So, he is also very brave. This Ona Drachir also seems mysterious, but very confident. Truly, I want to test all his capabilities! We even witnessed his fine skills as a deadly archer. And he saved us both from a poor fool's death.

"Elbe, remember your promise! He is mine, mine alone!" Rina continued voicing several other complimentary observations or thoughts about Ona Drachir to her elder cousin. However, Elberithe was not listening to her younger cousin's quiet, incessant outpour of infatuation.

Reza'Di and Je Danei's battle renewed with greater intensity and rage. The Aboveworld felf's third counterattack was a hard blow with her left fist to the face of Reza'Di. This blow knocked the dark felf backwards two steps and momentarily stunned the dark felf who then reengaged the battle with greater enraged fury. The dark felf next attempted several Rocha'Li attack variations which were all expertly blocked. Je Danei's last two counterattacks inflicted Reza'Di with cuts upon her face and left hand. Blood too now ran freely from Reza'Di's nose.

"I do not think you will win your bet with Jooba's brother," Reza'Di haughtily proclaimed.

"No, I will not. I conceded that wager when I decided to break your nose with my fist. That blow indeed felt too satisfying. Maybe I will just bludgeon you to death. What say you? Shall I just pummel you to your hell?

"Shall we put aside our weapons and just fight with our bare hands, knees and feet? What say you? Pity. Can you even fight without blades? Were you too arrogant to study and train in the martial arts?" Je Danei vainly questioned.

Another loud tremor shook the ground.

Je Danei sighed, regrettably. "Sadly, your lesson must be shortened. So, are you now ready to witness the Rocha'Li sixth and seventh attacks, fool? Observe carefully. This will be your only and very last chance," Je Danei further taunted, displaying a vain evil smile.

In the next series of strikes and counterstrikes, Je Danei broke the blade of Reza'Di's long sword with her lefthand battleaxe, reversed her grip on her righthand battleaxe to "power" through a weakened, short sword defense to inflict a severe, grievous cut across Reza'Di's left arm and torso. Close quarters combat was another specialty of Nui Honei who shared her knowledge and incessantly trained the daughters and sons of Houses Je Luneefa and Nui Vent. Reza'Di just received the benefit of Nui Honei's teachings from her prized student. Je Danei thought confidently, *"My beloved Auntie and Godmother would be quite pleased!"* With each shakily breath, lifeblood flowed freely from the dark felf's several grievous wounds.

Je Danei took two steps back and acknowledged, "Yes, your magical wards and pitiful armor will not protect you from my blades nor my wrath. Your death comes next." Je Danei quickly advanced and released a flurry of strikes whose blinding speed was unlike before. Now fueled by her profuse, completely unbridled rage, Je Danei's attacks inflicted numerous cuts upon Reza'Di's arms, torso and legs, essentially immobilizing her most hated enemy. Reza'Di was even pommeled several times with the shafts of Je Dane's battleaxes.

"Forgive me. I lied a moment ago; your death was certainly delayed again. I wanted you to suffer more merciless, excruciating pain before delivering the final death blow. I hope you use your last moments learning from your mistakes while I am very much alive!" Je Danei declared with extreme hatred for the dark felf. Je Danei concluded the battle with an attack Nui Jooba had used against her in previous battle training sessions. She hit Reza'Di with two last strikes, one vertical that cleaved a savage blow from Reza'Di's shoulder to her abdomen and one horizontal. The latter took her head cleanly. Ona Drachir smiled slightly.

Again, the ground trembled a bit more violently reminding all the elves that they were still in very grave danger. Elberithe smiled at the corpse, saluted Je Danei and proudly confessed, "Know that I would have killed my cousin had she emerged the victor. Thank you for saving me the inconvenience. Also, your battle was far more enjoyable to witness."

Now with a puzzled look, Elberithe turned to address Ona Drachir, "Thank you again for killing those would-be House Elra'Ki assassins. Unfortunately, Rina and I had been far too distracted by the felf's soon-to-be, epic battle. I now have five questions: How did you cause the explosions at each Tol'Tarei ruling House pavilion in the Coliseum, killing the Houses' first great mothers seated in those pavilions? What magic allowed your arrows to pierce the magical shields those House battlemages conjured?"

With a deeper furrowed brow, Elberithe continued, "Just before coming here, we fled from the Coliseum where I managed to salvage a few drops of Dan-Rei's blood. I gave each of us a drop of that blood after we reached the city's northern tunnel. We all fought our way here and we were all faster in our *movements*. No one born of the Underworld can move as fast. Again, I witnessed my cousin's battle movements to be much faster than ever before; however, that Aboveworld felf's movements were faster. How is that possible?"

After another few moments of silent reflection, the dark felf battlemage relaxed a bit. With growing excitement and sincere curiosity, Elberithe renewed her inquiry more earnestly with spirit-uplifting enthusiasm, "In our battles to get here, I had to cast eight very powerful spells. Six of those spells normally deplete all of the energy stored in my crystals. The last two spells should have completely depleted all of the remaining magical energy within my life's blood; yet, I had little ill effects. Why? Did the taking of Dan-Rei's blood somehow greatly increase my blood's magic energy?

Now even more excited, Elberithe relentlessly persisted her hurried inquiry, "Also, I detected all the Aboveworld blades are somehow magically enhanced with a power unknown to me. What magic is this? Reza'Di even wore the best steel armor made in Tol'Tarei and was also shrouded in magical spells of protection; yet they all failed to protect her from the revengeful pernicious cuts of the Aboveworld felf.

"Even though you, my Aboveworld savior, were cloaked invisible, I still could not detect your presence as you approached us. I am an experienced and highly skilled battlemage; yet I could not even sense your presence until after you removed your cloak of invisibility. How is this? Even your magical aura belies you are a mage; yet you are magically skilled. I do not understand this mystery either."

Looking lovingly at the Aboveworld melf too, Rina also finally interrupted Elberithe's onslaught of questions, "Ona Drachir, please forgive my dear cousin; mysteries of magic are some of the few things that truly excite her. Elbe lost herself in her very selfish, precious time-consuming inquisition. She asked seven questions, not five. However, I will only burden you with one: have you too been deeply marked by an Aboveworld felf? If so, whom must I kill to claim you?"

Rina's seductive intensity increased as she next said, "Why do you favor curved blades, like your scimitars and long knives? Tol'Tarei's greatest seer foretold of the 'very deadly melf whom I would meet on this last day of the Abaramerle. He is different, mysterious and carries eight blades.' We all know you have a most unique and mysterious nature; this alone makes you different from most males. Still, I wager you have more characteristics that make you *different*. And I see your four blades; do you perhaps also carry four more hidden blades? If so, then you are indeed my true *one*!"

Rina then gasped, after looking more deeply into the melf's eyes. She then exclaimed, "You are indeed very different; you are of mixed blood, are you not? Elbe, look closely at his eyes! Dark elf blood flows through this disguised, Aboveworld rock melf! Yes, my beloved, you will surely be mine!"

Ona Drachir just maintained his stoic, ever vigilant posture in silence, not choosing to answer either of the dark felfs' untimely questions except with his slight, mysterious smile that slowly turned to a scowl.

Upon hearing and confirming Rina's discovery, Elberithe evilly smiled in return. She then happily acknowledged, "Like his brother, he does not speak much. This is truly a very fine family trait. Still, I will certainly enjoy getting your answers to all my questions when we next meet."

Lastly, Rina said, "Ah... Drachir, you do have an enchanting, mysterious smile, but I like your scowls far more. Behind your scowls I know there are hidden mysteries and secrets, I wager; and I like mysteries too. So, I must now uncover all your mysteries! I too will certainly enjoy wrestling answers from you to my many questions. Know too you will undoubtedly greatly enjoy wrestling with me. Know too I am *your* beautiful, marvelous, perfectly made dark felf who will gladly share the hidden secrets of Aliyya's tribute. Until we meet again, wait for me my beloved Ona Drachir."

Immediately again, the ground trembled a bit more violently for a short while from the distant earthquake.

Elberithe laughed, "Surely, I do not understand how you can fall for a melf so quickly. Again, you are a love-smitten, insufferable fool. We need to go now."

"Ha! You are just jealous because I have chosen the more mysterious brother!" Rina countered victoriously. Elberithe then led her younger cousin quickly away through one of the side tunnels. Moments later, both dark felfs could be heard still laughing in the distance.

Looking at Je Danei, Ona Drachir sighed, offering a "congratulatory" nod and then said with a small smile, "You owe me a copper from our wager!"

"Ha! Yes, but I surely will not pay you this time since you do not want me to tell Leena how you somehow managed to receive a proposal of love here. Am I right? That will be a most difficult explanation, I *wager*. So, a copper for my silence is a heavily discounted price for your great debt to me," Je Danei responded, laughing heartily. "Now, let us also make haste and leave this foul place."

Ona Drachir scowled and said, "Agreed." The Aboveworlders quickly resumed their escape through the northern tunnel.

Je Danei laughed as they ran. "Tell me truthfully, how many blades do you carry?" she inquired. After running another hundred steps, Je Danei announced, "I am still waiting patiently for your answer. I truly must know."

Ona Drachir reluctantly replied, "Unfortunately eight! Argh!" Ona Drachir yelled as he continued to scowl, acknowledging his debt will most likely be used against him repeatedly in the future... Je Danei's laughter increased slightly.

The great dragon took aim at one of the great pillars supporting the cavern's high ceiling. Summoning her full rage and powerful magic, Keiku released a blue flame-ball at the lower half of the House Norkula pillar. That section of the pillar was completely blasted away. After Je Leena had described the House Norkula heraldic sigil to the great dragon, Keiku wanted to destroy that great supporting column first.

The surrounding ground even shook from the devastation. More jets of fiery lava spewed forth from several horrendous fissures, hailing the annihilation of that once great Underworld House. The noise emanating from the blast was gloriously thunderous and echoed loudly throughout the enormous cavern. Keiku was pleased. The upper portion of that blasted pillar, now with no supporting bottom section, started to crash down upon that noble House. That section of the ceiling too started cracking, signaling the beginning of another forthcoming catastrophe. Keiku resumed flying around the city breathing a revengeful mother's, terrible dragon-flame upon Tol'Tarei.

The great dragon blasted away two more bottom sections of great pillars. As more of the ceiling cracked and started crashing down upon the city, lava, from the now angry, abruptly awakened volcano, freely flowed into the city from three of its four main tunnels. The ground shook and cracked too, spewing more lava and fire rocks from the awakened volcano seeking revenge for its long excessive slumber. The cacophony of the city's doomed citizens became less and less as the volcano's fury escaped through large crevices in the ground and more of the ceiling continued to crash down upon the city.

Keiku proclaimed angrily, "Dark elves of this most

unfortunate city, today will be your final, glorious stand. This day, Tol'Tarei will pay the full price for attacking Houses Nui Vent and Je Luneefa! Bear witness as this legendary city of the Underworld is annihilated!"

Another earthquake, even more violent than before, shook the ground beneath Tol'Tarei for a few moments. Multiple, uncontrollable infernos raged around and throughout the city. The long dormant volcano spewed its lava and deadly gases throughout the cavern's broken floor. The fiery river of molten rock now moved steadily through the city destroying everything in its path. The long sleeping volcano had now been fully awakened with the great dragon's help.

Reconciliation and Redemption

Nui Jooba, Nui Kei Dan-Rei Ryuu, and Je Danei made their way quickly through the city's north tunnel. After blasting away the Je Kei specified, second and third giant pillars supporting the ceiling high above Tol'Tarei, Ona Kei Kuri Ryuu made her escape passing back through the same hole she had entered earlier in the gigantic cavern's ceiling. As Je Kei foretold, the remaining five giant pillars could no longer support the enormous weight of the ceiling supporting the great Ararateken's mountain. So, the remaining ceiling above Tol'Tarei savagely cracked, imploded and crashed down upon Tol'Tarei.

    In addition, the volcano near the great Underworld city was no longer dormant. It raged uncontrollably after being violently awakened from its centuries-long sleep. The volcano erupted through the ground, engulfing the city with its fiery, molten embrace. All of Tol'Tarei was utterly destroyed either from the falling rocks from above or the erupting inferno from below.

    Je Kei had also told the rescue group that taking the northern tunnel away from the city would perhaps be the safest route, at least for a short while. Dan-Rei also strongly encouraged her group to take this escape route too; for it had another, unique quality she learned.

    When Nui Jooba, Dan-Rei, and Je Danei were about a league from Tol'Tarei, they could all hear the distinctive sounds of battle ahead. The small group now rushed hoping to aid their family members. After rounding a bend in the tunnel, they could see Ona

Noirar, Ona Drachir and Je Leena were all fighting a larger contingency of House Elra'Ki soldiers. Ona Noirar was wounded, bleeding from a hand wound and covered in blood.

Je Danei mentally issued a command to her sister, *"Encshi!"* This battle command ordered Je Leena to encapsulate herself and group within a magical shield." The elder sister then quickly issued another command to Nui Jooba and Dan-Rei to touch her. In the next instance, Je Danei quickly spun her battleaxes while citing an incantation. She ended pointing both battleaxes at the unsuspecting enemy soldiers saying, "Eitl aithorn Je Teinori and Je Zeinori Wei." Like Nui Jooba's battleaxes, a raging storm's thunderous sound boomed loudly, and the stored lightning bolts shot forth from her battleaxes into the unshielded, enemy soldiers. The multitude of crooked, evilly jagged lightning bolts killed all the unprotected House Elra'Ki soldiers in their paths.

"I see more fine enhancements have been made to my gifts," Nui Jooba remarked as he gazed upon the charred remains of all the fallen enemy soldiers. "You must tell me all that was done to your weapons."

"Surely. Your mother is an invaluable blessing to our families," a pleased Je Danei responded.

Dan-Rei turned around looking at their escape route behind them and hurled a red flame-ball back down the tunnel.

"Yes, that is a wise precaution," Je Leena said as she cited a spell to cause some large rocks to also fall into the same tunnel from which they just passed through.

More tremors occurred reminding them that they still were not safe being close to the doomed city of Tol'Tarei.

Though covered in blood too, Ona Drachir and Je Leena were not seriously wounded. After Je Leena applied some healing magic to Ona Noirar's wound, the Houses Nui Vent–Je Luneefa group resumed a quick pace.

After traveling about another league in the tunnel, Dan-Rei saw their destination a short distance ahead. The excited young dragon then hastened her pace towards the gate and simply commanded the others, *"Follow me."*

"What is that and why go there? Is it not just another gate like the Luna Fendasse we saw on the first part of our journey to the Underworld?" Ona Noirar asked. They all walked up a few steps away from the gate.

"All, it is much more than a mere gate; it is also a transportation portal!" Dan-Rei responded mentally with some excitement. "If what I suspect is true, our escape ends here. This gate is Luna Eronnarsi. I will explain more later. Nui Jooba, please place your bracer in that hole on the lower left side of the gate."

Nui Jooba had learned from Ona Noirar that his dragon earned his trust long ago. A dragon rider's life often depends upon fast decisions or directions made by the dragon; so, trust is crucial between a rider and bonded dragon. Nui Jooba trusted Dan-Rei; so, he did what was requested without question or hesitation.

Dan-Rei next requested for the melf to extend his right hand, palm up. Nui Jooba immediately complied, again trusting his dragon. With her foreclaw, Dan-Rei swiftly cut his raised palm.

The young dragon then instructed, "Now touch the following runes around the gate starting from the left: the third, fourth, sixth, and eighth. Lastly, with your bloodied palm, touch the rune on the far right of the gate."

A low humming noise started to emanate from the Luna Eronnarsi. Each touched rune was backlit. After the last rune was touched with Nui Jooba's bloodied palm, a low beam of light emanated from each touched symbol and met at the center of the gate. From the gate's center, circular, shimmering waves of silvery light moved across the gate after the last rune was touched. Like waves on an ocean or lake, the waves quietly ebbed and flowed.

"Now, let us go through quickly," Dan-Rei said. With no fear, the young dragon bravely walked through the portal without hesitation. Nui Jooba swallowed hard first and then walked through. Je Danei walked through next. Before walking through, Je Leena extended her hand to Ona Drachir and they both walked through the portal together, hand in hand. Ona Noirar walked through last.

Moments later, the rescue party all emerged from the Luna Fendasse portal. They had just instantaneously and magically teleported an eight-day journey away from Tol'Tarei.

"Nui Jooba, please now touch that rune on the far left of the gate with the same bloodied hand," Dan-Rei requested. When the melf did so, the portal closed and reverted to being just a simple gate again.

"Well met, family!" called a familiar voice from a distance. Walking quickly to the Houses Nui Vent–Je Luneefa rescue group were the three House Je Luneefa brothers, and the one hundred House soldiers ordered to stand guard by the gate. After all the greetings, a bewildered Nui Jooba turned to Dan-Rei and said, "Dan-Rei, first we owe you many thanks for saving us from an eight-day walk. Thanks to you, we quickly got away from the doomed city of Tol'Tarei. Please tell us what you learned about these gates."

All eyes turned upon the young dragon. Nui Jooba moderated Dan-Rei's tale, "First, know that I am a devout student of the ancient Elvish language. Upon first arriving here at this Luna Fendasse gate, I studied the runes. These ancient Elvish runes were believed to have been created by the dark elves. However, there were other runes present that were not of dark elf origin. I believe those unfamiliar runes were created by ancient rock elves who also inhabited caves and other mountain dwellings.

"From my ancient Elvish lessons, I recalled the distinct differences and surmised that the dark elves "covered up" some of what the ancient rock elves originally wrote around the gate. The dark elves, through centuries of twisted folk lore, took credit for all the runes written.

"Given the runes pattern and symbology, I further surmised that the rock elves used these portals in ancient times of need, maybe to escape from their enemies, perhaps the dark elves. The instructions for operating the portal are also cleverly hidden in a poem's "warning" carved in stones by the portal. Certain other symbols gave clues that diachrom was the source of energy needed to provide the portal's power. Lastly, since these devices were originally built by rock elves for rock elves, logic dictated that only a rock elf's blood could activate the magical portal."

"And how did you know all of you would arrive here?" a very intrigued Je Kei inquired.

Dan-Rei replied, "Each portal has a unique identifier. By selecting the appropriate runes identifying the Luna Fendasse portal, it became the destination indicated on the Luna Eronnarsi portal, the point of origin." Still bewildered, most of the small war group remained shocked in silence. After many silent moments of sheer amazement, a long, hearty round of applause and cheers slowly erupted across the group congratulating Dan-Rei for her knowledge and excellent reasoning capabilities. Promises of delivering eight days' worth of her favorite food and luxurious scrubbings were pledged as well to the delight of the young dragon. Nui Jooba beamed with pride for his dragon. Dan-Rei humbly bowed several times to the group thanking them.

Ona Noirar got the attention of Commander Somai and asked how quickly they could start their return journey home. Ona Noirar wanted to leave the underground as soon as possible. Even after receiving additional healing magic and more attention from a House army healer, he was not feeling well. Ona Noirar was anxious to return home to see his beloved too. As expected, all the House army soldiers were more than ready to return to the surface and home. Preparations were immediately made to leave after the rescue party got some rest.

Nui Jooba joined Je Leena when she contacted Nui Honei using a magical scrying bowl. She told her aunt that the rescue mission was a success, and everyone was returning home. Nui Honei also asked her son several questions to confirm his mind was no longer being controlled. She ended the communication with tears of joy welcoming him back to his rightful family and saying, "Now hurry home, my son."

The House army soldiers' spirits were high and festive now that Nui Jooba and Dan-Rei had been successfully rescued from captivity in the Underworld and no one had died. Stories were told and re-told by the rescuers of the sights and sounds of Tol'Tarei. Details of the rescue were requested and conveyed many times too.

As Ona Drachir and Je Leena were giving their third account of their unique adventure perspectives, Dan-Rei observed that the House Je Luneefa first daughter was aloof and sullen throughout most of the evening. Dan-Rei looked at the young felf and asked if she would want to take a walk with her. Together the young dragon and Je Danei walked in silence away from the main camp of soldiers.

Dan-Rei looked at Je Danei, then closed her eyes for a few moments, and sat down so her eyes easily would meet the eyes of the standing felf. *"Fear paralyzed me after receiving my first serious wound in battle. I want you to know that I am eternally grateful for your heroic intervention after I was bashed breathless to the coliseum's sands. You surely saved my life. Thank you,"* Dan-Rei humbly confessed.

"You are most welcomed," Je Danei responded mentally. "I too was very afraid fighting such ferocious beasts that I had never encountered before. Yet, we are family Dan-Rei; it was my sacred duty to come to your aid in time of need. You know well that Houses Je Luneefa and Nui Vent stand together despite the odds as well as any fears."

"Yet after achieving victory, you are still disturbed this evening. What troubles you so?" Dan-Rei asked.

"Some old fears and doubts are returning. How do I ask Nui Jooba for his forgiveness after I repeatedly and deliberately hurt him due to my insecurities of being unsure about love and not being courageous enough to return his love? I am starting to fear I will fail again and fall victim to my fears and doubts," a tearful Je Danei confessed. "Hard training, long difficult fighting, and even killing enemies do not unsettle me. In truth, training, fighting, and killing enemies seem too easy to me at times. However, properly loving someone frightens me. I do not instinctively know what should be done or said. Somehow, my innate doubts and fears warn me that love will diminish me as a warrior."

"Maybe treat your fears and doubts like an enemy and bravely face them like you confronted those velociraptors. You undoubtedly trusted your skills, your training and your weapons. You trusted those who fought beside you. You can use that same great faith and trust to help you overcome your fears and doubts. I can even help you. Close your eyes. Place your faith and trust in me again now," Dan-Rei requested.

"What do you know of love? Why should I trust your words in this matter? Why would Jooba ever forgive me?" a doubtful Je Danei asked.

"Because I witnessed a brave felf stand against incredibly fearsome beasts. That same felf would have fought against all the House armies of Tol'Tarei to reclaim the melf whose love she thought she had lost. Reconciling one's torn heart can start simply with one's acknowledgement of fears and doubts. We all have some. Those who love us will oftentimes help make the path of reconciliation less difficult.

"Now, close your eyes and trust me," Dan-Rei insisted again. "Remember too I was celebrated this night for my exemplary reasoning skills. So, trust me, stand still and close your eyes. I need to perform some magic you should not see."

After a few more moments, the reluctant felf closed her eyes. After another few moments, Je Danei sensed another familiar presence very close and then felt some familiar strong arms embrace her from behind.

"A young, very intelligent dragon gave me good counsel this evening. She said I may need to first reach out to you to reconfirm my love for you. I too still have my fears and doubts. But my love for you is far greater than those obstacles. Have faith. Trust her and my words," Nui Jooba whispered. "Take a deep breath, turn around, and open your eyes. Dan-Rei's magic is completed."

Je Danei complied. "Will you now let me go?" she asked.

"No, I will never let you go. You captured my heart long ago and are still my *one*. Though you hurt me many times, you can also mend this same torn heart," Nui Jooba said. "Overcoming your fears and doubts may still not come easy but know that I will share my fears and doubts with you. By sharing our feelings together, I believe we can both overcome our challenges by having a far greater love for each other. So, will you be brave enough to dare to love me more than your fears and doubts?"

"How? How do I do that?" Je Danei pleaded with tears falling from her eyes.

"By being brave with me and trusting in *our* love. Together, we will overcome our fears and doubts by having and sharing love that will overcome those challenges," Nui Jooba replied. "Also, did your elders not tell you often that love would make you greater and not lessen any of your warrior's essence? Your grandmother and grandfather were very wise."

Je Danei stood there still wrapped in Nui Jooba's warm strong embrace. After continuing to deeply gaze into his eyes, she said, "Can you ever forgive me for all the hurt I caused you?"

"Yes, if you kiss me like I must again face death from ravenous velociraptors this night, Nui Jooba quickly replied.

Puzzled, Je Danei asked, "How can you so easily and quickly forgive me?"

With a bold, devilish smile, Nui Jooba replied, "Both first great mother Je Buel and great father Je Taeliel forewarned me I would have to be courageous and patient, very patient. With time and good emotional armor, I knew I would eventually win my great war for your heart.

"Also, how do you know you will beat me at our next battle training challenge? You did lose the last four contests. So, you do not know; yet you will still courageously meet me in the next challenge nonetheless will you not?"

"Release me!" Je Danei quietly ordered.

"No. You have not yet met my condition," Nui Jooba remarked, reminding her of his criteria.

"But I will gladly comply after you release me. Now you trust me and close your eyes," Je Danei said, returning an equally devilish smile.

"I have seen that look before. You duped me then," Nui Jooba said as he partially released Je Danei from his embrace. However, he was cautious remembering how she then took flight in a similar situation. Thus, he continued to hold her partially captive with just one hand. And he closed his eyes.

"You can be so annoying at times!" the felf exclaimed after some time passed. "But I do love you and want to share my love's journey with only you. You are my *one* Nui Jooba. I do not ever want to lose you nor this opportunity to become a greater warrior and have a more fulfilling future." After her declaration, Je Danei embraced the melf affectionately and kissed him like she never did before. Her kiss shook him to his core, conveying the message that she would fight any beast or anyone to save him. Her kiss foretold of her renewed love, a much stronger, committed love going forth. Her kiss conveyed her love for him would become another strength and she would not fear or doubt love and its blessings any longer.

After silently admiring the two young elves who finally reconciled and redeemed the love for each other, Dan-Rei announced, "*My work here is completed. I now go to rest. Night's blessings upon you both, my dear ones.*" The young dragon walked back to the main camp humming another tune of triumph.

A while later, Je Danei and Nui Jooba retired to the same tent where Dan-Rei was finding rest too. Overjoyed, but still cautious, Nui Jooba kept his beloved wrapped within his powerful arms, not wanting to let her go for the rest of the night.

Homecoming

The next morning, Nui Jooba awoke with Je Danei still wrapped in his arms. For several long moments, he just gazed at her, again lost in her quiet beauty – beauty that is strong, courageous, humble, intelligent, loyal, and now, finally less fearful of love. He smiled next also knowing that Je Danei's battle rage can be frightening. He chuckled to himself realizing she had indeed become stronger and more formidable since their last encounter. *"First great father Je Taeliel warned me about this feeling; I want your love now more than ever before Je Danei,"* Nui Jooba concluded.

To Nui Jooba, Je Danei was "perfect"; she embodied all that he could ever hope for in his "one true love." The melf marveled at the felf who had completely captured his heart. Again, he questioned how he, a commoner, an orphaned rogue, an uneducated "nobody" could have such good fortune. *"Had I died in the Coliseum of Tol'Tarei, I still would have considered himself having a life of mostly good fortune. Truly, miracles do happen. And again, I commit himself to cherish and love you unconditionally, fearlessly and completely all my life. Through the lessons I learned from Je Taeliel, Je Maron and Ona Noirar, I again promise to make the House Je Luneefa first daughter feel how much she is loved each day. I know I will make mistakes loving you, but I will do so fearlessly,"* he silently acknowledged again to himself.

Nui Jooba tried not to disturb his beloved; but unfortunately, he did after attempting to quietly rise. Je Danei had a tight grip on his jacket, and she immediately opened her eyes when she sensed his initial movements. She laid there beside him for a few more moments, looking into his eyes and then said, "I love you, Jooba."

The melf returned her warm smile along with a heartfelt "I love you too." Moments later after looking deeply into her eyes and removing some disheveled hair away from her lovely face, Nui Jooba whispered, "Will you now let me go?"

Je Danei said, "Why? No, I think not, especially without my escorting you. You have a way of attracting potentially harmful attention and mischief. Afterall, I must now provide greater protection for Nui Kei Dan-Rei Ryuu for she is a highly valued prize others may try to seize. She saved my life at the coliseum; so, I owe her a debt of blood. Dan-Rei, I strongly suspect, was the intended true prize those dark elves wanted; you were just a mere pawn, a very important pawn too, I might add." A few moments later, Je Danei frowned at Nui Jooba and remarked, "Why must all the young males of our Houses be the source of much trouble?"

Nui Jooba, puzzled, returned her frown and replied, "In truth, most times we do not cause trouble. It finds and overtakes us. To our credit though, my brothers, cousins and I overcame all those troubles."

"Yes, but with aid from the females of our Houses most times," Je Danei countered quickly.

"Not all the time. In fact, I helped rescue you when you were held captive by House Si Moina. Ah yes and if my memory serves me correctly, I killed many more enemies of that House than you did," Nui Jooba remarked.

Feeling challenged, Je Danei felt compelled to respond accordingly, saying, "And as I recall, I even killed more velociraptors than..." Before she could continue, Nui Jooba kissed her, not wanting to continue a banter he would most likely lose.

After some loving and playful wrestling, they finally rose. Nui Jooba and Je Danei soon learned that Ona Noirar's condition had gotten worse during the night. After another examination, it was discovered the great warrior had been cut by a poisoned blade. Commander Somai dispatched half of the advance party to return to the surface as quickly as possible. There, they could rendezvous with Ona Kei Kuri Ryuu who could fly Ona Noirar home faster in order to receive greater medical attention.

Anxious to put the Underworld behind them, everyone wanted to return to the surface, to the Aboveworld quickly; so, the return trek required only one-day's journey with the aid of some administered dragon's blood. When the advance party finally emerged from the Ararateken mountain, they all cheered. Dan-Rei immediately took flight after finally returning to *her* world. The fresh air, sun, trees, sky, grass, birds, animals, hills, and all that characterize the Aboveworld were very much welcomed sights, sounds and smells.

Keiku had already started her journey home with the injured Ona Noirar. She was able to apply more healing magic to her wounded rider before starting their journey. The great dragon expected that their return trip would only require a day's flight with the aid of her magically enhanced, greatly accelerated speed. She could also continue to radiate his damaged body with more healing magic during their flight. After flying for half the day, Keiku mentally reached out to Alleina and Nui Honei informing them that she was nearly home with the wounded Ona Noirar.

"Beloved, how are you feeling this day?" Ona Noirar mentally asked.

Nui Honei replied, "Pregnant, very pregnant and very uncomfortable. I have been studying melf anatomy with Alleina. I will impregnate you the next time and have you carry our next one for twelve long moons. That will be fair!

"Your little ones inside me are again waging war against some enemy. They need to hear their father's voice. After you land and Alleina attends to your wound, you must sing to these unborn warriors to calm them. It is very difficult for me to rest when they want to battle enemies."

"I have a request too beloved. Will you marry me this evening? I no longer wish to wait to become your husband. So, please honor me by becoming my wife today. Afterall, tomorrow is not promised to anyone," Ona Noirar asked.

Nui Honei hesitated before responding; she sensed something was wrong, very wrong with Ona Noirar. He had been wounded many times in the past and even poisoned. The great warrior had been very close to death several times in the past. Now, his tone of voice reminded her that he seemed to be near death again. *"Yes, let us no longer delay our marriage. So, we will wed this night beloved but only after you sing to our unborn, young warriors,"* she replied.

After rejoining with the main House army, Commander Somai ordered they would depart the next morning to return to Torondell. The next evening, Je Leena and Ona Drachir left the main group to return home by a different path. The battlemage offered the excuse of gathering some unique plants and herbs she needed from a market at a local village. She refused to accept an offered escort citing she and the melf could travel faster alone and should be able to rejoin the main group the night before they entered Torondell.

Je Leena and Ona Drachir did stop at a local village to purchase some medicinal herbs and plants. After leaving that village though, they had one additional stop to make before rejoining the main group. Good fortune was again upon them, for their detour required only one day's inconvenience. After resuming their ride towards Torondell, they felt confident they could easily overtake the larger, returning rescue group within a day.

As the sun was setting the next day, they could see the light from the campfires of their main group in the distance. Je Leena sat side-saddled in front of Ona Drachir. She rested there leaning against her *formally unacknowledged* beloved melf. With a rapidly pounding heart, Ona Drachir whispered, "Leena."

"Yes?" Je Leena said.

Ona Drachir continued, "I am very grateful we are both returning from another very dangerous mission, perhaps our most dangerous. By Fate, we again survived seen and unseen perils. We are indeed most fortunate."

"Indeed, mischievous fickle Fate has truly blessed us with unusually remarkable elders who willingly shared their great knowledge and skills with us, as well as relentlessly trained us all for such a terribly unusual and frightening mission," Je Leena responded. "I too am very grateful for returning alive with all my family. And I will ensure you and I celebrate our return from this successful mission for three days, like the Abaramerle. I will remind you each of those days why you should deeply and unconditionally 'love but hate this beautiful, marvelous, perfectly made felf.'" Je Leena then surprisingly kissed the melf passionately.

Now, a bit shocked from the felf's response, Ona Drachir hesitantly remarked, "You know how I feel about you. I confessed my love for you moons ago. My heart too was fully committed to you then, as well. Now again, my heart is pounding mightily within my chest because of your closeness. Using words to express my feelings does not come easily for me. Using my blades is far easier than skillfully speaking the many thoughts that are now rampantly running through my mind. Please forgive me for not using the right words to have you feel what I want you to feel now.

"Before leaving on this mission, I said we are not each other's first love. Let us no longer shackle ourselves with our pasts' insecurities nor with the recent insignificant mishaps. Instead, let us bind our futures together as each other's last love. I want you to commit your heart fully to me now and cease being insecure without just cause.

"You are the second most incredible felf I know. You never cease to amaze me. You are strong, intelligent, beautiful, brave, and evil at times too. Your many mysteries continue to fascinate me. You know you are my *one* and I could never love another in this lifetime. I know if I had been captured and taken to the Underworld, you too would overcome the dangers of that evil realm to try to save me..."

"Stop!" Je Leena abruptly interrupted his honest and sincere confession, kissing him upon his lips. "Forgive me, but I must speak now before I lose my courage. Under normal circumstances, not being the *most incredible* felf you know might offend me. But knowing our aunt *is* the most incredible felf we both know and ranking me second is truly a great honor. I am grateful. Thank you.

"And thank you again for still wanting me despite my faults, hurtful words and doubting heart. I was wrong, very wrong. Love this deep is still quite new to me. These feelings frighten me. Again, please forgive me for being so foolish.

"Yes, I know your joys and sorrows. I do love you despite your few faults. And you too are an incredible melf. You are my *one* and there will be no other in my lifetime. And I would not let anyone ever steal you away from me. I would surely kill her first."

Then with an evil smile, Je Leena continued, "And if I could not still have you, I would surely kill you beloved. You are mine only, like I am only yours! So, know full well who I am. I do have faults which I try to correct; but it will take time and patience. So, can you still truly love me knowing my shortcomings and the evil I have done and can do?"

"With all my heart, now and forever," Ona Drachir pledged solemnly. "But I still want to be much more for you..."

"Shhh," Je Leena interrupted him again, kissing him tenderly upon his lips. "More? How much more can you be? Do you truly even know what that *more* may even be? Foolish, foolish male, what have I ever said or done that made you think *I* wanted more from you? Stop setting self-imposed, unjustified obstacles before you. Surely, I have not given you reasons for your doubts and insecurities. You are now already *more* than I could ever hope for. Besides, we have the rest of our lifetimes for both of us to become more for each other."

After a few more moments gazing deeply into the melf's

eyes, Je Leena said, "Ona Drachir of House Ona Feiir, will you greatly honor me by becoming my husband? I promise you I too will become a greater *constant* like your cherished weapons."

The next day, Houses Je Luneefa and Nui Vent welcomed the triumphant return of Nui Jooba, Dan-Rei, and the rest of the rescue group. There was also much more cause for celebration. Nui Honei and Nui Noirar had married two days earlier. Nui Honei and Nui Noirar's twins had been born the night before. Both baby elves, a female and a male, were healthy and strong.

A bed-ridden Nui Honei was well too after the delivery but angry again, very angry. Between feeding her infants and sometimes resting, the felf would receive visiting family members. Her beloved family provided little comfort to the House Nui Vent great mother. Throughout the day, she continued several different tirades all mostly aimed at her gravely ill husband who bravely shared the same bedchamber with his wife.

"Husband, Nui Noirar of House Nui Vent, how can we remember you as an elite warrior if you could not vanquish a mere three House soldiers in battle? Why do you males of my House continue to defy me? I have already lost two sons; soon, I will lose you and my dearest sister too. Why must you disobey my orders? If by some miracle Alleina can heal you again, I may just kill you!

"You will not lead any more missions. The only battles you will have from hereon will only be those against me in training. I need to keep you closer to me to protect you better.

"Tell me again, how those three soldiers managed to get inside your Sun'Chi fourth defense? I still do not understand. Were you tired? Or just careless?" ranted Nui Honei.

"Sister enough! This melf, your beloved husband, the father of your miracle newborn elves is dying. Must you be so angry with him now?" Alleina asked. "You know that I will continue to do all I can till the very end, but I do not think your tirade is comforting him at all."

"Yes! He must now hear and feel my anger, despite his condition!" Nui Honei yelled back. "I still want him to hear me even after he dies! His pain too is light compared to mine.

"Husband, I carried your unborn elves for eleven moons and just delivered them. You males can never share the pain of that experience. So, do me the honor of letting you experience the wonders, the miracle, the pain of childbirth before you die. I am still a great mage. Or should I just simply ease any further *small* pain and suffering you have by just killing you myself now?" Nui Honei asked with tears falling from her eyes. "That would surely ease some of my pain."

"No, I think not beloved wife. Stay your merciful hand. Let me annoy you a short while longer, my dear Honei. Beloved wife, I want to love you and our family till I do draw my very last breath. Love me till then too. Death comes for all of us. My time finally approaches. And I do not regret that my time is before yours either," Nui Noirar managed to whisper.

He took his wife's hands in his, kissed them, and continued, "With Keiku's healing magic, I hope to evade Death's mighty grip another day; so, let us rejoice this day. We have so much to be thankful for. Now, help me join our families this evening in the hall to recount again our adventure to the Underworld." With the aid of Alleina, Nui Honei helped Nui Noirar out of his bed and dressed him for a family gathering.

In the stronghold's great hall, Houses Nui Vent and Je Luneefa family members congregated. Commander Somai and some of the rescue party's soldiers were there also. Keiku was outside in the garden by her favorite window where she could peer into the hall, as well as hear all the discussions. Her offspring were inside the hall sitting quietly together.

Beforehand, Nui Jooba privately gave the ring he had received from Aysun'Di to Nui Samu. The young melf explained, "While there in House Norkula, I recognized the unique pattern of the ring's bloodstone and realized it may be the lost heirloom of House Nui Vent you had mentioned long ago." Upon seeing his deceased wife's ring again, the House Nui Vent great father quietly wept, overcome with renewed pain of his lost cherished ones.

After Nui Noirar had been seated near the hall's fire, Nui Honei greeted everyone. She then asked Nui Jooba to start telling the first portion of the Underworld adventure. The young melf first presented more rare flowers, his mother's favorite, to Nui Honei as another peace offering. Like his stepfather, Nui Jooba had been scolded several times each day after he returned home.

With each offering and warm hug, the House Nui Vent great mother became less angry with her son. Nui Jooba again apologized for his foolish behavior and promised to be a better son. He also thanked everyone again for their rescue efforts.

Others contributed too as more of the great tale unfolded. Nui Jooba communicated Nui Kei Dan-Rei Ryuu's contributions, except for how the young dragon countered the dark felfs' failed seduction attempts. Nui Honei verbally communicated her husband's portions of the tale since he could do so mentally and not overtax his already diminished physical condition.

Je Danei offered a toast to the Houses' elders for imposing their long, rigorous training regimen and uncompromising discipline upon them all. From battle to academic, their training prepared them well for the ordeals encountered in the Underworld.

The House Je Luneefa sisters both also cited their respective roles in the rescue mission. However, Je Leena did not share all her detailed interactions with the sentient beings of the spider fang daggers nor her secret detour before rejoining the main House army returning home. Je Danei and Je Leena both pledged to their mother and Nui Honei that they both would extend more attention to their respective beloved melfs to further protect the dragons of their families.

Ona Drachir too contributed more to the great adventure by describing Tol'Tarei as well as their battles upon the sands and in the spectator stands of the famed Coliseum.

With the aid of Je Kei, Keiku mentally communicated her role in the rescue story. Je Kei first told all about the great cavern's structure and the eight gigantic pillars supporting the great cavern's ceiling. He then explained his theories and assumptions about those pillars. Afterwards, Keiku retold how she collapsed the great cavern's ceiling upon the doomed city of Tol'Tarei. The great dragon especially enjoyed citing her role. She did so with such verve and vigor to rival any bard in the kingdom.

To the House Nui Vent great mother's satisfaction, she was most pleased to hear Keiku's account of Tol'Tarei's utter destruction. The House Nui Vent great mother knew her time living amongst the dark elves had indeed influenced her... Those experiences surely enhanced Nui Honei's propensity to inflict her evil. She too learned from her own grandmother and Mother Je Buel when enemies dared to harm her family, only complete death and destruction are the most satisfactory responses and antidotes to quell one's rage.

The great dragon first recalled awakening the sleeping volcano by bringing forth several of her most devastating blue flame-balls which were hurled into the sleeping, inactive volcano. Keiku conveyed how the ground beneath the city of Tol'Tarei violently shook and broke into many pieces releasing the volcano's intense molten fury upon the city. Continuing, she cited through Je Kei, "Deadly gases spewed forth from numerous, ghastly ground's fissures and earthquakes killing the living above.

"Je Kei's recommendation of destroying certain giant pillars holding the ceiling proved to be the finale of Tol'Tarei's annihilation. After destroying the designated, three great cavern's pillars with her most destructive blue-flame fireballs, the remaining five could not adequately support all the enormous weight of the mountain above. So, the entire mountaintop imploded and crashed down upon Tol'Tarei."

Nui Honei then raised her glass, "Hail to all of you in the rescue party. I give thanks to everyone who obeyed my command not to die and returned home safely. I praise my nieces and nephew for their exemplary courage and bravery. I thank my husband too for his leadership on the successful mission and returning." Like her son, Nui Honei scolded her husband less intensity each time the great adventure was retold.

She also took the opportunity to toast everyone – praising the might and fury of Houses Nui Vent and Je Luneefa. Nui Honei also praised Dan-Rei, "All, let us also give special thanks and praise Keiku's first born. She too is a hero of this great adventure. Her courage and reasoning skills are profound." Nui Honei strongly encouraged all to make time to learn more of the ancient Elvish language. She concluded praising her sister, the great dragon, for her extraordinary and excellent representation of the House Nui Vent great mother's wrath. Nui Honei also privately again praised Keiku for achieving another "first" – crashing down an entire great mountain top! *"Well done, sister. Very well done indeed,"* Nui Honei said. More toasts were given accompanied by more congratulatory cheers.

Lastly, with the group's mood shifting and spirits raised, other happier announcements were presented. First, House great mother Nui Honei and Nui Noirar's twins, Nui Honeiku and Nui Noirarku were presented to all the family members. Both infants had been blessed by Keiku earlier that day. Keiku rejoiced with a mighty roar and flame burst too because both infants looked more like their mother and dragon aunt!

Keiku then "smiled" recalling their "mildly heated" debate, the last battle Keiku and Nui Honei would wage against their beloved Nui Noirar. That debate took place right after the birth of the twins. The battle started over the naming of the male twin.

Keiku wanted his name to be "Keihonei" which Nui Honei also liked and supported. On the other hand, Nui Noirar quickly objected citing his name should also be memorialized. The females suggested a contest and the winner selects the male twin's name. Nui Noirar declared any contest would be unfair given his present condition. More silent staring ensued and muffled grumbling. The famed warriors of Canae eventually ended their last battle after more debate and laughter. Keiku conceded reluctantly citing, a "dying father's wish should carry more weight" in the final decision.

Announcements were made of Zhen Lae and Nui Samu's engagement, as well as the engagement of Je Leena and Ona Drachir.

Pi Liu also announced that she finally realized that her life's path is to become a healer. She would officially become an apprentice of Alleina instead of going to the Rhodell Medical Academy. Even though she could receive a formal, ten-year medical education at the Academy, working directly under the world's foremost healer for the next thirty years greatly surpassed any benefits Rhodell and the Academy could offer. Besides, Pi Liu admitted she did not want to risk being far away from her beloved Je Tero for long, extended periods of time.

Plans to return to the Blood Tears Mountains for Je Annaei and Je Kei's Dwarven wedding celebration were finalized.

Nui Jooba said Dan-Rei was happy being rejoined with her brothers Ona Tae Kuri Ryuu, Je Ri Kuri Ryuu and their mother. They plan to share some needed time together too, recounting Dan-Rei's personal adventures in the Underworld. Dan-Rei had to promise to demonstrate several more times that she could now breathe fire, which caused her brothers to be in awe as well as a bit jealous.

Nui Honei thanked and toasted the group again for their successful mission.

Nui Noirar concluded the gathering with a toast giving thanks for being home and alive another day.

Inheritance

Several days later, news arrived from Rhodell that both King Rho John and Queen Rho Jiedae had died. Mysteriously, while in their sleep, the Majesties had been bitten by an extremely venomous phonelentari spider. Several old webs of the deadly tiny spiders had been found within the walls of the royal bedchambers. Prince Rho James was to now become the new king; he, not his elder brother, Prince Rho Paul, would inherit the Crown of Canae.

When the elders of House Je Luneefa received word of the king and queen's deaths, Je Pagi and Je Maron went to the sitting room where a portrait of her parents, the first elders of House Je Luneefa, hung on the wall. As they walked into the room, they saw that Je Leena was already there, staring at the portrait again, and seemingly having another personal, silent conversation with her beloved grandparents. While standing there, the elders could see tears falling from their daughter's eyes as she mouthed silent words to her grandparents' images.

The elders went to their daughter and placed supporting arms around the young felf. Je Pagi softly said, "Your grandparents would be thankful. The families of the other stolen and slain sons would be thankful too. Your father and I are also very thankful you made those truly responsible repay our family's blood debt in full." Je Leena thanked her parents for their words of comfort. With an uplifted spirit, Je Leena then dried her tears and left the sitting room still wrapped in her parents' strong, supporting arms.

Again, the youngest daughter of House Je Luneefa

demonstrated the evil nature she has; a trait that had long been nurtured by the House first great mother Je Buel. Again, Je Leena silently thanked Dilara and Dimara for sharing their secrets of how to use the deadly spiders as her angels of death...

Houses Je Luneefa, Nui Vent and Ona Feiir were all unmoved by the tragic deaths of the kingdom's royal Majesties. These Houses' elders were far too familiar with the former queen and king's treachery. These elders knew firsthand much of the evil Queen Rho Jiedae and King Rho John caused, directly or indirectly. Far greater sorrow was upon these noble Houses for Nui Noirar's health had indeed worsened after leaving the Underworld. He had been cut by a magically enhanced, poisoned blade and the poison had spread to certain vital organs slowly causing irreparable damage. At some point, those targeted organs and his noble heart would completely fail. Alleina could do no more for the great warrior. Even healing magic from the great dragon could not reverse all the damage that had already occurred. The radical treatment he needed had not been administered soon enough.

Now Nui Noirar, enduring great pain, continues to die slowly. Nui Kei Kuri Ryuu's daily application of healing magic does ease some of his pain. The miraculous magic of the great dragon still prolonged Nui Noirar's life; yet death's slow grip continued to be patient and ever relentless, killing the realm's famed dragon rider little by little.

Despite his grave situation, Nui Noirar is remarkably peaceful and happy. With the little time he had left, he first spent time with Keiku and Nui Honei retelling stories of their many adventures. Keiku reminded them too that their adventures together had been well documented in her *Chronicles*. Though the great dragon and her sister had received most of the writings' attention and praise, some words regarding Nui Noirar's feats had also been captured. Much laughter was shared too recalling their many personal contests which Nui Noirar typically lost.

Nui Noirar joyously remarked aloud, "Keiku, know too that I personally made my first and last entry in your Chronicles as well. I testified to all that you are truly perfect by any measurement. You have been one of my greatest blessings. Thank you for all that you have done for me."

Nui Noirar then said mentally as he dearly hugged his great dragon, "Honei, are you sure there is no way you could release Keiku's bond from me and rebind her to you? I know you are one of the world's renowned mages. Besides, those close to us know she really was and is your dragon. I do not wish her to die with me."

His last few words were declared with falling tears of great sorrow.

Nui Honei quietly interjected, "You know that the magic binding a dragon to its rider is unbreakable. It is one of nature and magic's steadfast laws. However, I did try already a few times because she and I look much better together! Sadly, I cannot undo one of nature and magic's greatest obligations."

"Shhh... Hush great warrior and Sister; be at peace. My fate too is sealed; that binding magic cannot ever be undone; it was so commanded very long ago. Without regret, I too will join you in death with the next sunrise after your death my beloved rider," the great dragon nobly said. "I am unafraid."

Nui Noirar and Keiku both implored Nui Honei, as their dying wish, that the House Nui Vent great mother does not mourn them too long. They reminded her that she still had much to live for; her infant twins, Nui Honeiku and Nui Noirarku, greatly needed her for many years to come. Houses Nui Vent, Je Luneefa and Ona Feiir still needed her too. Nui Jooba needed her. Her future granddaughters and grandsons will also greatly need their grandmother too.

As was the Elvish family custom, Nui Noirar spent some personal time with each family member and several important soldiers of the Houses and northern kingdom armies. After speaking with everyone, saying his last farewells, he wanted to again speak with Nui Jooba and Ona Drachir.

Joining Nui Jooba was Je Danei. Nui Noirar also requested Nui Honei and Keiku to join them. In the late afternoon, the sun's rays warmed him with their magnificent radiance. House Nui Vent great father Nui Samu, his blood-brother, had joined him this afternoon along with Zhen Lae. Nui Noirar felt very blessed to have lived a noble and meaningful life for over four centuries, to have found and loved his true *one,* the renowned Nui Honei, and to have shared most of his life with the great dragon Nui Kei Kuri Ryuu. Though he knew he would die very soon, he held only one great sorrow; otherwise, he did not regret the life he chose and lived. Not being there later for his daughter and son grieved him. Yet, his sorrow was lifted knowing his surviving family and dear close friends would care for and protect his young ones. Just as important, he also knew they would care for his grieving wife.

House Je Luneefa elders Je Pagi and Je Maron went to the House Nui Vent stronghold to meet with their dying friend and brother along with Alleina and Commander Somai. Je Jero, Je Tero and Je Kei followed their parents. The sons of House Je Luneefa were accompanied by Zhen Laehua, Pi Liu and Je Annaei. Ona

Drachir and Je Leena next joined the small group.

Lastly, Nui Kei Dan-Rei Ryuu and her brothers, Ona Tae Kuri Ryuu and Je Ri Kuri Ryuu, landed in the garden. Unlike most times, the two younger, rambunctious male dragons followed their elder siter and quietly settled near their mother.

Shortly after all invited had arrived in the House Nui Vent east garden, Nui Noirar stood, greeted everyone saying, "Dear beloved family and friends, I asked you all to congregate here so I could bestow upon you my last blessings. I feel my death will soon overtake me; so, I wanted us to all meet again in celebrating my very fortunate and wonderful life."

A large table, covered with a heavy cloth concealing various items, had also already been placed in the garden. Nui Jooba moved to stand behind this table.

With a large smile, Nui Noirar humbly acknowledged, "All, be at peace for we are all blessed immeasurably, blessed by the Houses' first elders whose love was unconditional, boundless and unwavering. They loved us more than we know. We are all also blessed to have each other. Protect the bonds holding us together tightly. Our loyalty to each other and to our Houses must remain very strong. We are also the very fortunate few who are dragon-blessed! This too is a very rare, precious, mysterious and wonderous treasure. Guard this treasure too.

"First, to my beloved *one* and wife, I leave this book of portraits to you. These portraits capture special moments of you I hold dearest," Nui Noirar announced. Nui Jooba then recovered a large tome concealed on the table and presented the large book to his mother. Nui Noirar continued, "These drawings and paintings reflect some precious memories of our time together spanning well over two centuries. The artist devoted well over five decades to recreating these precious treasures of our past. Our infants, daughters and sons of Houses Nui Vent, Je Luneefa and Ona Feiir are our present legacy, and they will memorialize our future!"

Keiku, who was sitting next to Nui Honei in the garden, peered into the large book after Nui Honei opened it and started slowly turning the pages. Nui Noirar continued, "And Keiku, please do not kill the artist for not capturing more of your likeness throughout this book. Your *perfect* image is drawn and painted only twelve different times with Nui Honei or me. So, that is quite sufficient for this tome's thirty-two pages." The vain Keiku snorted in response, a bit disappointed. Quiet laughter emanated across the small group. Nui Honei closed the tome after gazing upon the third picture and reminiscing about that ancient memory. With tears falling from her eyes, Nui Honei rose and kissed her husband while thanking him for such a thoughtful gift.

After Nui Honei sat again, Nui Noirar said, "Secondly, to my blood-brother, I leave to you my two Nimru battleaxes and two Nimru battle maces, along with two magnificent shields. Like these shields, all four battleaxes and maces are of the Zhavir design; they should sustain your being extremely formidable when wielded by such a mighty warrior as yourself. I do sincerely apologize for these particular gifts being long overdue.

"Undoubtedly, you already know much of these weapons' respective histories, but the scrolls will also detail the weapons' special capabilities as well. Your sister will bond these weapons to you."

"Indeed, you are a bit late, maybe by a hundred years! However, I still accept these very late, rare, exquisite weapons with much gratitude. Thank you," Nui Samu remarked. Nui Samu quickly received the bequeathed weapons from Nui Jooba as the frowning Nui Noirar scoffed at his blood-brother. The others laughed quietly at the jest.

Nui Noirar continued, saying "Also, I give you more shields. These particular shields mark four of the most glorious battles we waged together against enemies of Canae. Further, my brother, I bequeath you a large bag of gold also. Lastly, as I recall, you have never ridden upon the great dragon. Keiku gladly has agreed to take you and Zhen Lae on your first dragon's flight after we conclude this meeting.

"Je Pagi, Je Maron, Alleina and Commander Somai, I must thank you all for being such loyal, dear and wonderful friends. You became my beloved family too. Your on-going support through the centuries made many of our adventures successful. I could not ask or want more from anyone. I leave each of you a large bag of gold. Further, Je Pagi, Alleina and Nui Honei will each receive a small chest of jewels captured during many adventures.

"Also, I leave another large bag of gold to Je Maron to use for the on-going maintenance of the Torondell Estelridhaus, the homeless shelter and farm the House Je Luneefa first elders established.

"Commander, I leave you a spear, shield, long and short swords, and long knives all forged by Master Nimru. Commander Somai too will receive a large bag of gold to distribute equally to all the soldiers protecting Houses Nui Vent, Je Luneefa and Ona Feiir. Despite many personal challenges and hardships, their unwavering loyalty to our Houses is very much appreciated.

"Nui Samu, you will also receive another large bag of gold to distribute equally to all the soldiers of the northern army. They too have shown great loyalty to our Houses and are fine fearless warriors, dedicated to you, the realm's North and their noble duty.

"Drachir your father left his remaining wealth to me to pass on to you to help you build a House stronghold. I now pass that inheritance on to you, as well as more gold I give you to help in that glorious endeavor. Consult with Je Kei and Duenor Heartstone to review and finalize the building plans. You will now find what wealth we wanted to bequeath to you in your bedchamber. Know too my dear nephew, your father, my elder brother, would be very proud of you. You have greatly honored him and our House. Lastly, you are the last of noble House Ona Feiir and I also bequeath to you all the weapons on the east wall of my private study. Scrolls detailing the weapons' histories and special capabilities are left there as well. Your aunt will bond the appropriate weapons to you through blood-magic."

Nui Noirar then turned and looked angrily at Nui Jooba. Nui Noirar addressed the young melf with a scornful tone, "Despite the fact you and your brothers tried to kill me when we first met, despite the fact you and your brothers also tried to displace my being my beloved's *favorite*, and despite those many times you and your annoying brothers would rearrange one or two weapons on my private study's walls, I learned to cherish all those moments. Except for our first encounter, those other moments became tokens of affection you and your brothers bestowed upon me. Thank you." The dying melf's persona had shifted to esteemed joy and pride.

"By the way, whose idea was it to annoy your stepfather by moving his weapons in his private study?" a puzzled Je Maron interjected directing his question to Nui Jooba.

"Was it not Rei's idea first?" Je Pagi responded.

"Of course, it was Rei," Nui Honei sadly disclosed, assuming her youngest was quite jealous of the beloved melf who was to become her husband.

"Yes, I agree. Rei was most disappointed when he learned that he could not be his mother's favorite any longer," Je Leena said. Quiet laughter rose across the small group as they all remembered Nui Honei's overly protective, youngest son.

"Hmmm... I agree Rei may have been the *first* to actually move a weapon, but I believe it was *not* his original idea. Danei, what say you?" Je Kei asked, turning to look at his blushing sister.

"Well, I may have planted the idea..." Je Danei hesitantly and quietly confessed. "I thought it would be most amusing. I actually did not think he would dare to move any of his stepfather's prized weapons."

Nui Noirar scoffed in amazement.

"Father, I believe you now owe me a few coins!" Je Kei declared. The group all laughed heartily aloud.

Continuing, a smiling Nui Noirar next said, "Jooba, I am so very proud of you for many reasons. Your birth father, I am not. As your stepfather, I could not want more in a son of my own blood. I can honestly say 'I love you Nui Jooba.' Though you were not born of my blood, we do share a bond that may be stronger than shared family blood." With tearful eyes, the great warrior winced for a short moment, closing his eyes in acknowledgement of the pain he just experienced. "I bequeath to you all my weapons on the west wall of my private study. Scrolls detailing the weapons' histories and capabilities are left there as well. Your mother will bond the appropriate weapons to you through blood-magic. Continue to master the off-hand attacks when you wield spear and shield.

"To my dear son, nieces and nephews, I bequeath each of you a large bottle of fully blessed dragon's blood. Please come to my study later and I will release and bind your bottle of dragon's blood to you.

"Drachir and Jooba, in Keiku's secret lair, beyond the magically warded, protective wall, you will find more worldly treasures that Keiku and I accumulated. As you know, treasure means little to us, but find good uses for this wealth. It is to be shared equally after procuring armor for her offspring at the appropriate time.

"To Keiku's beloved daughter and sons, I hope these gifts serve you well. Continue to train hard with your bonded riders. Be dutiful in continuing to acquire knowledge. Learn all you can from your master, Nui Honei. Lastly, understand and joyfully accept the profound burden and great honor of being the legacy of the world's, maybe even history's, greatest and most perfect dragon!" With that last declaration, the garden resounded with a loud "Aye!" from the small crowd, as Keiku rose to her full majestic height and roared mightily. In unison, her offspring followed suit and released their own, less intimidating roars.

Afterwards, Nui Noirar remarked, "My beloved Je Luneefa nephews, I am bequeathing to each of you a diachrom infused steel shield, spear, long and short swords. These too were all forged by Master Nimru. In addition, I am giving each of you a large bag of gold. I am so proud and privileged to have helped all of you develop into fine young melfs. Your grandparents were truly proud of you and your sisters too.

"My dear, beloved Je Luneefa nieces, I have been honored to know you both most of your lives too. You too have made me so proud to observe and help you develop into such fine felfs. You brought much joy and pride to the House Je Luneefa first elders. A large bag of gold will be left for each of you too.

"Je Annaei, Pi Liu and Zhen Laehua each will also receive gold and a pair of long knives as parting gifts. The knives are also from my famed Nimru collection of the second one hundred blades he made for me. They should serve you well and further ensure the females of our Houses are always armed with fine weapons.

"Please, when you bear an infant, consider naming her or him after my brother. He too needs a legacy. Remember who ever bears him a namesake, female or male, will receive future *special privileges* from the kingdom's and perhaps the world's finest weapons master."

"Some of the sons of your Houses seem to be slower than others in their progression towards engagement," Pi Liu quickly remarked, looking disappointed.

"Agreed. Some sons require further encouragement or direction it seems," Zhen Laehua added. "Great mother and fathers of Houses Je Luneefa and Nui Vent, please further instruct all your unengaged sons and nephews; they all desperately need further guidance. Their fears, whatever they are, are not justified and..."

Je Tero quickly interjected, "Please do not say Kei should instruct us also since he is the *perfect* husband."

"Father and mother, after having me and Tero, your true *perfect* sons, why did you challenge fate by having such an *imperfect* third son who is so annoying?" Je Jero asked. Laughter rose across the small group.

"Jealousy does not look good on you Jero and Tero. Me husband be still de best me could ever hope for and want," Je Annaei announced proudly. "And he be very, very dutiful in following House great mother Je Buel's last orders too!"

"By the way, if I remember correctly, the *female elders* did first present marriage proposals. My grandmother, mother, youngest sister and even my wife all proposed to their future husbands first. So, why are you unengaged females delaying your fate? Take control! As my grandmother once said, 'Go, git yer elf!'" Je Kei declared in defense of his elder brothers.

"Yes!" exclaimed Je Pagi happily. "Take heed daughters and sons of our noble Houses, Je Maron and I want to be young grandparents; so, make haste!" More laughter erupted across the group knowing that Je Pagi and Je Maron anxiously awaited the blessed news of future granddaughters and grandsons.

"Daughters and sons of our Houses, remember that my wife and I must be prepared in the future to counter other Torondell elders' boastings about their granddaughters and grandsons. And like our Houses' first elders, Je Pagi and I will not be petty, just victorious with our glorious counterattacks!" Je Maron declared loudly, raising his glass in salute to his family. More laughter ensued from the small group.

Nui Noirar took Je Danei and Je Leena's hands and said, "Unlike Kei who is nearly a *perfect* husband, more challenges await you with your chosen, less-than-perfect melfs. The least of which will be to love my son and nephew courageously and continually despite their faults. Please be patient. Please do not let your own insecurities and fears hinder you further from fully embracing and returning love. Whether you know it or not, you are the most important essence of their strength and their wellbeing. You can help them become greater than they are now by loving them fiercely, living honorably with them and being happy, sharing your lives together. Fear nothing, for they will always be there to support you. In doing so, I believe you too will become greater. House Je Luneefa first elders Je Buel and Je Taeliel were fine examples of a most wonderful and powerful relationship."

Now looking at all his nieces, stepson, and nephews, Nui Noirar said, "My only regret is that I will not be here to help raise my young ones. I humbly request that you help your elders with that very important responsibility. Show them fine examples of an elder brother and cousins." Each young felf and melf pledged to help their elders with raising Nui Honeiku and Nui Noirarku.

Looking at Je Leena, Nui Noirar said after wincing again in pain, "My last and final request is that you consider becoming the House Ona Feiir great mother. As you know, Drachir is the last of my noble family. I do not wish to see our noble House lost through marriage since it is customary for the husband to take his wife's House name. I wish for House Ona Feiir to be rejuvenated and flourish through your marriage. Please honor your beloved and *favorite* uncle by considering his very last, *dying* request." More sorrowful tears then fell from Nui Noirar's eyes.

After embracing her uncle and hugging him tightly for a long time, Je Leena responded softly with tears falling from her eyes, "Beloved Uncle, yes of course I will most certainly give your request a great deal of thought and consideration. Your request carries much weight and is of great importance to me too." After a few more weeping moments, the felf asked amidst her sorrowful tears, "Then will you bequeath to me your black dragon short swords, long knives and daggers if I now promise to do so?"

"Ha! I told you she would want something most precious in return. And you thought that dying would hinder my clever niece from negotiating? You are still a foolish male to the end. Those tears were a ruse, just added for dramatic effect!" Nui Honei interjected.

"Brother Samu, you were right. Leena is so very much like her grandmother. I could not easily bribe Mother Je Buel either," Nui Noirar confessed. Smiling, Nui Noirar returned his attention to his niece and said, "My dear Leena, those weapons you want are yours regardless of your decision."

"And you are *not* her favorite uncle either!" Nui Samu proclaimed as more laughter rose throughout the group.

Je Leena walked up to her dying uncle, hugged him tightly again, and quietly proclaimed, "House Ona Feiir will not ever be lost!"

Je Danei, with a pouting countenance, looked at her dying uncle extending her hands hoping to get a precious heirloom too. In particular, she knew of something very special that hung on the north wall of his private study.

"Of course, my dear eldest niece, I am leaving something very special for you too. All the weapons on the north wall of my study are yours. Leena, every weapon on the south wall I leave to you," Nui Noirar said. "Your aunt will bind the appropriate blood-magic weapons to you. The designated weapons' scrolls are there too."

In his best ancient Elvish language, Nui Noirar blessed them all. "Now, Je Danei, Je Leena, Nui Jooba and Ona Drachir, please meet me in my study so all my gifted weapons can be released from me and bound to you. Afterwards, I must go and rest for a while. I hope to still cheat Death yet another day," Nui Noirar said concluding the meeting. Before leaving the garden, Nui Noirar hugged Keiku dearly, as well as Nui Kei Dan-Rei Ryuu, Ona Tae Kuri Ryuu and Je Ri Kuri Ryuu. With labored breath, he blessed all the young dragons in ancient Elvish.

After many last thanks and more warm hugs from each of the young nieces, stepson and nephews, Nui Noirar, escorted by Nui Samu, left the garden to go inside the stronghold.

Just before sundown, Nui Honei returned to the garden. Now, only Keiku and Nui Honei remain in the garden. The great dragon eventually broke the silence of their sharing the sun's last brilliant, reddish gold rays, saying, *"Dear Sister, I too must bequeath something very precious to you also. My last unhatched egg is still hidden in my lair. I feel it will be like none of my other offspring. Please protect it."*

"Of course, you know I will," Nui Honei mentally responded. "That dragon is another member of our family, and we always protect each other to the end."

Nui Honei stood affectionately close to the great dragon as she wrapped a protective wing around the felf. Tears fell from their eyes. Nui Kei Kuri Ryuu and Nui Honei, beloved sisters bonded through immense endearing love, trials of hardship, long meaningful time and many battles, returned to their sorrowful silence, still wanting to share the day's last final glory together.

The Last Chapter

House Ona Feiir family traditions were strict and dutifully remembered, embraced and administered by the House elders upon the young ones. Hence, the House daughters and sons were well-disciplined and started training to become warriors at a very early age. Most achieved the long-standing standards established by the House founders centuries ago. Some of the House Ona Feiir daughters and sons even became renowned for their exemplary skills and knowledge. A very few further glorified this noble House, throughout its history, when they became noted, awe-inspiring legends, unlike other renowned warriors. These designated warriors became known as the elite!

  As an elite warrior and dragon rider of the Canae kingdom, Nui Noirar had witnessed and accomplished much in his four-hundred years-plus lifetime. Nui Noirar, after so many battles, was now truly dying; there would be no miraculous escape this time from Death's mighty, final grip.

  Over the next few days, Nui Jooba, his stepson, and Ona Drachir, his nephew, spent most of their time now with Nui Noirar. Other family members would join them too on his walks around the stronghold. With little of life's time he had left, Nui Noirar wanted that time to be joyous. Sadness and pity were unwanted. He would sometimes just sit holding his infants amazed by such wonderful and precious blessings. Yet, he often said that his infant elves were his life's most wonderous accomplishments and he was truly thankful.

After first conveying the condition of Nui Noirar to Urtha Dal of Clan Battle Hammer, Urtha Dal immediately notified the king and queen of her realm. King Djurdin Joerson and Queen Djurdin Marta immediately gave orders to their Clan that they needed to journey to Torondell. The Clan Battle Hammer royalty and their entourage set out to honor one of the Clan's dearest friends in his dying moments. All of the Clan felt greatly indebted to the great warrior for his assistance to help save the Clan from eminent starvation long ago.

So, Nui Honei was a bit surprised to hear news from Urtha Dal the next evening. The Clan's great battlemage said that a "small" representative group of Clan Battle Hammer dwarves were coming to Torondell to see Nui Noirar and Nui Kei Kuri Ryuu, hopefully before the dragon rider and the great dragon died. In turn, Nui Honei told the Houses Nui Vent and Je Luneefa elders that about one thousand four hundred Clan Battle Hammer dwarves were enroute. All the House elders laughed upon hearing the news of such a "small" group of representatives. Nui Noirar and Keiku were both filled with joy.

Je Pagi and Je Maron immediately warned the Houses' kitchen staffs. Kaetlyn, the Clan's royal cook, would also make the journey and would want *some* control of the House kitchen. Je Pagi cheerfully laughed as old fond memories erupted in her mind of when she and Je Buel first encountered the Dwarven royal cook at Blood Tears Mountains.

With the prompt and expeditious arrival of the Clan Battle Hammer dwarves, a great feast was held for all, upon the grounds inside the Toronwalein. King Djurdin Joerson and Queen Djurdin Marta honored Nui Noirar and Keiku. The Clan's king and queen thanked them again several times for answering their Clan's desperate call for help. Heroic stories of the past battles were told and retold. Even Commander Djurdin Roerson's retelling of friendly contests also made Nui Noirar smile often.

Old Kaetlyn also shared a few stories of how she, Je Buel and Je Pagi prepared new meals with the different food received from Gelae during those most desperate times at Blood Tears Mountains. Both Nui Noirar and Djurdin Roerson had gladly volunteered to first test all their new recipes. Despite some initial indigestion, both famed warriors proudly announced later that the cooks had achieved more great victories for Clan Battle Hammer! Under the open tents, the assembly roared with laughter, remembering the culinary delights served to the then nearly starved Clan dwarves. Nui Noirar and Djurdin Roerson gave several toasts to Kaetlyn, Je

Buel and Je Pagi for their outstanding culinary wizardry of transforming some of very different Gelaetan food into new, rare Dwarven delights!

The daughters and sons of Houses Nui Vent and Je Luneefa contributed stories too that helped Nui Noirar maintain his positive mood despite the agony of his poisoned body and impending death. For the next few days, Nui Noirar's spirits remained high.

When he was not resting, Nui Noirar had many visitors keeping him company. In his final hours, Nui Noirar again sought commitments from his blood-brother to teach his daughter and son ancient Elvish martial arts, weaponry and the "old ways" of honor, chivalry and nobility. Ona Drachir and Nui Jooba pledged to be an exemplary elder brother and cousin while watching over them too. Other family members again pledged their commitments in helping to raise his infants. Even the young dragons made pledges to help too. Nui Honei, of course, committed to tell them endless stories about their father. The entire Nui Vent and Je Luneefa Houses, as well as Ona Drachir, promised to keep the memories of Nui Noirar alive in the minds of his legacies.

King Djurdin Joerson, Queen Djurdin Marta, Commander Djurdin Roerson, Urtha Dal and Duenor Heartstone pledged that his young ones would always be welcomed into their second home and family, Clan Battle Hammer. Urtha Dal too pledged to maintain a motherly watch over and care for Nui Honei. Duenor and Tradjan Heartstone even pledged to personally train Honeiku and Noirarku should either want to become an architect or engineer.

Je Pagi, Je Maron, Alleina, Commander Somai, Nui Samu and Urtha Dal also committed to watch over his beloved Nui Honei and help her to live on and not prematurely or impetuously seek her final peace...

Nui Honei seemed to remain in a very sullen mood when Nui Noirar's condition did not improve after returning from the rescue mission and receiving medical attention from Alleina. Alleina had worked tirelessly for days to counter the poison, but even after many attempts, she could not remedy her beloved brother's dire condition. The world's most renowned healer had finally confessed, with tears freely falling from her eyes, she unfortunately had no more miracles left to perform. Nui Noirar just bravely smiled upon hearing his dear sister's tearful confession and had then remarked in good spirits, "Dearest Alleina, my beloved sister, I know you tried your best and I am very grateful for your efforts. You have already performed more miracles for me than you know... Thank you."

On the other hand, at that time, Nui Honei was greatly saddened that two more, dear loved ones would proceed her in death. Though robbed many times in the past, now Death will surely take the life of the ones she loved most.

Now sensing his wife's unpleasant mood, Nui Noirar suggested she and he should take one last flight with Nui Kei Kuri Ryuu. The three comrades in arms, dearest friends and most beloved took flight together again, gloriously flying through the skies high above Torondell. No words were spoken. Unable to bear the shackles of silence and grief any longer, Nui Honei screamed mentally *"Please, let me die with you!"* As she then profusely cried, Nui Honei wailed, *"I can no longer bear this pain..."*

"How can you possibly abandon our little ones now?" Nui Noirar angrily questioned.

"Pagi would be happy to care for Honeiku and Noirarku. She would be..." Nui Honei sadly started to retort.

Keiku roared back vehemently, "No! You must live on! You now have a greater duty to all our young ones! You must live on, raise all our young ones and lead our House! I will not accept your death now; you will not receive my blessing!"

Nui Noirar added, "Nor will you receive my blessing either. Keiku and I can courageously meet our deaths knowing that you will still live to be a good mother to our young ones and a beloved leader of our Houses. There is still another yet to be born and you must protect and raise my last offspring too.! You must continue to honor us greatly through your life as the first great mother of House Nui Vent! The commitment you made long ago to being the best mother you can must be fulfilled! Keiku and I still hold you to that great, binding promise!"

Nui Honei reluctantly acquiesced, ending her plea.

Keiku concluded, "Know too Noirar and I will always love you and be with you in spirit. So, be at peace, beloved Sister."

Calming silence returned. All enjoyed the sun's western rays slowly announcing the end of the day. After the short flight, Keiku landed, returning to the House Nui Vent western garden. Nui Noirar hugged his dragon tightly again and then bid her farewell.

Moments later, Nui Honeiku and Nui Noirarku could be heard. Nui Jooba and Ona Drachir got the infants and met the infants' parents when the great dragon landed. "The little ones told me they wanted to see you and their dragon aunt too," Nui Jooba declared happily.

"So, you now speak *infant* Elvish, as well? That is good, very good. Your mother will always appreciate your help with those two," Nui Noirar jested. He looked upon his young ones again and marveled at the miracles staring back at him with their smiling faces. When Keiku and her young ones gathered around to see the infants, Nui Honeiku and Nui Noirarku continued smiling while waving their hands and kicking their feet. Both infants then started gurgling. Nui Jooba said to the dragons that the infants greeted them too.

Nui Noirar looked long at his young ones and sang a song to them. Nui Honeiku and Nui Noirarku fell asleep shortly thereafter. Nui Noirar returned his daughter and son to his nephews. Next, Nui Noirar took Nui Honei's hand. Keiku and they started walking slowly around the garden. When they stopped, Nui Noirar looked at his family members and closest friends and said, "Thank you all for the great honor of your presence here in what I feel is my last few moments of life. It has been my great privilege to know you, battle with you and achieve many of life's victories with you. My blessings be upon you all."

Nui Noirar wrapped his arms around Keiku's neck and hugged her tightly as tears fell from his eyes. Nui Noirar looked upon his wife, smiled and said, "You have made me so very happy. Thank you." Nui Noirar then sat in his favorite chair to watch the final rays of sunlight disappear slowly welcoming a new night while he softly sang his last song of praise:

> I die with the blood of enemies on my hands.
> I die knowing we were protecting our House and our lands.
> May our black dragons fly me home.
> May our ancestors welcome me home.
>
> Yes, my sons and daughters,
> May you too die with the blood of enemies on your hands.
> I know this will be your final stand.
> Die well my sons and daughters for our black dragons to carry you home.
> And for our ancestors to welcome you home.

Finally, after having a sudden revelation, he shared, "I now realize why the House Je Luneefa first elders died at peace. The wise Je Buel and Je Taeliel knew their decisions and efforts expended protecting Houses Je Luneefa and Nui Vent would remain strong after their passing. The first House Je Luneefa elders had accomplished much in their lifetimes. The great noble Houses

Je Luneefa and Nui Vent are the House first elders' lasting, monumental testaments and legacies."

Nui Noirar, Nui Honei's beloved, famed rider of history's greatest dragon Nui Kei Kuri Ryuu, and an elite warrior of the Canae kingdom finally succumbed to his grievous poisoned wound. Nui Noirar died that early evening at peace too with a smile on his face when he closed his eyes for the last time. He too knew he had accomplished much in his lifetime and his families would also continue to honor him by their living well and loving and protecting each other.

Nui Noirar was especially pleased that House Ona Feiir would again be restored, rejuvenated, and replenished. Further, House Ona Feiir will be established within the Toronwalein where it will be well protected like the House Je Luneefa and House Nui Vent strongholds.

Later that evening, a small funeral service was held for Nui Noirar in the eastern garden at the House Nui Vent stronghold. Dressed in his finest House army uniform, Nui Noirar's body was cremated by Nui Kei Kuri Ryuu's dragon flame. His ashes were gathered, placed in a special urn, and presented to Nui Honei. The elders, daughters and sons of the noble Houses Nui Vent, Je Luneefa and Ona Feiir had also joined their elders too to bid Nui Noirar and the great dragon farewell. The Clan Battle Hammer royalty and elders, as well as certain commanders and soldiers from the Houses and Canae northern armies, were there too to extend their final respects and farewell.

Outside of the stronghold upon the grounds inside the Toronwalein, a memorial service was later held with the larger, remaining contingency of the soldiers from the Houses Je Luneefa and Nui Vent, northern Canae and Clan Battle Hammer. Soon thereafter, King Djurdin Joerson and his queen started leading the dwarves in singing an ancient Dwarven song. As Urtha Dal explained to the Houses' elder and younger elves, "Our song be both a lamentation and a paean sung only to greatly honor a fallen hero. Nui Noirar and Nui Kei Kuri Ryuu be such esteemed and honored heroes of me Clan."

After the last service that evening, the elders of Houses Nui Vent, Je Luneefa and Clan Battle Hammer congregated again privately in the House Nui Vent's garden with all the dragons and the daughters and sons of Houses Nui Vent, Je Luneefa and Ona Feiir. At the request of Keiku, Nui Honei drew six large barrels of blood from the great dragon. After she fully blessed the drawn blood, Keiku bestowed a barrel as a last parting gift to Nui Honei,

Nui Samu, Alleina, Je Pagi, Je Maron and Urtha Dal. Nui Honei then cut each recipient's hand and let the recipient's blood mix with the recipient's given barrel of dragon's blood. Through a blood-magic incantation, only the recipient thereafter could call forth the full power of her/his given dragon's blood. Also, only the recipient could further release and bind her/his freely given blood to another.

When Keiku gazed upon the legacy of her family, she knew noble Houses Nui Vent, Je Luneefa and Ona Feiir would be in good hands. These noble Houses would remain strong and thrive. Keiku bowed to the Clan's royalty and blessed them as well. Keiku's ancient dragon blessing was translated by a tearful Nui Honei. Keiku next bowed first to the Houses Nui Vent, Je Luneefa and Clan Battle Hammer elders and then to the Houses' young ones. All the young ones bowed and saluted Nui Kei Kuri Ryuu paying their honor and respect.

In the very early morning before dawn, other than the dragons, only Nui Honei still remained in the stronghold's east garden capturing the last thoughts of Nui Kei Kuri Ryuu within the dragon's great tome:

> The great warrior and dragon rider, Nui Noirar formerly of House Ona Feiir, died as the second great father of House Nui Vent. He died from the wound he received in rescuing Nui Jooba and Nui Kei Dan-Rei Ryuu. Nui Noirar fought his last battle bravely and died with honor and with the blood of enemies upon his hands.

"I still have a short time before I must meet my fate with Death," Keiku said to Nui Honei. *"Promise me Sister, you will not seek your death. Promise me again now!"* Keiku's last words had been shouted with uncommon anger within the felf's mind.

Nui Honei looked at the dragon with red, desperately pleading, tears-falling eyes and slowly pledged, *"My dearest and most beloved Sister, I promise."*

Keiku relaxed her angry countenance, then remembering an old story Nui Honei shared with her long ago. Keiku remarked, *"Sister, do you remember the great Tol'Tarei seer foretold of your destiny, particularly your becoming the mother of nine little ones? With the birth of my last dragon, that great prophecy will be fulfilled! Indeed, Suphan was very skillful. From all that I have read and heard, no other felf has ever been the mother of four dragons. Beloved Sister, you will be the blessed first!"*

Now with less anger, Keiku continued, *"Live long for our*

offspring! Live long for our beloved families! Please, do not shed any more tears for Nui Noirar and me. We all must die, and my time is now upon me."

The great dragon next turned her head to gaze upon her offspring. Keiku greatly admired her daughter and sons; they were all beautiful, young, "perfect" dragons; and they would continue to honor their Houses and her with their distinguished accomplishments. The great dragon bared her deadly fangs smiling, filled with immense motherly pride.

"Young dragons, remember what Nui Noirar and I have taught you. Remember what it means to be a great dragon and my progeny. Live honorably, love fiercely, and care for each other. Remember Nui Noirar and your mother. We dearly loved you all. Now, stand before me and receive my last, final blessing." With that directive, each young dragon stood before Keiku. The mother dragon bowed her head to touch the forehead of each young dragon. As Keiku did so, she cited an ancient Elvish incantation and a soft golden light momentarily shone where their foreheads met. This act was repeated for each of the young dragons.

"Sister, as you requested, I placed your last entry into your Chronicles," Nui Honei mentally communicated quietly with tearful eyes. The House Nui Vent great mother presented the last page of the dragon's *Chronicles*. Even in the near complete darkness, both the felf and great dragon could clearly see what had been written. The magic of dragon eyes gave them the ability to see things well even in complete darkness. Keiku dipped one of her foreclaws into the container of ink and stamped her foreclaw's imprint onto the very last page of her *Chronicles*.

"So, it is now finally done," Keiku said. *"My dear little dragons, honor our legacy by chronicling your own feats. Your offspring should also know our wonderous and noble history. Lastly, honor my sister and our Houses; for Nui Honei is now your beloved mother, as well as your aunt! Never doubt; I will always be watching you!"*

Keiku turned her head towards Nui Honei and said, "Dearest Sister, I now entrust my offspring, my most beloved treasure, to you. Please take good care of them." Nui Honei stood, wrapped her arms around the great dragon's neck, and wept openly.

"My blood was the last, second-most precious gift I bestowed onto you. Please now accept my very last gift and blessing," Keiku said with great sadness. Nui Honei stood before the great dragon who bowed her head for their foreheads to touch. Keiku again cited the ancient Elvish incantation and a soft golden

light momentarily shone where their foreheads met. *"I now must go to my final resting place high atop Mountain Toron before the morning's dawn."*

The great dragon stepped backwards, looked lovingly at her family one last time, and took flight. Keiku flew high atop Mountain Toron to its highest peak. There, she looked around one last time upon the pre-dawn moon. As legend foretold, when a great dragon is about to die, the moon and sky turn red. When Keiku landed upon the mountain's peak, the rocks and even the clouds at that great height had already turned blood-red in the pre-dawn darkness welcoming the great dragon to her final peace. It was Nature's way of honoring and bidding a great dragon farewell...

After surrendering almost all of her remaining magical essence and blood to her family, Keiku's body withered. Rightfully so, she was now just a small portion of her former, magnificent "perfect" self. Her magical essence and blood were her final gifts to bestow unto those she loved most in the world. For this final honor and privilege, she was pleased.

A short while later, for the last time, her family could hear the great dragon's ferocious roar in the far distance and see Keiku's final, great burst of dragon flame. This was her final prelude, just before she kneeled to accept Death, her final peace.

Nui Kei Kuri Ryuu greeted the pre-dawn's glorious sunrays without fear or regrets. Like those dear loved ones who had died before her, she welcomed the sun with her lament of praise:

> *I die with the blood of enemies on my hands.*
> *I die knowing I protected our House and our lands.*
> *I joyfully greet the sun knowing that today is my final stand.*
> *May our black dragons fly me home.*
> *May our ancestors welcome me home.*

Death upheld nature and magic's righteous and binding commitment a dragon has with its rider - the great dragon, Nui Kei Kuri Ryuu closed her eyes for the last time.

Her young dragons began wailing loudly, and Nui Honei wept, falling to her knees. Her strong, powerful, ever-present mental bond she had with the great dragon slowly faded away. An agonizing and terrifying emptiness now replaced her ever-reassuring bond. Looking towards the East, Nui Honei, for the first time in her life, cursed the new day's sun.

The House Nui Vent great mother then prayed, "Blessings

be upon you at your final peace, my dear, beloved Sister. Be at blessed peace Nui Kei Kuri Ryuu."

A short while later, dawn's rays shone brightly through the mountain range. The heartbroken Nui Honei rose quietly and returned to the table where she had been writing. The last chapter of the world's greatest dragon's history book was now regrettably completed. Still weeping, her tears fell upon the great tome, staining Keiku's last act of consecration and remembrance. Nui Honei looked at the great dragon's claw print and reverently closed the magically sealed, *Black Dragon's Chronicles* of Nui Kei Kuri Ryuu.

Still United and Strong

Moons later, it is early Spring. Sad, mournful peace is still relentlessly clinging onto the noble Houses Je Luneefa, Nui Vent and Ona Feiir. Yet, the families of these Houses live on despite their enormous sadness.

The daughters and sons of Houses Je Luneefa, Nui Vent and Ona Feiir now met in the study of Nui Noirar to share personal memories of their honored, beloved Uncle. Though they spent the least amount of time with the House Nui Vent elder, Je Annaei, Zhen Laehua and Pi Liu also contributed their few personal memories of noted interactions with the famed warrior. Zhen Laehua and Pi Liu were especially appreciative of the warrior's great patience with them as he devoted additional personal time to their battle training. These young felfs were not warriors; yet they knew they must be ready to face unknown battles. So, they were diligent and trained hard, being very grateful for the warrior's attention.

Similar meetings had previously been held to regularly commemorate their Houses' beloved fallen Je Buel, Je Taeliel, Je Onyxia Ryoshi, Nui Danka and Nui Rei. Like their personal memorial meeting for Nui Noirar and Nui Kei Kuri Ryuu, the daughters and sons of Houses Je Luneefa, Nui Vent and Ona Feiir would congregate in the favorite rooms of the honored decease. Sometimes this group will meet in a particular House Je Luneefa sitting room or the kitchen, Je Buel and Je Taeliel's favorite places, respectively. Je Danei also tearfully shared that the kitchen had also been her panther's most loved room in their House. Other times, this group will meet in the great hall of House Nui Vent to commemorate Nui Danka and Nui Rei. Nui Jooba explained that the House hall was the single place where his and his brothers' lives had been most dramatically affected.

Je Jero had first proposed the idea of such memorial activities to his sisters, brothers and cousins and that they should meet once during each moon for the event. With the overwhelming acceptance of his proposed tribute, he further suggested that the "leader" of their memorial activities should also rotate amongst the daughters and sons of Houses Je Luneefa, Nui Vent and Ona Feiir. Je Jero emphatically told them too that he strongly "felt" his deceased elders would want them to do this so as a means to help keep the daughters and sons of Houses Je Luneefa, Nui Vent and Ona Feiir remain united and strong!

On this late afternoon, Nui Jooba concluded their commemorative activity for Nui Noirar with thanks to his stepfather, the Houses' elders and to his other family members. He reminded them too, "We all have duties and responsibilities to our esteemed fallen Houses' elders to live honorably, love fiercely, and care and protect each other." Emotionally stirred, Nui Jooba took Je Danei's hand and first left his stepfather's study.

Later that evening, like on other recent nights, Nui Jooba would just hold Je Danei in his strong arms as they both stared at the room's fire or the star-filled sky. Neither would speak much; they just enjoyed the closeness and warmth of being with each other without their previous emotional encumbrances. On some occasions, Je Danei would ask, "After all my unkindness, why did and do you choose to love me still?"

Nui Jooba would look lovingly at the felf and place her hands upon his chest above his heart. He then simply smiled and replied, "My heart will not ever beat so strongly for any other felf. You were and are still my *one*." His response was like that of the wise House elders who had confessed to their respective "ones".

Nui Kei Dan-Rei Ryuu spent a great deal of time with Je Danei too, just walking and communicating. Sometimes Nui Jooba was invited to join them; sometimes, he was not. Since escaping the Underworld, the bond between the young female dragon and felf became stronger. Their trust in each other increased as well.

On one night while the three of them were together, Nui Jooba told Je Danei of how the three dark felfs tried to seduce him on different occasions. Though thoughts of Je Danei had been magically "blocked" from his mind, he was able to concentrate on the memories he had of the three melfs he admired most and the relationship each had or has with his respective wife. Those memories gave him the strength he needed to not ever yield to the dark felfs' sexual desires. Those memories of the same three melfs were also a constant reminder that something far greater, something *more* yet awaited him beyond the dark Underworld and those three dark felfs.

Nui Jooba also confessed, "Then I did not know why my mind was so focused upon Je Taeliel, Je Maron and Ona Noirar; but I have realized that only Dan-Rei could have helped me recall those precious memories. Thank you, Dan-Rei, for protecting me when I was so emotionally distraught and vulnerable."

"Dan-Rei, I too must thank you for shielding Jooba against those dark felfs' desires. In protecting him, you also protected our noble Houses," Je Danei proclaimed profusely praising Dan-Rei as well.

Building upon their stronger relationship, the two females would even train together more often. The young female dragon was adamant about being ready to fight another velociraptor or any other such formidable beast. Dan-Rei and Je Danei would often challenge Nui Jooba, Ona Tae Kuri Ryuu and Je Ri Kuri Ryuu in battle training. Dan-Rei used these contests to remind her younger brothers that they too must be prepared to fight and fight well regardless of the enemy and their numbers. The females versus males contests were especially enjoyable – the females won most and would sometimes flaunt their victory prizes of meals or scrubbings, a *bit* more than the males.

Days later in the House Nui Vent west garden, Dan-Rei walked alone with Je Danei late in the evening. Now about half the size of her mother, Dan-Rei has become a fine, beautiful, young dragon that very much resembles her renowned mother in many ways. She still bears the scars from her battle with the velociraptors in the Tol'Tarei coliseum. Dan-Rei wears those scars as a serious reminder to herself and her younger brothers that they must be ready to always fight against any odds even to their glorious deaths. Knowing now how their older sister suffered, but fought bravely, Taeku and Riku both now listened more attentively to their Houses' elders, as well as to their "annoying" older sister. Their learning more of the ancient Elvish language had become a welcomed necessity too. Life, in general, had become a bit more serious and precious to all the young dragons.

After walking silently with Je Danei for some time, Dan-Rei mentally remarked, *"We have fought well together. You even saved my life. I will be eternally grateful to you."*

"*Yes, our enemies died by our hands and claws; we are both formidable warriors,*" Je Danei responded. They continued to walk together in silence enjoying the comfort and peace that silence brings.

"*Like our Auntie Honei, she shared the love of a great warrior, Nui Noirar, with my mother, the great dragon Nui Kei Kuri Ryuu. We too now share the love of a great warrior, Nui Jooba. My jealous feelings of you, I have no more. I have also learned to love you too Je Danei of House Je Luneefa. And now, I wish to make our bond even stronger. I wish us to become sisters, like my mother was with Nui Honei.*

"*As you well know, brothers are quite irritating and I want a female relative who has certain admirable qualities superior to most males,*" Dan-Rei declared with her dragon's "smile." Both females laughed quietly to themselves as they watched the two younger dragon brothers continue to play-fight, somewhat recklessly, around the garden. Je Jero and Je Tero were also attempting to secretly play some prank upon Nui Jooba in the distance.

Je Danei remarked, "*I too have come to love you Dan-Rei and would welcome and be honored to be your blood-sister. Thank you.*"

"*Je Danei,*" the young dragon responded. "*I will then ask our aunt to perform the blood-magic ritual to join my blood with yours.*" With that acceptance, Dan-Rei turned and faced Je Danei. Je Danei leaned forward and touched the forehead of the dragon with hers while hugging her affectionately.

Now larger and stronger, Dan-Rei and Nui Jooba would fly together. At times, Je Danei would join them. On one occasion, the three flew to the great forest not far from Torondell where Nui Jooba wanted to show Dan-Rei the place where he first saw and fell in love with Je Danei. There he shared with Dan-Rei and Je Danei his first feelings for the felf. Later, Nui Jooba caught fish from the lake and prepared their evening meal. Few words were spoken that evening, but much was said between Je Danei and Nui Jooba with their love-filled hearts, eyes, and touch.

After a long period of silence just looking at the stars in the moonless sky while wrapped in his strong embrace, Je Danei whispered, "Tonight is a very special evening; for I will mark you Nui Jooba; I will mark you very deeply. You will then be completely mine." Je Danei then kissed Nui Jooba passionately. Even after their campfire had gone out, their love was still dragon-flame ablaze, and kept them both very warm throughout the cool night under the protective wing of a mighty young dragon.

In the morning, Je Danei and Nui Jooba took flight upon Dan-Rei and returned to Keiku's former secret lair. Nui Jooba had told his most beloved females he had something he wanted to give them. It was a secret the young melf had kept from them for several moons. Now, he thought it was time to reveal his secret to them both. After flying high atop Mountain Toron where they landed at the entrance of the dragon's secret lair. They all easily passed through the magically protective walls into the Keiku's private, inner sanctum. There, Dan-Rei first heated some firestones in a pit to make her elf family members more comfortable. The young dragon then looked upon her rider with very inquisitive eyes.

Taking that cue from her sister, Je Danei impatiently then inquired of the young melf, "You first treated us to a wonderful evening meal you prepared and then you wanted us all to come here this morning. Why? Do you have more presents you wish to give us? Or are you seeking our forgiveness for some wrong you have committed? Speak quickly," Je Danei impatiently demanded.

"We both promise to still love you regardless of your answer. However, you may not leave here unscathed," Dan-Rei quickly warned.

Je Danei quickly added, "That may be true if you have fallen again under the magical spell of any other felf. You have been warned many times to be more careful. Dan-Rei is now my precious sister and must be protected too. Lastly, if both of us are not pleased, we both will punish you." The felf remarked menacingly her last words with a cold, flat matter-of-fact tone. And, as if by magic, two exquisite Nimru long knives suddenly appeared in her hands.

"Yes, yes, I know. You two now have this unbreakable bond between yourselves and stand united. Like before with Nui Honei and Nui Kei Kuri Ryuu who battled against Nui Noirar, you two now will wage battles against me. This I know, accept, and gladly welcome the many challenges I have yet to encounter. You two, like Nui Honei and Nui Kei Kuri Ryuu, will plot against me and even bend contest rules. But I know you both will still love me unconditionally; so, I will persevere through all your annoyances. Afterall, I have the support of my grandfather and grandmother, the first great House Je Luneefa elders, Je Buel and Je Taeliel. They both had blessed me with their love, support and wisdom. Hence, I too will continue to be strong and love you both unconditionally till I draw my last breath," responded Nui Jooba. He was now accustomed to the felf's "threats," now understanding it was one of her ways to display sincere affection for him.

"As you have already guessed, I do have special gifts for you both," the young melf continued. "First, walk with me to the far side of the lair." Upon reaching the destination, Nui Jooba cited an incantation and four large boulders transformed into meticulously carved images of the great dragon Nui Kei Kuri Ryuu. The details were exquisitely accurate, being scrutinized repeatedly and approved by the most discerning Nui Honei. The images captured the mighty dragon standing upon her rear legs with wings spread apart. Keiku's image is ferocious looking, displaying her frightening deadly fangs and foreclaws. Yet, the great dragon's likeness was captured in all her "perfect" majesty.

For several long moments, young Dan-Rei stared at the identical images as she slowly walked around each black steel statue. Though all the statutes, standing eight fahs in height, were a fraction of the size her mother, they were all "perfect." After her silent scrutiny of the statues, Dan-Rei looked at Nui Jooba and bared her fangs after she bowed to her bonded rider. *"Thank you. These are very precious gifts to me and my brothers. We will now have constant reminders of our mother's esteemed presence. She will always be fondly remembered, and we will pay sacred homage to our mother as long as we live. Thank you again,"* Dan-Rei said.

"You are most welcome Dan-Rei," Nui Jooba remarked. "The second and third statues will be moved and placed in the great halls of House Nui Vent and House Je Luneefa. There, the statue will become another guardian of our Houses. The fourth statue will be moved into House Ona Feiir when completed. The first will remain here in remembrance.

"I do have one more gift for you too." On a nearby table, another gift was magically hidden. Nui Jooba cited another incantation and an invisibly veiled, large tome appeared. "This tome, like your grandmother and mother's, is to become your *Chronicles* for capturing your adventures, feats and history. I suspect you will want to continue that family tradition your dear grandmother started."

"I will also cherish this great book as well. Again, thank you dear warrior," Dan-Rei said. The young dragon next looked at Je Danei with high hopes.

"Yes, of course, I will be your dutiful scribe to capture your thoughts, should you desire. As your sister, I will ensure too all your significant accomplishments and greatness are properly and accurately recorded," Je Danei said, smiling at Dan-Rei. Nui Jooba scoffed at his beloved females while slowly shaking his head with a dejected countenance.

"*Thank you, dear Sister. It is an honor to have you fulfill that duty,*" Dan-Rei said joyfully. "*Later today, we shall begin chronicling my life and our journey to the Underworld.*"

Je Danei replied, "As you wish, dear Sister." Turning to Nui Jooba, she asked, "And what will you be doing while Dan-Rei and I are working?"

Nui Jooba replied, "Perhaps exploring this cave or just observing you." From the same table, Nui Jooba uncovered a box and presented it to Je Danei saying, "Beloved, I wish to gift you something very special as well. Behold, our *Chronicles*." The felf opened the box and found inside a diachrom bracelet holding three small bloodstones. "The larger, center stone represents me. On the left is your stone and the right stone represents Dan-Rei. In time, more stones will be added."

"And why will there be a need to add more stones to this already beautiful and magnificently crafted bracelet?" Je Danei asked quietly after she removed the bracelet from the box for her close inspection. She smiled after a few moments, very pleased with her gift.

"One stone will be added for each of our little ones we will have in the future..." Nui Jooba replied. And before he could say anything further, Je Danei pulled him close and kissed him deeply.

The next morning, Nui Jooba rose from his deep sleep and walked to the entrance of the dragon's lair. As the sun's rays announced the wonderful new day, the blustering winds howled loudly, welcoming a new day. Nui Jooba raised his arms, took a deep breath and released a mighty battle roar. Feeling very blessed, he too wanted to announce his thankfulness for being loved by two mighty females. His resulting smile rivaled the vast mountain range he thought.

"*Sister, was that supposed to be a mighty roar? I thought it was quite harmless and not intimidating at all. You?*" Dan-Rei asked as she and the felf silently joined Nui Jooba at the cave's entrance.

"I too was not impressed by this great warrior. Surely, he needs much more practice," Je Danei added. "But I also crave more of you," she whispered, biting his ear as well as wrapping herself around the melf. "Now!"

A moon later, the House Je Luneefa family, Nui Jooba and Ona Drachir journeyed to the Blood Tears Mountains along with a House army escort. There, Je Annaei and Je Kei finally were to celebrate their Dwarven wedding celebration which is a glorious two-day event. Je Annaei, a woods elf, is the adopted granddaughter of the Clan's first great mother Urtha Dal. The Clan's renowned battlemage and Commander Djurdin Roerson represented the bride's family in their participation in the marital ceremony. Je Pagi and Je Maron performed similar duties in representing the husband's families. King Djurdin Joerson and Queen Djurdin Marta presided over the wedding event. All of Clan Battle Hammer and many others of the Mountains clans' dwarves attended the joyous event along with the party from Houses Je Luneefa, Nui Vent and Ona Feiir.

All the clans residing at the Blood Tears Mountains stronghold "claimed" to be related directly or indirectly. The clan and family connection "details" were vigorously argued and debated oftentimes, especially in times of wedding celebrations. By Dwarven social standards, all "family" members required no special invitation and are "informally" invited to weddings. This social standard can make celebration planning arduous, given the "unknown" number of guests who might attend.

So, Je Annaei and Je Kei had well over six thousand Dwarven "family members" attend their wedding. Less than one hundred honored guests from Torondell, including three young dragons, also attended their wedding celebration.

House Nui Vent great mother Nui Honei could not travel to the celebration given the recent birth of her twins. Alleina, Zhen Laehua and Pi Liu all remained in Torondell to help Nui Honei with the care of her infants. Nui Samu also remained in Torondell to manage certain important Warden duties, as well as, to aid in his sister's recovery and care for his new niece and nephew. Though not at the celebration physically, they all attended in "spirit" through scrying sessions with Urtha Dal and others.

Urtha Dal would also privately scry daily with Nui Honei. At the first magical, scrying communication session, Urtha Dal said privately, "Honei, ye know Bueli and me be not only blood-sisters, we be more like real family. Ye be part of dat family too. She loved ye like ye were her own blood daughter. So, me be yer Auntie now cause me love ye too! If ye ever be needin' anythin', just let me know."

Both elders recalled and exchanged memories of the House Je Luneefa first great mother. Both cried and laughed, especially over those incidents when the elder females won wagers against the male elders. Afterwards, Urtha Dal informed Nui Honei of all the day's important activities, news, and upcoming bets to be won!

Since Prince Dajald and Moira were to marry in the Fall, Nui Honei promised to attend their wedding celebration and collect her winnings from the king personally then. It seemed Urtha Dal continued to make wagers with the king even on House Je Luneefa and House Nui Vent great mothers' behalf.

When the refreshments were served at their first evening meal in the Dwarven stronghold, the Houses Je Luneefa, Nui Vent and Ona Feiir party heard many stories about Je Buel and Je Pagi's excellent trail cooking. These memories were still fresh in many of the Dwarven soldiers', now extended family, minds. The House Je Luneefa mothers' cooking reputations had also been elevated to "legendary" status even before any ale or brandy had been drunk. Even some highly contested arguments ensued that led to a few friendly fights over the House Je Luneefa great mothers' cooking skills. Stories were told and then retold to such lofty heights that the House Je Luneefa second great mother gladly accepted the cooking bribe by Jaso Ironfist who presented her with a whole small garden's worth of her favorite mountain flowers. Fortunately, the House Je Luneefa party had planned well and arrived three days early before Je Annaei and Je Kei's wedding celebration event. House Je Luneefa great mother Je Pagi gladly helped cook for all the wedding guests.

As with most wedding celebrations, some issues did arise and required immediate attention and quiet, discreet resolution. After first arriving at the Blood Tears Mountains stronghold, the House Je Luneefa great father requested that the eight wagons of their highly special and confidential cargo should be placed under immediate royal protection and guarded both day and night.

Later that same afternoon, when the females of House Je Luneefa left to meet privately with Queen Marta, Urtha Dal and Moira, Je Maron and his sons and nephews met privately with King Djurdin Joerson, Commander Djurdin Roerson, Prince Dajald and Duenor Heartstone. The males all met in the king's third, secret private sitting room where Je Maron wanted to share a "family" secret with the king.

After introducing his other sons, Nui Jooba and Ona Drachir, Je Maron shared a "secret" with the Dwarven royalty. Je Maron declared brazenly, "Through hearty determination and skillful negotiations, I procured, unbeknownst to my dear wife, the entire season's first batch of Napa brandy, the kingdom's most renowned drink. The entire lot of the brandy has been safely brought here to the wedding celebration to share with all the guests."

"Many throughout Canae will not be pleased!" Je Kei announced. "But Mother will be pleased, I assure you, despite the great cost." Turning to the Dwarven king, Je Kei happily declared, "Me king, dis first batch amounts to eight entire wagons' load of de fine precious liquor!"

Upon hearing this family secret, King Djurdin Joerson was overjoyed and immediately issued orders to his Guard Commander, waiting outside of the room. The king opened the room's heavy doors and commanded, "Double de guards now be watchin' de Torondell wagons and be especially alert fer possible 'royal' dieves!"

Djurdin Roerson quickly added, "Triple de guards be better, me dink. Dali's stash be very low now."

"Broder, ye be right! Guard Commander, triple de guards!" the king ordered, smiling joyfully.

Four cases or twenty-four bottles had been secretly brought to the king's sitting room for his Majesty's first "royal inspection." Just after the first case of liquor had been opened, Je Maron immediately replenished the king's cape with four bottles of brandy. Like the House Je Luneefa capes, the king's gifted cape had secret compartments in which precious items could be magically compacted and concealed.

Shortly afterwards, the guarded doors to the king's third private sitting room burst opened. Standing at the room's entrance was Queen Marta, Urtha Dal, Je Pagi, the daughters of House Je Luneefa, and Moira. Queen Marta first walked in and appeared perturbed. "Me king, brother-in-law, prince, Duenor and royal guests, well met and welcome again," she said as she walked into the room followed by her female entourage. "What ye be celebratin'? And why ye be hidin' so far away from us?"

"Oh me lovely queen, ye still amaze me after four hundred years!" King Joerson said, greeting his wife.

"Hah! Ye be caught hidin' somedin'; so, please do not deny it," Queen Marta charged enthusiastically.

"Me queen, if me can..." Roerson started to say.

"Silence, Commander! No, ye may not speak. Ye always be tryin' to protect yer broder! Instead, me want dat most handsome melf over dere, me new dird cousin to now explain," commanded the queen pointing to the third son of House Je Luneefa.

Without any hesitation, Je Kei proudly stepped forward, bowed, and addressed the queen with his honest, innocent and disarming smile, "Me queen and highly honored elder of me Clan Battle Hammer, we be seekin' de king's private counsel on a very special matter of great importance. Dis time be so very special and not just fer me weddin' celebration. We be wantin' de king's counsel on de gifts we bear fer ye, yer Majesty!"

"Hmmm... Gifts fer me? Really? Please continue and stop yer smilin'; me know yer tricks. Yer handsome smile be not workin' on me," a scowling Queen Marta declared.

Now smiling a bit less, a disappointed Je Kei continued, "Me Queen, many years ago dis day bein' about de time when den warrior Djurdin Joerson of Clan Battle Hammer first went off to save ye and de oder members of de Clan from dose thievin' and maraudin' Clan Adanrock dwarves. Ye and de king be our beloved family elders too. So, we be wantin' to celebrate dat time for his courage and bravery fer fightin' fer his *one* and beloved future wife and queen.

"So, me family wanted to honor ye and de king wid some special gifts. First, me want ye to know me precious wife, Je Annaei be pregnant wid our first elf. Our Clan be growin'! Ye, be de first here to know!"

"Second! Me be de first even widout yer tellin' me!" declared Urtha Dal, the renowned battlemage and Je Annaei's adopting grandmother. An overjoyed Je Annaei, who could finally share her secret, first hugged the queen affectionately and then all the other females.

When Je Annaei, with open arms and a big smile, went to hug her male family members, Queen Marta stopped her saying, "No! No hugs yet fer me king and de oder males till me hear more explanation."

Je Jero quickly stepped forward next and retrieved a present hidden inside his cape. "Queen Marta, as the eldest sons of House Je Luneefa, Je Tero and I would like to present you with bottles of precious dragon's blood. My aunt, Nui Honei, bonded this bottle to me and Auntie Urtha Dal can release it and bond it to you," Je Jero said after bowing and greeting the queen with his handsome smile. Similarly, Je Tero, the House Je Luneefa second son, presented Queen Marta with another bottle of dragon's blood taken from inside his magical House cape.

The queen looked at her husband and remarked, "Hah! Me dink ye got some more very good allies here to help ye out of a tough spot. Dey all be quick and smooth wid dere gift givin' too." Looking carefully at all the young House Je Luneefa sons there, the queen declared, "And Anni, ye still got *de* best-lookin' House Je Luneefa son too!" All the other females quietly laughed as Je Jero looked disappointed.

"Queen Marta, second great House mother of Clan Battle

Hammer, I am Ona Drachir. As the nephew of Nui Honei, Nui Noirar, Nui Samu, Je Pagi and Je Maron, I would like to gift you and King Joerson with a dragon's flight. My dragon, Ona Tae Kuri Ryuu, is the son of the great Ona Kei Kuri Ryuu and we want to also honor you and the king. As I recall the story, you two could not see the night's stars when you were rescued. Even without their guidance to lead you back home, King Joerson never lost his way. So, tonight, you can fly above the clouds for you to closely greet and witness the wonders of the stars that fill the night's sky," Ona Drachir presented after bowing to the queen.

First bowing to the queen, Nui Jooba quickly presented next, "My queen, well met. I am Nui Jooba, the second son of Nui Honei and Nui Noirar and nephew of Nui Samu and the House Je Luneefa elders. I too would like to also gift you a special meal prepared by my own hands. I learned how to prepare some of your favorite dishes from House first great mother Je Buel. She told me how the king prepared that first meal for you after your rescue. So, I will prepare that same memorial evening meal for you and the king tonight."

At this point, the queen was no longer upset with her husband and the House Je Luneefa great father. Queen Marta then looked at Je Maron with great anticipation. She inquired, "So Je Maron, great fader of House Je Luneefa, me see some bottles of brandy be missin' from dat case. Me guess ye personally be givin' me king dose four bottles fer his cape. What ye have to say now?" the queen asked.

"First, I do wish to sincerely apologize for any possible misunderstanding. Secondly, I too bear gifts for you and Urtha Dal," Je Maron replied quickly after his royal greeting. The House Je Luneefa great father then pulled a bouquet of rare, red flowers from his magical House cape and presented the flowers to the queen. Je Maron then said, "I believe the king gave you one of these rare roses after your rescue and safe return to your family and Clan. His love for you continues to burn brightly and true still. We all wanted to honor you for being the essence of his inner strength. You both, like my House first elders, are amazing inspiration to us all." Glasses were then expeditiously handed to the females by Je Kei and Je Tero. Je Jero then followed quickly pouring brandy to all the females, except Je Annaei who graciously accepted water instead. All the males then immediately raised their glasses and toasted the queen, "Hail, Queen Marta!"

Next, Je Maron quickly gave Urtha Dal her "payment" of six bottles of brandy for her invaluable assistance with the Nui Jooba and Nui Kei Dan-Rei Ryuu's rescue efforts, along with many thanks. As more brandy was being poured, and toasts given, Urtha Dal, a very wise elder and elite battlemage, quickly removed her payment of brandy from everyone's sight lest they fall victim to more celebratory toasts. She simply explained as she magically made her six bottles of brandy disappear, "Mine!" Laughter erupted in response.

The queen, now beaming with a huge smile, shouted, "Silence. Je Kei of Clan Battle Hammer, come forward." The young melf did as commanded. "Anni said on many occasions 'ye be clever, real clever.' Dough me know ye and yer kin be here secretly *inspectin'* de brandy wid me king, me be not angry fer yer not invitin' us females to join yer first inspection. Dough dat be not proper manners fer excludin' us. But yer gifts and de recalling old, treasured memories of de king's time courtin' me made me very happy. So, dank ye, dank ye all."

Looking at Je Maron, Queen Marta then sternly announced, "Me too want an equal share of brandy like de king received as a personal, royal gift." She then scolded the House Je Luneefa great father, citing that favoritism is not fair nor favorable in maintaining good family relationships. She even threatened that Je Kei could be expeditiously expelled from her clan for such a slight.

Smiling, Je Kei approached the queen and again sincerely apologized to her and to the other females. After a brief private conversation with the queen, he quickly left the gathering to run a royal errand to rectify his family's "misunderstanding." After a short while, Je Kei returned and privately reported to the queen he had been successful on his "royal mission." So, the newest member of Clan Battle Hammer had promptly followed a royal order without questions and secretly helped eighteen bottles of the newly arrived Napa brandy abscond their way into a secret hiding place in Queen Marta's third private sitting room. The queen of course greatly appreciated that the newest Clan Battle Hammer member promptly and successfully obeyed her orders and proved he was also adept in thievery without getting caught. Lastly and most importantly, Queen Marta also privately complimented Je Kei too for demonstrating his exemplary mathematical skills of "properly" calculating her personal, "equal share" of the famous, exquisite Napa brandy. Queen Marta now returned the young melf's big smile and thought, *"Yes, Je Kei be very, very clever indeed! Oh Bueli and Taeli, we do love yer family very much!"*

Queen Marta was thereafter very pleased and encouraged the males to continue with their private gathering while she led the females to her private sitting room where they would take the last case of Napa brandy there and privately "inspect" it themselves.

After the females had all left, King Joerson refilled the glasses of all his guests and declared, "Me new dear family, dank ye. Ye be savin' me from an unpleasant situation wid me queen. Dank ye all."

"And Kei be clever me sure when he left, secretly takin' and stashin' away some bottles of brandy just fer de Queen. Me right?" Duenor Heartstone inquired. "Me king, dose bottles be helpin' ye later too, I wager."

"And me reckon her required 'fair share' be more dan four bottles too!" Djurdin Roerson declared, laughing heartily. "Me sure Kei also wanted ye Broder to have no more squabbles; so, he stashed away at least eight bottles of brandy fer de queen! Me right?"

"Oh! Dat be clever, very clever!" King Joerson remarked, smiling while rubbing his hands. "Ye definitely be savin' me. Dank ye all!"

"Bah! We are all allies in our battles against the females of our Houses. Your battle is our battle too. Our Houses stand with Clan Battle Hammer, and we all stand united!" declared Je Maron.

"Aye!" roared the males in triumphant response.

"How did ye know 'bout me early courtin' time wid me queen?" a puzzled King Joerson asked the youngest House Je Luneefa son after the vocal fanfare finally subsided.

"Broder, me told Kei dat story long, long ago too. He be usin' it today very cleverly," Roerson acknowledged.

"Ah, me king. Me knew dose females would find us. Grandmoder Dali be a great mage, and she be havin' an ever-present *watch* over ye and Queen Marta. Me broders and cousins battle our Houses' females on a regular basis; so, we be accustomed to supportin' each oder at a moment's notice. Befer we left home, me told dem to be prepared to present gifts should we be needin' dem. So, we be ready! Our broderhood must remain strong and united! And ye be our family and in our broderhood too; so, we had to help ye," Je Kei explained.

An amazed King Joerson raised his glass and declared loudly, "Me will say it again, ye be kinfolk word havin'! Dank ye all!"

Again, all the males responded with a thunderous "Aye!"

On the day before the Houses Nui Vent and Je Luneefa party was to return home, Je Leena thanked Urtha Dal again for all her past mentoring and pledged to return in the Fall to learn more magic directly from her. Je Leena knew there, at Blood Tears Mountains, was a great library. In particular, there are old tomes there of the ancient Elvish language which was essential to study and learn in order to invoke certain magic.

Je Danei and Je Leena spent some time in that great Dwarven library which had been a place of refuge for their grandmother long ago. Je Buel had told her granddaughters and grandsons that she had spent much time in the great Dwarven library studying, as well as exploring the vast treasury of precious scrolls and tomes. Urtha Dal even shared with the House Je Luneefa daughters the secret hiding place of hers and their grandmother. There, the battlemages and blood-sisters would find some peace from the madness of the world's chaos.

Je Kei also spent some private time with his mentor Duenor Heartstone and shared some possibly important observations he had made while in the Underworld. Much of their discussions were centered around the two gates/portals the rescue party encountered and used. The renowned dwarf engineer and architect was both very puzzled and intrigued with the idea of further exploring other mountains that might contain similar gates/portals.

Je Kei and Ona Drachir also reviewed the initial plans for the House Ona Feiir stronghold with Duenor Heartstone. The necessary Dwarven resources were also finalized and committed. Heartstone lastly committed to visiting Torondell, along with Tradjan, several times to review the progress of the construction.

On that evening, Queen Marta and King Joerson privately presented Je Pagi and Je Maron with two bags of gold. The gold was payment for the next two years' first batches of Napa brandy, if not the entire vineyard. "Joeri, ye know me be just jokin' when we arrived here and gave ye dat brandy first fer yer royal inspection. Me be dinkin' dat me should just buy dat dern vineyard and save some coin in de long time," Je Maron had confessed to King Joerson late the first night while sitting in the king's first private sitting room with his entire family and the royal hosts. By then, four additional bottles of brandy had been thoroughly "inspected" after dinner to ensure the brandy was still of the highest quality and deserving of the highest praise.

"Me know Mari, me know; but dat be a very good idea. Dali and Marti heard ye and dought so too; so, now ye got partners!" With all the laughter that soon followed, somehow a deal was struck to everyone's satisfaction. The king then whispered privately to Je Maron, "Besides ye, yer sons and nephews rescued me from possible big trouble wid me Queen dat day. Me be very grateful."

Days later after returning safely home to Torondell, Nui Honei welcomed her family with food and drink. In the House Nui

Vent stronghold's eastern garden, tables had been placed there and upon these tables were a variety of fresh fruits, cheeses, and baked goods. Different wines were there too, highlighting the season's best varieties. The female elders of Houses Je Luneefa and Nui Vent decided to meet there on a regular basis now that the weather was warm and pleasant. House great mothers Je Pagi and Nui Honei were there along with Alleina. Zhen Lae joined them too along with all the daughters and soon to-be daughters of House Je Luneefa.

"Honei, please do not wait for the others. You need not be so courteous; eat if you are hungry." Alleina encouraged after spying that Nui Honei was again personally "inspecting" all the delicious food. "Your young ones will soon be awake, and they will want to nurse again."

"Those two seem to be hungry all the time when they are not sleeping," Nui Honei said. "They can be so tiring. Having dragon's blood running through their veins may account for that. Despite their dragon-like appetite, Honeiku and Noirarku are truly blessings and their mother's joy."

"Do let me know when they wake up. I will be happy to go and get them for you," Je Pagi gladly offered.

"After raising five infants of your own, you still never tire of wanting to hold, helping me feed, or caring for my infants. Bless you sister for wanting to be so involved. I appreciate your help more than you know. Again, thank you," Nui Honei said so very gratefully.

"Dear Sister, don't thank me. If our mother was here, you might have had to relinquish care to her. She absolutely would oversee all the infant care activities to absolutely *ensure* they were performed properly. Even by the time Leena was born, you would think I would have mastered how to properly care for my infants; but Mother was still very involved even then. Yes, she was a great nuisance at times, but a very loving one.

"Oh, how she loved presenting her granddaughters and grandsons to the grandmothers of the other Torondell noble Houses. House first elder Je Buel was extremely proud of all her granddaughters and grandsons. Father and mother were truly wise; our granddaughters and grandsons, their daughters and sons and so on are wonderful blessings and bring much joy to our hearts and Houses. I do love young ones and want all of our daughters and sons to bless us, the House elders, with many more infants," Je Pagi said.

Alleina proclaimed, "Yes, I agree too. That would be welcome blessings. As you know, the Rhodell Academy continues to want me to relocate there to teach at the Academy's medical school. Ha! I shall not do that regardless of their many generous bribes. So, having to oversee the medical attention of our nieces and deliver more infants here, as well as overseeing the medical requirements of the Houses' elders, continue to require my personal attention, unique expertise and commitment to stay in Torondell!"

"Aye Sister! For at least another two to three hundred years, maybe even four hundred years," Je Pagi said reflecting her parents' protective natures not to ever let Rhodell break their families apart.

"Besides, I am sure Rhodell is very interested in knowing more about our two dragon-blood little ones," Nui Honei added.

"Yes, of course," Je Pagi concurred. "Rhodell still fears our great Houses and our dragons. House Rho still secretly cowers in fear that our Houses are greater than their royal House. Pray we never have to go there, or they come here."

Nui Honei smiled evilly, thinking, "And should House Rho ever declare war against our united Houses, all within that heinous family will be mercilessly killed by my hand and my angels of death..."

"Look, Nui Kei Dan-Rei Ryuu and her brothers, Ona Tae Kuri Ryuu and Je Ri Kuri Ryuu, will be joining us soon," Alleina observed. High above in the sky, three young dragons could be seen flying toward the House Nui Vent stronghold. Dan-Rei too wanted to take advantage of opportunities to spend more, non-training time with her Houses' elders. With the death of her mother, Dan-Rei also wanted to continue her dragon education from Nui Honei, her mother's closest living friend.

Since the dragons and House elders all shared Nui Kei Kuri Ryuu's blood, they could still enjoy mental communications amongst themselves. After the dragons landed, they all went to the House elders, bowed, and greeted them. Dan-Rei thereafter quickly shooed her brothers away telling them that only females could participate in their upcoming meeting. Gladly, her brothers left to enjoy haunches of deer meat that had been left for them on the far side of the garden.

Nui Jooba emerged from the House stronghold to enter the garden. Upon seeing his elders, he walked toward them smiling. The melf first greeted his mother, the other House elders and then the other young females gathered there. Lastly, he greeted Je Danei with a bigger smile. In response, this felf pulled him very close and kissed him. "Would any of you like any additional food or drink?" Nui Jooba asked after recovering from his beloved's surprising public behavior.

"No, thank you. Please just leave now. We need privacy to discuss a new House matter that greatly concerns us," Je Leena quickly said after witnessing her older sister's audacious public response to Nui Jooba's "smile."

Not at all annoyed with his inelegant, mildly rude dismissal, Nui Jooba departed from the company of the females to join his uncles and cousins who had congregated at the other end of the garden.

"Jooba has been in extraordinarily good spirits lately. Maybe escaping from the Underworld greatly lifted his spirits finally perhaps?" Alleina offered.

"No, I think not. Unless one, very special felf had something to do directly with *uplifting his spirits*. What say you Danei?" Zhen Lae asked.

Now, all the females turned and looked directly at Je Danei who was caught smiling as she gazed lustfully at the departing Nui Jooba.

"Sister, what ye be dinkin' right now?" Je Annaei asked.

"Yes, what *are* you thinking about right now?" Pi Liu also asked.

"Any secrets you want to share with us?" Zhen Laehua quietly asked.

"Danei, I have also observed that my son has been smiling much more lately. Why is that?" Nui Honei probed.

"I believe his change in mood coincided with my unleashing my recently discovered *female powers*," a more mature and confident Je Danei proudly announced. "Those long-hidden mysteries are slowly unfolding before me."

"And from what I could surmise, you unleashed those powers several times quite well last night and again, a few moments ago. Well done, sister. Well done," Je Leena quipped. Laughter erupted around the table; except Je Danei remained silent momentarily, captured by thoughts of her wonderful experiences last night.

"Leena please, don't embarrass your sister further," Je Pagi urged when she noticed Je Danei blushing. "Finally, this day has arrived when my eldest daughter is confident enough to embrace and acknowledge her female powers. Daughter, you still have yet to discover fully how wonderfully exciting and mighty you can be. More mysteries will unfold in time. You too will become greater. So, beware Nui Jooba. Beware."

Je Danei smiled again and recalled a certain memory of the Underworld she now cherishes. She told her House elders and sisters of the dark elf warrior-songstress, Aliyya, she had encountered and the song she sang:

> Know your wonders; embrace your powers.
> Know her pleasures; delight her body and mind.
> Master your treasures; know your wonders.
> Discover all her pleasures; deeply love her body and mind.
> Be forewarned, escape her loving, deadly embrace.
>
> She is filled with mysteries unknown.
> She is the epitome of evils untold.
> She's grace, beauty, and hell's fury embodied.
> Beware not to lose your heart to a dark felf.
> Beware not to yield your mind to a dark felf.
>
> She is the favored daughter of Valdearaneida
> Her sultry evil ways have no bounds.
> Once embraced, there is only one escape.
> Beware not to lose your heart to a dark felf.
> Love but hate the beautiful, marvelous, perfectly made dark felf.
>
> Know your mysteries; know your rage.
> Learn her mysteries; fear her rage.
> Love with passion; love fiercely without care.
> Love her completely without boundaries.
> Love but hate the beautiful, marvelous, perfectly made dark felf.

Je Danei said, "Before hearing the song, I had witnessed the songstress in battle against two assailants earlier. This warrior-songstress was fierce in battle and sensual while she sang; her passion seemed to have no limits whether fighting or singing. Her song glorified the dark felfs, as well as issue a warning to those who dare to love a dark felf, an extremely fierce warrior." Je Danei concluded, "I learned that I too can be both warrior and a passionate, loving felf. I also finally believe love will not lessen my prowess as a warrior; in fact, it gives me more power."

Nui Honei raised her glass and proclaimed, "I will say again, 'Hail to us females!' Remember this day and rejoice. Our Danei has truly become a full grown felf!"

House Je Luneefa great mother Je Pagi's smile widened as

she looked upon her daughter with admiration, great pride and said, "Then Danei..."

"Yes mother, before you even ask; I believe next year, you will have at least one other granddaughter or grandson. You will be the fourth to know after I conceive," Je Danei said, anticipating the next question about to be asked by her mother.

"What? And why would I be the fourth?" That is not right, dear daughter. I should at least be second, the same day when Alleina confirms your pregnancy!" Je Pagi earnestly protested.

"Mother, please do not forget that we have two distinguished battlemages in our family. Their dragon-blood enhanced powers are quite formidable and awe inspiring. Their overwatch of our families is always present, and I do not think I could ever keep such a secret hidden from either of them. They may even know before Alleina," Je Danei humbly admitted.

In acknowledgement, Nui Honei and Je Leena raised and clinked their glasses together and nodded. All the females joined in laughter. Nui Honei looked at Je Pagi and the two elder felfs smiled knowing that the bonds between the females of their Houses remained very strong. And they both expected their sisterhood to continue to get even stronger.

Epilogue

It is mid-Spring, and the Je Luneefa, Nui Vent and Ona Feiir families all gather in the House Je Luneefa's east garden for their midafternoon meal. Je Pagi stood and proclaimed, "Take heed Houses Je Luneefa, Nui Vent and Ona Feiir. I am no mage; but I too can wield powerful magic. This magic I started learning from the elders of my family long ago and I still continue to perfect my great skills." The great mother of House Je Luneefa then nodded at a nearby servant who then left to go inside the stronghold. "Let us now go to the tables to eat."

A special covered plate was presented to Je Annaei and Je Kei. Empty plates were placed before everyone else. These other family members had a wide variety of seasonal fruits, cheeses and breads to choose from for their midafternoon meal.

"Youngest brother, why are you so special to have received a covered plate?" Je Jero noticed and asked.

"Hmmm... Would you care to place a wager Jero? I bet I have received a large piece of pear-apple pie. As you know, pear-apples are quite rare, exquisitely delicious and difficult to prepare properly," replied Je Kei smiling innocently at his eldest brother.

"Jero, do not bet against Kei. He calculates everything very well. Even without looking underneath that cloth, somehow, he has already somehow managed to determine that the odds are in his favor. You will lose elder brother... again," Je Tero cautioned seriously.

"Kei, do you already know what is under that heavy cloth

either through knowledge or smell?" queried a rash Je Jero who hated losing a wager, especially to his youngest brother. Being the eldest of the House Je Luneefa daughters and sons, Je Jero always wanted to set a good example for his siblings; so, he tended to place himself in either the "all-knowing" or leadership position, warranted or not. He also had a highly competitive spirit.

Kei simply answered, "No, I do not." After a long pause and more thinking, Je Jero impetuously accepted the challenge.

"Mother, did *you* prepare whatever is hiding on Kei's plate?" Je Jero further inquired, trying to increase his odds of winning.

"No," Je Pagi replied laughing. "Nor was Alleina involved in the preparation of that covered treasure." A smiling Alleina shook her head in confirmation when Je Jero looked at her.

"Master Katsu?" Je Jero quickly added.

"No," Je Pagi quickly answered.

Feeling confident that only his mother or Master Katsu, both renowned cooks, would only be skillful enough to prepare a pear-apple pie, Je Jero now felt his winning the wager was assured. Furthermore, as he looked around the table, he knew who did not possess the baking skills required to make such a delicate and complex treat. When he looked at his aunt, Nui Honei, Je Jero asked, "Was any magic used in the preparation of your treat?"

"Jero, all here know I do not cook nor bake well," Nui Honei admitted sadly.

"And before you ask Leena, no magic had to be used either," Je Kei proudly stated.

So, Je Jero boldly said, "Then I will wager my duty of cleaning the eastern stables tomorrow for your mysterious, no doubt delectable, wonderful food dish. Agreed?"

"Done!" responded a pleased Je Kei. "And if I win, you clean those same stables in three days when it is my responsibility."

Je Jero said, "Agreed."

By this time, all the family members had quieted in order to listen to the friendly wagering exchange between the Je Luneefa brothers. After Je Jero's agreement, other family members started wagering enthusiastically. During all the noisy, verbal jostling, Je Kei remained silent just displaying his handsome innocent smile. Eventually, all eyes returned and settled upon Je Kei again for him to reveal his secret food dish. When all were silent, Je Kei removed the heavy cloth hiding his food dish. There on his plate was a very large piece of pear-apple pie. Je Annaei also lifted the cover on her plate to find another large piece of pear-apple pie.

Je Jero slumped back into his chair with his defeat. Not only was he in great disbelief, but he also now questioned if his honorable youngest brother had actually cheated... He hung and shook his head slowly. Laughter arose from some; other family members were also saddened with their lost wagers. When Je Jero looked up and fixed his gaze upon Je Kei, the youngest Je Luneefa brother's smile increased. Je Jero just said, "Explain."

"Brother, you were not betting just against me; you were also betting against an old, well established family tradition set by our grandmother. Most everyone knew that if you expect to win, one does not ever bet against Je Buel, the first great mother of House Je Luneefa!"

"But she is not here; nor did mother, a fabulous cook herself, prepare your dish. Magic was not used either. None here, I assumed incorrectly now, has the skills to prepare such a rare delicacy. The odds of winning should have been in my favor. So, I foolishly thought," Je Jero responded. "Who then prepared that pie?"

"Other than Mother and Alleina, who else was Je Buel's most dedicated disciple in the kitchen?" Je Kei queried.

"Our sisters were devoted disciples of Grandmother. But neither of them fares well in the kitchen. Unfortunately, Danei and Leena did not inherit their culinary skills from our elders," Je Jero proclaimed.

Leena quickly retorted, "Nor did any of the sons of our House!"

"Besides even if Leena and I had, why would we cook for such an annoying elder brother?" Je Danei quipped.

"More importantly, Kei will you share just one spoonful of your pie? Afterall, I am your favorite sister?" Je Leena asked.

"No, absolutely not! I do still love you, dear sister," Je Kei replied. "This has been a well-earned victory! And it is a victory I *will* relish to the very last morsel!"

"Me cannot eat such a large piece of pie. So, me will share my piece," Je Annaei offered. She then cut a smaller portion of pie for herself and placed it on a small plate at her setting. She then was about to pass the larger portion to an anxiously waiting Je Danei sitting at her right but stopped and asked, "Moder and Fader Je Luneefa, ye won most of de wagers and were laughing; so ye know who den baked dis pie. Me right?"

"Beloved, my one hint should have been sufficient to disclose the identity of grandmother's devout follower," Je Kei interjected between bites of eating his rare, delicious treat. He also smacked his lips loudly several times testifying to his great enjoyment and appreciation for his wonderful pie.

Nui Samu, who also won a wager with Commander Somai, started laughing. Je Danei, holding a small spoon from her setting, kept her eyes focused upon the plate holding the piece of pie Je Annaei would hopefully soon pass to her. Je Jero, sitting next to Je Danei, had already retrieved a large serving spoon from a bowl on the table. Though defeated, he planned to make good use of his anticipated "one spoonful" share of the Je Annaei's pie remainder to be passed.

Moments later, Zhen Laehua, sitting across the table from Je Jero, pulled her hidden Nimru long knife, stabbed the table in front of her and looked menacingly at Je Jero. Zhen Laehua then handed him a regular spoon which the defeated melf took in hand, after returning the serving spoon. Zhen Laehua continued to smile evilly at the eldest son of House Je Luneefa. More laughter erupted from this gesture.

After more careful thought, Je Tero declared, "Brothers, I believe we have been tricked by one of our own."

"How so, dear beloved son?" Je Pagi asked, laughing at her eldest son.

"Jooba! Jooba baked that pie?" a surprised Je Leena exclaimed.

Je Kei's face was now smeared with the delectable juices from the pie he quickly devoured. He wore a huge smile upon his face, a great smile of victorious satisfaction. He remarked, "Did he not suggest to us all daughters and sons of Houses Je Luneefa and Nui Vent to spend more time with the first elders of Je Luneefa, especially in the kitchens? Clearly his investment paid off well again. He learned his cooking skills from our House first elders, and they are indeed quite good. In fact, they are, very, very good." Je Kei emphasized his last compliment while vigorously claiming the last remnants of his desert from his spoon and plate.

Je Pagi and Je Maron joined Nui Samu in laughing with their victory too.

"Dearest sister, when will you pass me your plate of the pie you wish to share? I too want to take my one spoonful of that wonderfully delicious pie," Pi Liu inquired.

"But I am your favorite sister; so, I should take mine first," Je Danei quickly countered.

"Pear-apple pie is a rare delicacy most of ye have not ever enjoyed. So, dis pie be of great value me dink? Who den will do me small chores, de few chores I have?" Je Annaei asked after seeing the anticipation on Pi Liu's face.

"Hold! Daughters and sons of Houses Je Luneefa and Nui Vent. Should you not first inquire if more pie exists before you let Je Annaei's auction cause discord amongst you?" Je Maron asked between his laughter.

"No more pie exists. I, unfortunately failed with my early attempts," Nui Jooba sadly reported.

"Wait. I just recalled a conversation with grandmother explaining *why* Annaei and Kei received that rare treat..." Je Jero started to explain.

Je Pagi quickly interjected with a beaming smile, "Yes. On my mother's behalf, Jooba offered to restart a family tradition my mother began long ago. My beloved husband and I greatly enjoyed many wonderful and extraordinary meals my mother prepared throughout each of my pregnancies. So, daughters and sons of Houses Je Luneefa, Nui Vent and Ona Feiir, make me a granddaughter or grandson. Then, I, our Houses' second most renowned cook, will wield my great culinary magic and prepare your favorite meals twice per moon. Ponder that treasure if you would."

"All hail Je Pagi, the second great mother of House Je Luneefa and archmage, the great wielder of wonderous, culinary magic!" Je Maron declared. In response, Houses Je Luneefa, Nui Vent and Ona Feiir raised their glasses in toast and roared "Aye!"

Je Danei looked at Nui Jooba and just frowned. Nui Jooba winked one eye in response with a small smile.

Je Leena loudly remarked, "I saw that! Jooba, what are you hiding? You may not have any more pear-apple pies – I do not think you would deliberately lie to all of us – but do you have any other delicious desserts you prepared?"

Suddenly, a barrage of questions, wagers and remarks erupted from the House Je Luneefa daughters and sons. Nui Jooba immediately took a defensive position against the immediate, verbal attacks. Renew requests were made for Je Annaei's pie remainder; offers and counteroffers were vigorously made. The elders of Houses Je Luneefa and Nui Vent started laughing again at the joyous noises.

The next day welcomed blessed peace and great hopes reign over noble Houses Je Luneefa, Nui Vent and Ona Feiir of Torondell.

Nui Honei resumed teaching all the young dragons and dragon riders dragonosophy, including the history of the dragons' mother and Nui Noirar's adventures. Nui Honei would also read from the *Chronicles* of Nui Kei Kuri Ryuu as well. All three of Nui Kei Kuri Ryuu's offspring even urged Je Danei to read the exploits of their grandmother, Siida, another great dragon. The young dragons now yearned to learn more of their proud noble lineage.

The elder felf would also oversee the dragons and dragon riders battle training. Everyone also devoted more time to also learn more of the ancient Elvish language. After the Underworld experience, everyone felt compelled to earnestly learn magic's ancient, first language. Through the magic of scrying, even the great mage Urtha Dal would lead lessons in this and other language arts.

It has been just over a year since the passing of the great warrior Nui Noirar of House Nui Vent and his great dragon, Nui Kei Kuri Ryuu. Two days ago, on a beautiful spring day, a memorial service was held for these renowned warriors and dear family members of Houses Nui Vent and Je Luneefa. The lives of the House Je Luneefa first elders, Je Buel and Je Taeliel, and Je Onyxia Ryoshi, Nui Danka and Nui Rei were also commemorated.

Though a very sad day, some sounds of joys could be heard throughout the House Je Luneefa garden. Both great noble Houses Je Luneefa and Nui Vent were blessed with new family members. Je Annaei, Je Kei's wife, recently gave birth to their first elf, an infant male they named Tae'Duen. This name was taken from Je Taeliel, first great father of House Je Luneefa, and Duenor Heartstone, an elder of Je Annaei's Dwarven family and Je Kei's beloved mentor. Duenor Heartstone's wife and sons had been killed in battle long ago; so, Je Annaei and Je Kei wanted to pay him a great honor.

As promised, Je Pagi prepared twenty-four special, extraordinary and wonderfully delicious full meals for Je Annaei and Je Kei's throughout Je Annaei's pregnancy. On those particular days, the daughters and sons of Houses Je Luneefa and Nui Vent were quite disgruntled for not being able to partake in those amazing meals. Je Pagi also used those times to remind and encourage her daughters and sons too of her only requirement to receive a similar glorious reward.

House great mother Nui Honei and Nui Noirar's twins, Nui Honeiku and Nui Noirarku are still very healthy, happy, strong, and growing. These infant elves too brought welcomed, new joys to the great noble Houses Nui Vent and Je Luneefa every day.

House Je Luneefa great mother and father, Je Pagi and Je Maron, are now finally grandparents. This is a role, duty, and responsibility they take very seriously. High standards were set by their House Je Luneefa first elders, Je Buel and Je Taeliel. Je Pagi and Je Maron feel duty-bound to not only maintain those high standards but also try to enhance them even further. Je Pagi, like her mother, is constantly providing loving oversight to the care given to all three infants. She gives all three much of her affection and attention daily.

House Nui Vent great father Nui Samu married Zhen Lae, last Winter. Contrary to the Elvish societal tradition, Zhen Lae took the House name of Nui Vent. Hence, Nui Lae became a great mother of that noble House. Afterwards, Nui Samu became the victim of small, occasional "mishaps." Like his blood-brother, Nui Samu also had a private study where he kept and displayed all his most cherished weapons on the room's walls. Nui Samu too was very orderly and each of his weapons had a distinct, designated reserved space. He also would find that some of his precious weapons would be slightly moved from time to time. And like Nui Noirar, Nui Samu was quite annoyed, but quietly enjoyed the displayed tokens of affection bestowed upon him regardless of the annoyance. "Some family traditions just had to be maintained", the daughters of Houses Nui Vent and Je Luneefa joyfully and secretly decided.

House Je Luneefa second daughter Je Leena and Ona Drachir's wedding is scheduled to take place later this Spring. Je Leena joyfully decided to fulfill her uncle's dying wish by taking her husband's House name, Ona Feiir. In addition, Je Leena decided that she would follow another old, House Je Luneefa family tradition. Each granddaughter of House Je Luneefa who inherited the gift of magic was named "Buel." With her wedding, Je Leena would also take her grandmother's first name as her own. She will be known then as House Ona Feiir great mother Ona Buel Leena. This too was another old family tradition she promised her grandmother she would maintain.

The House Je Luneefa sons, Je Jero and Je Tero, are both now engaged to Zhen Laehua and Pi Liu, respectively. Both couples are to wed in the upcoming Fall. Zhen Laehua and Pi Liu also decided to break Elvish societal tradition and will take the House name of their future husbands too like Je Annaei. Though the House Je Luneefa "lost" its first and second daughter in name, House Je Luneefa gained two more daughters. Je Pagi and Je Maron were very pleased with the possibility that House Je Luneefa would indeed flourish with more granddaughters and grandsons to carry-on the House name and fill their lives with much more joy.

Construction of the House Ona Feiir stronghold began this year as well. This castle, like strongholds Je Luneefa and Nui Vent, would be constructed inside the Toronwalein and integrated into

Mountain Toron. Je Kei developed the construction plans himself and leads the construction efforts too. Master Duenor Heartstone provides architectural engineering and construction oversight. The dwarf master engineer refused to miss another opportunity to work directly with his prized student; so, he frequently visited Torondell. His personal guard escorting him to the House Je Luneefa home was a "small" army of workers and soldiers all intending to partake of the "legendary" meals prepared by the House Je Luneefa second great mother, Je Pagi.

Houses Je Luneefa, Nui Vent and Ona Feiir families gathered in the House Je Luneefa eastern garden to share another early afternoon meal. As usual Keiku's sons, Ona Tae Kuri Ryuu and Je Ri Kuri Ryuu were flying above the garden, lost in battle play.

"Look there Jooba, are you losing your dragon?" Je Jero asked observing his sister Je Danei and Nui Kei Dan-Rei Ryuu were affectionately close together. Je Danei was also attired in all black clothing and light armor again to match her dragon sister.

"I am not concerned; they both truly love me!" Nui Jooba responded.

"Yes. That is true; but Auntie's relationship with Keiku seemed a *bit* stronger than Uncle's," Je Tero added, supporting his elder brother's jest. "We all knew the great dragon *favored* Auntie a bit more. Even in their contests, Keiku and Auntie secretly helped each other."

"Those two females do look amazing together. Whose dragon is she?" Je Kei asked.

"My dear cousins of House Je Luneefa, should you not be more concerned that the females of your House are *still* far more formidable than the males?" Ona Drachir interceded.

"Oh, my beloved speaks truth! And that statement applies to all our great noble Houses!" an evil smiling Je Leena said as she looked at Ona Drachir with blazing emerald, dragon eyes and small fires raging in both her hands.

Ona Drachir quietly remarked, "You have only won just one contest against me; but I have won many against you beloved. Do cherish your single victory; it will be your last for a long time I imagine."

Je Leena quickly retorted lasciviously, "I think not! So, you beware, *beloved*. Tonight, another great battle will be waged, and I will be victorious!" Ona Drachir just smirked in response to her challenge.

The elders of Houses Je Luneefa and Nui Vent all came out then and joined the younger family members as jests continued to be exchanged between them. Joyous laughter echoed throughout the garden. House Je Luneefa great mother Je Pagi carried her sleeping niece, Nui Honei's twin infant while Nui Honei walked in carrying her sleeping twin son. House great fathers Je Maron and Nui Samu also arrived shortly thereafter followed by Je Annaei, Nui Lae, Zhen Laehua, and Pi Liu. Commander Somai arrived last, escorting Alleina.

Dan-Rei looked around and gazed upon all her dear family members and felt great pride. She last looked at Je Danei who had a question on the forefront of her countenance, "*Is this truly my time?*" Je Danei privately asked mentally.

Smiling as only a dragon can, Dan-Rei replied, "*I believe so. You promised too. Be reassured and do not fear; I am here standing with you, dear sister.*"

Je Danei requested everyone's attention. After a few moments to let everyone settle into silence, she took Nui Jooba's hand and walked to the front of the small group. After taking a deep breath, she looked at her beloved and was about to speak when Je Jero, interjected, "Jooba, why are you standing dangerously close to my sister without wearing your armor?" Laughter erupted again amongst several of the family members. Laehua poked the eldest House Je Luneefa son in the side, warning him to be silent. As a sign of solidarity, Dan-Rei looked at and bared her fangs at the House Je Luneefa eldest son.

"Continue dear sister. Dan-Rei has also just threatened him. And our brother now knows I will cast a harmful spell upon him if he does not keep quiet and stop interfering with your marriage proposal," Je Leena encouraged.

"Leena!" exclaimed Je Danei loudly, now embarrassed that her "secret" was no longer secret.

"Why else did you want us assembled here and commanded our attention while you affectionately hold hands with Jooba?" Je Kei rightfully questioned. "But please, do continue. We have all been waiting a long time."

Looking at Nui Jooba, Je Danei continued, "As I was about to say, I had been greatly challenged by some things. I do not always have the right words to express certain feelings I oftentimes do not understand. Nor do I sometimes easily show or reciprocate affection as much as I should. Please forgive me. But know that I have finally realized through these past few years of joy and pain, you have remained very true and been patient with me. I am forever grateful to you for many things. Before all my family, I now openly confess my complete, devout love for you. I do love you with all my heart. As always, I will battle beside you till my last breath. I want to spend my life with you and raise a family with you too. You are my *one* and if you will still have me, I want to be your wife and become a great mother of House Nui Vent. I vow to be the best wife and mother I can be. Nui Jooba, second son of House Nui Vent, will you marry me?" Silence hovered over the garden. With a timid smile, Je Danei looked at Nui Jooba with great anticipation.

Responding with a puzzled look, Nui Jooba replied, "Cousins, please join me in conference." With that request, Nui Jooba started walking away to the far side of the garden with an entourage of the initially hesitant young melfs following him. Je Danei stood there frozen in place, utterly astonished and speechless.

Je Maron, Nui Samu and Commander Somai started chuckling which immediately received scornful looks from all the females. "Please look away; we are innocent and know not why he suddenly called for such a conference," Je Maron said.

"Nothing seems to go easily with those two. I shall greatly enjoy my nephew's response though. Another battle could start. Should we take wagers on the first and second strikes?" Nui Samu quizzically remarked.

"Let us hope he will not require any healing this day; Alleina and I have plans to visit our granddaughters and grandsons later," Somai said. The three male elders just laughed while all the females remained stunned in silent puzzlement.

Je Annaei finally broke the shocking silence amongst the felfs, "Jooba be waitin' fer Danei a long time. He endured a lot of pain too. Be he really afraid now after all dis time? Me do not understand." The other young felfs just maintained their silence, still totally surprised and perplexed by Nui Jooba's response to Je Danei's marriage proposal.

Recovering from her state of shock, Nui Honei asked, "Danei, are you armed?" The elder males resumed laughing quietly.

"Always!" Je Danei replied slowly, with growing anger.

"Then please do not severely cut him. Punish him, if warranted; but please do not hurt him too much," Nui Honei remarked. "I now want granddaughters and grandsons too and want to join your mother and Alleina in being a young grandmother."

Je Pagi and Alleina, still perplexed, unenthusiastically said, "Aye."

Nui Samu, Je Maron and Commander Somai renewed their laughter upon hearing Nui Honei's last comment. Nui Samu even bravely remarked, "Of course then all my sisters would intimidate all the other Torondell grandmothers who surely would not dare to boast about their granddaughters and grandsons..." As Nui Samu laughed, Je Maron and Commander Somai stepped away from the House Nui Vent great father when Nui Honei turned her fully angry attention at her brother. He too ceased to laugh when he saw his sister's dragon emerald eyes of anger.

After arriving at a destination far away from the Houses females' dragon-sensitive hearing, the young males huddled together by the noisy water fountain.

Nui Jooba looked at each of his dear cousins and remarked, "As the last unengaged son of our Houses, I am somewhat at a loss for the proper words to respond to such an important request. Do please advise me."

"After all this time, surely you are not surprised by my sister's proposal. Why do you now hesitate?" a puzzled Je Kei remarked.

Je Jero quickly stated, "It is good, I think, to delay your response. After all that you have been through to court my annoying sister, she can wait a bit for you to formulate all your demands you first want to present to her."

"So, what do *you* want? Be totally selfish too," Je Tero insisted.

"How many little ones do you want? State that now for all to hear," Je Jero quickly suggested. "Mother will gladly support you as long as you want at least three. She wants enough granddaughters and grandsons to fill all three strongholds! She thinks that among the five of us, we should give her at least fifteen granddaughters and grandsons. Mother and Father would then have the most granddaughters and grandsons in all Torondell, an esteemed honor *they* really want and would cherish! I assure you Mother will definitely be disappointed with any number less than that."

"Also, if you want anything else, you need to negotiate that now. Danei is vulnerable and will yield to your wishes without much difficulty. Take all the victories while you can. Your victory is our victory too this day," Je Tero advised. "Also, I just remembered that Danei, Leena and Liu all need to spend more time in our kitchens learning to cook better. Negotiate that too somehow," Je Tero urged. "I suffered from stomach pains for an entire day after eating some soup Liu prepared."

"Drachir and Kei, any advice for me?" Nui Jooba inquired.

"Brother, I will support whatever decision and response you

give. However, know that I, like our other brothers, must account for any counsel we offer to you. Our respective females will seek revenge if you give a response that they *all* deem less than satisfactory. Even now, we may be held accountable and punished for *your* delayed response. Lastly, do realize that I am the only one here who is betrothed to a battlemage, a very powerful battlemage. She can be utterly evil and ruthless! Leena is very much like her grandmother and auntie. So please be considerate of us too," Ona Drachir jokingly pleaded.

Je Jero added, "Any fault Danei finds in your response will be shared by all of us too, except for Kei. Somehow Annaei still thinks he is still a *perfect* husband and has done no wrong."

Je Kei responded, "Thank you brother, for you are correct. Lessons learned from grandfather and father keep me in *perfect* standing with my beloved wife. These lessons I vigorously practice daily too.

"Jooba, you have loved and still love my oldest sister despite her flaws and deliberate hurtful intentions at times. Your strength, determination and patience are commendable. I assume you are only delaying your response as part of your ploy to inflict some *annoyance* or *irritation* upon Danei for the many times she needlessly caused you pain? One day, she may eventually understand that and may even find some humor in your tactic. But do make it up to her quickly. We all want lasting peace with all the young females of our Houses."

Nui Jooba looked around at each of the melfs he considered to be far more than his cousins; these were his true brothers, like Nui Danka and Nui Rei. Nui Jooba smiled and earnestly thanked them for their counsel. "Let us now return; I am now better prepared," he said. Nui Jooba turned around and led the melfs back to the others.

As he approached, each of the young females drew a hidden weapon. Each young felf pulled her finely crafted Nimru long knife. "Why must *all* the females of our Houses *always* be armed? And why did Uncle gift them all such fine weapons. Even the finest armor wouldn't protect their victims from those weapons' dragon blood-enhanced, deadly cuts," Je Jero wondered aloud for his brothers and cousins to hear.

Alleina too announced loudly, "Sisters, brothers and nieces, this should be quite entertaining to watch. Since I am now retired, Liu will be responsible for any medical attention required." That declaration caused all the elders to laugh. The young healer was just one year into her long apprenticeship and was pitifully not yet skillful at all.

Je Danei, clearly annoyed, held a prized Nimru long knife in each of her hands. Then Je Leena sheathed her long knives. With an evil smile, brilliant emerald dragon eyes and menacing, small lightning bolts crackling from her hands, Je Leena looked directly at Ona Drachir with a cold, ominous stare.

"I gave good counsel beloved," Ona Drachir said, hoping to deter any preemptive attack.

Je Annaei put her weapon away as soon as Je Kei smiled innocently at her. The other young females scoffed at Annaei and whispered "Traitor" under their breaths.

"Me husband gave Jooba good counsel too, me certain," Je Annaei declared in defense. Je Kei continued smiling just before he joined and lovingly kissed his wife.

"Nephew, you do realize that you are not wearing armor, not that it would provide adequate protection from my angered niece. So, please think carefully before you respond," Nui Samu cautioned.

"Jooba, know that if you respond with the *wrong* answer, I will not even oversee Liu's attempt to heal you either when Danei cuts you this time," Alleina warned, jesting quietly.

Scowling, Nui Jooba boldly walked up to Je Danei and gestured with his head to return her knives to their sheaths. He then took her hands after she handed her blades to Je Leena, for he was undaunted by the felf's unpleasant demeanor. After a few silent moments of gazing deeply into her eyes, Nui Jooba took a deep breath, smiled and said, "Danei, since the night when I first met you, I have loved you. I then first promised my heart to you. Since then, I can honestly say, my love for you has never faltered, but has grown stronger. Even when I competed against those nobles at your Day of Adulthood celebration, I feared not loving you less. I only dared to dream of loving you more. Even when facing certain death in that Underworld coliseum, my thoughts were of you. You are still my *one* and I would be immeasurably honored and proud to be your husband. However, I do have some conditions."

"Conditions! What conditions? Danei, do you want your blades back?" an impatient and angered Je Leena asked. "Say the word and I will gladly hit him with a *conditional,* proposal acceptance-pending, lightning bolt. I promise it would only be as painful as you may be hurt now. What say you Sister?"

Dan-Rei bared her fangs and deadly claws and declared to the entire group mentally, *"Remember, my mother even intentionally wounded her dear rider, your stepfather, for his wrongdoing. I too will punish you if you dare hurt my sister!"*

"Wager?" Je Maron asked, looking at Nui Samu and Commander Somai who had both started chuckling again.

After taking a deep breath and continuing to return the gaze of Nui Jooba, Je Danei said, "Stay your hands dear sisters; I will first listen to his conditions. I owe him that at least." She extended her hand to Je Leena who returned her long knives. Je Danei sheathed both deadly weapons. "I want them closer should I have cause to need them," Je Danei calmly forewarned in response to Nui Jooba's puzzled look. She also instinctively took a step back and assumed a fighting preparation stance. Instinctively too, the gathered family members, except Dan-Rei, also stepped back away from the potentially combative couple. Undeterred and unafraid, Nui Jooba stepped closer to his *one*. Je Danei continued calmly, "Now please, state your conditions."

"First, I want us to marry this Fall, the most beautiful time of the year. There is no need for us postpone our destiny any longer," Nui Jooba stated.

"Agreed," a surprised Je Danei slowly responded with her initial anger subsiding and her initial frown slowly transitioning to a small smile. The felf then placed her shaking hands onto Nui Jooba's extended open hands.

"Very good my son," Nui Honei said, very pleased with her son's initial response. "You may yet survive this day unscathed." The elder males quietly laughed again.

"I want us to have at least three little ones, all females," Nui Jooba requested and continued to fearlessly hold Je Danei's gaze.

"No, no, no, I object. Only one female! We need more males in our Houses. I want many nephews I can train! And they will all appreciate me as being their favorite uncle too," Je Jero exclaimed. Je Tero and Je Kei scoffed, shaking their heads. Ona Drachir frowned too.

Zhen Laehua then elbowed the House Je Luneefa eldest son hard in his stomach. He barely flinched; she added a stern "Shhh! Please, do not interfere. And do not take my threat lightly. Though I am no warrior like my sisters and the least intimidating, I will extract revenge! Heed this final warning and remain silent, foolish male!"

A loud "Aye!" was pledged by all the other young felfs; Dan-Rei roared her supporting commitment as well. Both Je Pagi and Nui Honei just stared menacingly at the eldest Je Luneefa son to reinforce his future wife's warning.

"And why would you possibly want more little, annoying *Daneis* running around?" an annoyed and bewildered Je Jero inquired.

"Because Cousin, they would all grow to be strong, fearless, beautiful felfs like their mother and their other female elders. They would all love me unconditionally despite my faults too," Nui Jooba said.

"Yes, we agree!" a beaming Je Pagi declared. The entire group started laughing with the House Je Luneefa great mother now that one of *her* primary objectives will have serious great importance and priority. She indeed wanted to be surrounded by as many granddaughters and grandsons as possible. Her pledge to her parents must be fulfilled! "Remember your grandparents' request and your responsibilities. Daughter, please do not protest! They will all be *my* granddaughters and grandsons! And remember too, he said, 'at least three.' You two should also have a son too. So, if you have five or six, that would be more than sufficient to fulfill his condition. You can overachieve in bearing young ones like you excel in other areas!"

"Does anyone else in our families want to help my soon-to-be betrothed negotiate further?" Je Danei asked the family assembly.

"Yes, there is something..." Je Tero started.

"Tero, know that if you continue speaking, you will not be able to sleep comfortably for a long time since I will have several different, hideous, crawling creatures visit you," Je Leena warned. With that warning, Je Tero succumbed to silence immediately since his sister knew of his fear of spiders.

"I also agree with your second condition too. Anything else, Jooba?" Je Danei inquired with a radiant smile.

Nui Jooba replied, "Yes, just one. Something small and simple. I wish for both of us to prepare meals together for all our families on a regular basis, at least once per moon."

Beaming, Je Danei embraced her betrothed and kissed him deeply. She then returned his loving gaze and said, "Yes, I agree to all your conditions." Cheers erupted around them while their pact was sealed with another long kiss. For the remainder of the afternoon, a celebration continued honoring the newly engaged couple.

Late that evening when alone and sitting closely together in the House Nui Vent great hall before the fire, Je Danei asked her betrothed why those particular conditions were requested.

Nui Jooba looked at Je Danei lovingly, smiled and replied, "I want to become your husband soon before you possibly change your mind. Out of consideration for our elders to prepare for our wedding, I thought Fall would be soon enough. Secondly, building a good family, especially with you, will be a near-impossible dream fulfilled. I truly believe we will be exemplary parents like your elders. Your parents and grandparents are truly remarkable. They have taught me much and I want to carry forth their teachings and legacy through our wonderful daughters and sons. Lastly, I wish to continue the cooking tradition your elders started. Cooking and eating together are indeed excellent opportunities to strengthen our relationships with family members. Also, some of your grandparents' most cherished memories took place in the kitchen while they prepared meals. Your grandfather and grandmother both told me that 'great magic' can be found and made there. I still trust the first elders' wisdom."

Je Danei, a bit sad now, declared, "Though I truly loved my grandparents and love my parents, there were times when I did not fully appreciate their sacrifices and wisdom as much as I should have. I wish I had devoted more time to them to learn their wisdom. It took you and your brothers to remind the daughters and sons of House Je Luneefa that our elders are indeed truly remarkable. I pledge to honor them by being a better daughter, a very good wife and a very good mother. Why did it take me so long to learn such a valuable life lesson?"

Je Danei started to softly cry while kissing Nui Jooba. Through her joyful tears, Je Danei sincerely promised, "Know that no other will ever be my husband, only you. I will not change my mind. I will be the best wife and mother I could possibly be. I promise to love you passionately and fiercely. I will still become a great warrior and will always fight beside you anytime and against all odds. So, be forewarned great warrior, my future husband and father of my little ones; you cannot ever escape from my love while we both live."

Deeply touched by her sincere words of commitment, Nui Jooba cleared his voice and started softly singing:

> I will learn more of your mysteries; I will fear not your rage.
> I will love you with great passion; I will love you fiercely without fear.
> I will love you completely without boundaries.
> I will love you endlessly, my beautiful, marvelous, perfectly made felf.

"I too vow to be the best husband and father I can be. Know

that I also vowed to your grandparents I would maintain many of their traditions," Nui Jooba said while smiling and pulling out the scroll hidden in his boot. "I received this scroll from the House Je Luneefa first great father at the reading of the House Je Luneefa first elders' will," Nui Jooba said. "I always kept this important letter close. This letter provided me much needed comfort and encouragement during my times of great despair."

Nui Jooba handed his letter to Je Danei who then read the scroll:

Dear Jooba,

Even before your declaration at Danei's Day of Adulthood celebration, I knew, I hoped for, and wanted you to become our granddaughter's 'one.' Of all our granddaughters and grandsons, we knew she would be the most difficult to love because she is foremost a warrior and is dedicated to becoming an elite warrior someday. Being anything other than a warrior frightens her. Training, fighting, and killing have all been easy for her and she has excellent talents in all those areas and more. So, your fortitude and patience with her will be tested time and time again.

When Danei is deliberately hurtful or unkind, withholds needed affection due to her doubts and fears, and/or pushes you away, know that she is just afraid. Loving will not be easy for her. It is not instinctive nor an integral part of her being like mastering martial arts and weaponry. Her actions or inactions may lead to your heart being torn many times. If you are truly strong enough to withstand the sharp blades she wields, physically, emotionally, and verbally, you will find a deep, unconditional love in her that will last for centuries. Of this, I am certain.

So, please grant this old melf three requests: First, forgive her and help her overcome those challenges. She is very much worth the effort, and you are indeed strong and patient enough to persevere on your journey of love with her. I believe you will be richly rewarded as a result.

Secondly, commit to raising a family with her. Have at least three daughters. Our families need more warriors like her. Imagine the joy of having three little "Daneis" also giving you their unconditional love. (Disregard whatever objection Jero will have to this condition when you announce it.)

Thirdly, always, always protect our families! Evil abounds in this world along with jealousy and hatred. Be vigilant and a merciless guardian of the Houses Je Luneefa and Nui Vent. House Ona Feiir will also need your same protection too when Je Leena marries Ona Drachir. No doubt my daughter will be overjoyed, and perhaps a tireless nuisance, with the challenge of caring for three strongholds filled with her granddaughters and grandsons.

Lastly, but just as important, I love you as if you were truly my beloved blood grandson. I wish you and Danei much happiness.

Your grandfather,
Je Taeliel

"My grandfather was very wise," she whispered while tightly hugging the melf. Je Danei then looked at Nui Jooba affectionately and told him that her grandfather's personal letter to her also greatly encouraged her to win the heart of the only melf who truly would love and remain by her through all of life's troubles and challenges. "My grandmother also urged me to pledge my heart to the only one who would always fight by my side till he drew his last breath. Both of my grandparents wanted the second son of House Nui Vent to become my husband.

"They further requested that I take Nui Vent as my House name when I married you. The House Je Luneefa first elders also wanted House Nui Vent to flourish through such a blessed union. Upon discussing this request recently with my parents, Nui Honei and Nui Samu, all the elders were very pleased to support such a great honor. I hope you too beloved will be pleased with my taking your House name."

"Yes, of course my future wife and second great mother of House Nui Vent. I am very happy with your decision. Thank you," responded Nui Jooba, beaming a smile confirming his gratefulness and joy.

After more long moments of quiet thinking, Nui Jooba reflected aloud, "By the way, House Je Luneefa first elder Je Taeliel was very crafty too. I just realized he actually made four requests, not three." Before Nui Jooba could comment further, Je Danei kissed him deeply.

"Then does that mean you will only fulfill just three of his four requests?" inquired a curious, devilishly smiling Je Danei as she started to further enhance her passion-filled kisses.

With a faster beating heart and panting a bit heavily, Nui Jooba replied, "Again, you continue to hone your female powers which are indeed becoming more formidable. Know that I am... and will be... first elder... Je Taeliel's dutiful grandson. All requests made... will be fulfilled without hesitation and to the best of my abilities."

Je Danei whispered, "I loved my grandparents very much. I love you very much too Jooba. You are and will be my only one!" Her kisses became more heated with growing passion igniting more of Nui Jooba's unbridled passion in kind. "Today, I believe, is my first day of estrus. So, Nui Jooba, second son of House Nui Vent, my beloved and betrothed, would you like to help me fulfill my grandfather's third request this night and the next nine days, as well? Let us not postpone fulfilling another dream for another ten years till I can conceive again."

After softly kissing her hands, forehead, and each closed eye, a devilishly smiling Nui Jooba suddenly picked up his betrothed and carried her to his bedchamber where he planned to completely fulfill their grandfather's third request with joyful and fully committed determination.

As Nui Jooba was happily bounding up the great stairway of House Nui Vent, he still carried a laughing Je Danei effortlessly.

"And do not dare attempt to distract me by showing me any more enhancements your mother made to your prized weapons. There is only the one weapon I wish to see you wield this night, mighty warrior!" Je Danei ordered amidst her now heighten lascivious laughter.

In the far distance, Nui Honei smiled along with Je Pagi and Alleina as the elder felfs watched the young couple. The House elders had just left the bedchamber of the sleeping twins of House Nui Vent. Alleina remarked, "Tonight may be another momentous occasion for our Houses!"

Je Pagi's face reflected a huge smile, a smile that radiated unusual great joy. "Why are you smiling like that; you might hurt your face," Nui Honei quietly observed. Alleina shook her head and responded with a near-silent snicker. Je Pagi pulled a small scroll from her robe's side pocket and handed it to Nui Honei who unrolled the assumed missive and scrutinized the mysterious runes organized in neatly arranged rows and columns. After a few moments, Nui Honei raised her head and looked at Je Pagi in disbelief. "What is this? I do not understand the meaning of this writing. Please explain." Je Pagi seemed not to have heard the last request; she was deeply lost in thoughts as the House Je Luneefa great mother caught the last glimpse of her eldest daughter and Nui Jooba turning a corner at the top of the staircase. Tears of joy swelled in her eyes.

Alleina quietly laughed and replied, "Honei, Pagi just handed you one of her most treasured documents. Pagi is maintaining another family tradition our first House elder Je Buel started centuries ago. That scroll holds family secrets even though it is written in such a way that most could not understand. That scroll documents the estrus cycle of each young felf of our Houses. Given how Pagi reacted to Danei and Jooba's actions and giddy laughter, I believe they intend to bless our Houses this night with the miracle of sacred conception of another descendant.

"So, beware. If Pagi is like her mother, which we all know she very much is, Pagi will uncommonly cater to those particular young ones to a point where it will seem quite annoying to others. Understand that right now, those two are now her *favorites*; most others will have less priority for the next ten days. She will greatly inconvenience me after the ten days' time to confirm Danei's pregnancy." Alleina then sighed heavily about the great, near-future pestering and annoyance that awaited her.

"Yes, I do hope more pear-apples will be needed very soon!" declared a smiling Nui Honei.

"Agreed, dear Sisters. Afterall, promises must be kept!" Je Pagi said, beaming with joy, hoping to fulfill her obligation soon, very soon.

About The Author

M. R. Lucas is a former business management consultant, legal project manager, and legal electronic discovery consultant. His professional work experience has spanned over three decades.

Although he formally studied mathematics in college, he then began to develop deep interests in information technology and computer programming. While in college, Lucas was also a four-year varsity athlete on the college fencing team. He also was an active member in the college's gospel choir and volleyball club.

After college, Lucas started working full-time with a leading information technology and services corporation. He later married and raised a family with his wife of over three decades. His current hobbies mostly include playing strategy games, especially trading card games, and reading a wide range of fantasy books. After transitioning into semi-retirement, Lucas started devoting more efforts to his newly developed hobby: authoring sword and sorcery fantasy stories.

www.ingramcontent.com/pod-product-compliance
Lightning Source LLC
LaVergne TN
LVHW041747060526
838201LV00046B/937